THE UPSTAGED CORONER

THE UPSTAGED CORONER

A FENWAY STEVENSON MYSTERY
NUMBER FOUR

PAUL AUSTIN ARDOIN

PAX ARDSEN BOOKS

To Murph

TABLE OF CONTENTS

The quality of mercy is not strain'd,
It droppeth as the gentle rain from heaven
Upon the place beneath: it is twice blest;
It blesseth him that gives and him that takes:
'Tis mightiest in the mightiest: it becomes
The throned monarch better than his crown;
His sceptre shows the force of temporal power,
The attribute to awe and majesty,
Wherein doth sit the dread and fear of kings;
But mercy is above this sceptred sway;
It is enthroned in the hearts of kings,
It is an attribute to God himself;
And earthly power doth then show likest God's
When mercy seasons justice.

—WILLIAM SHAKESPEARE, *THE MERCHANT OF VENICE*,
ACT IV, SCENE 1

I

WEDNESDAY

CHAPTER ONE

FENWAY STEVENSON SAT UP IN BED. SHE GRIMACED AND TAPPED HER fingernails against her teeth, then turned to her bedside table and looked at the clock—3:43.

Oh, what the hell. She picked up the mobile phone on the bedside table.

Before she could unplug it from its charger, it rang and vibrated in her hand. She almost dropped it and blinked hard. The screen read *Craig McVie.* She chuckled and pictured him tossing and turning for the last few hours, too, wondering if *he* should call *her* to finish what they started last night—before Fenway found out her father had been arrested for murder.

She cleared her throat and answered, her heart fluttering.

"Hey, Sheriff," she said in her best sultry voice. "Couldn't sleep either, huh?"

"It's not that." He sounded professional and serious.

Fenway's heart sank.

"The night janitor at Nidever University called. There's a body at the bottom of a stairwell in the theater department. We need to get over there right away."

———

Fenway filled the coffeepot with water and started the coffeemaker. It took her twenty minutes to shower and throw on one of her less rumpled business pantsuits. She grabbed a commuter cup, pulled the carafe from the coffeemaker—it was just hot water. She'd forgotten to dump the coffee in the filter.

She walked out of her apartment before she remembered that the crime scene unit hadn't processed her Accord yet.

Fenway frowned as she ordered her Uber. Not many drivers were up this early and the closest one was fifteen minutes away. She confirmed the pickup and went back into the apartment. She was getting her coffee, dammit.

She scooped the coffee into the filter and turned things over in her mind. Her Accord should have been the first car processed—surely there were other cars with more ash, with some *real* evidence from the explosion. She'd have to speak to the idiots who ran the impound yard.

She shook her head as she pushed the start button. This was no way to start off the day. She knew the people who ran the yard. She *liked* the people who ran the yard. They weren't idiots.

What the hell was wrong with her?

Maybe it was the interrupted romantic evening. After having to spend the whole election season apart, Fenway and McVie could finally, finally, *finally* date. He'd just been served divorce papers, and she'd won her election, and no one would care that they were dating.

Before the election, it had been too risky. McVie wasn't technically divorced, and the voters could reject both of them, although it probably would have affected his candidacy for mayor more than her candidacy for coroner. There was the age difference too, but fourteen years' difference hardly seemed like anything to clutch one's pearls over.

Neither of their campaign managers said it, but they didn't have to: he was white and she was black. Half black. *Perceived* as black. Whatever. Fenway's nose twitched as she poured the coffee into a mug. That didn't seem like anything to worry about either, but elections brought out the worst in people.

She was halfway through her second cup when her phone dinged. The Uber was here.

The ride was devoid of conversation; the driver had Johnny Cash on the sound system, but at such a low volume Fenway could barely hear it.

The last several hours had been surreal. McVie was right to leave the apartment. When Fenway had seen her stepmother's name on the screen at midnight, she thought Charlotte wanted to bug her about dinner or maybe congratulate her on her election victory.

But no. It had been serious.

Fenway sank lower in the back seat. She didn't want to think about it. But she couldn't help it. She hadn't been able to stop thinking about it since the midnight call.

She shut her eyes tight.

A decade earlier and a thousand miles away, at Western Washington University, Fenway had approached Professor Solomon Delacroix after class about her upcoming essay in Russian Lit. The professor had invited her to his office. And he had locked the door.

Fenway shut her eyes tighter.

Fenway had switched majors and gone into nursing. She hadn't told a soul about it before her mother passed away and she moved here from Seattle. She hadn't even told her mother. She'd pushed down the humiliation, pushed down the anger and sadness.

But three months ago, Barry Klein—the opportunistic narcissist on the county board of supervisors—had approached her. No, he'd tried to *blackmail* her. He'd found a video of her assault on the dark web. Delacroix hadn't just raped her, he'd recorded it, and Klein threatened to go public with it if she ran for coroner.

All the humiliation and the pain and the powerlessness and the hurt came flooding back. As much as she hadn't wanted to, she'd told her father. She'd gone through that humiliation again, telling her rich, white, entitled, spoiled brat of a father. As much as she hated telling him, she didn't want him finding out from anyone else.

And as far as Barry Klein was concerned, she wasn't worried about him. It was mutually assured destruction. It was illegal for him to possess the video. It would be humiliating for her if it got out. It would kill his career, too, if anyone found out he'd tried to blackmail a rape victim.

Ignoring Barry Klein. Informing her father. Those were the right decisions. The *high-road* decisions, even.

Within days of those right, high-road decisions, Professor Solomon Delacroix's body was found floating in the Squalicum Waterway, right near where the Western Washington crew team practiced.

Last night, they'd arrested her father for his murder.

She opened her eyes.

Charlotte could barely get the words out when she called a few hours ago, ping-ponging between anger and worry and panic and shock.

Fenway had tried in vain to calm Charlotte down. After ten minutes, Fenway looked up at McVie, and saw it in his eyes: their romantic evening was over. She knew he could see it in her eyes, too.

"I'll see you tomorrow," McVie had said.

"I'm so sorry, Craig," Fenway whispered, and he kissed her on the cheek. "No," Fenway said into the phone, as McVie let himself out of her apartment, "Charlotte, don't mess around with this. Get a criminal lawyer. My father's corporate attorneys *must* have some great contacts. Get one first thing tomorrow morning, and he'll be out by the end of the day. His money and power still count for quite a bit in this town."

Charlotte had finally stopped crying. "I'm so impressed how calm you are under pressure, Fenway. I know this is hard for you, but I appreciate it."

But Fenway wasn't calm. She'd had to pretend. Every mention of the murder of Professor Solomon Delacroix started playing the humiliation over and over and over in her head.

Fenway stared out the window as they passed the exit for Highway

326. She tried to slow her breathing and relax, but she could feel her veins pulsing, as she was both wired and exhausted from lack of sleep.

She'd wanted to call McVie as soon as Charlotte hung up. Have him come back over. Get him to stop the images playing. But, it had been so late by then.

Besides, McVie had been through enough with the mayoral race. The night before, McVie had a glimmer of hope as he won the late voters, but Klein's lead had officially been insurmountable. McVie, decent, kind, Eagle Scout McVie, had lost.

Mayor Barry Klein. The bile rose in Fenway's throat and she almost screamed in frustration.

Ah, what those right decisions had wrought.

And what would McVie do now? With the impending divorce, the loss in the mayoral race, and his term as sheriff expiring on January first, would McVie even want to stay in Estancia?

The driver exited onto the George Nidever Expressway.

The darkness and artificial lights played havoc with the shapes in the shadows on the side of the expressway as Fenway watched the trees and hills go past. She looked out the driver's side too. Beyond the evenly spaced palm trees, with no hills on that side of the car, lay a footpath running parallel to the ocean. She closed her eyes and tried to hear the ocean's thunder.

Some days she just wanted to sit still, or take a run through the butterfly grove, out to the ocean cliffs. Out to where her mother had painted the seascape two decades ago, now hanging on Fenway's wall. To see the cypress jutting from the rock—the impossible tree taking root in the midst of saltwater and sand, battered by the Pacific Ocean and the sea winds, but still standing tall and proud.

The Uber maneuvered through two roundabouts and pulled into a yellow zone in a nearly empty parking lot in front of DiFazio Hall. A blue Acura ILX stood in a space marked Reserved, next to McVie's beige Highlander. McVie waited by the double doors at the hall's entrance, his tall, muscular frame silhouetted against the lights in front of the theater.

Fenway got out of the car, grabbing her forensic kit and putting the strap of her small purse over her shoulder. She looked up at the squared-off four-story building of graying concrete and adobe brick.

McVie walked toward her with a quizzical look on his face. "Fenway? What are you doing here?"

"What?" She looked at McVie as if he were crazy. "Don't you remember? You called *me.*"

"Well—yeah, but I assumed you'd give this one to Dez or Mark."

"You said *we* needed to get over here right away."

"I meant—I meant 'we' as in the police, the authorities, the CSI units. Not *you.*"

"Then why didn't you call Dez or Mark?"

A frown played at the corners of McVie's mouth, and the realization hit her.

"Oh," Fenway said. "Because *I'm* their boss. Not you. I'm the one who needs to decide who to assign to this case."

"I'm sorry, Fenway—I guess I wasn't clear. But you've been running nonstop for almost a week, plus you've run an election campaign, plus your father is in jail. You need to go home. Give yourself some time. Delegate."

Fenway nodded. "You're right—I wasn't thinking. I'll call Dez now." She shifted her weight. "But—the university will get busy in a couple of hours, right?"

"Well, yeah."

"I'm here. I might as well tag and bag stuff until Dez gets here." Fenway motioned to the building. "Is this the theater?"

"No," McVie said. "Well, kind of. The theater itself is around the other side—DiFazio Theater. It's connected to this building, which is all classrooms. Drama and English, a few other classes in liberal arts."

"You went here?"

"No. Fresno State."

"Why do you know so much about it?"

"Megan took a tour a few months ago. Loved the drama department."

"Oh, she wants to go to Nidever?"

McVie shook his head. "We don't have the money."

Fenway grimaced. There was that *we*. Craig and Amy. Even in the middle of the divorce, they were a family. She toyed with her hair. "She wants to major in drama?"

"If you've seen her latest parade of loser boyfriends, you'd think she was *already* majoring in drama," McVie said under his breath. "Anyway, Dr. Pruitt said he'd meet me at five. Let's head over to the theater."

They walked along the side of DiFazio Hall. Fenway pulled out her phone and called Dez.

It rang three times before Dez picked up. "Roubideaux." Dez sounded like she just woke up.

"Hey, Dez. It's Fenway."

"Hey, rookie. It's early. Something going on?"

"Yes. There's a body at Nidever University. At DiFazio Hall, near the theater."

"All right. Do you know who's responding?"

"Uh—yeah. McVie and I are both here."

"You're... you're there?"

"I know, I know." Fenway grimaced. "McVie already told me."

"Yeah, well, I'll tell you again. You'll burn out if you keep going like this, Fenway, and you won't do anybody any good if you have a nervous breakdown." She paused and chuckled. "And don't expect me to visit you in the loony bin, either. Those places give me the creeps."

"I got it, Dez." Fenway coughed. "How long till you can get here?"

"Let's see—it's almost five, right? I can be there in half an hour."

"All right. I'll hold down the fort till then."

"Fenway?"

"Yes?"

"Next time, you call me right away. You can't take this all on yourself."

"Okay, Dez. Sorry."

"You don't need to be sorry. Just do better."

They hung up as McVie and Fenway came to a large quad. The

DiFazio Memorial Theater jutted, loud and unapologetic, from the rest of the building.

A slender white man, sporting an unkempt salt-and-pepper Vandyke on his chin, walked across the quad to meet them. He was in a parka, crisp dark blue jeans, and penny loafers, and he carried himself like he'd be more comfortable in a suit. Fenway didn't recognize him at first, and then he opened his mouth and his thin, reedy voice kicked Fenway's memory into gear. "Sheriff, hello," he said, reaching out and shaking McVie's hand. "I'm so glad you could come on such short notice."

"Dr. Pruitt," Fenway said. "I'm so sorry. Where do you need us to collect evidence?" After six months, Fenway knew there was no variant of "Where's the dead body?" that made people feel at ease. She was still trying different tacks, and it wasn't even out of her mouth before she winced internally.

"Ah, Coroner," Dr. Alfred Pruitt said. "I didn't think I'd be seeing you again so soon." The words came out of his mouth with barely contained contempt, as if Fenway could have somehow prevented the disastrous evening at the university's political dinner. "Poor Jessica is this way."

Dr. Pruitt stepped between McVie and Fenway toward the double doors at the front of the theater. He pulled out a ring of keys, selected one, and opened the door. They all went into the foyer, then Pruitt nervously led them down a corridor off to the side.

They passed three blue doors with small rectangular windows. Fenway looked through one window and saw student desks and a table pushed halfway into a corner. Ahead of them loomed a large gray door, and Dr. Pruitt approached it carefully, slowing down as he got closer.

He stood in front of the door for a moment, then turned the handle and pulled it open, revealing a stairwell. Whitewashed concrete-block walls and a metal staircase. The foot of the staircase was on the far side from the door, and Fenway could see, partially hidden by the metal stairs, a crumpled form at the bottom. Even at this angle, the pool of blood around the figure's head grabbed the eye and drew it in.

McVie and Fenway both took several steps forward, and Fenway snapped on a pair of blue nitrile gloves, while McVie slipped on a white pair. "This is Jessica Marquez?"

"Yes," Dr. Pruitt said, running his hands through his hair.

Fenway squatted down next to the body.

Jessica Marquez lay on her left side, her shoulder blades against the wall, her left arm splayed at an awkward angle behind her head. Her eyes were open, and her lips were slightly parted. Her legs still partially rested on the stairs, with her left foot on the second step and her right foot on the first.

She wore a navy blue blazer and charcoal gray slacks with tan high heels.

"I think she fell," Dr. Pruitt said.

Following procedure, Fenway felt for a pulse, knowing it was useless. She tried to keep her tone as conversational as she could. "What makes you say that, Dr. Pruitt?"

"I mean," Dr. Pruitt stuttered, "she's lying at the bottom of the stairs. Look at those high heels. Surely she caught her heel on something and lost her balance."

"You're saying she must have hit her head on the way down?" Fenway asked.

"I suppose," Dr. Pruitt replied in a low voice.

Taking care not to step in the pool of blood, Fenway took out a small penlight and shined it on the back of Jessica Marquez's head. McVie stepped forward and craned his head so he could see better as well. The light from the small flashlight reflected off the coagulated blood and the dead woman's thick, shiny black hair. Fenway could see a bloody wound visible near the crown of her scalp.

"What is it, Miss Stevenson?" Dr. Pruitt said, straining for a look.

"Sheriff," she began.

"Dr. Pruitt," McVie said, snapping to life, "perhaps it would be best if you waited outside."

"Outside? It's cold out there."

"I mean anywhere outside the stairwell," he said. "Until we know for sure that this was an accident, we need to treat it like a crime scene."

"A crime scene? You think she was—"

"We don't think anything yet, Dr. Pruitt. Perhaps you would be more comfortable in the theatre lobby."

"I don't feel comfortable without someone representing the school here," Dr. Pruitt said.

McVie stared at Dr. Pruitt. "You're telling me you want me to put in my report how you insisted on being at the crime scene where you had the opportunity to contaminate the evidence?"

"I don't—that's not—" He sighed. "Okay, fine. I'll go wait in the theater lobby."

"I'll join you," McVie said.

"Hey, McVie," Fenway shouted.

McVie turned to Fenway.

"Alibi," Fenway mouthed, pointing at Dr. Pruitt.

McVie rolled his eyes and followed Pruitt out, leaving Fenway alone with the body. Fenway looked for other wounds on the scalp, as closely as she could without touching it, but found nothing.

She gingerly tried to lift the lifeless arm, but rigor mortis had set in; it was cold in the stairwell—maybe fifty-five degrees Fahrenheit at most, something to consider in fixing the time of death.

Fenway stood up and shined her flashlight on the stairs.

The stairs were painted a medium gray with a slight undercoating of yellow, a nauseating combination that was enough to make Fenway a little sick to her stomach. She was glad she hadn't had breakfast yet.

The stairwell, though poorly lit, was clean and well cared for: the paint on the walls looked a year or two old at most, with no papers, trash, or old gum. The stairs of the nursing education building at Western Washington had been constantly dirty and often full of litter.

Fenway took out a few clear evidence bags and looked carefully on each step, taking care to step around the body as she went up the first set of steps. There was blood on both the wall and a few steps above the body. A small, hard-edged object sat in a large splatter of blood on the fourth step from the second-floor landing. She bent down. It was an off-white, somewhat triangular shape, with a tinge of pink on one edge.

"Maybe it's a pebble," Fenway murmured, although she was certain it was a piece of bone. She pulled her phone out and took pictures, both a wide shot and a close-up, and then used a pair of tweezers to pick up the fragment and drop it in her evidence bag.

She continued to scour the steps, and on the second-floor landing she discovered another small object covered in blood. Slightly larger than the previous bone fragment she had found, it lay halfway between the door and the step. She took pictures of it, not sure of what it was as it lay on the floor. Fenway picked it up with tweezers and shined her flashlight on it—a piece of glass or crystal.

She heard the stairwell's bottom door open and close, and then Dez's voice. "Fenway?"

"Up here."

"Oh, damn. That's a lot of blood."

"Head wound. Looks like a blow from an object with an edge, possibly glass or crystal."

"You found a piece of evidence?" Dez stepped around the body and began to climb the stairs.

"I found a *few* pieces of evidence," Fenway said. "A shard from the possible murder weapon. Also, body's in early rigor. That means about four hours given this temperature. We're probably looking at sometime between eleven thirty last night and one thirty this morning."

"So this is a murder scene."

Fenway nodded. "I think she was hit up here, near the second-floor landing. This is where the blood spatter starts. We'd have to get CSI here to be sure, but it's a good bet."

Dez set her mouth in a line. "All right, thanks for starting me off on the right foot. Now get out of here and get some sleep."

"I'm fine."

"You're not fine." Dez lowered her voice even though it was only the two of them on the stairs. "I heard what happened to your dad. Go home. You're dealing with way too much right now."

Fenway snapped her fingers. "I should have secured the area before now. I'll go get the police tape and start. I'll get McVie over here."

As if on cue, McVie opened the door and stuck his head in.

"Hey, Sheriff," Fenway began, "it looks like the lethal blow was struck on or near the second-floor landing, so we'll have to cordon off the whole stairway, and probably part of the second floor—"

"Seriously, Fenway, go home," McVie said. "Dez is here now."

"I know. I just wanted to make sure Dez saw what I saw." Fenway started walking down the stairs, as slowly as she could get away with. About halfway down, she pulled out her phone. "I'll email you the photos."

"Thank you kindly." Dez nodded. "Go home."

"You know I don't have my car, right?"

"You want me to drive you home? What are you, seven years old?" Dez folded her arms. "You want me to check under the bed for monsters before you go to sleep, too?"

McVie took his car keys out of his pocket and handed them to Fenway as she reached the bottom. "Take my car. Dez can drop me off at your place to pick it up later."

Fenway nodded. "Yeah, okay." She opened the door and stepped into the hallway toward DiFazio Hall, and as the door was about to close, McVie pulled it open and stepped out with her.

"Oh—what is it?"

"Are you okay, Fenway?"

"Why wouldn't I be?"

"Because your dad got arrested for murder, and you're making excuses not to go home."

Fenway blinked. Of course she didn't want to go home to the same endless circle of thoughts that had kept her awake for three hours. Of her father in jail. Of her former professor and what he did to her. Of her father *knowing* about what her professor did.

Of what he might have done after he found out.

Fenway shuddered. "It's not—I'm fine. I'll be fine. I didn't sleep well. I'll call Charlotte when I wake up. We'll make a plan. I'm sure he'll hire an expensive lawyer and make sure my father doesn't spend another night in jail."

"Okay." McVie stepped closer to her, and for a split second Fenway thought he might hug her. "Call me if you need anything. I mean it."

"Sure." She turned to go, then perked up. "Does Pruitt have an alibi?"

"Home asleep. He says his wife can vouch for him. Now go on."

Fenway looked in McVie's eyes; they were kind and gentle, but Fenway had the strange urge to turn and run away. "Thanks, Craig."

She went through the foyer, not even stopping to acknowledge Dr. Pruitt where he sat on a wooden bench, and she rushed out the door. Her heart pounding in her ears, Fenway pushed the unlock button on McVie's key fob before she even got halfway through the quad. She kept on pushing the button until she saw the flash of the Highlander's parking lights.

She pulled the door open, started the engine, and backed out of the space without adjusting the seats or the mirrors. She heard a squeal and looked down, then released the parking brake. The SUV lurched backward, and Fenway slammed on the brakes. She looked through the windshield and turned the highlights on, closed her eyes, and took several deep breaths.

What the hell is wrong with me?

When she opened her eyes again, her vision seemed to open up a little, and she took two more deep breaths before she realized she was shaking. She swore at the top of her voice, drawing out the vowel sounds, feeling her throat go raw, then closed her mouth.

Putting the Highlander in Drive, she navigated the campus roads to Nidever Expressway and the safety of the freeway. A wave of exhaustion flowed over her. Maybe that's all it was: fatigue.

She hoped she'd be able to catch a few hours of sleep at her apartment.

CHAPTER TWO

FENWAY TOSSED AND TURNED, FLITTING IN AND OUT OF A LIGHT doze for a couple of hours, then she gave up getting back to sleep. She called Charlotte, who was beside herself that Nathaniel Ferris's expensive corporate lawyers had failed to get her any information.

"They don't have to arraign him for forty-eight hours," Fenway said, "and with someone who's a flight risk like my father, they might petition for seventy-two."

"This is ridiculous," Charlotte snapped. "What do we have these lawyers on retainer for if they can't even tell me what's going on?"

"I can ask around."

"You haven't *already* asked around?"

"It's barely eight o'clock, Charlotte. I'll call around, see if anyone knows anything." She paused. "Do you know if he's being held in the county jail, or did they move him somewhere else?"

"I didn't ask. I just want him home."

"Okay. I'll do everything I can to find out why it's taking so long."

"If you find out where he is, please let me know. Maybe you could even go visit him."

"I'm sure he'd rather see you than me."

"He'd love to see you, and you can see him outside of visitors' hours, can't you?"

Fenway stared at her feet. "Yes. Yes, of course I'll let you know where he is. As soon as I find out."

Charlotte's voice caught, but she coughed and gained control. "Thank you, Fenway."

Fenway squeezed her eyes shut and took a deep breath. "Sorry you're going through this. I know how much you mean to him, and I'm sure this is hard for you."

"He's your *father*, Fenway. It should be hard for you, too."

Charlotte's words were a punch in the gut. Fenway had gone out of her way to say something nice, something supportive to Charlotte, and all she got was grief that she wasn't worrying enough. "Yeah, well, we all have different ways of processing this stuff. Doesn't mean it's easy for me. Anyway, I need to go. I'll keep you informed."

She hung up before Charlotte could get another word in, and she seethed. Everyone *does* process stressful situations differently. She'd seen plenty of diverse reactions from the families of the injured, or dead, when she worked in the ER in Seattle. She hadn't cried right away when her mom died. She remembered her mother's hand slipping from her grasp with a shuddering last exhale, then she was driving home from the hospital in a daze, eyes dry. The tears didn't come until she was in the house her mother had bought, in bed with all the lights out, sensing but avoiding all the voicemails coming in from friends and lovers she didn't want to see.

She shook her head. She'd gotten through hard situations by herself before. She could get through this too.

———

Fenway took her time getting ready, daydreaming in the shower, pulling out five outfits before picking the first one she'd touched. She wandered around the kitchen for ten minutes before deciding she didn't want to have breakfast. McVie hadn't come to the apartment to claim his car yet, so Fenway figured she'd drive it to work.

It was almost ten as she circled the block. She rarely got to work so late, and with the parking garage unusable, Fenway had trouble finding a parking space. She finally found a spot several blocks away, in front of the Phillips-Holsen Grand Hotel, just outside the valet area.

Getting out of the Highlander, Fenway felt the first drops of rain on her face. She wanted to take cover next to the building, but she didn't want to deal with the valets who already eyed her suspiciously. She pulled her purse higher up on her shoulder.

Next to the hotel stood a boutique bakery, where a cup of coffee and a pastry would take the chill off the morning. She'd passed the bakery several times—she drove by it on her way to work almost every day—but hardly ever went because it didn't open early enough. The few times she walked past, it smelled divine. Today was no different.

She ducked into the bakery as the skies opened and it started to pour, and the smell of dough and espresso teased her nose as she went up to the counter.

"*Bonjour*," said the woman behind the counter. The white apron offset her dark skin and the multicolored African wrap around her head.

"*Bonjour*," Fenway responded, her gaze landing on the pastries. She ordered a latte and a *pain au chocolat*, and after she paid, she turned from the counter with the pastry in her hand and almost dropped it.

Detective Deshawn Ridley from the Bellingham Major Crimes Unit sat ten feet in front of her.

"Coroner," he said, nodding in greeting. He had a half-eaten croissant on his plate and a large cappuccino cup in front of him.

"Detective," she said warily.

"Care to join me?"

Fenway didn't want to but couldn't see a way around it without being confrontational—which she considered for a moment.

"Sorry," he said. "I'm sure you've heard of your father's arrest by now. I understand if you don't want to sit."

Fenway started to take a step away from the table and then reconsidered. "No, it's okay." She walked up to the table, slid the wooden chair back, and took a seat.

"I've had breakfast here every morning since I got here. It's a good place." He took a sip of his cappuccino.

"You're staying close by?"

"The Phillips-Holsen next door."

"Wow, fancy. I didn't think you could swing that as a public servant."

Ridley shrugged. "I stay where they tell me to. I guess November isn't a busy time of year here." A corner of his mouth turned up. "But, yes, it *is* a nice hotel. Nice bar. Swanky. Makes me forget that I hang out in the crappy parts of town all day."

The woman behind the counter called *Joanne,* and Fenway went to pick up her latte. She took a deep breath, then promised herself she'd finish her pastry and her coffee and be on her way. She walked back to the table, plastering what she hoped was a calm look on her face.

"Oh," Ridley said as she sat down, "congratulations on the election, by the way. I read an article that it was the biggest margin of victory by a black candidate ever in Dominguez County."

"Thank you. I'd like to take all the credit, but it sure helps when you have a weak opponent who can't get out of his own way."

Ridley grinned. "And when you have a top-shelf campaign manager."

Fenway gave him a tight-lipped smile in return. "That too." She took a sip of her latte. "I see you've gotten what you came for."

"What, finding Professor Delacroix's killer? I go where the evidence leads."

"You have evidence that my father hired someone to kill the professor?"

Ridley kept grinning but said nothing.

"Of course, you can't share with me what you have."

"We'll leave that for discovery at trial, or however the district attorney wishes to proceed."

"You must be eager to get back to your family."

Ridley chuckled.

"What's so funny?"

"Divorce, that's what's funny," Ridley said. "I've got a five-hundred-square-foot third-floor walk-up. Wife got the house. My hotel room is bigger than my apartment." He coughed. "And I'll be here a few more days, anyway."

"Why's that?"

"Just tying up some loose ends."

Fenway narrowed her eyes.

"You're not one of those loose ends, don't worry. I want to make sure we have all our ducks in a row, that's all."

Fenway leaned back in her chair. "You must be a tenacious son-of-a-bitch. No one's ever gotten anything to stick on my father before."

Ridley looked into Fenway's face, then dropped his eyes and took another bite of croissant. He chewed carefully and swallowed. "I take it there's no love lost between you two."

Fenway shrugged. "It's a complicated relationship. I didn't see him a lot when I was growing up."

"I hear he put you in the position you're in now."

"It wasn't my idea." Fenway looked at her *pain au chocolat* but had lost her appetite. She took another drink of her latte.

"You're telling me it was *his* idea?"

"Don't get me wrong—it helped me out. I needed to take the California nursing exam before I could get a job in the state. They needed a coroner, and I needed a paycheck. It was supposed to be temporary."

"I heard that, too. Your dad picked a pharmaceutical executive to be coroner, right?"

"I see you've done your research."

Ridley glanced up at Fenway briefly before staring into his cappuccino cup. "I heard you showed your dad up. That must have pissed him off."

"'The dear father would with his daughter speak, commands her service.'"

"What?"

"It's from *King Lear*. Lear expects his daughter to obey him without question."

Ridley laughed.

"What's so funny?"

"Yeah, I heard you're on the murder of the manager of some local Shakespeare group. You sure internalize this stuff, don't you?"

Fenway stiffened. "How did you find that out? The body's not even cold yet. Do *you* have a connection in our department, Detective?"

"A gentleman never reveals his secrets."

Fenway stared out the window; the squall had turned into a drizzle. "What *can* you reveal? Maybe where they're holding my father?"

Ridley shook his head. "I hear they'll arm wrestle over that for the next couple of days."

Fenway nodded. That must be a loose end—Ridley must want him extradited to Washington state.

Her phone dinged, and Fenway dug it out of her purse. It was McVie.

We're all done here I'm coming to get my car

"I've got to go," she said, standing. "Have a safe trip back to Bellingham."

Fenway was halfway out the door when her stomach rumbled—she had left the *pain au chocolat* on the table. "Settle down," she told her stomach, as she texted McVie to tell him to meet her in the office.

———

With one eye on her phone, she walked into the building. It was a few minutes before ten o'clock. The latte staved off Fenway's exhaustion, at least for now. Walking down the hall, she opened the door to Suite 150.

Migs sat at the front desk and looked up from his legal paperwork.

"Fenway!" he said, and he began clapping. Applause burst from every corner of the room: Migs, Sergeant Mark Trevino at the back desk, Rachel in the far corner, Piper Patten from IT sitting next to Migs, and five officers from the sheriff's department. It was only a handful of people, but their applause was loud enough to catch Fenway by surprise.

"Congratulations on the win," Migs said, standing up with a broad smile on his face.

Mark stepped in front of Fenway and held out his hand. She took it, and he pulled her into a hug. "Congratulations, Fenway," he said. "Couldn't have happened to a better coroner."

"Aw, thanks, guys," Fenway said, a little dumbstruck.

"Mark brought in donuts," said Piper, "but you were two hours late. We only have the ones with the nasty pink sprinkles left."

"You party a little too hard last night?" Mark grinned at Fenway.

"The murder case at the university," Fenway said. "I—uh, I went over there before I called Dez."

Mark nodded, and Fenway read his look. Not only had Dez and McVie started telling her to manage her team instead of doing everything herself, but they seemed to have told everybody else.

"I couldn't sleep anyway," Fenway said. "At any rate, I'm here now, and thank you for everything. Even the donuts with the gross pink sprinkles."

She felt a tap on her shoulder and turned.

Rachel stood smiling, a pink-sprinkled donut in her hand. "I've got to get back and finish a press release," she said, "but I just wanted to tell you how happy I am you won." She pulled Fenway into an embrace.

"I miss you not working in this department," Fenway said.

"Yeah, me too. But I like the pay raise, and my own office." She pulled away first. "Maybe we can get drinks this weekend? Happy hour or something?"

"We'll see. We just got another murder." Fenway caught Mark looking skeptically at her. "But I'll manage my time better. So yeah, let's plan on it."

Rachel opened the door to leave, and Dez walked in. "Oh, man! Just like me to miss my own surprise party." She guffawed and chucked Fenway lightly on the shoulder. "Great job, rookie," she said. "Quite the landslide."

"Thanks, Dez."

"Four more years of you being the boss here," said Dez. "Sheesh, what was I thinking, encouraging you?"

"Okay," said Piper, "I guess everyone's fine making you think there are just disgusting donuts left, and I guess *I'm* the only one nice enough to tell you there's *cake*."

Fenway perked up. "Cake?"

"Dammit, Piper." Dez folded her arms in mock annoyance. "We wanted that cake all to ourselves."

"It's got Nutella filling," Piper said.

Fenway smiled. "Oh, hell yes. I'll have a piece."

Piper hopped off Migs's desk, her green dress clinging to her willowy form. Migs watched her walk all the way to the door of the office suite.

They must have made up, thought Fenway, a pang of longing for the sheriff in her stomach. Although he had stayed over the night before last—putting the end to months of simmering emotion between them —she was nervous. Was it because the specter of officially dating was looming over them? He and Amy had been separated for three months now, she'd served him the final divorce papers, and even after waiting for weeks through the election season, he still wanted to date her. And she wanted to date him.

Piper opened the door into the main foyer and almost ran into a short Latina woman, about forty years old, hair pulled back into a bun, in blue jeans and a puffy aqua jacket. She had an angry look on her face.

"Is this the coroner's office?" she demanded of Piper in a heavy accent.

"Uh—yes," Piper stammered.

"I need to talk to Fenway Stevenson *now*," she said. "You know where she is?"

"I'm Fenway Stevenson," Fenway said, letting Piper scoot around the angry woman and into the foyer, presumably to get the cake from the refrigerator in the IT office's break room. The woman looked familiar, although Fenway couldn't place her.

"You!" The woman stomped into the outer office, her large beige purse smacking against her hip. "You are supposed to work on suspicious deaths. But nothing! You've done *nothing* about my boy?"

"About your—" Then the answer clicked in Fenway's mind, almost audibly. "Oh—you're Rory's mother." She had seen her from a distance, and had seen photos, but she hadn't spoken to her face-to-face before. It took Fenway a couple of seconds before the name came to her—Marisol Velásquez.

"I say I have heard nothing!" the woman said, raising her voice. "You make me think you care about people and justice. But no. Just like all the others. You care only about popularity and your election." She stepped right up to Fenway and looked up into her face, her eyes flashing with anger.

"I don't—" Fenway began.

"Hey, hey," Dez said, stepping around her desk and holding her hands out, palms up. "I think there's been a misunder—"

"Oh, *somebody* doesn't understand," Rory's mother seethed. "My boy is dead for five days, and I hear nothing. No calls. Nobody coming by the house. *Nothing!*"

"That's because Coroner Stevenson isn't in charge of this investigation," Dez said, trying to position her body between Mrs. Velásquez and Fenway. "The sheriff is leading it."

"No, no. It is the *coroner* who—"

"The coroner was injured in the explosion," Dez said. "She was in the hospital for the first twenty-four hours. The sheriff took over the investigation."

Rory's mother shook her head. "Rory was a good boy. He worked for you. For your—how do you say—your *campaign*. He died because he helped you. Because he did something *nice* for you."

The rock of guilt in Fenway's stomach dropped. "I know," Fenway said, "and I'm—"

"You and I? We will talk *now*," Rory's mother said.

Fenway stole a glance at Dez. "It's okay," Fenway said. "I'll take care of this."

Dez looked sideways at Fenway. "Okay, rookie," she murmured. "It's your funeral."

"Why don't we go into my office?" Fenway suggested, though it was more like a statement. "You can tell me everything you want to know about your son's investigation. Even though I'm not leading it, I can find out where we stand, and I'll be sure that someone gets back to you by the end of the day."

"You think I have anywhere to be?" Mrs. Velásquez said. "My son is murdered. My husband is gone, left town. No. I stay right here until I get answers."

"I understand," Fenway said. "Come on in. Take a seat."

"Don't think you can sit me down in your office and tell me nice stories. It's been five days. *Five days,* Coroner. No patting me on the head and telling me to go away."

"No," Fenway said, "I won't do that."

Fenway led the way into her office. She barely knew the place because for two months she'd always been out in the field, or at a campaign event. The room had an almost ethereal quality to it. It wasn't too different from when she had first walked in after her predecessor was murdered. The window to the outside was closed, but it was colder here than in the main office space, and the leafless trees and the high gray clouds contributed to the gloom.

Rory's mother closed the door and turned toward Fenway, a different look on her face. "Okay," she said, quietly but quickly. "I don't think I have much time. My husband is in a lot of trouble, I think."

"What?" Fenway creased her brow in confusion.

"Out there—I am not mad. *Estoy fingiendo.* It is all fake."

"Fake? You're not angry?"

"I don't know who to trust. But, I make a bet I can trust you,

Coroner." She pulled a file folder out of her large purse and put it on her desk. "I find these in a locked file cabinet in the backroom of the shop. I can't figure it out. I think I see a lot of money going around, going to other accounts. Money from I don't know where."

Fenway opened the file folder with the Central Auto Body name and logo at the top. It was a spreadsheet and it looked generic. No company name, and no context for what the spreadsheet could be for, but she recognized the unique look of a payment ledger and balance sheet. The name on the first line was *Global Advantage Executive Consulting*.

"I'll be damned," Fenway said under her breath.

"*¿Qué es?*"

"I recognize the name of this consulting company," Fenway said. "We've seen payments to this organization from quite a few of the businesses here in the area."

"Are they all hidden like this one?"

"They—" Fenway started to say, and then stopped herself. "I don't think I can comment on an ongoing investigation, Mrs. Velásquez."

Rory's mother gave a pained smile. "Call me Marisol. But not out there. You say there were payments from this consulting company to the two other dead men who were killed last week? Then, I think, maybe *they're* the ones who killed my son, too."

Fenway nodded. "We're getting warrants on as many financial records as we can."

Marisol Velásquez looked Fenway in the face. "What do you think it is?"

"It may all be interconnected illegal activity." Fenway shook her head. "But I've told you as much as I can right now."

"Take these files. You see many, many payments in there. Payments with information. Use it to find out who killed my son."

"Information like what?"

"Names! Names on the checking accounts, names on receipts, names on forms. Sometimes there is only an account number, maybe a fake company."

"Like what we found out so far."

"*Es verdad,*" Marisol said, "but look for the names of people. People you can connect with fake company names, yes?"

Fenway paused. "Is my father's name in here?"

"I don't look," she said. "The more I know, the more they can get to me."

Fenway glanced through the file. There were over seventy pages of not just spreadsheets, but email printouts and text message logs, too.

"Your husband liked to keep records of these activities."

"Domingo, he doesn't trust anyone. He always says he can only trust himself. I think he doesn't even trust *me* to know."

Fenway flipped through the last few pages. "This might be helpful, Mrs. Velásquez. Marisol."

"I want to help. I found this, and I think it can help. Yes?"

Fenway nodded, flipping through the pages. "So," Fenway said slowly, "that was all an act?"

"*Lo siento.* I had no choice. Some names in the files are powerful people. Like I said, I don't know who I can trust."

The woman was right to be wary, especially since McVie still hadn't figured out who the mole was in the sheriff's office.

"If somebody sees me, are they going to think, 'okay, she found the files'? Not if I come in here and start yelling." She tapped her forehead. "Okay, Coroner, put them somewhere safe." She turned to go. "And find out who killed my boy."

Fenway nodded.

She opened the door and raised her voice. "Maybe if you weren't so worried about winning the election you'd know something."

Dez appeared behind her. "All right, Ms. Velásquez, that's enough. You want to yell at someone, the sheriff has an office right across the street. I'll even escort you over there if you like."

"I'm going," Mrs. Velásquez snapped. "It's nice to see my tax dollars going to people who only care about getting re-elected."

"We'll be in touch," Fenway said.

"I hope so." Mrs. Velásquez sniffed, then turned on her heel and left.

"What was that about?" asked Dez. "She was upset."

"Her son is dead," Fenway said.

"Think she'll come back with a shotgun?"

Fenway shook her head. "No. I calmed her down. She just wants answers."

"Man, I can't *believe* Sheriff McVie would blow her off," Dez said. "Normally he's so good about doing stuff like that."

Fenway stopped for a moment, considering.

"Come into my office for a minute, Dez," she said.

CHAPTER THREE

DEZ ROLLED HER EYES. "I'M NOT GOING TO MISS OUT ON CAKE FOR this." She zipped to the center table where a few pieces of the *Congratulations Fenway* cake were on small paper plates. Dez took two pieces of cake and two forks and followed Fenway into her office.

Dez closed the door behind her with her foot. "Let me guess," she said. "You want to be brought up to speed on the Jessica Marquez murder."

"Yes." Fenway sat down in her chair behind the desk. "But first, I want to talk about payments from the global consulting firm."

"Wait." Dez placed the two plates on the desk but remained standing. "I'm on a new murder, and you want to discuss the consulting payments from the *last* murder case?"

"I do," said Fenway. "Jeremy Kapp, Domingo Velásquez, Dr. Tassajera—they all got payments from Global Advantage. We don't have much else to go on for Dr. Tassajera's murder."

"And why Domingo Velásquez disappeared after his minivan blew up with his son behind the wheel."

"Exactly."

Dez tapped her foot. "Don't tell me you think Jessica Marquez is part of it too?"

Fenway shook her head. "No, no, there's nothing to suggest that," she said. "Not yet, anyway, but I haven't seen any evidence from this morning."

Dez nodded. "I'll bring you up to speed."

"And because Jessica Marquez's death happened so soon after the others, I think we better at least *look* into her accounts and see if there's anything from Global Advantage. Even if there isn't, you might find a motive."

"Even if we find evidence of Jessica Marquez being paid by Global Advantage, keep in mind those payments had nothing to do with Jeremy Kapp's murder."

"I know," Fenway said. "But when we were talking about the murders all being related, we thought Jeremy Kapp's murder was the first domino, remember?"

Dez nodded.

"What if it was *still* the first domino? What if whoever is behind the payments and the money laundering and everything—what if they thought Kapp's death meant something?"

"Like what?"

"Maybe that Domingo Velásquez and Dr. Jacob Tassajera were, I don't know, skimming off the top, or had somehow betrayed someone."

"You'll see if there are any payments that involved Jessica Marquez, too?"

Fenway shrugged. "I'll at least look into it. A Shakespeare troupe manager involved in a money laundering ring is *crazy*."

"True," Dez said, "but it's crazy to think your shrink would be caught up in it, too. And now Mark is investigating his murder." She motioned her head at the door. "What information did Rory's mom have about the killings?"

Fenway stared at her. "How did you know?"

"I was there when McVie made the first phone call to her," she said. "She's been in the loop. I knew there was something else going on than her being mad at you."

"But you played along."

Dez clapped Fenway on the shoulder. "I've been doing this a long time, rookie."

Fenway's phone buzzed. It was a message from McVie.

Coming to your office to get my car

"That McVie?" Dez said.

"Yeah. I need to give him his car keys." Fenway put her hands on her hips. "Seriously, has Dominguez County ever had this many open homicide cases at one time?"

"Hey," Dez said, "Listen, I know I call you 'rookie' all the time, and I ride your ass. But don't beat yourself up over this. You solved one murder while winning an election. That's something. You've got the highest close rate on homicides of any coroner in this county's history."

"If you don't count the last three."

"Which have been active cases for less than a week."

"Still, it's a small sample size," Fenway said.

"It's always a small sample size."

"Not if we don't catch the person who's responsible for the other murders last week. I'm afraid it'll keep multiplying."

"I don't know," said Dez carefully. "Look, Jeremy Kapp's murder was a family thing, personal. Now that that fact is public, that it had nothing to do with money laundering, maybe whoever killed Dr. Tassajera and Rory Velásquez will realize the killing can stop now."

Fenway shook her head. "Maybe, but we still need to investigate whether Jessica Marquez got herself involved with these other payments."

"You can't jump to conclusions that Jessica Marquez's death had something to do with the other murders. Don't get ahead of yourself. And remember—you've assigned *me* to the Marquez case. I happen to think I *should* dig through her financials, but you better believe I'll keep an open mind."

"Look for payments like the ones Jeremy Kapp and Dr. Tassajera received."

"Hey—no. I'll look for evidence of motive. If anything is connected, I'll point it out. But I won't have any preconceived ideas of what I might find."

Fenway nodded. "Right—yes. I know you're right."

Dez cocked her head and looked at Fenway. "Did you get any sleep when you went back home?"

Fenway shrugged. "I tried. Couldn't sleep. I called Charlotte, which was a mistake."

"Your dad out of jail yet?"

Fenway shook her head. "No. I'm not sure what's going on. I ran into the detective from Bellingham on my way over here, and I think there's a jurisdictional issue. I guess my father's rich lawyers can't seem to make any headway on getting him out. Maybe I can talk to the D.A. and find out what's going on."

"You should take the day off. Try to get some rest."

"I need to be briefed on the Marquez case."

"Yes, and we need to get Piper started on the financial records, and we need to keep the feelers out for Domingo Velásquez. But you won't do any good if you're exhausted."

"We've got three open homicides," Fenway said.

"Listen, rookie," Dez said, "*you're* for real now. You're not babysitting the position anymore. You're not here to keep everyone happy. You're here to make sure that we do everything we can to get to the bottom of every suspicious death. But you've got a staff. A *good* staff I know you believe in. Mark and me—you know we're good. And you know we've got your back—Migs too. But you've got to realize the rest of us can shoulder an equal amount of the load. If you let us help you, you'll be in a position to do your best work."

"You're right," Fenway said, avoiding Dez's eyes.

"Hah!" Dez said. "Of course I'm right. I got a couple of write-ups for insubordination over the years to prove it, too." She lowered her voice. "Listen, Fenway, I'll make you a deal. You show me you're okay letting your team handle their share of the work in these homicides, and I won't call you 'rookie' anymore."

"Not at all?"

Dez grinned. "Well, not in front of other people."

Fenway paused. "Look, Dez, I've never managed anyone before. I've always had to rely on myself, think on my feet. I'm not used to it."

"Are you making an excuse to keep being a control freak? Or are you asking for help figuring out what you can assign to me, Mark, and Migs?"

"Uh, I guess I'm asking for help."

"No problem," Dez said. "I've done some management in my time. If I see you drowning in work, or you feel yourself pulled in a bunch of different directions and you don't know what to do, talk to me."

"All right, it's a deal." Fenway smiled at Dez, then picked up the folder that Mrs. Velásquez had given her. She walked out with Dez. Piper was sitting on Migs's desk again, dangling her legs as he smiled at her through a mouthful of cake.

"Thanks for the cake, Piper," Fenway said.

"You're welcome," she said. "By the way, the warrant came through for Jessica Marquez's financials. I should be getting access to the files soon."

"Those warrants came through fast."

"There wasn't much to consider against it," Piper said. "McVie ran into a judge on his way in and dragged him back into the building to sign it."

"Even getting the application for the warrant done that quickly? Someone was sure on the ball."

"You're welcome," Migs said.

"Ah," Fenway said. "I should have guessed. Thanks, Migs."

"See, Fenway?" Dez said. "We've all got your back."

"You'll miss me when I'm a real lawyer," he said. Piper lightly punched him on the shoulder.

"Hey, Piper, walk with me, would you?" said Fenway.

"Oh. Sure." She hopped down from the desk. "I'll see you after work, Migs."

Dez said, "I'll do some paperwork and head to Nidever in about an hour. Catch me before I leave, if you want a briefing."

Fenway nodded, walked around the front desk, and held open the door; Piper went through.

"Everything okay?" Piper said in a low voice.

"We got something, but we can't let anyone know we have it," Fenway said. "Because it might endanger the person who gave it to me."

"Oh, okay, understood."

Fenway stopped and looked Piper in the eye. "I mean *anyone*," she repeated. "That means no one else in the IT department. That means talk to me, and me only about what you find. Make sure you do your research so it can't be tracked."

Piper's eyes widened. "You think someone on the inside—"

"I don't know what I think," Fenway interrupted, "and I won't play around when I don't know what the risk is. I trust you, Piper. Keep this between you and me. Not even Migs."

"But Migs is—"

"I know. I trust Migs too, but the more people know, the more this could go off the rails. I'm not telling Mark. I'm not even telling McVie."

"Wow." Piper paused. "Did you tell Dez?"

"Dez figured out what was going on already," Fenway said. "But I wouldn't have told her if she hadn't."

Piper was quiet for a moment.

Fenway tapped the folder. "There are more financial records in here, so you need to be careful with it."

"More financial records? From who?"

"This is a ledger and a bunch of spreadsheets from Central Auto Body."

"That's the shop owned by Rory's father, right?"

"Right."

"I've already got a bunch of their financial records. Lots of sketchy payments back and forth."

"Right, but I'm hoping we can connect some of those payments and shell companies to real people. I think Domingo Velásquez made some notes. We might get some insights—and hopefully, some real names."

They walked down the hallway and stopped at the door to the IT office.

"You okay?" asked Fenway.

"Uh, yeah," said Piper, reaching out to turn the door handle, then pausing. "Actually—no."

"What's wrong?"

"Last week, we've had *four* murders in Dominguez County," she said. "Sure, violent crime has risen the last few years, but we only had one murder *all* of last year."

Fenway shook her head. "Carl Cassidy and Lewis Fairweather are getting reclassified as homicides," Fenway said.

"Okay," Piper said, "but that's still three last *year* and four last *week*. The people involved in this money laundering scheme for the oil that supposedly isn't coming in and isn't being shipped out? They're *all* dropping dead."

"But Jeremy Kapp's murder wasn't because of that," Fenway whispered. "He was involved, but the money laundering didn't factor into the motive."

"I know," Piper said, "but I know you think the other murders were. I think whoever is behind *those* murders started to freak out when Jeremy Kapp was killed, and they started putting a plan in motion."

Fenway smiled. "That's exactly what I told Dez."

"And you're not freaking out?"

"Why? You're afraid you'll get caught up in it?"

"Yes! I'm just a computer geek. I'm not on the front lines. I'm not carrying a gun to work every day. I'm happy sitting in front of my PC and getting overtime if I don't leave by five. I'm going a little crazy."

Fenway paused. "Okay," she said after a moment. "I'm not sure what I can do, but I'll figure something out." She paused. "You know what will make us safe?"

"Catching this guy," Piper said.

"Right."

"And I'm the only one who can help."

Fenway shrugged. "I guess we'd figure out a way to get it done if you weren't here—actually, no, we probably wouldn't. You're crucial. You have a unique skill set here."

"I wish my paycheck reflected that."

"That's the spirit." Fenway handed her the folder. Piper took it, opened the door, and stepped into the IT office, shutting the door behind her.

Fenway turned, intending to go back into her office and get a briefing on that morning's activities, but instead walked down the hallway and went outside.

The gray of the morning had settled into midday as well, and the wind had picked up, coming cold and damp off the ocean. She stood close to the sidewalk, breathing the wet air, and decided she was ready to go in. She turned—and a sharp pain in her knee almost made her lose her balance. She caught herself, wincing, then gingerly felt her knee; it still hurt to the touch, but the sharp pain receded and then it was fine again.

Fenway straightened up, and it hit her, all at once, how tired she was. The lack of sleep—not only from the night before, but all week—descended upon her, and she was so overwhelmed for a minute she had to hold back tears.

She couldn't remember the last time she had a good night's sleep. Fenway was often used to being exhausted at the end of the workday with the coroner's responsibilities, but she was usually able to fall into a deep, heavy sleep quickly, even when she had a full day ahead of her, or a problem she couldn't solve. But this was different. The explosion in the parking garage. The vandalized car. The brick through her window. Now she had to—as McVie put it—delegate responsibility, making sure her team did the job right without doing it herself. All while showing the world that she was calm and levelheaded.

But she didn't feel calm and levelheaded anymore. The last few days were clawing at the back of her mind, and more than anything, she wanted to pull up the covers and forget about life for a few hours. Or maybe even a few days.

She didn't want to quit, though. The job had its hooks in her.

She wondered what would have happened if she hadn't run for coroner. If she had just babysat the coroner's office like she was supposed to. That had been the deal with her father, after all.

Maybe the last two killers she caught would have gotten away with it.

Maybe her father's handpicked candidate would have won the election instead.

But it *still* wouldn't have gotten her away from the four murders in the last week. Granted, she wouldn't have had to deal with the election at the same time, but without the election, she might not have known about the refinery's political deals. And that might be the key to solving the case.

Of course, McVie might not have run for mayor without Fenway running for coroner. He might be looking forward to four more years as sheriff instead of staring bleakly at an unknown future. In fact, she and McVie would probably already be dating, with neither of them needing to hold off on anything because of the election. She'd be applying to hospitals and clinics for open nursing positions, maybe a few not even in Estancia.

Maybe it would have been good. Maybe she would have been happier.

Her phone rang.

It was McVie.

"Hey," she said, trying to sound calm and happy.

"Hey," McVie said. "Sorry, I got waylaid."

"Yeah. I got waylaid, too. Rory's mom came into the office when I was there and she—"

Fenway bit her tongue. She had almost told McVie about the ledger.

"She what?"

"She was angry with me for not doing more to help out on her son's investigation."

"What?"

"I know. I told her you were handling it, but she read me the riot act in my office."

McVie grunted. "I guess I should have been keeping her more informed. I mean, I thought I was doing okay with her, but we don't have much to go on. A bunch of leads haven't led anywhere, and we're still waiting for the lab results." He paused. "And I checked—you won't get your car for another few days, but they'll make sure it's at the front of the line for processing."

"They haven't even started processing it yet?"

"Sorry. The lab is backed up. You know how it is."

"What the hell are they doing with it? My car didn't even get covered with that debris from the bomb. I mean—the blast totaled a couple of cars on either side. Mine was at least fifty feet away."

"Ask them. I don't know what's taking so long."

Fenway opened her mouth to rant some more, then closed it. "Okay, sorry. I know it's not your responsibility. Come on over. Your keys are on my desk."

"Okay. I'm going back to Nidever and interviewing a few of the students now. Pruitt finally agreed to make them available."

"That's good."

McVie was silent for a moment.

"So—I'll see you in a few minutes?" Fenway prodded.

"Yeah. A few minutes."

Fenway hung up and went inside.

"Okay," Dez said, cutting herself another slice of cake and following Fenway into her office. "So. The evidence from this morning."

"Right," Fenway said, settling into her seat.

"Open up your email. You should have the photos in there by now."

Fenway woke up her PC and found several dozen photos in her email.

"Okay, rookie," Dez said, "the first few are the fragment of bone and the piece of glass you found. The techs have them now. Just one other item I found in the stairwell—a stray hair, visual match to Jessica Marquez."

"Okay. Did you cordon off the second-floor hallway?"

Dez smirked. "Yeah—that university president sure got his panties in a twist over that one, let me tell you."

"I'm sure you handled him with your usual charming diplomacy, Dez."

"You know it. My voice is the music that soothes the savage beast."

"Uh-huh."

"Well, something like that, anyway." She turned Fenway's monitor so she could see it better. "Now, at the side of the hallway, photo 6A."

Fenway squinted. "Is that a big earring?"

"Nope. It's a button."

Fenway enlarged the photo until it filled her screen. The metal button had been treated to look like brushed nickel, with a small emblem on the front: a stylized K and an equally stylized Q, intertwined in a latticework pattern. It was a famous logo on an expensive-looking button.

"Not just any button, either," Dez said.

"Is that a Kendra Quinlan logo?"

"Sure is. I see someone was paying attention during Fashion Week."

"Well, rich-kids' school, right?"

Dez nodded. "Right."

"But who knows how long that button was there?"

"I can't be sure," Dez said, "but I talked with the cleaning staff, and that hallway got cleaned last night at six thirty. They might not clean the corners the way my mother would have wanted, but they do okay. And they wouldn't have missed this button. It's not like it was hidden or wedged in a corner. I think someone dropped it there last night. You can't see this in the photo, but there's not much dust on it. It hasn't been there long."

"Okay. What else?"

"So have you heard of this group that Jessica Marquez managed?"

"Uh, no. You mean the theater group?"

Dez nodded. "She was the—let me see." Dez flipped through her notebook. "Here it is. She was the general manager of the North American Shakespeare Guild."

"Wow, that sounds fancy."

"I think it's intentional that it sounds fancier than it is. But Nidever agreed to have this professor run things—you might have heard of him. Professor Virgil Cygnus?"

Fenway shook her head. "But I've only been around here for six months, remember?"

Dez nodded. "Yeah. I see their plays every year. They're student-led —I guess there's a class associated with it—but it's a lot more professional than most local theater I've seen. Certainly around here, anyway. Not a whole lot of cultural experiences in Estancia, and Professor Cygnus seems like he cares about the text. He gets a little crazy sometimes, though. They did a production of *The Merchant of Venice* last year that—I swear to God—had a live capuchin monkey."

"A live monkey?"

"Yeah. It was a whole thing. Don't get McVie started." Dez straightened up. "Anyway, the offices of the North American Shakespeare Guild are on the second floor. They've got an outer office and a back office—that back office was for Jessica Marquez, and the outer office is where the students work and have their computers and files."

"Files?"

Dez nodded. "Yeah. They coordinate a London theater trip every summer, and they take checks for it. Professor Cygnus is kinda old-school, I guess." She leaned forward. "Click on the photos labeled 13A through 13K."

Fenway did. Immediately, eleven pictures of two ransacked offices came up. Files were spread across the floor, desks were overturned, trophies were knocked over, papers were strewn everywhere. On the wall was a large poster of *The Taming of the Shrew*, with stylized illustrations of Petruchio and Katherine holding hands with handcuffs encircling their wrists. The art was flat, like an old woodcut from the native Chumash. Fenway wondered if there had been some thematic purpose to the choice of artwork. The back office—Jessica's—had also been tossed, with drawers open, chairs on their side, and papers covering the floor.

Fenway looked through four pictures, marveling at all the bills and checks and file folders on the carpet. "They didn't keep any of those files on computers?"

"Oh, of course they did, but, you know, all those signatures, receipts, tickets—a lot of the information is still done by paper."

"What a mess," Fenway murmured.

"I'll tell you, the university president sure didn't like seeing those offices tossed," Dez said. "He looked like he was ready to kill somebody."

"Did they take anything?"

Dez shrugged. "It looks like there's a missing laptop, but we don't know if anything else is gone. We had to hustle Dr. Pruitt out of there. He wanted to come in and assess everything, but it was a crime scene, and we couldn't let him. We took pictures, and CSI was there fingerprinting, but we have to wait for a student who works there to tell us what's missing."

"When is that happening?"

"Late this afternoon, I hope. Dr. Pruitt is supposed to make the arrangements. The girl's name is Amanda Kohl, but we want to interview her first." She paused. "I think Dr. Pruitt believes we'll speak to all the students in a group."

"But we're not."

Dez shrugged. "I didn't want him to deny us access."

Fenway nodded and turned back to the pictures of the office. "Anything of Jessica's in there?"

"Her purse was there. Everything seemed to be in it, but it looked like someone had gone through it—things not in the right place, the clasp of the wallet undone—stuff like that. But she had a spot for a laptop, and no laptop. Not that we've been able to find, anyway."

Fenway brought photograph 13J to the front. It was a wide shot of Jessica Marquez's office. It, too, was a mess, although some of the shelves behind the desk were less untidy than the others.

"See, this is why I keep my apartment in a state of constant upheaval," Fenway said. "Anybody who comes in to toss the place will think they got there after someone else has already ransacked it."

Dez grimaced. "Don't quit being coroner to do stand-up."

"You're right, Dez, this job is so much more glamorous."

"Oh, bring up the photos in set fourteen."

Fenway clicked and saw three photos of an award.

It was a weighty, impressive piece of rock and heavy glass. The base was black onyx, with silvery veins running through it. The clear top was chunky, inch-thick crystal, in a kind of trapezoidal shape, but set at an angle into the base. Etched into the crystal were a logo and some lettering. Fenway clicked on another picture that had zoomed in on the inscription.

West Coast Theater Educators
Third Annual Shakespeare Awards
"The Bardies"
Professor Virgil Cygnus, Director
North American Shakespeare Guild
Macbeth
Best Shakespeare Production

Fenway clicked through the pictures of the award. The onyx base was scuffed, and the crystal had a large scratch across its face, which almost certainly wouldn't be fixable. But it looked like the damage had been done by something metallic, certainly not a human skull, and there was no blood on the award.

Fenway looked at the award again and noted the year. She clicked on the photo with the piece of bloody crystal.

"What do you think, Dez? Could the shard of crystal have come from this award, or is this one of those acrylics that look like glass?"

Dez leaned forward on the desk. "It's crystal for sure, and it might match, but there isn't a chunk out of this one. At least—I don't think there is. No blood that I could see. The lab will be able to tell for sure."

"If this Shakespeare program is supposed to be so incredible, maybe there's another award like this that *does* have a piece missing." She opened a web browser and typed *West Coast Theater Educators Shakespeare* and hit Search. The first link listed confirmed her suspicions.

"Last year," she said to Dez. "The Guild won for *The Merchant of Venice*. Did you come across that award too?"

Dez shook her head.

Maybe that award was the murder weapon.

A knock sounded at the door and McVie stuck his head in. "Hey."

In one fluid motion, Fenway tossed McVie's keys to him. He flinched and they bounced off his chin, landing on the floor.

Dez snickered. "This is why I didn't want you on my intramural basketball team, Sheriff. You might be able to hit those fadeaway jumpers, but you're a liability on defense."

He opened the door a little more, squeezing his shoulders inside and leaning over to pick up his keys. "You ready to go, Dez?"

"Where? Nidever? Already?"

"I got us a meeting with Professor Cygnus, too. He might be able to shed some light on things."

Dez shook her head. "I'm picking up the search warrant for Jessica Marquez's house, and I was going over there as soon as I could. CSI is meeting me there. I thought the students were meeting us later this afternoon."

"Oh," McVie said. "Well, never mind. I can go by myself. Although it's always good to have a couple of people interviewing."

"Maybe I could head over to Marquez's house." Fenway jutted her chin out, as if it were a substitute for raising her hand.

Dez shook her head. "I think you'll do better interviewing those kids." She stood up. "Besides, I had to dig through all the file cabinets in my brain to keep up with the Shakespeare references they made this morning. You can talk about that shit in your sleep, Fenway."

"Yeah," Fenway said, the two open homicides from the week before still bothering her. Then she remembered—*delegate*. "Okay. Let me get Mark working on the Tassajera case. I'll meet you at the car in about ten minutes."

"I'm taking a cruiser. Meet me in the yard."

————

Mark was eager to dig into the Tassajera case, and a weight lifted from Fenway's shoulders—she hadn't known where to start, but Mark immediately jumped on the computer to request phone records—with a zest she hadn't seen for a while.

She jogged across the street, squinting against the drizzle, and walked through the sheriff's office toward the transportation yard. All through the building, people congratulated her on the election win. *I didn't realize so many people liked me.* She chuckled. *Maybe they just hated my opponent.*

McVie was waiting for her at the edge of the transportation yard, a cruiser idling a few feet away.

"You ready?"

"Yeah."

"You look more relaxed."

Fenway bobbed her head. "I took your advice and I'm handing things off. Mark was more than happy to take on the Tassajera case. I don't know why I hadn't done it before."

McVie smirked, and Fenway shook her head. It was smart of him not to say anything.

They were quiet in the car as they got on the George Nidever

Expressway. Fenway turned to McVie a couple of times but couldn't think of anything to say.

McVie licked his lips and finally spoke. "Pruitt wasn't easy to deal with, you know, but he wound up getting to where we were."

"Not easy to deal with?"

The sheriff nodded. "Right. He's protective of the Shakespeare program. I don't know if you were old enough to remember, but Professor Cygnus put Nidever on the map. It used to be a tiny, rich-kids' liberal arts college. Cygnus and his grandiose ideas made national headlines a couple of times. People started recognizing the name. I mean—it's not Stanford, but it isn't tiny anymore. And the famous alumni haven't hurt, either."

"But Pruitt was uncooperative?"

McVie looked thoughtful. "Maybe uncooperative is too strong of a word. He sure didn't want to cordon off the hallway on the second floor, that's for sure, and he went ballistic when he saw that The Guild's office was tossed."

"The Guild?"

"Oh, yeah, sorry, that's what the Nidever people call it—not the North American Shakespeare Guild, or the NASG, or anything like that —they call it 'The Guild.'" McVie affected Pruitt's thin, reedy voice. "'Really, Sheriff, disrupting a whole morning of classes—is that necessary?'"

Fenway smiled. "Not that you were *looking* for ways to be a pain in the ass."

"That guy." McVie grimaced as he turned onto a university road. "He gets under my skin."

They pulled into the parking lot behind the DiFazio Theater and McVie turned the wipers off. "Okay," McVie said. "The first interview will be with the professor—Virgil Cygnus. He's been here for over thirty years, and he thinks he runs the place."

The image of her father's smug smile flashed in her head as they got out and walked quickly through the heavy mist toward the theater entry. "Don't worry. I'm used to dealing with people like that."

McVie looked at her out of the corner of his eye. "We'll be okay as long as we keep Dr. Pruitt out of our—"

The entry door swung open, and Dr. Alfred Pruitt stood in the doorway, taking a step out and folding his arms. Next to him stood a man who looked to be in his sixties, with straight white hair touching the tops of his shoulders, where it curled under slightly, like a medieval pudding-basin cut. He had small, keen brown eyes behind thick black-rimmed glasses, thin lips, and a strong jaw. He wore a polo shirt in spite of the cold weather, and his muscular arms stretched the sleeves around his biceps.

"Good morning again," McVie said. He didn't break his stride as he walked up to the pair, turning to the white-haired man. "You must be Professor Cygnus. Thanks for making the time to meet with—"

Pruitt stood between them and put up a hand. "I'm afraid you'll have to wait a bit on talking with the professor."

"Two days before opening night allows me no time for anything else but study and direction, Sheriff," Professor Cygnus said. "I'm afraid Dr. Pruitt overstepped when he promised my time to you."

"It won't take more than half an hour, Professor."

Cygnus put his hands out, palms up. "I don't have a half hour, sheriff. I may have some time on Saturday. I'll have all the time in the world after we close in two weeks."

"Not even to discuss the death of your general manager?"

"Not even for that," Cygnus said. "For the next two weeks, I will think of nothing but *Othello*. I wish it weren't this way, but I'm not one to multitask. Forgive me." He backed out of the doorway and turned, walking surprisingly quickly through the lobby.

"Professor—" Fenway called, but he was already through the theater doors.

McVie set his jaw. "Dr. Pruitt, this is a murder investigation. We can't allow Professor Cygnus to simply not make himself available."

Pruitt shook his head. "I don't believe that's necessary. I can tell you unequivocally that Professor Cygnus had nothing to do with—"

"With all due respect," McVie said, "you're not in a position to tell us what's necessary in a murder investigation."

Pruitt glared at McVie.

Fenway took a step forward. "No one is in a better position to give us information on Ms. Marquez's background and her relationship with the people she knew at Nidever than Professor Cygnus. He's first on the list."

Pruitt scoffed. "You saw his reaction. I'm afraid meeting with him is impossible right now. Surely you know how much Professor Cygnus and the North American Shakespeare Guild mean to this community."

Fenway cocked her head. "I moved here only six months ago, Dr. Pruitt, I'm sorry." She caught herself apologizing and clamped her mouth shut.

Dr. Pruitt looked at her above his glasses, and he clicked his tongue. "Professor Cygnus is quite possibly the most renowned American Shakespeare scholar alive. It was quite a coup when he agreed to teach Shakespeare here—and more than that, direct a play every year. Are you quite sure you've never heard of The Guild?"

Fenway set her mouth in a line. "Quite sure."

"The North American Shakespeare Guild is the university's star achievement. It's our way of giving Professor Cygnus a certain level of autonomy. The Guild not only puts on the Shakespeare play every year, but it also sponsors *Guild at the Globe.*"

"What's that? Something to do with the Shakespeare theater in London?"

Pruitt nodded. "Correct. A summer theater tour of London and Stratford-upon-Avon."

"Like a study abroad program."

"No—it's not just with Nidever students, but with students from universities all over the country, and with theater lovers of all ages."

Fenway raised her eyebrows; Pruitt sounded like he had memorized their sales brochure. He also sounded like he was trying to change the subject away from Professor Cygnus. "Dr. Pruitt, if—"

"They attend three weeks' worth of plays," Pruitt continued, as if

Fenway hadn't spoken. "The theater actors do lectures and workshops with all the attendees. It's the envy of every English department in California. Possibly the world."

"And my ninth level of hell," muttered McVie.

"While I'm always up for a good history lesson, what does that have to do with Jessica Marquez's death?" Fenway said, ignoring McVie.

"She's the general manager. For the last two years, she's run the business end of things for The Guild," Dr. Pruitt said. "All the marketing for the *Guild at the Globe* tours, as well as the bookkeeping, taxes—she was truly a one-woman show, making The Guild run smoothly." He harrumphed. "I'm not sure what Professor Cygnus will do without her, frankly. We'll have to get someone in here to take the business reins. I'm sure it won't affect the production or the summer tour, but it won't be easy." His voice faltered at the end.

Fenway paused for a moment while Pruitt composed himself, then continued. "So there's a Guild production going on right now?"

"Opening night is Friday, as I said." Dr. Pruitt said.

"Is this a professional company, or is it all students?"

"We like to think of it as both," Dr. Pruitt said, losing his defeated posture and puffing out his chest a bit. "You won't find a finer Shakespeare production on the West Coast. Oh sure, maybe in terms of fancy sets, but Professor Cygnus turns these students into better actors than they have at the RSC."

"The what?" McVie asked.

"The Royal Shakespeare Company," said Fenway. "Super-famous British Shakespeare group. Based in Shakespeare's birthplace, right?"

Pruitt nodded.

Fenway had her doubts that any professor at a small liberal arts college could turn ordinary American students into RSC-level actors, but she pressed on. "So Miss Marquez was also dealing with the marketing and publicity for The Guild's production?"

"Yes."

"What's the play they're putting on? Did the professor say they were doing *Othello?*"

"Yes," Dr. Pruitt said proudly. "It's a tough play, of course, but that doesn't scare anyone, least of all Professor Cygnus. The Guild put on *The Merchant of Venice* last year, and it was a huge hit. Even won a theater award. We're hoping for a repeat performance with *Othello.*"

Othello. Fenway tasted bile in her mouth. She swallowed hard and kept her face neutral. "How was the marketing and advertising being received?"

"What do you mean?"

Fenway shifted from foot to foot. "*Othello* is a controversial play. So is *Merchant,* for that matter. Has anyone seemed upset by the play, or by the way Marquez was marketing it?"

Pruitt chuckled. "All of Shakespeare is controversial, and I suppose there will always be 'social justice warriors' trying to pick a fight for the most ridiculous reasons."

Fenway bristled, but rubbed her nose and changed tack. "So that's a *yes?* Did Marquez get threats, or were there protests?"

Pruitt looked almost disappointed. "Well, no. There haven't been any protests, and Jessica didn't get any threats about the play. At least none I'm aware of."

Fenway understood why McVie found such glee in upsetting Dr. Pruitt; the university president spun everything in the service of his own ego. She moved to another line of questioning. "So she would have been interacting with who? Professor Cygnus? The stage manager? The ticket people?"

"Oh, that's the genius of The Guild," gushed Dr. Pruitt. "The staging, the costumes, the ticket process, the music—it's all done by students. You'd think it would reek of community theater, or amateur hour, but no—those who are expecting a typical college production are *shocked* by the professionalism of it all. A critic up from the *Santa Barbara News-Press* last year gave us five stars. 'I was stunned by the depths of betrayal and the thirst for justice that the actors were able to deliver in their captivating performances.'"

"Wow, you've memorized the review," Fenway said.

"I feel like a proud father, I don't mind telling you." He grinned, not picking up on Fenway's sarcasm.

Fenway tried to steer the conversation on track. "So Miss Marquez interacted with the students frequently?"

"Of course," Dr. Pruitt said. "In fact, several of the students work in The Guild office, helping with the tickets, the marketing, and all the coordination. It's part of how they pay for their travel when they sign up for the summer tour in the U.K."

I thought you said Jessica was a one-woman show, Fenway almost said.

"The students all report to her?"

"No, no, the play is an eight-unit Shakespeare class, taught by Professor Cygnus. The students who work in the business office all report to Jessica as their boss."

Fenway shot a look at McVie. "And Sheriff, you've set up time to interview each of the students, correct?"

Pruitt took a step forward. "We value our students' privacy here at Nidever. You said you needed to speak with the students, but I never said you could interrogate them."

"This is a murder investigation, Dr. Pruitt," McVie said. "Some of them may be witnesses. No one said anything about interrogation."

Dr. Pruitt closed his eyes. "You'll have to forgive me. I see that makes sense now, but I don't deal with murder on a regular basis."

"And it's also important we talk with Professor Cygnus," Fenway said. "I hope you can talk him into changing his mind."

Dr. Pruitt winced. "Of course," he said, faltering, "but Professor Cygnus is his own person. His *wife* could be the murder victim and he'd still spend all his time directing the play."

"Perhaps we can have a quicker, more informal chat?" McVie asked. "Does he have an office in DiFazio Hall?"

Dr. Pruitt shrugged. "He doesn't go into the office. His spot is in the theater, about six rows back. The *stage* is where he finds the voice of Shakespeare." Dr. Pruitt turned his head toward the theater entrance. "He won't be in there yet, though. The theater serves as a lecture hall until the afternoon. I'll try to reason with him, and I suppose I can't forbid you from trying to talk with him, but he'll be reticent."

"Reticent?" McVie asked.

"Hostile," said Fenway.

But Fenway wasn't thinking about the hostile Professor Virgil Cygnus. She was thinking about how Dr. Alfred Pruitt pretended to be easily distracted to mask how uncooperative he was.

CHAPTER FOUR

THE FIRST STUDENT WASN'T DUE FOR A FEW MINUTES, AND SINCE THE drizzle had finally let up, McVie and Fenway walked to the student union for coffee. There, McVie pulled a folder out of his case and showed Fenway a photocopy of The Guild's work schedule, and the name at the top had been scheduled for over twenty hours that week—more than twice as many as the other students. "Amanda Kohl," she read. "It looks like Miss Kohl is the lead office worker. She'd probably be able to tell Dez if anything is missing."

"She's also playing Desdemona," McVie said. "Pruitt said she's one of Nidever's scholarship recipients, too. Extremely dedicated. Dean's list. The only freshman in the play, which I guess is some kind of big deal."

"Why?"

"Professor Cygnus almost never takes underclassmen. Pruitt went on and on about it."

Fenway tapped the page. "She was the last student worker out of here yesterday."

McVie rubbed his arms, and Fenway looked up at him.

"What is it?"

"Well—now that the election is over, we can see each other. You know, *officially*."

Fenway smiled.

"So what would you think about having dinner tonight?"

"I think that sounds great."

"Not Dos Milagros. Someplace nice."

"Oh, Craig, don't insult Dos Milagros in front of me."

McVie smiled. "I remember you talking about that new Argentine steak house."

"Oooh," Fenway said, almost involuntarily.

"Gotcha. I'll make reservations. Is there a day this week that works for you?"

"No time like the present, right?"

"Okay. Seven tonight?"

"Sounds perfect."

"Great." McVie checked his watch. "Listen, I have to call the station. Can you head to the theater in case Amanda shows up a little early?"

"Sure."

Fenway walked to the theater, buoyant with the feeling of McVie asking her out—almost like she was in high school, and not a grown woman who had an on-and-off relationship with the sheriff.

When she opened the door to the lobby of the theater, a white girl of medium height stood nervously near a theater entry door. She had no makeup, but her skin was luminous, without the blemishes that Fenway had as an undergrad. Her eyes were wide and blue, her hair was shoulder-length and blond, very light with just a touch of goldenrod. She wore blue jeans that looked carefully torn in the right places, a bright red hooded sweatshirt unzipped down the front, and a fitted T-shirt underneath that said *If I be waspish, best beware my sting*.

"Katherine," Fenway said.

"What? No—I'm Amanda."

"Sorry, I meant your shirt. A quote from *The Taming of the Shrew*."

"Oh." She looked down. "Right. I didn't realize I was wearing this."

Fenway nodded. "Nice to meet you, Amanda. I'm Coroner Stevenson."

"You're the coroner?"

Fenway nodded. "You were expecting someone else?"

"I thought you'd be older."

"I guess you didn't pay much attention to the election."

"Oh, that. No, Professor Cygnus had us in rehearsals for, like, six hours every night for the last month."

"Dr. Pruitt told me you're playing Desdemona, right? That's a big part."

"I know. That means I'm in a *lot* of the rehearsal scenes. I barely even know what month it is. Between this play and my classes, I hardly have time to sleep."

"And work at The Guild office?"

Amanda nodded, a guilty look on her face.

"What is it?"

"I kind of feel bad for working so many hours when there's not that much work to do. There aren't enough computers for all of the student workers, so I usually do my homework. But Jessica always said we need someone to be in the office when it's open."

"And she scheduled you more than anyone else. Do you know why?"

Amanda shrugged. "I don't know, but I'm not arguing. I need the money, and I sure couldn't do my homework during work hours at most other places."

Fenway pulled a notebook out of her purse. "You were here until five last night, right?"

"Uh—no. I was *scheduled* till five, but I had to be at rehearsal at four thirty. I left at about four twenty."

"You and Jessica usually the last ones to leave?"

"Oh—no. It's usually just me. Jessica's out of here at three or four every day."

"Not at five?"

"This isn't a real nine-to-five kind of place," Amanda said.

"Are you okay with that? Your boss leaving early?"

Amanda shrugged.

Fenway realized she was tense; her shoulders were tight, her brow was creased, her right hand was even balled up into a fist. She remembered watching McVie interview reluctant witnesses. When they tensed up, he would relax his whole body, creating an easy, stress-free vibe, and he often got more forthcoming answers. So Fenway took a deep breath and exhaled slowly. She looked at Amanda and gave her a smile with what she hoped was the right amount of sadness in it.

"Listen," she said, "I don't know if you heard, but the office was ransacked. If we can figure out who did this to The Guild office, it might be important. Was there something valuable in the office? Maybe from someone who signed up for the tour?"

Amanda's shoulders dipped slightly, but her jaw was still tightened up, and her tone wasn't much different.

"I don't think so, but I just open mail, organize the checks, and enter stuff into a spreadsheet."

"People still pay by check?"

Amanda shrugged. "Probably about half. A lot of them are old. Seeing Shakespeare in Stratford is on their bucket list, I guess."

"How many computers are in the office?"

"Um... well, Jessica has a laptop."

"Does she take it home with her?"

Amanda nodded. "Oh, yeah. She never leaves it in the office."

"Do you know what kind of laptop it is?"

"What do you mean?"

"The manufacturer. The model. Stuff like that."

Amanda shook her head. "I mean, it's not a Mac. She wanted one, but the university denied it. Too expensive."

"Did she leave early yesterday?"

"Who? Jessica?"

"Right."

"No, for once she was still in her office when I left."

"What time was that again?"

Amanda's shoulders tightened up a little more. "Four twenty, like I said."

Fenway took another deep breath, hoping it would get Amanda to relax as well. "I noticed you called her 'Jessica.' You didn't call her Ms. Marquez?"

"Sure. We all called her 'Jessica.' She's not a professor or anything."

"What was her background?"

Amanda shrugged again. "I don't know. It's not like we're friends."

"Has she been acting strange at all the last few days?"

"Strange? Like how?"

"Maybe a change in her personality, maybe she's been jumpy lately, or particularly secretive?"

Amanda thought for a moment. "She *has* been secretive, but she's never been the type to open up. Of course, that might be because we're students. She has a friend who comes around every so often. Maybe you can talk with her."

"Do you have a name for this friend?"

"Um... no, I don't think so."

"What can you tell me about this friend?"

"Um... what do you mean?"

"Do you know if she works on campus? What does she look like? Stuff like that."

"Oh. I don't know where she works. She's older than the students here, but she looks younger than Jessica. About your age, I guess. And she's black. Good dresser. I noticed she had this beautiful suede jacket with a drape front on the last time she was coming out of The Guild office. I think it was a Chelsea Piers Original—it was the same one that Dana Bohannon wore on the red carpet at the Emmys last year."

"You follow fashion?"

Amanda shrugged. "Not religiously."

"You know anyone with a Kendra Quinlan blouse?"

Amanda's eyes lit up and then washed over with confusion. "I think I have a girl in my Psych class that has one. She's rich. Always bragging about her dad introducing her to celebrities. She likes to show off."

"Wearing a Kendra Quinlan blouse is showing off?"

"No, no. I mean, Quinlan is one of the few upscale designers who still cares about practicality in their clothing, sustainable practices, paying her workers a living wage, stuff like that. I've read a bunch of interviews." Amanda set her mouth in a line. "Not that the rich bitch in my class cares about any of that. She only cares that she's wearing an eighteen-hundred-fifty-dollar blouse."

"You don't have a Kendra Quinlan?"

Amanda looked at the ceiling. "Where would I get the money for that? If I hadn't gotten the scholarship, there's no way I could have come here. My mom works her ass off to make sure we have a roof over our head and food on the table, but a college fund wasn't in the cards. Designer labels weren't either."

"You seem to do okay."

"Last season's markdowns, and I'll let you in on a little secret— thrift store shopping in gentrifying neighborhoods. People don't know what they're donating half the time."

Fenway nodded. "Okay." She turned a page of her notebook. "Did Jessica have any enemies? Anyone who might have wanted to hurt her?"

"I don't think so. Like I said, I don't know her that well."

"Was she dating anyone?"

"Not that I know of."

"What about the woman in that suede jacket?"

Amanda cocked her head to the side. "I don't *think* so. She swooned over the hot male actors that Professor Cygnus would get to speak to our class. She liked their English accents. She's not into Shakespeare, so I kind of figured meeting the hot actors was the biggest perk of the job for her."

"No hot guys with accents visiting the office, then?"

Amanda shrugged. "Not while I was there, anyway."

Fenway nodded and turned another page. "Did Jessica owe anyone any money? Or did anyone owe her?"

"How would I know that?"

"You might have heard something. You work in the office more than all the other students combined."

"I only have that many hours because I'm trying to go on the summer theater trip."

"Oh, right—*The Guild at the Globe* thing?"

Amanda nodded. "Right. Not only do I get money, but my discount goes up the more hours I work."

"You're serious about acting, then?"

"Professor Cygnus and The Guild are the *only* reasons I picked Nidever over UC Santa Barbara. I got a full ride there, too, but their drama department isn't as good, and they don't have Professor Cygnus."

"Gotcha." Fenway looked through her notes. "Anything else that might have been unusual with Jessica over the last couple of weeks?"

"Not that I can think of."

"Okay, thanks. Let's go up to The Guild office and see if anything is missing."

"Now? I've got class in fifteen minutes."

"Oh. All right. We have other interviews to do. Can you come back when your classes are done?"

"Sure. I was supposed to work today anyway."

When they had settled what time they'd meet again in the theater lobby, Amanda picked up her bookbag and walked outside as McVie walked in. He held the door open for her, then crossed the lobby to where Fenway was standing.

"She was early," he said.

"She was waiting for me when I got here." Fenway pulled out her phone and brought up a web browser. "Answered all of my questions, didn't get angry, didn't push back."

"I sense a 'but' coming on."

"But," Fenway said, "I think she was lying."

"About what?"

The picture of the black-and-white silk tulip-sleeved blouse loaded onto Fenway's screen from the Kendra Quinlan website. And so did the price.

$1,850.

"I bet this blouse is hanging in Amanda's closet right now, with a button missing. She stated the exact price for it."

McVie folded his arms. "That doesn't prove anything. Maybe she likes Kendra Quinlan blouses. Megan sure does. Asked for one for her birthday."

Fenway screwed up her face. "Yeah, you're right."

"Even if she had it, she probably threw it away."

Fenway shook her head. "There's no way. She grew up poor—well, poor enough—and this is way too expensive."

"Not if there's Jessica Sanchez's blood all over it."

"True." Fenway tapped her foot. "Okay, let's see what some of the other students have to say. You said you scheduled meetings through Dr. Pruitt?"

"I did, but not till later. I thought we'd be talking to Professor Cygnus for a while, so I scheduled some of the student interviews after rehearsal."

"Maybe we can meet Amanda at The Guild office before rehearsal, and she can tell us if anything else is missing."

"Yeah, that might work." McVie paced the floor for a moment, thinking. "We might as well head over to administration. Get any files we can on Jessica Marquez. See which staff members might have been close to her."

They walked across campus to the administration building, only to find that the records office was closed for the lunch hour.

"I guess we should get some lunch, too," McVie said.

For once, Fenway's stomach wasn't complaining about missing a meal, but the cake she'd eaten a couple of hours before was still settling. She went to the student union with McVie, where a large Ernesto's sign hung in the middle of the food court.

"I didn't know they had an Ernesto's here," she said to McVie. "I've been to the one downtown. It's not bad."

"Don't tell me you *cheated* on Dos Milagros." McVie grinned.

"I was just there for the guacamole, baby," Fenway purred. "I swear, it didn't mean anything."

"There's a decent grill over there, too. I grabbed breakfast there this morning. They've got a Monte Cristo on the menu."

"I don't even like Monte Cristos." Fenway playfully elbowed McVie in the ribs. "You must be thinking of your *other* girlfriend."

The word *girlfriend* left her mouth before she could stop it. Oof—presumptuous. Too early. It might scare McVie off—hell, it might scare *her* off. Her cheeks burned as she stole a quick glance at McVie's face. He, too, was blushing.

But why—

Then it hit her.

McVie wasn't blushing at the implied girlfriend status. He was blushing because his *ex-wife* liked Monte Cristos.

"Ernesto's is great." Fenway's stomach lurched as their conversation train plummeted into a ravine. "I like their pollo asado tacos."

They stood in the short Ernesto's line in silence.

"Next," the cashier said.

McVie and Fenway stepped up to the counter, and a look of recognition came over the handsome cashier's face. He was taller than Fenway but shorter than McVie, with skin a terra cotta color, about as light as Fenway's, but much more red-hued than the predominant brown of Fenway's. His dark umber hair was cut close to his scalp, a long face and thick eyebrows above heavy-lidded, kind eyes. He wore a black polo shirt, tight on his lean, muscular frame, with a nametag that simply said x.

"Oh—you're Coroner Stevenson."

"Hi," Fenway said. "Have we met before?"

"Not really," he said. "I saw you speak at one of your campaign events. Congratulations on your win."

"Thanks," Fenway said. "Truth be told, I haven't had much time to think about it. Right into another investigation."

"Is that why DiFazio Hall has all the police tape on the second floor?"

Fenway looked at McVie, and he nodded.

"You have a class there?"

"Oh, no. I'm in a Shakespeare play. Opening night's on Friday."

"*Othello,*" Fenway said. "What part are you playing?"

The cashier smiled at Fenway. "Take a look around, Coroner. How many other black guys do you see on campus?"

"So you're in the title role, huh?"

"Yep."

McVie nodded. "So that must make you Xavier Gonsalves."

Xavier smiled. "Yes. Although my stage name is Xavier Go."

"Go?"

"Yep. My agent's idea." He straightened up, flashed a huge smile, and with both hands, pointed at Fenway. "It's Go time!" Xavier's face immediately went to its former serious state. "That was my agent's idea, too. I think he's getting a little ahead of himself, giving me a catchphrase before I've landed a serious acting role. He wanted me to shorten my first name to x, too, but fortunately, I got talked out of that."

"Not before they made your nametag, though, right?"

"Right." He paused. "Is, uh, everything all right with Amanda?"

"Your wife?"

The cashier jumped slightly. "My what?"

"Your stage wife. She's Desdemona, right?"

"Oh." Xavier looked relieved. "Yeah. She got the call that the police wanted to talk with her. I wanted to know if everything was all right."

Fenway nodded. "She's fine. Hey, do you have a few minutes to talk with us?"

"I've gotta get to rehearsal right after work."

"After rehearsal, then."

"Sure. Was that it, or did you want food?"

They ordered their food and paid, Xavier gave them a number, and they chose a hard plastic booth within sight of the counter.

"How do you suppose our Othello knew that Desdemona got called in?" McVie asked Fenway.

Fenway felt the curve of a smile at the corner of her mouth. "I can think of a reason. Happens in a lot of productions. You notice he looked like he might jump out of his skin when I called Amanda his wife."

"I did notice that. So you think they're an item? That they were together this morning when Amanda got the call?"

"I do." Fenway grinned. "And I bet they don't want anyone else to know."

CHAPTER FIVE

AFTER LUNCH—AND THE TACO WASN'T NEARLY AS GOOD AS AT THE Ernesto's downtown—McVie and Fenway went to the administration building to look at Jessica Marquez's files. The human resources department referred them to IT, who referred them back to human resources, who finally passed the buck to Dr. Pruitt, who spent twenty minutes behind his closed office door before his secretary let them in.

Fenway went in first. The room was huge, but by no means modern; too many walls and not enough glass. It radiated stateliness. Dark wood cabinets and end tables complemented reddish-brown leather upholstery on the chairs and sofas. Dr. Pruitt sat behind the large mahogany desk with gold inlays and carved wooden legs, thoughtfully resting his chin in his hand. Behind him, two large bookcases towered on either side of a window with dark plantation-style shutters, which were open to let in the afternoon light that weakly filtered through the clouds.

Dr. Pruitt, behind his desk, indicated two chairs. Fenway settled herself into the one farthest from the door. McVie began discussing access to the personnel files with Pruitt. The two of them pushed back and forth, and Fenway sat quietly, out of the conversation, and she studied Pruitt for a moment.

He only had his wife to confirm his weak alibi, so Fenway thought about the interviewing techniques from her forensics program. Nothing in Pruitt's demeanor suggested deception. He was looking straight into McVie's eyes, and after McVie's questions, didn't suddenly look away. He wasn't sitting in a defensive posture. His movements weren't fidgety or overly mannered, and his high, reedy voice stayed relatively even, although he was arguing over the access McVie asked for. Either he was a good liar, or he was telling the truth. Of course, it was about personnel files, not about the murder.

Fenway's eyes grew heavy and she lost focus for a moment.

When she caught herself tilting her chair back, trying to slouch, she pulled herself to attention. She looked at the bookshelves behind Dr. Pruitt. Academic texts were scattered among the knickknacks of both bookcases. The books were so pristine, Pruitt likely chose them for their impressive titles rather than their usefulness. The bookshelf on the right held an interesting wire sculpture of a man on an 1890s-style bicycle with a huge front wheel, and on the shelf above, a silver picture frame sat with what looked like a photo of Dr. Pruitt and his wife.

McVie abruptly stood up, holding his hand out. Dr. Pruitt remained sitting as he shook the sheriff's hand. McVie, a determined and grim look on his face, was already out the door as Fenway fumbled for her purse and found the strap was caught around the leg of the chair.

Pruitt cleared his throat.

"Sorry," Fenway said, lifting the chair and freeing the strap. She smiled weakly at him and walked out the door—

Right smack into a young, square-jawed white man with a deep tan, wearing a dark suit and a light blue dress shirt, carrying a black leather briefcase.

"Sorry," Fenway said.

The man snarled at her. "Watch where you're going!" He pushed past her into the university president's office, slamming the door behind him.

Fenway turned to the secretary. "Who the hell was that?"

The secretary shook her head. "I don't know. He didn't have an appointment. Just barged in." She turned to her left and hit the intercom button. "Dr. Pruitt, I'm calling security."

"No, no, Belinda," Pruitt said through the crackling speaker. "That won't be necessary. Mr. Grayheath needed to speak with me urgently."

Fenway looked up, but McVie was already halfway down the hall. She ran to catch up with him.

"This is like pulling teeth," McVie said. "I wonder if he's hiding something."

"If he is, it's not in the personnel files," Fenway said. "Who do you think that man was who went in to talk with him?"

"Uh—I don't know. I didn't see him."

"Young guy—white, but tan, which is weird for November. Wore a suit. Also, super-rude."

McVie scratched his neck in thought. "Sorry. I guess I wasn't paying attention."

They made their way to the human resources department, where an administrator, her mouth turned down at the corners, silently led them into a small office. She shut the door behind them.

"This looks so normal," Fenway whispered to McVie, "but when you start pulling the layers away, this university is rotting from the inside."

"Why are you whispering?"

"I don't know—I guess because it feels like we were sent to the principal's office."

The two of them sat, and the minutes ticked by.

"You think maybe we're on some game show and we're getting punked?" Fenway asked, pulling her phone out of her purse.

"This isn't my definition of cooperation," McVie grumbled.

He sat in his chair, staring straight ahead, while Fenway found the North American Shakespeare Guild online. She read interviews with several of the stage actors and directors who came to speak at Nidever. An article in *The Blue Dolphin Online,* the Nidever alumni magazine, focused on *The Guild at the Globe* trip, though it was little more than a sales pitch disguised as a fluff piece.

After nearly thirty minutes, the administrator popped her head in with two folders, handing them to McVie. "Here you go. Let me know when you're finished with this and I'll get you the next ones."

"I spoke to Dr. Pruitt about this," McVie said, exasperated. "He told me—"

"We have policies here in HR, Sheriff," the administrator said curtly. "One file at a time for each of you. I don't care if you agreed to something different with Dr. Pruitt, or Brad Pitt, or the pope. We don't make exceptions. You have an issue with that, I can take these files away completely and we can schedule a court date in a couple of months."

"This is fine," Fenway said. "Thank you for your help, Miss...."

The administrator stared daggers at Fenway before she slammed the door shut.

The two folders were labeled *Marquez, Jessica* and *Cygnus, Virgil.* The sheriff handed Fenway the Jessica Marquez folder, considerably slimmer than the one on Cygnus.

Fenway chuckled. "You afraid I can't handle the big, bad folder, Craig?"

"You haven't been in town long, Fenway. I've at least heard of—" He glanced up at Fenway's face. "Oh, you're kidding. Sorry."

"You lose your sense of humor?"

"Guess so. Pruitt sent us on a wild-goose chase, and it pisses me off."

Fenway opened the folder. The top page was a photocopied itinerary for next year's England trip. The next forty or fifty pages were older itineraries. She leafed through half of the papers and then came upon profit-and-loss statements for The Guild. She lifted the whole stack, but there was nothing else. No work reviews, no salary information, not even a résumé or background document. She lifted her head. "You have a résumé for Professor Cygnus, Craig?"

"Yep. Came here from the east coast thirty-two years ago."

"I don't have anything. Just travel plans for her interview and customer communications."

"Really?"

"Really." Fenway put down the folder. "That's odd, right?"

"Maybe we should ask."

"Right, because that administrator seems so *very* helpful."

Fenway stood up, stretched, and then grabbed the folder and walked out the door to the administrator's desk. The administrator was typing, looking down at a page of handwritten notes.

"Hey, I'm sorry to bother you, but the folder didn't have Jessica Marquez's résumé or any notes about her job perf—"

"Everything we have is in the folder," the administrator interrupted, not looking up.

"Well, I thought I'd be reviewing her personnel file. It's nothing but business papers."

"Everything we have is in the folder." Same even, flat tone.

Fenway felt her mouth twitch involuntarily. "That simply isn't possible. You can't have a personnel file without a résumé or a job application."

"I can take that folder for you if you don't want it."

"You're not concerned that there's a personnel file with missing information?"

"You'll have to take that up with Dr. Pruitt."

Fenway stopped. *Dr. Pruitt.* He had spent an awfully long time on the phone with human resources earlier. She'd thought it was because he was on their side, but now, it seemed he might have been circling the wagons and hiding information. "Did someone tell you to remove parts of the files you gave us?"

The administrator looked up, narrowed her eyes, and snatched the folder out of Fenway's hand. "Okay, that's quite enough. I'm rescinding your privileges."

"What?"

"You heard me. You can go out the way you came in."

"My purse is in the room!"

"I'll be happy to get it for you."

"This is ridiculous."

"Again, you can always schedule a court date if you disagree with how we run things here. Now, you'll need to watch that uppity mouth of yours if you don't want me to kick out your friend, too."

He's the sheriff of this county—not some random friend of mine! Fenway opened her mouth, then snapped it shut. It was pointless to argue.

The woman glared at Fenway, walked down the hallway, and entered the room where the sheriff sat, closing the door behind her. Muffled voices came from behind the door, each voice growing more agitated. The door opened and McVie came out, holding Fenway's purse.

He stepped to Fenway and handed over the purse. "I don't know what her problem is, but I need a few more minutes with the file."

"Did you find something interesting?"

"A recent leave of absence. It might be nothing, but I at least want to get notes down of where he's taught before, and cross-reference anything we find from Jessica's past. Assuming we find anything."

"I don't think we will. I think somebody messed with the files."

"You what?"

"There was nothing in the Jessica Marquez file. I think someone removed all the personal info—the job application, the résumé, all of it."

"Who would do that?"

"Dr. Pruitt had the means, and his alibi is weak."

McVie exhaled. "Maybe I'll ask for Dr. Pruitt's records, too."

"Okay. I won't keep fighting about the file here."

"We can always get a warrant."

"Shouldn't that be a last resort?"

McVie was quiet, then shrugged.

"Well," said Fenway, "let's see how many flies you can catch with honey instead of vinegar. The more background you can get through those files, the better, right?"

"Right."

"So don't piss off that admin like I did. I'll take an Uber to the office and meet up with you later." Fenway's phone rang in her purse. "See? I've already got something to keep me busy." She turned and walked out of the administration building, looking at her phone.

Charlotte.

Ah well, the lesser of two evils. She answered.

"Hi, Charlotte."

"Fenway?" Charlotte said. Her voice had none of the ice-queen calmness that Fenway was used to; instead, a hint of keening desperation lay beneath the surface. "Where are you? I haven't heard from you all day. I called you last night to tell you your father was in jail, and I expected you to do something about it, not leave me hanging here."

Fenway pinched her eyes shut. "I have been trying to solve a murder since four this morning, Charlotte."

"You're trying to solve *a different murder?*" Charlotte's tone turned harsh, but still had the underlying desperation. "You're in charge, aren't you? Don't you have deputies, or sergeants who can handle that? We're talking about your father! This isn't some regular low-life that you have to deal with."

"I know, I know," Fenway said, leaving the building. The gray daylight outside was again thick with mist. She took the phone away from her face and looked at the time: two thirty. "What did my father's lawyers say?"

"They're *all* getting the runaround. The sheriff's department says they're not holding him. None of the local police say they're holding him. A deputy I talked to said there was a jurisdictional issue. I don't know why they can't tell me anything. I've got one lawyer on the phone with the D.A. and another on the phone with the U.S. Attorney. This is crazy!"

"I'm sorry, Charlotte. So you don't know where they're holding him?"

Fenway heard Charlotte's voice start to break. "I bet those bastards are holding him at the jail in Estancia, but no one can tell me if he's there or not."

Fenway turned left, beginning to pace around the administration building. "I've heard of this before—losing paperwork, that kind of thing. They might be trying to buy themselves more time before the arraignment. If he doesn't get entered into the system until tomorrow morning, they won't have to arraign him until Monday—oh, wait, no, Monday's a holiday."

"A holiday?"

"Veterans Day. So Tuesday. That'll give them an extra three calendar days to build their case."

"Can they do that?"

"They usually don't try it with someone as powerful as my father is. And it looks like they're doing it on purpose, but intent is tough to prove. They're probably laying a paper trail, trying to figure out where they'll arraign him. If they're talking a jurisdictional issue, it's probably because the death occurred in Washington state, but they'll say that he hired somebody in California to kill Professor Delacroix. Hell, he might be on a bus, driving up and down the 101, to give them time before entering him into the system."

"Our lawyers will have a field day with that," Charlotte growled.

"They might. It's a pretty bold thing to do." Fenway wiped the mist off her forehead; her hair was starting to frizz. "Of course, they might truly be fighting over the jurisdiction, or they might be completely incompetent."

"You work for the sheriff's department and you're calling them incompetent?"

"Doesn't have to be the sheriff's department. Lots of blame to go around." Another possibility popped into Fenway's head. "Or—maybe they're assuming it's a single crime and it happened over state lines. They might bring in the U.S. attorney. Do you know who arrested him? Was it the FBI?"

"The FBI? I don't know. Why would the FBI be involved?" A note of panic crept into Charlotte's voice.

Oh. Charlotte didn't need to hear this right now. In fact, why wasn't *Fenway* more upset by the news of her father's arrest? Granted, their relationship was strained, especially in the last couple of months. Even so, Fenway was being overly clinical—the word *heartless* popped into her head—about his arrest. She shook her head to clear her thoughts. "I'm sorry, Charlotte. I shouldn't be speculating like this. I'll talk to some people and maybe I can figure out what's going on."

"Thank you," Charlotte said. "I know this would mean a lot to your dad."

CHAPTER SIX

FENWAY'S UBER TOOK FOREVER TO SHOW UP. THE FIRST DRIVER didn't know his way around campus, and after fifteen minutes of the driver reporting as either two minutes or three minutes away, Fenway cancelled the ride and requested another one—and no drivers were within a ten-minute drive. She texted Dez while she waited. *Delegating. Managing her team.* Fenway felt a surge of pride... or something. A little more like an adult, maybe.

By the time she got to the coroner's office, it was past three o'clock. She asked Migs to look up the legality of keeping administrative records from peace officers, but Fenway suspected that she and McVie had only flimsy arguments. By the skeptical look on Migs's face, he knew it too. Fenway typed up her notes as Migs researched it, and to no one's surprise, Migs found that nothing could be done without a subpoena, or at least a warrant.

She walked to the IT office, and at the sound of the door opening, Piper turned around. "Oh—great, Fenway, you're here. Just who I wanted to see. I'm concerned about some of the anomalies I see in the Central Auto Body records."

"That's great, Piper. Keep digging."

"Uh, I don't know. I think it's something *you* should see."

"Can I look at it tomorrow?"

Piper bit her lip. "I don't think so."

Fenway bobbed her head side to side and took a deep breath. "Okay, I promise I'll take a look at it later. Right now, I kind of need a favor."

"More important than the Central Auto Body thing?"

Fenway paused and closed her eyes. *Delegate.*

But this was a personal issue, not something to prioritize for Piper's work time.

"No. Keep digging on the financials. It's a personal thing. I'll try to figure it out myself."

Fenway started out the door when Piper's voice stopped her. "Wait, Fenway—at least tell me what you need."

She turned around. "I take it by now you heard my father was arrested."

"Yeah. It's all over the news."

"I don't know where they're holding him. His wife doesn't know, his lawyers don't know."

"What do you mean? He's lost in the system?"

Fenway shrugged.

"You want me to find out where he is."

"You can dig into county records, right?"

"Of course, but that won't tell me anything if the paperwork is lost. If it's never been entered into the system, breaking into the system won't do any good."

"Can we see what's out there? I don't know if he's been extradited to Washington state, or if he's in some FBI detention center somewhere."

"All right, but after you find your dad, you promise to look at the Central Auto Body problem? Like, before you go home?"

"Absolutely."

Piper listened as Fenway related the facts about her father's arrest: the professor at Western Washington, the MCU detective from Bellingham, the arrest the night before, and the team of high-priced lawyers who couldn't locate their client. Then Fenway's theories: Nathaniel Ferris on the bus that was killing time driving up and down the freeway, the possible FBI or U.S. Attorney involvement, the goal to get the arraignment moved to Tuesday.

"And, of course, Charlotte is going crazy," Fenway finished.

"Charlotte—that's your stepmother?"

"My father's second wife? Yes."

Piper spun her chair in front of her keyboard. "If their whole purpose is to delay your father's processing until tomorrow, they'd need to establish a reasonable paper trail for what's essentially a twenty-four-hour delay." Piper shook her head. "But honestly, Fenway, they don't need to book him tomorrow morning to establish his arraignment on Tuesday. They need to wait until after the courts close. That sets the clock at the start of tomorrow—that's the forty-eight hour limitation."

Fenway looked at the clock on her phone. "So I've got an hour to wait."

"Those are the county offices. They're open till five, but the courts close at four."

Fenway grimaced. "Yes. I knew that."

"So your dad might be getting processed right now."

"Or he might be on his way to Bellingham, or FBI detention."

Piper tilted her head. "Or he might be across the street." She smiled. "So come back here after you see if your dad is there. We've got to figure out if there are more financial ledgers at Central Auto Body. Also, I'm not sure if I made a mistake. I might have told someone something I shouldn't have."

Did Piper know there was a mole in the department? "Don't worry about it. I'm sure whatever you said is fine. You know everyone here—we're all police officers."

"No, Fenway, it wasn't a coworker. It was someone whose name I found in the ledger."

Fenway's eyes widened. "That might be a big deal. Maybe you should tell me now."

Piper hesitated. "Okay. I found a name in the ledger—a real one, not a fake one, not like I usually find in these sanitized financial records—and I thought it was a guy who had sold a boat to one of our nameless suspects."

"Wait—a boat? Why—"

"It's a long story." Piper waved her hand. "My point is, I was hoping I could get the *real* name of someone who could give me clues about who's behind the money laundering, so I called the guy with the real name in the ledger. But I don't think he's an innocent third party who sold a boat. I think *he's* involved. I think he's close to the people who run the whole thing, and I think I spooked him. Now I'm afraid he'll to try to steal evidence from Central Auto Body."

"What?"

"Listen—I know it's a crazy and convoluted story, but I'm almost positive there are more ledgers there, and I think this guy will try to steal them."

Fenway looked at her watch. On one hand, Piper's warning was time-sensitive. On the other, she sometimes overreacted to danger— and her sensors were on high alert. If Fenway's father had been given the runaround, maybe on a prison bus for much of the last twenty-four hours, was delaying a meeting with him worth it? She closed her eyes and heard Charlotte's nagging voice in her head, and made her decision.

"Okay, Piper," she said evenly. "I'll see my father, but I promise I'll come right back here, go through your evidence, and see if we need to take any action."

Piper looked more worried than Fenway had ever seen her before, but she gave her a pat on the shoulder. "Maybe an hour, an hour and a half tops."

"Okay," Piper said.

———

Fenway was keenly aware of her flats clicking on the concrete, a higher-pitched sound than she was used to, echoing off the buildings and the glass windows. She opened the door to the jail building, stepping into the vestibule, and glanced up at the guard.

"Hey, Fenway!"

"Hey, Todd—Officer Young," Fenway said. "I didn't realize you were on duty here."

"Yep, after my stint on your protection detail was over, they reassigned me."

"I thought you liked the night shift."

"Swing isn't that bad. I'm returning to night shift in a couple of weeks." Officer Young tapped the clipboard in front of him. "Who you here for?"

"Three guesses. The first two don't count."

Officer Young smiled. "You must have a sixth sense for these things. He's not even out of processing yet."

"My father's lawyers won't be too impressed if paperwork goes missing for twenty-four hours."

Young shook his head. "I don't know anything about that."

"What—you think this is all on the up-and-up?"

"Let me rephrase. They don't *pay* me enough to know anything about that." Officer Young opened the logbook. "You know visiting hours are over."

"I know," Fenway said. "I'm here in an official capacity."

"Sure you are." Officer Young chuckled. "And we *officially* lost the paperwork. I'll go get him. It might take a few minutes. Room four okay?"

"That's fine."

Officer Young opened the door behind him with his card key, and Fenway turned and walked down the corridor, going into the interview room.

All four interview rooms looked about the same—metal table, panic button, three metal chairs in various states of disrepair. Fenway sighed and sat in the only chair on the near side of the table.

She had to wait over forty-five minutes before Officer Young appeared at the door. An orange-clad Nathaniel Ferris followed him into the interview room, and Fenway stood up from her chair automatically. Her father looked old. The orange jumpsuit made his white skin look pink and sun-scorched, like a German tourist on a beach holiday. His shoulders were slumped, his head was down, and his eyes had little light in them.

"Hi, Dad," Fenway said. "Are you okay?"

He raised his head and looked Fenway in the face. Fenway saw, as if for the first time, the similarity in their noses and the shape of their eyes, in spite of the difference in their skin color. Ferris nodded, silently, and Officer Young led him to a chair on the opposite side of the table from Fenway.

"You know how to reach me," Officer Young said. "Just push that red button and I'll be in right away."

"I'm sure that won't be necessary, Officer."

Officer Young nodded and exited the room.

Fenway looked at her father. His chin was down again, his posture slouched against the metal chair. Not even when Charlotte had been arrested had the powerful Nathaniel Ferris been so morose. "I guess the official word is they lost your paperwork. I bet your lawyers will rip the county a new one."

Nathaniel Ferris looked blankly into Fenway's face, not responding. But then, after a few agonizing moments, he mumbled, "I've never been in a situation like this before, Fenway. I'm not sure what to do."

"Come on, Dad. Snap out of it. It's the same old dirty tricks you're used to playing, but instead of screwing over smaller oil companies with leveraged buyouts, *you're* the one who got screwed over. So how did they delay you from getting processed for so long? My money's on a supposed snafu that put you on a bus to Bellingham. Then the bus turned around *just* late enough where you'd miss the courts being open. And I bet all the paperwork is in place to make it look legit, too."

Ferris stared at Fenway with an odd look in his eyes, like he didn't understand what she had said.

"Dad, don't you see? It was all so they could have the long weekend before they had to arraign you. They want as much time as possible to build their case. But your lawyers will have you out of here tomorrow morning, right?"

Ferris dropped his head. "I had gotten Charlotte back, and I thought everything would be okay, and then the detective from Bellingham shows up at my door, with a couple of officers, tells me I have to come with them, that I'm under arrest for the murder of that professor."

"Yeah," Fenway said. "The murder of my professor."

Nathaniel Ferris looked her in the eye and slowly shook his head. "You think I did it, don't you?"

She couldn't believe how much fight had gone out of her father. The ruthless scion of the oil industry, vengeful ex-husband, subject of dozens of magazine articles about fearless leadership—he sat across from her, looking thoroughly defeated.

"What's going on, Dad? I thought you'd fight this."

"You think I did it."

"Well, so what if I do?" Fenway retorted. "Since when have you cared what I think?"

Ferris raised his eyes to hers. He looked like he'd been slapped.

She drew in her breath sharply. "That's not what I meant. I—"

"Listen, Fenway, I know you think I'm selfish. I know you think I don't care what happens to other people. But I never imagined you think I'd be capable of *murder*."

"Come on, Dad, you're the most powerful man in the county. I remember when I was in second grade and that boy called me the—uh, the n-word. You got him kicked out of school."

"I didn't have his parents killed," Ferris pointed out.

"Of course you didn't, but he was a kid. He might not have known any better."

"He knew better," Ferris said under his breath, and Fenway caught the gleam in his eye. Perhaps the fire in his belly had reignited.

"Maybe so." She coughed lightly. "What Professor Delacroix did to me is a hell of a lot worse."

Ferris leaned back in the chair, his hands on his knees, and nodded. "Okay," he said, "you want to know the truth?" He gritted his teeth. "I *would* have done it."

"You *would* have?"

"I even thought about doing it. I thought about paying my pilot out of my own pocket in cash, taking the turboprop to the Bellingham airport. I found out where he lived. I knew when his last class got out. I planned to go to his house, wait till he got home, then shoot him in the head."

Ferris's eyes unfocused for a moment.

"I know a gun dealer there," Ferris continued. "I left him a message the day after you told me about it. Untraceable. I'd pay for the taxi in cash. I'd wear a disguise."

"You wouldn't take the jet?"

"I don't have to file a flight plan with the turboprop." He laughed. "All that planning, and he was already dead."

"You wouldn't hire someone?"

"I don't trust anyone who works for me to kill someone. Sure, my employees don't always follow the spirit of the law, but exploiting the loopholes in contract law is a far cry from murder. It's not something you give your head of security twenty grand to do. It's something you have to feel."

"And you were mad enough to do it."

Ferris nodded.

"Why didn't you?"

"I went to double-check his schedule online," Ferris said. "I thought maybe I'd wait a few days—I had meetings anyway—and then when I searched for his name, I found an article in the *Seattle Times* about his death."

"You searched for his name? You would have left a trail on your computer!"

"I have an anonymizer."

Fenway narrowed her eyes. Her father was, surprisingly, even more savvy than she gave him credit for. "You're telling me that you would have tried to kill him if you thought you could get away with it, and someone *else* killed him before you figured it all out?"

Ferris set his jaw. "I *would* have gotten away with it, if I had done it." He looked at Fenway. "Which I guess means that I *am* a murderer. I just haven't murdered anyone yet."

Though she was skeptical, some parts of Fenway thought that was kind of—not terrible. Maybe even a little sweet. She had spent twenty years of her life separated by both distance and emotion from her father, and as much as she had dreaded moving to Estancia, she grudgingly admitted to herself that she was glad she'd returned. True, she and her father didn't get along well right now, but upon reflection, she got along better with him than she thought she would. "I don't think you're a monster or anything, Dad," she said. "I wasn't sure, when I lived in Seattle, how far you would ever go to protect me, or defend me, or even, you know, spend any time with me at all."

Ferris blinked rapidly several times and looked down at the table. "I know, I know," he mumbled. "I haven't been there. I wasn't there for you in high school, or at graduation, or in college—" His voice started to break, and he stopped speaking.

"What is it, Dad?"

Ferris sucked in air through his teeth. "I don't know if things would have been any different if I had, I don't know, taken a more active role in your life when you were at Western Washington."

Fenway lowered her voice. "Are you saying that if you had been a better father, Delacroix wouldn't haven't raped me?"

Ferris didn't raise his head, still staring at the tabletop and not meeting Fenway's eyes. "I don't know what I'm saying."

"Well, I hope you're not saying that, because you'd be giving yourself a lot more credit than you deserve," Fenway snapped. "You think that fucker raped me because my daddy didn't come to my high school graduation? You think I somehow let him know that without a big strong father figure I was *vulnerable* and he could get away with it?"

"He *did* get away with it," Ferris said.

"Not because of *you!*" Fenway roared, standing up. The metal chair scraped against the concrete floor. "Are you seriously so egocentric that you think the world revolves—" She stopped speaking midsentence, closing her eyes, opening and closing her fists, noticing her breaths coming short and fast, and trying to settle herself down. She opened her eyes and looked at her father. "I came here tonight because Charlotte didn't know where you were being held," Fenway said. "You need to get your shit together before Charlotte comes here tomorrow. I'll tell her to be here at straight-up noon. I don't care if you're wallowing in self-pity, but at noon, you'll be the overconfident, spiteful asshole that she fell in love with, and you'll tell her you can beat this thing. She's falling apart, and you have to be her rock now."

Ferris nodded. "But Fenway—"

"What is it?"

"You need to know I didn't do this."

"Have you found a good criminal lawyer yet? I mean the one who'll lead the murder defense, not the ones who'll get you out of jail first thing in the morning."

Ferris shook his head. "I'm working on it. We have recommendations from our legal team."

"Okay, Dad. I'll talk to you later."

"What, that's it? Five minutes and you're gone?"

"I've got a series of murders to take care of, and while I'd love to stay here and chat, the people of this county elected me to do my job."

"But you can call people, Fenway. You can see what the Bellingham detective has on me."

"Maybe I've already started." Fenway sympathized with him and swore at herself for letting him get to her. "I'll come see you tomorrow. Try to keep busy. See if they can get you some books or something."

"Books?"

"Sure. Maybe Charlotte can bring a few from your library."

He nodded.

Fenway got up and walked over to the rear door. She knocked firmly.

Officer Young opened the door. "Everything okay?"

"Yep. We're finished here."

"All right. Come on, Mr. Ferris."

"Hey, Todd," Fenway said, "see if you can find my father something to keep him entertained. Maybe a good book. An action thriller or something."

"We've got some John Grisham."

"Do you have the one where the rich guy with no soul gets his comeuppance?"

Officer Young smirked. "I think that's *every* John Grisham book."

"That should do, then," Fenway said, turned on her heel without looking at her father, and strode across the room and out the other door.

She walked down the hallway quickly, her heart beating in her ears, replaying the conversation in her mind.

She hadn't been nice, and she hadn't been kind, but she didn't care. She was pretty sure her father had hired someone to kill the professor, and she thought the kids from *Othello* could learn a lot from her father's acting.

CHAPTER SEVEN

Uber was much more responsive around the end of the workday, and Fenway was back on campus by six fifteen. All the light had faded from the sky. Streetlamps on posts, scattered at various points around the edges of the sidewalks, provided the only light for the parking lot. Their warm glow mingled with the harsh fluorescent white that leaked out of the double doors to the DiFazio Theater, held open with metal door stops. Nearing those doors, Fenway could hear voices from inside, with the unmistakable rhythm of iambic pentameter. She wondered if Cygnus gave his students a dinner break. With opening night in two days, this was likely a dress rehearsal. Fenway had never been in a theater production herself, at least not after fifth grade, but something about Shakespeare had always spoken to her. This particular play, as problematic as might be, was no exception.

She padded, almost tiptoed, through the lobby of the DiFazio Theater and reached for the door handle of the main auditorium. She pulled it open quietly, immediately regretting the harsh light that spilled into the dark auditorium. She didn't see McVie, but the blackness was so complete she couldn't tell who was sitting in the audience.

It was silent. Fenway held her breath. Had she interrupted the actors?

She looked up, and no, she hadn't broken their concentration. A standoff on stage had the air crackling with tension. Xavier Go, clad in a white military-style tunic shirt and fitted black pants, stood with his back to the audience. Amanda Kohl lay awkwardly crumpled on the bed before him. A rosy-cheeked woman, whose curled tresses fell in ringlets on either side of her face, had a sad, desperate look in her eyes and a horrified expression on her face. She pointed at Xavier.

> *"O thou dull Moor! that handkerchief thou speak'st of*
> *I found by fortune and did give my husband;*
> *For often, with a solemn earnestness,*
> *More than indeed belong'd to such a trifle,*
> *He begg'd of me to steal it."*

Fenway was transfixed. From seeing the play before, she recognized the Emilia character, fraught with emotion over Desdemona's death. She was disappointed that she hadn't seen any of Amanda's performance. Maybe Amanda's acting was as good as Amanda thought it was.

The rear of the stage was crowded, with the actors playing Iago, Emilia, Gratiano, and Montano behind the bed onstage, and the body of the dead Desdemona in front, with Othello nearest the audience. Iago, sword drawn, faced Emilia, only Gratiano separating them.

"Villainous whore!" seethed Iago.

Fenway tore her eyes from the actors for a moment and began to scan the audience. At a small desk behind all of the other seats, all the way on the far left-hand side, sat Professor Cygnus. He stared at the stage fixedly, his eyes concentrating heavily, his mouth drawn tight, the muscles in the side of his face pulsing. After a moment, Fenway figured out that his jaw clenched and unclenched in time with the actors' lines.

Fenway spotted a knot of students in the front seats. Their faces were rapt. On the stage, Iago ducked under Othello's knife.

Then he rushed toward Emilia and stabbed her.

Even though Fenway knew it was coming, she gasped.

Emilia fell on the floor, her look of sad desperation transformed to one of disbelief with a hint of pain.

So many murders in Estancia since her arrival in town six months ago.

Could she not feel any of it?

She even knew Rory. She had borrowed the minivan that morning, and Rory—innocent, hardworking, brilliant Rory—was just returning the minivan to his father's auto shop.

The bomb wasn't for him.

Yet Fenway was pissed off about *her* car not being processed after the explosion. Could she not even feel the tiniest twinge for Rory?

She knew she did. She knew she'd cried over his death, but she hadn't felt it for a couple of days. Not until she saw Emilia get stabbed on stage.

It took her breath away.

She turned her attention to the professor, who didn't look pleased at Emilia's stellar performance, and instead got to his feet and started stamping down the aisle, shouting and waving his arms. In his left hand was a flat cap, and he waved it around for emphasis as he shouted, "No! No! For the love of God, no!"

"What is it?" the woman playing Emilia snapped.

"Your blocking is all wrong, Denise," Professor Cygnus said. "If you land there, we can't see Desdemona's face. All the great acting in the world will be for naught if you block the audience from seeing the most important thing they can see in this scene."

Denise's lower lip trembled slightly, but then she set her jaw and steeled her gaze. "If I'm stabbed that way, I have to fall that way. Otherwise it's not believable."

"We are at *dress rehearsal*, Denise," the professor said through gritted teeth. "We have had conversation, after conversation, after conversation about the blocking in this scene. This won't be fixed by opening night unless you do it the way that we have all spent *hours* of rehearsal working on." He turned to the audience. "Company!" he said loudly, raising his arms, his muscles large and tensing. "Did we all work on the blocking for this scene?"

A low murmur of assent rose.

"I've heard you express louder opinions for a swipe-right on Tinder," the professor said. "I'm sixty years old, and I need to hear you. I said, *Did we all work on the blocking for this scene?*"

"Yes, professor," came the unified answer.

"Did we all *agree* to the blocking on this scene?"

"Yes, professor."

"Did *Denise Delatasso,* the diva from San Dimas, agree to the *fucking blocking?*" he screamed, and threw his cap across the room. The hat spun like a Frisbee, bounced against the wall above the lit exit sign, and dropped on the floor.

The professor turned and stared at Denise.

She pushed herself up, crossed her arms, and exhaled noisily. "Okay, Professor," she said. "I remember the blocking perfectly, so where do you want us to take this from?"

Professor Virgil Cygnus stamped the ground in disgust. "I'm done with you for tonight, Denise," he yelled. "I don't care if we *are* opening in two days, I will let all of you embarrass yourselves on stage if this is the way you treat the text—and each other as *actors*."

With that, he picked up a stack of papers and books sitting on the floor next to a theater seat, and heaved it across the theater. The books flew straight, and a student ducked out of the way. The sheaf of papers flew apart in midair, like startled seagulls taking flight from a sandy beach. The professor stomped up the aisle, opened the door to the lobby, and stormed out, slamming the door loudly. On stage, Amanda, no longer the dead body of Desdemona, pushed herself upright with one hand. Denise looked furious, and stomped off stage right. Xavier Go, who had not uttered a line since Fenway entered the theater, turned around to face the seats, a look of sheer exasperation on his face. None of the students' faces registered surprise or shock; maybe they were numb to the professor's outbursts. Perhaps this was how it went: rehearsals aborted by the professor's screaming, with the production in chaos, but everything destined to be all right tomorrow, as when families scream and yell and hurl insults at each other, but wake up the next day like nothing ever happened.

Fenway scooted along a row of seats and followed Dr. Cygnus out into the lobby.

She hadn't taken more than two steps into the brightly lit foyer when her eyes adjusted well enough to the harsh fluorescents to see the sheriff already talking to the professor.

Fenway walked up to the two of them, catching McVie's eye.

"Listen, sheriff," the professor said derisively, "I'm sure that there *are* normal people who would cancel a play or a movie or a sing-along if the general manager who ran the sponsoring organization were murdered, but I, dear sir, am proudly *abnormal*. I don't think you appreciate that I have been fighting with this text for thirty-five years, and as far as I'm concerned, the theater would have to be washed away in a tsunami before I would agree to cancel any of these performances. Do you think I can just get a look of betrayal to magically appear on Xavier's face during that last scene? I swear, next year I shall break my promise to my mother, God rest her soul, and direct Shakespeare in modern dress with guns. Xavier wouldn't need to learn sword fighting or dagger movement with a gun in his hand. Ah, for life to be simpler."

"I just need to know where you were—"

Cygnus put up his hand to silence the sheriff. "I'm in no mood to talk about where I was, or what I did last night, and even if you drag me kicking and screaming down to the police station, I shall talk about nothing but *Othello,* and how my best actress thinks she's too good to follow the—" and here he raised his voice, fairly echoing throughout the lobby "—BLOCKING WE AGREED ON WEEKS AGO!" He stormed off quickly out the side door of the lobby, leaving McVie staring after him.

Fenway walked up to McVie. "You okay?"

McVie wore a sour expression, one Fenway rarely saw. "I think that went well," he said. "I'm glad I was able to make him see the importance of the investigation."

"Maybe you need to speak his language."

"I'm not going to start using *thou* and *prithee,* Fenway."

"Very funny, Craig. No, I mean—all he loves is Shakespeare. Maybe tell him one of his awards is missing, maybe say we found that Jessica, I don't know, planned to sabotage the play or something. Hit him where he lives—not with the language, but with the drama. Then you can get him up to the office to see if anything is missing, and interview him there."

McVie squinted, his eyes unfocused across the room. "That's not a half bad idea."

"Hey, I've been doing this for six months now. Pretty soon I'll get the hang of it."

Xavier came out of the theater and ran toward the side door.

"Xavier!" Fenway shouted.

He stopped. "Sorry, Coroner, but I've gotta get the professor back in here. We're opening in two days, and we can't give up when a rehearsal goes sideways."

"What about Denise?"

"Amanda's working on her." Xavier gave a little half wave, then ran out the door.

"We won't catch them in a good headspace until after rehearsal's over," McVie said.

"What else can we do?"

"Right now? Dez is going through Jessica's house. Piper's working on Jessica's financials. So I think the only thing left to do is go eat some Argentine steak."

Fenway felt her heart swell. She had been so focused on the murder of Jessica Marquez and the plight of her father that she'd forgotten they had a date that night, and it was their first *real* date. Even though the election was over, she'd still kept her mind away from him, banishing any thoughts of romance with McVie was simply second nature. "I'm not sure I'm dressed for a fancy dinner."

"I'm not, either, but it's a steak place, not the Vatican. I bet they'll take our money."

"Okay, I'd like that," Fenway said. "I'm sorry. I've gotten so used to the election season that I feel like my finger is still holding down the pause button on our first date."

"I know—I feel like that, too. Like I have to deny that I want to go out with you." McVie ran his hands through his hair. "Listen, Fenway, I haven't dated in a while. I don't even know if it's a good idea to start dating so soon after my separation. And—for the time being, anyway—I'm still sheriff and you're still coroner."

Fenway felt the hair on the back of her neck stand up. "Wait—you asked me out this morning—and you said you wanted to go with me to get some steak. Now it sounds like you're trying to back out." She folded her arms. "Or maybe you're telling me you just want sex and that you don't want to call me in the morning."

"No!" McVie said, and he pulled her to the side of the lobby and lowered his voice. "I'm trying to tell you that I'm bad at dating. I'm out of practice. That I don't know the rules. I might come on too strong, or not come on strong enough. I'm telling you that I want to date you even though I'm bad at this, and even though common sense might say I'm not ready."

"Oh." Fenway dropped her arms to her sides. "Well, I don't know if you've noticed, but I kind of suck at this myself. and it's not because I'm out of practice. It's because I suck at dating."

"All right, then," McVie said. "We can suck together."

Fenway gave McVie a dirty look out of the corner of her eye, then burst out laughing.

"We can suck at *dating* together." McVie rolled his eyes. "And things will be less complicated after January first. I won't be sheriff anymore, and our relationship will be exclusively unprofessional." He paused. "I mean, *non*professional."

"I certainly think some behavior inappropriate for the workplace is in order," Fenway said, a coquettish tone in her voice.

"Great," McVie said, "and now that I'm thoroughly embarrassed, let's go to dinner. We can talk to the actors after rehearsal."

They exited the theater and walked toward the lot.

"We going in the cruiser?" Fenway asked.

"Oh, I forgot I still have it. We'll have to switch before I take you out to dinner."

"What, you can't use the cruiser to stop for dinner on the way home?"

McVie was silent for a moment, and Fenway looked at his face. *Yep. Boy Scout.*

Fenway fell into step with McVie as they walked. She liked that he was taller than her, even though she was okay dating shorter men. She listened to the sound of their shoes falling into a rhythm, His legs being longer, their footfalls were in syncopation, or even a polyrhythm: every six steps for him and every seven steps for her, they would step at the exact same time. This was jazz, the realm of Dave Brubeck and Steve Coleman and Dave Holland. This was Carnatic music from India.

Turning the corner past the theater building, she felt him tense with every step. They had been silent since they began walking, when she started counting the rhythm of their steps. Maybe McVie needed the conversation to flow, to move forward. She could sense the responsibility land on his shoulders now that they were on a real date, and when they got to the visitors' lot and the cruiser was in sight, she reached out and took McVie's hand in hers. She slowed her breathing down, the same way McVie did when they were interviewing a nervous witness. She breathed more deeply and slowly, and she could feel the blood slow down its pulsing in her veins. And McVie's hand, so tense when she first touched him, started to relax.

"We've been looking forward to this for so long," Fenway said softly. "I don't want us to overthink it."

McVie looked at her and smiled, taking his key fob out of his pocket. "Is it that obvious?" he said sheepishly.

"That the buildup is making you all weird?"

"I didn't even expect there'd be a buildup. Not after the other night."

"Yeah, but this isn't just sex, is it?" asked Fenway. "This is—this *could be*—us at the starting line."

McVie nodded. "Am I all weird?"

"I'm weird, too." She dropped his hand and turned to go around to the passenger side.

McVie put his hand on her shoulder, and she stopped. She closed her eyes and the electricity from his fingertips cascaded in waves down her body, from her shoulders to her hips, all the way to the soles of her feet and the tips of her toes. He took a step closer, and she breathed in his scent. He pulled her gently, and she started turning with his hand, into his body, as his other hand wrapped around her waist and drew her close.

She tilted her head up and looked into McVie's eyes. The blood in her veins was pumping faster, more urgently. Neither of them was relaxed now. McVie's body was alert, and Fenway moved her hand up his arm, touching his bicep and moving to his muscular chest, where she placed her open hand, wondering if she'd be able to feel his heart, wondering if she could feel the rhythm, wondering if she could feel a polyrhythmic syncopation with her own.

Their heartbeats crashed together on the downbeat.

He took her face in his hands and kissed her. She closed her eyes and leaned against the driver's door of the cruiser and let him control her, taking his tongue into her mouth, feeling the hunger from the months of waiting, the months when they could have been together all along.

The kiss took a few seconds, or maybe a few hours. Fenway lost herself and fell backward through a cascade of emotions. She was hiding things from him, she knew. She was hiding what the dead professor had done. She was hiding what she had almost done with

Akeel in Seattle—even though McVie had been trying to patch things up with his wife. She'd been hiding a lot of things.

None of that seemed to matter; or rather, it mattered, but she no longer wanted to hide from him. He'd be leaving the sheriff's office soon, and all they would have together would be their personal connection. There would be no professional relationship to worry about, no awkward glances in the bullpen of the coroner's office, no knowing looks from the officer at the front desk, no smirks from Quincy or Callahan, no more snide comments from Dez about Fenway having a boyfriend.

McVie broke from the kiss, and Fenway opened her eyes.

"That was nice," he murmured.

"Yeah," she whispered. "That was nice."

"Maybe we can skip the fancy dinner and continue this at my place?"

Fenway's stomach rumbled.

"Never mind," McVie said. "We'll get some steak in you."

———

Signing in the cruiser took longer than they expected, and they walked to the Highlander together, hand in hand. It was a short drive to the restaurant, and when they entered, it was noisy and most of the tables were full, but no one was waiting in the front for a seat.

"Good evening," the maître d' said. "Can I help you?"

"I had reservations for six thirty," McVie said, "but unfortunately, I had some police business to attend to, and we're a little late. I wonder if you can still accommodate me and"—he lightly elbowed Fenway —"my date."

The maître d's smile didn't fade. "Not a problem, sheriff," he said. "Of course we'd love to accommodate you. I'll make sure we have a table available."

Fenway took a step closer to McVie. "I'm your date," she said, halfway into his ear. He leaned closer to her and Fenway's upper arm rested against McVie's chest. She put a little of her weight into him, and McVie put his arm around her waist.

"You're my date," he said.

The maître d' rushed over. "Your table is ready," he said, grabbing two menus. "Follow me."

He led both of them, McVie still with his arm around Fenway's waist, to a four-person table at the side of the restaurant, with a booth on one side and chairs on the other.

Fenway looked at the table and blinked hard.

"Do you want the chair side or the booth side?" McVie said.

"We could, um," Fenway stammered. She cleared her throat. "We could both sit on the booth side."

He looked at her like he might say something—maybe make a clever remark—but he smiled instead, released her, and they both went around opposite sides of the table to sit in the booth.

The maître d' handed them their menus. "Your server this evening will be Mateo. Can I get your drink order to him?"

"Bourbon, neat," McVie said quickly.

His immediate order surprised Fenway, especially since he had gone out of his way to be a traditional gentleman, but she smiled at the maître d'.

"Is there a particular bourbon you had in mind?"

"Do you have Buffalo Trace?"

"We do. Very good, sir. And for you, miss?"

"A glass of the house red," Fenway said.

The host nodded and turned away.

Fenway looked at her menu. She already knew she'd order the Gaucho steak, with the fried plantains and the sautéed mushrooms. She looked over at McVie and scooted a little closer to him, so that their knees brushed against each other. He looked up from his menu and smiled.

"You're getting something crazy, aren't you?" he asked. "They have conch here. I've never had conch. I thought that was something they only ate in *Lord of the Rings*."

Fenway chuckled, suppressing a strong desire to correct him to *Lord of the Flies*. "They've got sweetbreads, too," Fenway said, as the server came to deliver their drinks.

McVie smiled and leaned closer to her. "You order sweetbreads and you're not getting any action tonight."

A thrill ran up Fenway's spine and stopped at the base of her skull. She put her hand on McVie's knee and turned her face to whisper into his ear.

"If I order sweetbreads and I want a little action tonight," she breathed, "I'm pretty sure you won't say no."

The grin on McVie's face widened and his ears darkened.

"Oh," Fenway said, pulling back a little with her head, but moving her hand to the top of his thigh. "I didn't realize I was embarrassing you, Sheriff."

McVie took a sip of his bourbon.

"Am I sitting too close to you?" she whispered. "Am I making you uncomfortable?"

McVie closed his eyes, nodded slightly, and shifted his weight. "In a good way."

The phone in Fenway's purse rang.

McVie grunted.

"It's like the universe knows we're on a date," Fenway said, "and it doesn't want us to get together. First, they had to arrest my father. What do you think it is now? Nuclear war?"

"Damn Puritan universe," McVie said, taking another drink.

Fenway pulled the phone out of her purse. The call was from the 805 area code, but she didn't recognize the number. She pushed her phone in front of McVie. "You know this number?"

He screwed up his face. "Is it someone telling you not to order the sweetbreads?"

"I'm serious, Craig."

Craig shook his head. "It kind of looks familiar, but I don't know it off the top of my head."

Fenway answered, grimacing as if she expected to be hit. "This is Fenway Stevenson."

A whisper came through. "Fenway?"

"Who is this?"

"It's Piper. And I'm in trouble."

Fenway sat up straight and pressed the phone to her ear. "What's going on?"

"I'm at Central Auto Body," she said. "Someone is here. If they find me, I think they're going to kill me."

CHAPTER EIGHT

"Wait," Fenway said, "how can we—" But the silence on the other end of the line was ominous. She looked at her phone—the call was no longer connected.

Alarm was in McVie's eyes. "What was that?"

"Piper." Fenway debated calling the number back, but thought if Piper was in danger, the last thing she needed was her phone going off in a silent room while she was trying to hide. "She needs help."

"Where is she?"

"Central Auto Body."

"What's she doing there?"

"I don't know why—" Fenway started.

McVie paused. "What is it?"

"Shit." Fenway smacked her hand on the table. How could she forget something like that?

"Out with it, Fenway."

"Piper had something to tell me before I left. She said she found something. She was worried."

"You didn't get any more information than that?"

Fenway almost started talking about the ledger, then remembered

Marisol Velásquez hadn't wanted to trust him. "Uh—I was planning to go to the office and talk to her after I saw my father. But I forgot."

"You forgot?"

"Yes, I forgot. Oh, no." Fenway held her head in her hands. "My father accused me of—well, never mind, it's just a dumb excuse. I let myself get distracted. I went straight over to Nidever."

"And, what? Piper took the law into her own hands?"

"She *did* say it was time-sensitive." Fenway covered her eyes. "Oh, shit. If something happens to her, it's all my fault."

"Piper wouldn't go anywhere without a warrant," McVie said, "and even if she had a warrant, she wouldn't go anywhere by herself, would she?"

Fenway got up from the table. "We need to go. I don't know exactly why she went to Central Auto Body, but she wouldn't do it on a whim. She must have thought it couldn't wait."

McVie put two twenties on the table and stood. "Did she say why she was in danger?"

"Someone else was there." Fenway paused but just for a moment. "We need to get going. Now."

They walked through the restaurant, and the maître d' had a look of shock on his face as they passed by. "Hold on, sir, miss—"

"Emergency," McVie said gruffly. "I hope that's enough to cover our drinks."

The cold November evening air revitalized Fenway as soon as they pushed open the door to the outside. She stole a glance at McVie's face, creased with concern.

McVie unlocked the car with his key fob, and they pulled the doors open.

"Okay," Fenway said, as McVie started the engine and drove out of the lot before she could even put her seat belt on. "What's the plan?"

McVie pulled the radio from under the seat. "Possible two-four-oh at Central Auto Body on Thirtieth. Repeat, possible two-four-oh in progress. Sheriff requests backup." He clicked off. "You're staying in the car."

Fenway was quiet. She wanted to help Piper, but without a gun, she was more likely to put herself in danger than she was to help out. It struck her that McVie probably shouldn't have brought her along.

The Highlander was an older model and radiated dad vibes, but when McVie stamped on the accelerator, the car shot forward. Fenway glanced at the speedometer; it passed seventy as McVie put the siren ball on top of the SUV.

"Yeesh," Fenway breathed, "this car *moves*." She thought of the time a few months before when there had been a shooting at the hospital, and how McVie had driven on the freeway. At the time, it had seemed wild, but not particularly fast, but this, with empty streets at nine at night, as opposed to a crowded freeway in the daytime, pushed Fenway down in her seat.

"I'm not sure what the plan is yet," McVie said. "I don't think we'll have a plan until we get there. I don't know who else is there, or what the threat to Piper is."

"What do you want to do to figure out if Piper is safe? Do you think we should kill the siren?"

"No," McVie said. "With the siren going, whoever is after Piper will hopefully leave. If they're trying to catch Piper breaking in or some-thing, they they'll think we'll be on their side. Either way, the other person will want to keep Piper unharmed."

"Gotcha." Fenway braced herself as they squealed around a corner onto Thirtieth Street. She looked behind them; a police cruiser was four or five blocks away, also coming up Thirtieth.

"Not a bad response, Craig," she said.

"It's not my first rodeo."

They pulled up next to a red Toyota Prius with a bumper sticker that said *My Other Car is a Quantum Computer*. In the lot, next to the Prius, was a black sedan without markings. Fenway couldn't tell if it was a Ford or something more upscale.

"Stay down," McVie hissed at Fenway.

"No problem." Fenway ducked in her seat.

"And stay here. No rushing in and trying to play hero for Piper."

"I know I don't have a gun or anything. I'll stay safe."

McVie shot a warning look at her. "Stay in the car, Fenway."

She sighed. "I promise."

McVie opened the door and got out, standing in the noise of the blaring siren. The police cruiser screeched to a halt on the other side of McVie.

He closed the door and she heard him speak to the other officers, but she couldn't understand any of the conversation above the noise of the siren. The top of McVie's head bobbed toward the front of the car where it disappeared from view. She heard two car doors slam and assumed it was also the police cruiser.

And then Fenway heard nothing but the wail of the siren. The red and blue of the lights cast harsh, swirling shadows around the inside of the SUV. For several moments, Fenway concentrated on the sound of her own breathing so the siren wouldn't drive her mad. She looked at the phone in her purse; it felt like half an hour had passed since she got the call, but it had only been five minutes.

She heard voices again and poked her head above the sight line of the dashboard, and McVie and Callahan came into view. Piper Patten, her shoulders covered in a red-and-black plaid blanket, stepped out from behind Callahan to stand next to McVie, who took her by the elbow. On the other side of Callahan stood a man wearing a dark suit and a light blue dress shirt, talking a stream of words, his brows knitted, his eyes dancing in agitation. Fenway recognized him, but wasn't sure where from. She pulled her phone up and took his picture.

McVie looked at Fenway, and she pulled the phone down quickly. He made a quick cutting motion in front of his neck with his whole hand. She looked down at the siren controls on her left and fumbled with them for a moment before toggling the switch. The siren, thankfully, went silent. Callahan walked to the cruiser, reached inside, and turned his siren off too.

"—certainly *will* press charges," the man in the suit finished.

Fenway remembered. That rude, entitled tone of voice belonged to the man who had pushed Fenway out of the way when she was leaving

Dr. Pruitt's office. She tried to remember the name she heard Pruitt say over the crackle of the intercom—Gray something.

McVie shook his head. "This property belongs neither to you, nor the company you work for. *We'll* decide if we'll arrest this young lady or not."

"I was hired to protect this property, and I have every ri—"

"Mister Grayheath," McVie said, his speech growing more curt, "your supervisor may have asked you to keep an eye on this property, but you have no more right to be here than this young lady." He turned to Piper. "If this is some sort of prank—"

"No, I swear, Officer—" Piper said.

"*Sheriff*," McVie said.

Fenway cocked her head. They were pretending they didn't know each other. Was this for Grayheath's benefit?

"Sorry, Sheriff," Piper said, looking down at the ground. "I swear, I didn't know I wasn't supposed to enter the building. I thought it was a public space until I went into the offices."

"Perhaps if we all go to the station, we can discuss this," Grayheath said.

"If you own, or lease, the property, sure," McVie said. "As it is, you can't even make a citizen's arrest."

Grayheath frowned.

"This is ridiculous. I haven't—"

"You're not law enforcement, Mr. Grayheath. If you had concerns about this young lady trespassing, you should have called the police, not tried to confront her yourself."

"That's nonsense. She was accessing some—" Suddenly, a pinched look came over Grayheath's face and he clamped his mouth shut.

"Accessing some *what*, Mr. Grayheath?"

"Accessing some computers that obviously didn't belong to her," he continued. "I couldn't let her do that. What if she were a hacker and she was stealing social security numbers or credit card information?"

"I'd say it was a good thing that we came when we did, then," McVie said. "If you hurt or injured this woman, we'd be taking you down to the station, too, and you'd probably get free lodging for the evening."

Grayheath didn't say anything else.

"I'd suggest you get in your car and figure out how to explain this to your boss so that you look like the hero," McVie said.

Fenway looked over at the unadorned sedan and typed the license plate number into her phone.

Grayheath glanced from McVie's face to Piper's, back to McVie's. A snarl formed on his lips, his hands curling into fists, and then he closed his eyes and breathed in and out. Finally, he gave a short nod. "Gentlemen," he said, "you're right. I'll head to work. Thank you for taking care of this unfortunate situation, and I appreciate your sensitivity in this matter."

McVie and Callahan both watched him walk all the way to his car. As he got in, Callahan put Piper in the back seat of the cruiser. Grayheath nodded at McVie as he drove out of the lot.

McVie motioned for Fenway to get out of the car, so she joined him. Piper, looking up at them guiltily, sat on the rear seat.

"McVie," Fenway said, "*that* was the guy."

"What guy?"

"The guy who was going into Pruitt's office while we went out."

"Really?"

"And you'll never guess who he works for," Piper broke in.

"Who?" asked Fenway.

"Global Advantage Executive Consulting."

"Oh no," said Fenway.

"Am I supposed to know what that is?" said McVie.

Fenway and Piper looked at each other.

"It's kind of a long story," said Fenway.

"I hope the story ends with me knowing what Piper's doing here, and why she played it like she didn't work for the county."

"I had to come here," Piper said. "Everyone else had left, and Fenway didn't come back, and I didn't have a choice."

"You didn't have a choice?"

"Not without risking Grayheath destroying the evidence." Piper shifted on the seat uncomfortably.

"Okay," Sheriff McVie said, "start at the beginning."

Piper looked from Callahan to Fenway to McVie and took a deep breath. "I looked into the payment book that Fenway gave me earlier today," she said.

"Payment book?"

"Mrs. Velásquez brought it in," Fenway said. "It was from Central Auto Body."

"I thought you already looked into those finances," McVie said.

"I did," replied Piper, "but these were records of transactions I hadn't uncovered, and there were some account numbers I hadn't heard of, too."

"And that led you here?"

"No—not yet. I saw the name *Grayheath* in the book."

Fenway cocked her head. "Regarding what?"

"That's what I was trying to find out. I came across some new bank account numbers and some big transactions. One was marked *Grayheath,* then a dash, then the word *sea,* then a notation for one hundred thousand dollars."

"Whoa," Callahan said. "That's a lot of money."

"The word *see* as in *look and see?*" asked Fenway.

"No, *sea,* like the ocean." Piper pressed her lips together. "I got excited. I thought maybe Grayheath had sold Mr. Velásquez his boat, and he was using it to go out to the oil tanker and disguise it before it came into the Ferris Energy port, or maybe disguise it after it went out. Or maybe he's hiding on the boat. I thought if we could get some sort of nautical ID on it, we'd know what we were looking for."

"Wait," McVie said, "what? Oil tanker? Disguise? What's going on?"

Piper looked at Fenway, and Fenway looked at Callahan.

McVie could know about this, but Callahan was an unknown. True, Fenway had gotten to know him pretty well over the last few days when he was on her protection detail, but that was only a few days, and McVie still thought there was a mole in the department. Fenway didn't think Callahan was the mole, but still, it paid to be cautious, even though Piper had said too much already.

"Brian," Fenway said, "I'm sorry, but the rest of this conversation needs to be for McVie only."

"Seriously?"

"Seriously, Brian. I'm sorry."

"It makes it hard for me to do my job if I don't know the whole story."

McVie looked Fenway in the eyes, and she tried to communicate her fear of the mole telepathically.

"Fenway's right, Callahan," McVie said. "Sorry, but you'll have to go out of earshot for this."

"I could just take the cruiser back," Callahan said. "You can all catch a ride with the sheriff."

"Thanks for understanding, Callahan," McVie said, although no understanding registered on Callahan's face.

Piper got out of the rear seat of the cruiser, and Callahan closed the door behind her. He walked around to the driver's side without another word, got in, and drove out, leaving the three of them in the dark parking lot.

McVie watched the cruiser leave.

"Okay," Fenway said. "Here's what's going on. A supertanker goes into port at Ferris Energy and leaves a few days later, but that particular dock is supposed to be out of service the whole time. And the ship shows up on the Ferris Energy manifest, but it doesn't go where it says it goes, and it doesn't always hold the type of cargo that the manifest says it does."

"You're saying Ferris Energy is *hiding* a tanker twice the size of a football field for three days?"

"*Three* times the size," Piper said, "and it's more like four days."

"I think it's why Carl Cassidy and Lewis Fairweather were killed," Fenway added.

McVie looked at Fenway, then at Piper, and then back at Fenway.

He opened his mouth, closed it again, and finally spoke. "What could they possibly be doing that would get two people murdered?"

"Embargoed oil," Piper said. "Getting oil from La Mitad, then selling the refined gasoline and diesel to customers under U.S. sanction —we're pretty sure it's rebels in East Timor."

"And it's making someone billions," Fenway said.

"And your father is involved." McVie folded his arms.

Fenway shook her head. "I can't be sure, but I don't think so. I haven't come across his name yet in this investigation."

"But the buck stops with him," McVie said. "He *is* the CEO, after all."

"Possibly," said Fenway. "I guess he's either involved, or he should have known and didn't, but I haven't seen his name come up."

McVie put his hands on his hips. "So, out with it, Piper. What are you doing here, and how is this Grayheath guy involved?"

"Well," Piper began tentatively, "there's only one *Grayheath* in the county—in the DMV database, anyway. Peter. So I called him up, and I asked him if he sold a boat recently."

"You didn't think that he'd be involved?"

Piper's eyes went wide. "Honestly, Sheriff, no. Whenever I've come across records, the real names are always hidden, or in code, or missing completely. The only way I've been able to uncover the names I have is through account numbers and cross-referencing information. When I saw a *real* name in that ledger, I assumed it was because he wasn't involved at all."

"At what point did you think he *was* involved?"

"Let's see," mused Piper. "When he asked why I wanted to know, I told him I was looking into some old records—I think I said it was part of a routine audit—and I noticed a payment for something related to the ocean, and I thought it was a boat or something, and he said, 'The ocean? I can't think of what that would be,' and I said, 'This clearly says *Grayheath* with the word *sea* after it'—I even spelled it. He got quiet for a minute, and then he said I must be mistaken, that he never owned or sold a boat, and said it must be another Grayheath. He wanted to get me off the phone, fast. That's when I knew I had screwed up and that he was in on it."

"And that's when you told me about it," said Fenway. "I'm sorry I didn't come back when I promised I would."

Piper didn't say anything.

McVie nodded. "Okay. So why did you show up *here?*"

Piper screwed up her mouth. "I think he realized that I had the ledger. I think he knew that 'Grayheath-dash-sea' could only have been written in a few places, and I had a hunch he'd check if the ledgers were where they were supposed to be."

"But *this* ledger wasn't where it was supposed to be."

"No," Piper said, "but this is only one ledger book. The dates only cover a few months. The last page in this book ends in the middle of September. I knew there must be more, and I thought the other ones —the ones where we could keep building our case—would be at Central Auto Body. In a warehouse, or in a locked filing cabinet, something like that."

"So you came here."

"Um," Piper said, "I might have called Marisol Velásquez first. She told me where the other ledgers might be."

"Mrs. Velásquez is the one who gave me the ledger in the first place," Fenway said to McVie. She turned to Piper. "But she didn't trust anyone in the department except me. How did you get that information out of her?"

Piper turned red.

"Did you tell her that you were me?" Fenway asked, an angry edge to her voice.

"Not exactly. I said I had some questions about the ledger, and she called me 'Miss Stevenson,' and she told me there was a backroom with a loose floorboard."

"And you didn't correct her."

"Well—no. I thought Grayheath was on his way, and I didn't want to spend the time convincing Mrs. Velásquez that she could trust me."

McVie frowned. "You're skating on thin ice, Piper. Burglary and impersonating an officer."

"Don't blame her," Fenway said. "I should have gone back to see Piper before I left. I knew she was concerned, and I knew it was time-sensitive, and besides, she had no intent to impersonate me."

McVie was still looking at Piper. "You broke in with the intent to steal those ledgers."

"But Mrs. Velásquez told me I could take them," Piper said, a desperate note in her voice. "She told me where to find them."

McVie exhaled loudly. "You know she thought she was telling Fenway, not you. That still makes it burglary—and that's still a felony."

"Oh, come on," Fenway said. "It's not like she did a home invasion. This is a commercial building—it's a misdemeanor at most."

"Misdemeanors are for *shoplifting*, not for breaking into a commercial establishment after hours."

"You can't be serious, Craig." Fenway's tone was sharp. "You honestly think Piper wouldn't get a jury of her peers to disagree with that?"

"It's still not ethical, Piper," McVie said, "and now we can't use any of that in court."

"But—but I *didn't* get it," Piper said. "I didn't even make it into the backroom. If the ledgers are there, I didn't see them. I didn't touch them."

McVie shook his head. "We'll deal with your criminal acts later. It's a good thing you *didn't* get into that backroom."

"I still think Grayheath will destroy those ledgers as soon as he can. He was about to go into that backroom when he heard the sirens."

McVie set his jaw. "That's why we'll get Marisol Velásquez out here to make sure nothing was taken."

CHAPTER NINE

PIPER PROFUSELY APOLOGIZED TO BOTH MCVIE AND FENWAY, AND as it dawned on her the seriousness of what she had done, her face grew ashen. Fenway felt bad for Piper because McVie was treating her like a disappointed father would.

After McVie woke up Marisol Velásquez, and she agreed to come to Central Auto Body, Piper slunk into her Prius and drove off.

McVie leaned against the driver door of the Highlander and watched the Toyota's taillights disappear. "I don't know what she was thinking," he muttered, staring into the darkness.

"That she needed to save evidence from getting destroyed," Fenway said. She stood next to McVie, and looked at the parking lot exit where Piper's car had vanished around the bend.

"She doesn't usually take risks like that."

"She wouldn't have if I had gone and talked to her like I promised. This is a big deal." Fenway wrung her hands. "We're talking about a billion-dollar conspiracy, national security, lots of people high up getting a piece of the pie." Fenway looked over at McVie. "And you haven't even heard about the money laundering yet."

"Money laundering?"

"You don't think a billion dollars in profit can just show up without tripping alarms, do you?"

McVie's eyes widened. "No one can launder a billion dollars."

"I said the same thing when Piper told me about it." Fenway looked around. She didn't see anyone, but she lowered her voice anyway. "She said there are a bunch of companies in Estancia that are laundering a few million each—and she's right."

"That would have to be dozens of businesses."

"Right."

"Are there even that many businesses *in* Dominguez County?"

Fenway shrugged. "Maybe not, but Dr. Tassajera was in on it. So was Jeremy Kapp's landscaping company, and so was Central Auto Body. Piper's sure there are more."

McVie looked at Fenway. "Why didn't you tell me this before?"

"When, Craig? When would I have told you? Piper uncovered all of this—jeez, I think it was the day before the election." Fenway smirked. "As I recall, when you came over that night, neither one of us were that keen to talk about work."

McVie smiled and elbowed Fenway. "We weren't that keen to talk at all, if I remember right."

"Yeah. You remember right." She looked sideways at him. "I sure didn't think we'd talk *this* much tonight, either."

"Hazards of the job."

They were silent for a few minutes.

"So," McVie said, "you think Grayheath is involved in this whole thing?"

"Piper's right a lot more often than she's wrong," said Fenway. "But her judgment might be a little off on this one because I think she's scared."

"Scared?"

"Yes. She uncovered what looks like a massive conspiracy. A billion dollars in laundered money. Frankly, I can't believe that there aren't alarm bells going off with some big law enforcement agency somewhere—Interpol, the u.s. Attorney's Office, Homeland Security."

McVie furrowed his brow. "Yeah. It seems like this is too big to go under the radar."

"Which means someone high up in law enforcement either isn't doing their job, or is on the take."

He shook his head. "Don't jump to conclusions. If this is spread out among a hundred businesses, like you say it is, that means there are a hundred businesses showing the same sort of financial transactions. If the system is built to report anomalies, maybe it doesn't think a hundred businesses showing the same transaction types are anomalous."

Fenway nodded. "I hadn't thought of that."

McVie turned toward Fenway. "It's not that you shouldn't worry about it. You and Piper are smart to be careful."

"But you're saying we might not need to look over our shoulders."

McVie was quiet.

A Dodge Ram pickup, one of its headlights dimmer than the other, drove into the lot.

"I think that's Mrs. Velásquez now," Fenway said.

The pickup ground to a stop in front of them and the door opened. Marisol Velásquez jumped to the ground.

"Hi, Mrs. Velásquez." Fenway nodded at her.

"I'm so sorry, Miss Stevenson. I swear I thought that was you on the phone when you called. I didn't know I was—"

"No, no, don't worry about it. We're dealing with her later," said Fenway. "The sheriff and I just have to know if anything else is missing."

"We can trust the sheriff?" she said to Fenway, but eyeing him.

McVie gave Mrs. Velásquez a tight smile.

"We can," Fenway said.

Marisol scrutinized McVie's face. "Okay," she said. She pulled a large keychain out of her purse and opened the front door. "Who did you say was here earlier with that woman who works for you?"

"A man named Peter Grayheath," McVie replied. "He said his

manager told him to keep an eye on this place, but he doesn't work here."

"I've never heard of him," Mrs. Velásquez said. "I mean, he might work for Domingo, but I don't think so. I know most of his mechanics."

"He's not a mechanic," Fenway said. "At least, he doesn't *dress* like a mechanic. He was in a suit. Blue dress shirt, top two buttons undone. The kind of guy who thinks he's so handsome he can get away with anything."

"Is he?"

"Is he what?"

"Handsome."

Fenway looked sideways at McVie. "Yes, but not as handsome as he thinks he is."

"I would have remembered a handsome man in a suit who worked for...." Marisol frowned.

"What is it?" Fenway said.

"On Friday, I come by the office to see if Domingo wants to go to lunch, and I see a strange car in the driveway, and a strange man in the office, too. Handsome, yes, but he looks arrogant."

Fenway pulled out her phone. "Hang on," she said, bringing up the photo of Peter Grayheath. "Is this the guy?" She turned the screen toward Mrs. Velásquez.

She looked carefully and then nodded. "I didn't get a long look at him, but yes, that could be him."

"What kind of car?"

"A big sedan. Maybe a Lincoln or Cadillac. It looked fancy, but *estadunidense* fancy, not like a German car."

"He was in Mr. Velásquez's office?" Fenway asked.

"Yes," Mrs. Velásquez said. "Neither one of them looked happy. They were arguing about something."

"Did you hear any of the conversation?" McVie said.

Mrs. Velásquez closed her eyes tight and was silent for a moment. "The other man said that they had a good thing going, I think. That wasn't exactly what he said. Maybe 'too good of a thing going.' And Domingo said that it wasn't him, or that he wasn't at fault, or something like that. Honestly, I thought he was from your father's company." She nodded at Fenway. "I thought maybe a car had crashed, or had come in with damage on the inside, and Domingo said that he hadn't done it."

"Has that happened before, that kind of confrontation?"

"Not usually with Mr. Ferris," Mrs. Velásquez said. "He is a great client. Domingo usually likes working with him." She lifted her head and stared at the wall. "You know he gives us a bonus at Christmas, every year. It's big, too, about twenty percent of what we charge him throughout the year. No questions asked, won't let Domingo refuse it, so we always make sure your father's fleet is top priority."

Of course, that's why he does it. And then, Fenway remembered that it had been her father who went over to the Velásquez house to give them his condolences about Rory.

She looked at Marisol. The woman was strong, standing up straight, not in a defeated or depressed posture, and yet there was a sadness behind her eyes, and when Fenway recognized it, suddenly it was all she saw. She cleared her throat.

"How long did Mr. Grayheath stay?" Fenway asked.

Mrs. Velásquez shook her head. "I don't know. With Domingo busy, I waited around for about five minutes, but then I left. I didn't know how long that meeting would go on, and I had errands to run."

Fenway almost asked if her kids were in school that day, but then she remembered that Rory had had a teacher in-service day, and decided that she didn't want to open a fresh wound with that question.

"Grayheath didn't tell us he was here on Friday," McVie said.

"No," Fenway mused. "You would think that would be something he'd have mentioned."

"You would think."

Mrs. Velásquez dug through the large number of keys on her ring, and she unlocked the door with a large copper colored key.

"All right," said Fenway, "shall we see if the ledgers are in here?"

"Are you sure that man didn't take them?" Mrs. Velásquez asked.

"Almost positive," McVie said. "He didn't have anything in his hands when he left, and I don't think he got into the backroom."

"But he got inside?"

McVie nodded.

"Why didn't you arrest *him?* He is trespassing. This is my property. I don't want him here."

McVie harrumphed. "He had a key. I'm not sure where he got it, but he said his supervisor asked him to keep an eye on the place. It seemed like he knew what he was doing."

Fenway grimaced, and out of the corner of her eye she saw Mrs. Velásquez grunt. Grayheath *was* trespassing, and neither McVie nor Callahan had batted an eye. Of course, Fenway hadn't either, but she was also stuck in the car the whole time.

"I don't understand," Mrs. Velásquez said. "You know this building is owned by us. You know our employees are all mechanics. Why do you just assume he belongs here? He might have stolen cash, tools, customer lists, computer equipment. Just because he was in a suit?"

Fenway heard the unspoken words, too—*just because he was a white man?*

McVie seemed to hear the subtext as well because he paled and shifted uncomfortably. "I, uh," he said. "I suppose I made some bad assumptions." He looked at Mrs. Velásquez. "Do you want to press charges against him?"

Mrs. Velásquez sighed. "For what? Will that bring Rory back? Will that bring Domingo home?" She shook her head adamantly. "The time for that has passed. Whatever he took, whatever he stole—now he's had plenty of time to hide or get rid of it."

"I'm sorry, Mrs. Velásquez," McVie said.

She didn't say anything but walked inside the building.

"If you find anything missing," McVie said, following her inside, "just let me know. We can still make an arrest."

Fenway stepped in and closed the door. The front office was clean but industrial, with linoleum floors that looked like tile, desks a little too low to the ground, task chairs with dusty black upholstery, and PCs and monitors a few years old.

Mrs. Velásquez looked around the office.

"Anything missing?"

"I'd have to check more closely, but it looks like the computers are all here," she said. She walked over to a filing cabinet and pulled on the handle of the top drawer; it clanked but didn't move. "The cabinets are locked, too. That's a good sign."

She strode across the room to the rear door, and turned the handle; the door clanked with almost the same noise the file cabinet had made. "This is locked, too. That's good." She pulled out a key and unlocked the door, pushing it open.

"Where did you find the ledger that you gave me?" Fenway asked.

"It was in the bottom drawer of Domingo's desk."

"Should we look there for the other ledgers?"

"I already looked through all the drawers the other day. You can see if I missed anything."

McVie walked over to the desk with DOMINGO VELÁSQUEZ, OWNER on the nameplate. He pulled on the top drawer.

"Locked," he said.

"You can look in here while I unlock the desk for the sheriff," Mrs. Velásquez said to Fenway, motioning to the room she had opened. "The loose floorboard is in back, under that stack of boxes."

Fenway looked at the stack of white file boxes five high. "Jeez. Are those heavy?"

She turned, but Mrs. Velásquez had already left the room.

Fenway looked at the floor. Instead of the cheap linoleum of the front office, this room had plank flooring—old but good quality. The wood was scratched in places, and the protective coating had worn off in several areas. One floorboard, sticking out an inch in front of the stack of boxes, was lighter in color than the surrounding boards. Fenway pushed the top box about half an inch. It slid easily.

She picked up the first two boxes and set them against the wall, but the next two were significantly heavier, and the box on the very bottom was so heavy that Fenway couldn't even pick it up. She tried to push it with her foot but it didn't budge. Kneeling, she pushed the box with her shoulder and moved it all the way off the discolored floorboard.

She tried to get the board up using her fingernails but couldn't get a good grip on it. She finally stood up and found a flathead screwdriver on a shelf next to the door.

After retrieving the screwdriver, she lifted out the floorboard. Setting it gently to the side, she pulled blue nitrile gloves and her phone out of her purse.

She turned on her phone flashlight and shined it in the hole where the floorboard had been. A gray bag, about twelve inches by fifteen, and a few inches thick, lay on its side, with a "fireproof" label clearly visible. Fenway quickly put the gloves on and reached down to grab the bag. It was surprisingly light.

Undoing the Velcro enclosure over the top revealed a black zipper, which Fenway quickly opened.

The space inside was divided into six sections, each large enough for a spiral notebook, a dozen file folders, or a decent-sized ledger.

But the bag was empty.

"You've got to be kidding me," Fenway muttered under her breath. "Piper put her ass on the line for an empty document bag."

Fenway got to her feet and walked out of the backroom. McVie was leafing through a drawer full of files in Domingo Velásquez's desk, and Marisol was looking through a cabinet.

"Mrs. Velásquez, who else knew about the place your husband kept those ledgers?"

She looked over at Fenway and bit her lip, thinking for a moment. "I don't know," she said. "I knew about it because Domingo said I might need those ledgers in an emergency. Why?"

"The ledgers aren't there. There was a fireproof bag in there, but it's empty."

"I don't know who else my husband would have told," Mrs. Velásquez said. "He didn't talk about those ledgers."

"Who did the books for Central Auto Body?"

"I did, for a long time," Mrs. Velásquez said, "but maybe two years ago, we get someone full-time. Domingo said with all the changes in the tax laws, and all the clients we got, we need an accountant." She sniffed. "I was happy. I work too many hours, and I have trouble with numbers anyway. I can manage the Ferris Energy car fleet, but *¡ay!* the consulting service, complicated. No matter how many times Domingo shows me how to do it, the balance is always wrong."

Fenway's ears perked up. "Consulting service?"

"Yes, *claro que sí.* Domingo told me that this consultant group talked to other energy firms to help them start up, find oil or gas, how to structure the company for tax laws, all that. They had a fleet that was three times the size of the Ferris Energy fleet. I figured that pretty soon they'd make more money off their consulting than their oil."

"Was this under the Ferris name? Ferris Consulting, something like that?"

"You know, that's the first thing I said to Domingo—that with a name like Ferris Energy, you'd think they'd want to take advantage of their name for their consulting firm. But no, they went with something generic. I guess they didn't want anyone thinking they were hiring a competitor to consult with them."

"A generic name?"

"Yes. Let me think. It was *World* something."

"Maybe *Global?*"

Mrs. Velásquez eyes widened. "That was it. *Global.* Not *World.*" She thought another moment. "Global Advantage."

"Did your husband keep those ledgers from when you first started working with the consulting company?"

"Oh, no. Only Rose's ledgers were kept here. After we did our taxes that year, they went home with me."

"Rose—that's the accountant?"

"Yes."

"Where did she come from?" Fenway asked.

"What do you mean?"

"I mean, did someone recommend her? Did you put out an ad, or get a recruiter, or what?"

"Oh. I'm not sure. Domingo told me we'd hire a full-time accountant, and he did. She was in here pretty quickly, I guess. Within a week."

Fenway nodded, although it struck her as odd. "What's Rose's last name?"

"Morgan."

"Did your husband do a background check on her?"

Marisol Velásquez shook her head. "No, I told you, I don't know anything about her hiring."

"What about her HR file?"

Mrs. Velásquez smiled. "Most of it's on the computer, but anything she signed is in the file cabinet there. You looking for her W-4 or something?"

"No, her address."

"Her address?"

"Sure. If she knows about the financial ins and outs of Central Auto Body, she might know something about what happened with your husband. He might have emptied some account before he disappeared." Fenway cleared her throat. "You took your ledgers home with you?"

Mrs. Velásquez shifted uncomfortably. "Well, yes. I mean, I suppose I should have left them here in case Rose ever had to reference them, but she never asked."

"And the ledger that you gave to me, Rose was the one who maintained it?"

"As far as I know," Mrs. Velásquez said. "It looks like her handwriting."

"How do you know what her handwriting looks like?"

Mrs. Velásquez waved her hand. "I read a note she wrote to one of our mechanics. She's young. She only got her degree a couple of years ago and this is only her second real accounting job."

"Note to one of your mechanics? What kind of note?"

Mrs. Velásquez laughed. "A love letter, if you can believe it. The man is young—he's probably a year or two younger than she is. He's good looking, too. More handsome than that arrogant *cerote* who was here on Friday." She lowered her voice conspiratorially. "If I was young like Rose, I'd make a play for him."

Something itched at Fenway's brain. "What's his name?"

"We don't need to get him involved, surely."

"I don't know yet."

Mrs. Velásquez paused. "Rafael."

"So Rose wrote a love letter to Rafael?"

"Yes."

"And you—what? Intercepted it? Found it on his desk or something?"

"No, no, Domingo caught her sneaking it over to Rafael's desk. He took it away from Rose and gave her a warning about workplace romance."

Fenway thought for a moment. "Does Rose have a desk here?"

"Yes. It's that one—third one from the end."

Fenway walked over to the desk where a newer monitor was set up, and she looked at the two framed photos next to the phone.

The first picture showed three women in hiking clothes, all in their early twenties, standing shoulder to shoulder in front of a waterfall. In the second photo, a young woman in a cap and gown stood between a man and a woman in their late forties or early fifties. All of them were grinning ear to ear. Fenway looked at the pictures more closely. The woman in the middle of the hiking picture was the same as the woman in the cap and gown. She was black, with large, bright eyes and high cheekbones, and tight, dark brown ringlets cascading out of her cap in the graduation picture. In the hiking picture, she wore no makeup and her hair was hidden under a Dodgers baseball cap.

"This one's Rose, I take it?" Fenway held up the graduation picture so Mrs. Velásquez could see it.

"Yes, that's her. A few years ago, but she still looks the same."

"Has she been into work this week?"

Mrs. Velásquez shook her head. "No, with Domingo gone, there's no point. She told me her mother was sick anyway and she could use the time off."

The itch in Fenway's brain grew more insistent. She looked under the desk.

"Did Rose have a laptop?"

"No. She worked on a PC."

"Like everyone else?"

"No, most of the mechanics had these workstations that connect to a central system. It was just for customer information, invoicing, orders, inventory, that kind of thing. Rose had one of the only real PCs."

"Do you know where it is?"

"What?" Mrs. Velásquez sounded shocked and hurried over to Rose's desk, and McVie looked up from the cabinet he was leafing through. Fenway ducked underneath the keyboard tray and found the monitor and keyboard cables dangling.

"The PC's gone," Fenway said.

"The PC's gone?" Mrs. Velásquez asked faintly.

"Do you think Peter Grayheath took it?" McVie said. "I know most of the other equipment is here, but if Rose's PC was the one with all the accounting files on it, he might have taken it." McVie looked at Fenway. "You were asking Mrs. Velásquez who else knew about the floorboard hiding space. Was it empty?"

Fenway nodded. "I found a fireproof document case, but that's it— no ledgers, no documents, no nothing."

"We should probably pay a visit to Mr. Grayheath," McVie said.

Fenway looked at McVie, again trying to convey information to him telepathically, but this time his attention was divided between the missing PC, the missing ledgers, and the mysterious man who had shown up to "keep an eye on" a business that wasn't his.

———

After they all performed a more careful search of the office, they found nothing else missing—nothing obvious, anyway. Mrs. Velásquez showed McVie and Fenway the door and said she needed to get paperwork taken care of. "I'll bring everyone in tomorrow," she told them wearily. "We have cars to service, and I can't delay the customers any longer."

Fenway got into McVie's car and they drove out of the parking lot. Once they were a couple of blocks away, McVie glanced at her. "You've got something on your mind, Fenway."

"Yep."

"You don't think Grayheath took the PC?"

"I don't think he took the ledgers, either."

"Who, then?" He paused. "You think it was Rose?"

"That's who I think it is, yeah," Fenway said, "but didn't it strike you as odd that Domingo Velásquez had that love note from Rose?"

McVie was quiet.

"I wonder if that love note was *really* for the young mechanic, or if it was for Domingo Velásquez."

McVie slowly nodded. "And if Domingo took the ledgers, and if Rose took the PC, and Rose wrote that love note to Domingo... maybe they're holed up together someplace?"

"It's just a theory," Fenway said. "I couldn't ask too many more questions without freaking her out."

"Your gut's been right before."

"My gut's been wrong before, too," Fenway said, "but it's an avenue of inquiry worth pursuing, right?"

"Right."

"What do you think? Should we go to Rose's house now?"

"I don't think so," McVie said, glancing at his watch. "It's almost midnight. They'll be there in the morning."

They were silent for a moment, and the unasked question hung heavily between them.

"Um, Craig," Fenway said, at the same time McVie said, "Listen, Fenway."

"Oh, sorry," Fenway said. "You go."

"No, no, go ahead."

Fenway took a deep breath. "I know tonight was our first real date, and it got all kinds of crazy-messed-up."

"But it's okay," McVie said quickly. "I mean, we like—I like, anyway, working with you. It wasn't a normal date, but I always like, uh...."

Fenway cocked her head to the side. "You always like what?"

"It's cheesy."

"Cheesy? That's stopping you from talking?"

He coughed. "I like seeing how your mind works."

Fenway smiled. "Thanks. Me too. I mean, I like working with you. It's not the same as a date, though."

"Right."

"And sometimes, at the end of a date, if things are going well, some people stay over at the other person's apartment." Fenway tapped her fingers on the console between the two front seats.

"And sometimes people don't even need to go on a real date to do that," McVie said, a little cautiously.

"Sometimes."

"So," McVie said.

"So," Fenway said.

McVie turned onto Estancia Canyon Road, only about a half mile from Fenway's apartment. "You're wondering about what'll happen the rest of the evening."

Fenway nodded. "Kind of. Yeah."

"But?"

"It's late."

"Yeah."

They turned into Fenway's apartment complex. McVie pulled up slowly into Fenway's parking space. He debated for a moment, then put the car into Park.

Fenway smiled. "Awfully bold move, Sheriff."

"I didn't think we were done talking." He smiled slyly. "Can't be rolling out into the middle of the parking lot. Safety first."

"Of course."

Fenway returned McVie's smile, and then leaned over and kissed him.

The kiss was gentle at first, but it ignited something in Fenway. She pulled him closer with her right arm, their kiss growing more intense with each second. Her left hand moved from his bicep to his chest, finally tracing the line of his uniform shirt from his collarbone, slowly snaking down to his sternum, down to his navel. She put her palm flat on his stomach, her fingers inside his shirt between the buttons. He wrapped his right arm around her, moving from her shoulder blade, and then down, in time with her hand moving down his stomach. Then Fenway broke from the kiss. Her heart beat quickly and she gasped to catch her breath.

"Wow," said McVie to himself. Fenway could feel his abs tighten, and his hand was tense on the small of her back.

"Dammit," she said. "I wasn't going to invite you up tonight."

"You don't have to," McVie breathed, kissing her lightly on the lips.

"No," she said, "no, I kind of have to."

McVie kissed the side of her face. "Maybe I don't want to come up," he said playfully.

Fenway's hand traveled from his stomach to his thigh. She could feel him tense with the movement. She leaned forward and breathed in his ear. "Lying to a peace officer is a serious crime, Sheriff."

"Guilty as charged," he said, kissing her neck.

They pulled apart from each other and got out of the car, not speaking, the electricity between them pulsing in delicious anticipation as he followed her up the stairs, while she fumbled in her purse for her keys.

II

THURSDAY

CHAPTER TEN

FENWAY WOKE UP, THE SIDE OF HER FACE HOT, AND OPENED HER eyes. Weak gray light came into the room, washing out the colors of the dresser and nightstand. She blinked; she was lying on top of McVie, her head on his chest. Her cheek stuck slightly to his skin before separating as she pushed herself up.

"Hey," McVie said. "Good morning."

That had been the third night they had spent together, but for the first time, he was still in bed when she woke.

"Hey yourself," she said, attempting a playful tone but hearing brusqueness in her voice. Her tongue tasted awful, she needed a shower, and she was keenly aware that both of them were still naked. She turned her head to look at the bedside clock. It was 6:20.

"I've gotta get moving," she said. Her heart pounded in her ears and her shoulders were tight. She rolled off McVie onto her back, and she covered herself with the sheet.

McVie looked surprised. Fenway had pulled the covers off him and she tried to keep her eyes on his face. "What do you mean, you've gotta get moving?" he asked.

"I—uh—there's a lot of work to do. We missed the interviews with the students after rehearsal last night, for one thing."

McVie nodded. "Pruitt gave me their schedules. I bet we can get one or two of them between classes."

"And we still need to talk to Cygnus."

"And we will. What's gotten into you?"

"Me?" Fenway rubbed the back of her neck and tried to calm down. "Nothing. I'm just—just ready to get the day going. That's all."

"You seem tense."

"Maybe I slept wrong."

"This is the first time I've stayed all night. Does that have anything to do with it?"

"No, of course not." Fenway lied, eyeing the floor, the bedroom door, the dresser—anywhere but McVie. "Don't be silly."

"It's okay, Fenway. This is kind of a big step for us. It feels a little more real than what we've done up till now." He put his arm around Fenway's shoulders.

She closed her eyes and fought the urge to throw his arm off. "Really, McVie, I'm fine." She avoided his eyes but felt his gaze on her.

McVie exhaled audibly, taking his arm away. "See what Dez has to say when we get in. I don't think there's a break in Amanda's schedule until nine thirty, and I want to talk to that Xavier kid, too."

"What about Denise?"

"Denise?"

"Yeah, you know, Cygnus called her 'the diva of San Dimas.'"

"Oh, right. The one with the problem being at the right spot onstage."

"Right."

McVie put his hands behind his head. "You could give her to Dez, and you and I might talk to Rose Morgan this morning, considering what Piper found out yesterday. We want to know what she has, and if Domingo is there, what he has, too."

Fenway paused. "Maybe we should see about getting a warrant before we visit Rose Morgan. If she's got the PC, or if Domingo

Velásquez is hiding out at her house, we should have a warrant in hand when we knock on the door."

McVie nodded. "I don't know that we can get one, but we'll see."

"Sure," Fenway said. "Talk to Migs. He's good about figuring out stuff."

"I've gotten warrants before."

"Yeah, but if you want it to stand up in court, you should talk to him." She wanted to get up. She wanted to get into the shower and spend time on her hair treatment and wash the night off.

"We're not in any hurry this morning," McVie said. "You can relax. We've got a couple of hours before the judges even show up."

"I have to do my hair," Fenway said, willing her shoulders to drop. She got out of bed and wrapped the sheet around herself. She inwardly grimaced because she hated pulling the sheet off her bed, but felt compelled to cover herself up.

"Your hair?"

"Takes a while." For all of Amy's faults, she probably didn't have to take forty-five minutes to apply three different products just to get her hair not to frizz on damp fall days.

"I can't imagine anyone taking longer than my, uh," McVie hesitated and then finished lamely, "*ex-wife* did in the bathroom." He put a smile on his face, but it looked a bit stricken.

Fenway forced herself to smile. "I'm quick like a ninja when I don't have to do my hair."

McVie chuckled.

Fenway kept smiling, too, begging herself not to say the thing that was itching her brain, but she couldn't stop it. "Is that the first time you've called Amy your ex-wife?"

McVie glanced up at Fenway, a slightly worried look in his eyes, and nodded.

"Did you sign the paperwork yet?"

"My lawyer's looking it over. In fact, I'm supposed to call him this afternoon."

Fenway paused, then quickly drew a breath. "I wasn't trying to pressure you into—"

"No," McVie said, holding up his hand. "I know you weren't." He pulled himself up into a sitting position. "I could get in the shower with you."

Fenway realized the smile had left her lips and forced it back. "That sounds nice, but you don't have clean clothes to change into."

McVie blinked and studied Fenway's face. "No," he said slowly, "no I don't. I guess I'll head out so I can get ready. I'll see you at the office?"

Fenway hesitated but then nodded. "Sure. See you there at—I don't know—eight?"

"Sounds perfect." He grinned, a little unevenly, and then swung his toned legs out of the bed and stood up, facing away from Fenway. She took in the whole of his body and mentally kicked herself. What was wrong with her? Yes, McVie was older and in the middle of a divorce, but he was kind, he was gorgeous, he was *cut*. But Fenway was wound so tight she might snap inside.

Fenway stepped around him as he pulled on his boxers—cute, playful ones, with jalapeño peppers on a black background, which she noticed with a mixture of amusement and annoyance. Paying attention to his boxers and not looking where she was going, she stepped on the edge of the sheet and almost tripped.

The heat rose to her face as she padded to the shower and turned it on.

"Let me go to the bathroom and I'll get out of your hair," McVie mumbled.

Fenway started to open her mouth, but that was exactly what she wanted. So she stepped out and let McVie slip past her and close the door.

Good, Fenway thought, with a trace of relief. She had wondered if McVie was so used to being married that he'd use the bathroom with the door open out of habit. She wondered if most couples were that gross with each other, or if it was just something on Netflix shows.

She stepped on the sheet again but kept her balance. The sheet was wet. Fenway sat down on the bed. She must have gotten it wet when she turned the shower on.

She heard the toilet flush, then the sink turn on and off, and McVie came out. He gave her a smile, reached down, and got his trousers off the floor. He looked at them and shook them out; they were wrinkled, but certainly good enough to wear to his car. He put them on, then walked out to the living room where his uniform shirt was thrown over the chair. Buttoning up his shirt, he walked back into Fenway's bedroom and kissed her on the cheek. "Okay," he said. "See you at eight. Remember to lock the door behind me."

She nodded, watching him go out to the front room, slip his sock-less feet into his shoes, and grab his wallet and keys off the table.

Then he was gone.

Immediately a weight lifted off Fenway's shoulders, and she cocked her head to the side, as if listening for a strange noise, but the only strange noise was in her head.

She dropped the sheet and walked out to the front room, turning the deadbolt of the front door, then went right into the shower.

As she ducked her head under the cold water, she berated herself. It was no way to treat a boyfriend, or whatever McVie was. This is what she wanted—and when she got it, she couldn't get him away fast enough.

She went over the night before in her mind. Did she feel weird about anything McVie did?

No. She felt pretty good about most of the things McVie did.

Except the fact that he was still in her bed in the morning.

She shook her head to get the cobwebs out and turned the tap to warm. Whatever was wrong with her, Fenway decided, working the investigation with McVie would put it all right again.

———

She requested an Uber and stood outside in the parking lot. The morning was cold, and frost rimmed the hoods and roofs on all the cars. The Uber had trouble finding her address, so she got to work ten minutes late.

Dez sat at her computer and looked up as the door shut behind Fenway.

"Well, someone finally got a good night's sleep," Dez said, grinning. "I barely recognized you without the circles under your eyes."

"Gee, thanks, Dez." Fenway rolled her eyes. "You look like a million bucks, too."

Dez scoffed. "I do not. I was searching Jessica Marquez's house for hours last night, and I found nothing except pizza boxes and trash. The girl may have looked good, but she was a slob. Lots of fingerprints, though. We'll see if any of those are interesting."

"No laptop? No weird financial ledgers or anything?"

"Nope. Oh, I almost forgot. I did find one interesting piece of evidence."

"What was it?"

"It was a class ring. Rio de Palmas High School."

"Interesting." Fenway paused. "Where did you find it?"

"Ooh, twenty questions. I like this game." Dez cackled. "Underneath the bed. Wedged a little under the headboard."

"The bed in Jessica's room?"

Dez nodded.

"And I take it Jessica didn't go to Rio de Palmas."

"We're still having trouble getting background on her, but it was a man's class ring."

"Under the bed. I see. A gentleman caller."

"That's what I'm thinking."

"Was there a year on it?"

Dez shook her head. "No, but it's got two theater masks on the side of the band."

"That would suggest someone who's into the dramatic arts."

"Right."

Fenway folded her arms and smiled. "And would you like me to ask you which of the *Othello* actors graduated from Rio de Palmas High?"

"I would be delighted."

They were both quiet for a moment.

"You have to ask, Fenway."

"Yeah, yeah. Okay, so which of the *Othello* actors—"

"Xavier Gonsalves. The leading man himself."

Fenway closed her eyes and shook her head. "I was so hoping he wouldn't be like that." She grimaced. "Okay. I think we need to question him and Amanda Kohl. Especially Amanda. She's now the last one out of the office except for Jessica, and the first one with a motive."

"I'll drive," said Dez, grabbing her purse.

"Hang on, Dez. I want to wait for McVie. We thought we might have a lead on the Velásquez case—the accountant who did the books for Central Auto Body."

Dez set her purse down. "I suppose I should call first. I'd hate to give the students warning, but I also don't want Dr. Pruitt breathing down my neck."

"I need to get my kit anyway," Fenway said. "By the way, has anyone notified Jessica Marquez's next of kin?"

Dez shook her head. "Jessica Marquez is an enigma so far. The university has no next of kin listed in her file. We may have to do some digging. I thought maybe we'd find something at her house, but no such luck."

Fenway grabbed her equipment kit and hesitated, and then opened the second desk drawer from the bottom and pulled out an old dictation recorder. She checked the record button—it still worked.

When she came out to the main office, Dez hung up the phone. "We have to hurry. Xavier's got about an hour and a half to talk to us before his next class. They're having him meet us at the admin building. Amanda too. We can divide and conquer if we leave now."

CHAPTER ELEVEN

WHILE DEZ SPED DOWN THE EXPRESSWAY IN HER RED IMPALA, IN the passenger seat Fenway texted McVie that they were on their way to Nidever. They parked in the same visitors' lot as McVie had the day before, and the two of them walked into the admin building.

"How do you want to play this?" Fenway asked Dez in a low voice, walking through the carpeted hall toward the president's office.

"I say we interview both of them at the same time," Dez said. "That way they can't compare stories, or even—I don't know—shoot each other looks."

"Shoot each other looks?"

"Or semaphore, or carrier pigeons. You know what I mean. I wish they weren't coming in together."

Fenway tilted her head. "Why *are* they coming in together?"

"I don't know."

They arrived at the anteroom in front of the president's office. The secretary, typing with perfect posture, radiated efficiency, and she didn't raise her head to look at them.

Dez cleared her throat.

The secretary didn't look up. "Can I help you ladies?"

"Sergeant Dez Roubideaux," Dez said, showing her badge. "This is Coroner Stevenson."

Fenway smiled. "It's Belinda, right?"

The secretary looked up and returned her smile. "That's right."

"Dr. Pruitt made a couple of students available to us for interviews. Is he in?"

The secretary shook her head. "He's meeting with the board of regents, but the two students should be in shortly. I'll put you in one of the conference rooms."

Fenway shot a look at Dez. "If you don't mind," she said slowly, "we were hoping to interview them separately. Do you have a second room we can use?"

The secretary frowned. "Well, I suppose so. There's a workroom in the back, if you're okay with the mess."

"That's fine."

The secretary walked the two of them down the hall and put Dez in a glass-walled conference room, with a huge mahogany table and leather chairs. She showed Fenway to a small office farther down. A photocopier was against one wall, and a bar-height worktable cluttered with papers, scissors, and more stood against the other. There were two folding chairs, but no desk or table in front of which to sit.

Fenway looked around at the beige walls, devoid of personality—no wall hangings, no posters. It was a blank canvas in this unwelcoming building on this unwelcoming campus.

Fenway sat in the office for several minutes waiting, then there was a knock at the door. It opened and Xavier stuck his head in.

"Hi, Coroner," he said. "I heard you wanted to see me."

"I did." Fenway motioned to the chair across from her. "Do you have a few minutes?"

"Class in an hour. Our last dress rehearsal tonight. I've got a little time."

"Great." Fenway pulled the dictation recorder out of her purse and set it on the worktable. "You mind if I record this?"

"Uh...." Xavier eyed the ancient machine warily. "I guess not."

"Cool." Fenway hit the record button. "Coroner Fenway Stevenson, interview with Nidever student Xavier—I'm sorry, did you officially change your name to Go, or is it still Gonsalves?"

"Go is just my stage name. My real name is still Gonsalves."

"Great." She said the date and time and then looked up at Xavier and smiled.

"You excited about the opening of the play? This is your first lead role, right?"

"I don't know—I should be excited about it, I guess." He rested his elbows on the table. "I—uh, I don't feel so great about it with Jessica, Ms. Marquez, dead. I thought maybe the play would get postponed, but no—Professor Cygnus isn't changing a thing." He leaned back in his chair. "I guess it's better to keep working through this."

Fenway shrugged. "Everyone processes it differently."

"Yeah, I guess so. You've probably seen a lot of stuff since you've been coroner."

"That I have." She smiled. "Did you know Jessica Marquez well?"

Xavier looked up at the ceiling and exhaled long and slow and loudly. "Not as well as some of the other actors."

"Like who?"

"I mean, I never worked with her. Amanda and a few of the other students—they knew her a lot better than I did."

"Hmm," Fenway said. "That surprises me."

Xavier brought his gaze down from the ceiling and fixed his attention on Fenway. "Everyone in The Guild knew her. All the actors were in and out of the office, not just the student workers. Jessica would come watch us rehearse, maybe once or twice a week. She was trying to get us all to do the theater tour in London."

"Were you going?"

"Me? No. I'm trying to get out of the audience and onto the stage. I don't have the time to take three weeks and travel to London when I could be auditioning and making money. Plus, it's crazy expensive."

"How expensive is it?"

"The special student price is six grand."

Fenway winced. "That's a lot for a college student."

"It's a lot for *me*, anyway. Most of the actors are having their parents foot the bill."

"You don't think you could learn from the London stage?"

"I'm sure I could," Xavier said, "but I want to be a working actor here—or in L.A., anyway. Shakespeare's okay, I guess, but I don't want to make it my career."

"Why are you in this play, then?"

"Are you kidding? With Professor Cygnus's name recognition? This should get me some auditions on some serious films. Art films, the kind that get buzz at Toronto, maybe even Cannes. They're always doing Shakespeare adaptations. Nothing better on a young actor's résumé than a Cygnus production."

"Especially when you're the lead actor."

"Right." He nodded. "Othello. Big, juicy part. Trying to convince directors and producers to drive up from L.A. to see it is a pain, but Professor Cygnus wrote letters for us."

"Really? Who else besides you?"

Xavier shifted uncomfortably. "Uh, Amanda Kohl got a recommendation letter. She plays Desdemona."

"Right, we talked about Amanda last time. Is she your girlfriend?"

"Uh, no," Xavier said. "I mean, you might get a different answer from her, but there's nothing like, uh, you know, the kind of relationship you have when you're in a play together. Kind of does a number on you."

"How long has it been going on?"

"A month or two. I don't think it's that serious."

"You sleep with a lot of your leading ladies?"

Xavier smiled. "I've never been the leading man before."

Fenway smiled back. "Fair enough. Did you go to the office the day before yesterday?"

"The Guild office? No."

"Not even to see Amanda?"

He smiled. "She and I want to keep it quiet."

"Keep it quiet? Professor Cygnus doesn't like his actors to get romantically involved with each other?"

"It's not that," Xavier said. "We just don't want to make it a big thing. Reduces the drama."

"Does the professor care about his *general manager* sleeping with his lead actor?"

Xavier blinked hard, then looked down at the table.

"You have anything to say?"

He rubbed his hand over his face, from forehead to chin. "No one was supposed to know."

"That you and Jessica were having an affair?"

Xavier laughed, although a little sadness rounded off the corners. "An *affair*. That sounds so *bourgeois*."

"What would you call it?"

He leaned forward, elbows on his knees. "I don't know. I guess I'd call it having a good time."

"What do you think Amanda would call it?"

Xavier was quiet. Fenway let him sit in the silence for a moment. He shifted uncomfortably in his chair.

She was the first one to speak. "When was the last time you saw Jessica?"

Xavier looked up toward the ceiling. "Let me see. Uh—I'm not sure. It must have been earlier in the week. I was trying to get one of my costumes taken care of. There was an issue with the fit in the shoulders, I think."

"When was that? Monday? Yesterday?"

"Maybe it was last week. It definitely wasn't yesterday." Xavier groaned. "We're right up against opening night. The days are all running together for me. I'm at rehearsals for six or eight hours every night."

"Okay," Fenway said. "How about Tuesday night? What did you do?"

"We were rehearsing the early scenes," Xavier said. "Amanda was out of there by eight o'clock. I didn't get out of rehearsal till eleven. And I, uh, I texted Amanda just before I left."

"Ah. So it was a booty call."

He grinned sheepishly. "I wanted to see her. I got home and made myself some dinner. She got to my place about midnight and we—uh, went to bed."

"It took her an hour to get from her dorm to your apartment?"

Xavier shrugged. "She texted me that she was on her way, but then I told her I was eating dinner, and she said she'd see me in a little while."

"Where do you think she went?"

"I don't know. I figured she just stayed in her dorm and did homework. And we're not exclusive—for all I know she was with another guy until she came to my place."

"Would that bother you?"

Xavier shrugged. "A little, I guess."

"But you think it might bother her a lot to find out about you and Jessica?"

"Maybe." He paused. "You—uh, you won't tell Amanda that I was sleeping with Jessica, will you?"

"You don't think she knows already?"

"Uh—I hope not. Like I said, we're not exclusive, but I don't want to hurt her."

"If she knows already, do you think she'd have a motive for hurting Jessica?"

Xavier put his hands on his knees. "No. No way. She'd never hurt anybody."

"But you just said she wouldn't like it if she found out about you and Jessica. She wouldn't confront her about the affair?"

"It wasn't an affair! It's not like Amanda and I are official or anything. For all I know, she's seeing other guys."

Fenway narrowed her eyes at Xavier. "Now, come on, Xavier. I can tell just by the way you said that. She's only seeing *you*, and you know she thinks it's exclusive. It absolutely *would* devastate her to find out about you and Jessica. That's why you don't want me to say anything."

"Yeah, fine, all right, but she still wouldn't confront Jessica. She'd confront *me*."

Fenway stayed silent for a moment, but Xavier offered nothing else. Fenway leaned forward slightly. "Have you seen the Bardy award that The Guild won for *Merchant of Venice?*"

Xavier screwed up his face in thought. "Those ugly awards? Man, if I never see another Bardy again, it'll be too soon. Yeah, I know it. The Bardies are on the shelf in The Guild office."

"That sounds right."

"I mean, I've seen them before, and Professor Cygnus talks about them a lot, but I don't know when the last time I noticed them was. Why?" Then a light ignited in his eyes. "Oh. One of them is missing. Or maybe it was the weapon. That's it, right?"

"Have you seen it in the last couple of days?"

"No."

"Not on stage, not in the theater—nothing?"

"Right."

"You have a roommate or a family member who can confirm where you were between eleven thirty and one thirty?"

Xavier shifted uncomfortably. "That's when Jessica was killed?"

Fenway pressed her lips together. "We're just trying to establish some timelines, that's all."

"Then, uh, I don't know. I *think* my roommate was home, but he was asleep in his room. Maybe. He might have been staying over at his girlfriend's. If he was home, he might have heard me come in, or he might have heard Amanda come over."

"I'll need your roommate's name and contact information."

"Um—yeah, sure, that shouldn't be a problem."

Fenway took her notebook and pen out of her purse and handed it to Xavier, who scribbled the name and number down, then handed them back. Fenway glanced at it.

"His name is Tony?"

"Yeah."

"He around now?"

"Should be. He's got a break between classes."

"Okay, thanks." Fenway stood up.

"All right," Xavier said, getting to his feet. "Let me know if you need anything else."

"Okay. Thanks."

Xavier started to leave and then turned his head back. "Coroner," he said, "look—I know I wasn't real forthcoming with you about my relationship with Jessica, and I know I wasn't serious about her, but, still, I liked her. Not the same way I care about Amanda, but still—she didn't deserve to be killed. So, please, find out who did this."

Fenway nodded. "That's just what we're trying to do."

Xavier opened the door, hesitated a moment, then exited into the admin building.

CHAPTER TWELVE

FENWAY TURNED OFF THE RECORDER AND PUT IT BACK IN HER PURSE. Should she go join Dez, or leave her alone? After a few minutes of waiting, she stood up and stretched her arms above her head and walked down the hall to the glass windows of the conference room.

Amanda looked stricken, her face melting in grief. Dez sat at the head of the table, watching Amanda through narrowed eyes. She got up and walked to a side table where she picked up a box of tissues and handed it to Amanda.

So much for Xavier not wanting Amanda to find out about his affair with Jessica.

Fenway returned to the workroom and sat down on the folding chair. She called the number in her notebook for Xavier's roommate, who told her that on Tuesday night Xavier had come home, and then Amanda came over. He didn't know exactly what time either of them arrived. She ended the call in disappointment.

After another ten minutes, Fenway heard the door of the conference room open and the muted voices of Amanda and Dez. After a moment, Dez came into the workroom.

"That looked rough," Fenway said.

"I hated to do it. She bawled."

"He asked me not to tell her."

"Too bad for him. It gives her motive."

"You think Amanda knew about Xavier and Jessica being together?"

Dez shrugged. "She's a great actor. I couldn't tell if she knew or not. Of course, she said she didn't—she even denied it, and said how stupid she was, on and on."

"You find out where she was the night of the murder?"

Dez nodded. "She said she stopped at a convenience store. Bought a couple of lottery tickets."

"Lottery tickets?"

"The last refuge of the hopes and dreams of kids who grow up without money," Dez said.

"I never bought lottery tickets when I was in college."

"Yeah, well, you're the exception that proves the rule."

"Should we go see if any other students are over by the theater?" asked Fenway.

Dez chuckled. "Surely you're not suggesting we go talk to them without Dr. Pruitt's permission."

"I mean, if we just *happen* to run into Professor Cygnus, and if we just *happen* to ask him questions—"

"Yeah, well, good luck with that."

"Maybe I could take a look at the ransacked office."

Dez nodded. "That's not the worst idea. Maybe something will click."

"Has anyone cleaned it up?"

Dez shook her head. "I think we have until Monday. The students and the professor are too busy with *Othello*."

They walked across campus, students on bikes whizzing by on the paths. The two of them diagonally cut across the quad near DiFazio Hall.

Afternoon classes were in full swing, and the empty first-floor hallway echoed with their footsteps. They wandered into the lobby, and Fenway started to pull the door to the theater open before she realized a lecture class was in session. She quickly let go of the door handle.

"I guess we struck out," she said.

"Did you want to see the office while we're here?"

"Might as well."

They went to the stairwell, where the body of Jessica Marquez had lain. The cleanup had been thorough; there was no sign of blood. Dez and Fenway were silent as they walked up the metal staircase to the second floor.

The Guild's office was at the other end of the hallway, past several classrooms and offices. They walked past quietly, Fenway feeling as if she were in a library. Stopping in front of the office door, Dez pulled a key out of her pocket and unlocked the office to the North American Shakespeare Guild.

The room was in half darkness; the gray sky filtered weak light through the drawn blinds. Even in the shadows, Fenway could tell that the room had been tossed. She carefully reached out and with a single gloved finger flicked the light on.

The fluorescents sparkled and snapped, then came on with a low hum. Blue-tinged light washed over the space.

Four desks were in the room, one at each corner. The drawers in each desk were either pulled open or missing, and two tall file cabinets stood on the other side of the room from the window, each with a drawer pulled out. Folders and paper covered the floor.

"Looks a lot like the pictures, Dez."

"I'm a talented photographer. I changed my last name from Liebowitz."

"Only one PC tower in this front office?"

Dez nodded.

"Hmm," Fenway mused.

"What's wrong?"

"I don't know. Something seems off."

"What?"

"If I knew, I'd tell you." Fenway shook her head back and forth, as if to get the blood flowing. "Jessica's office is behind that door?" she asked, pointing.

Dez nodded.

Fenway pulled her phone out of her purse and picked her way over the papers and furniture to Jessica Marquez's office. She opened the door, revealing open drawers, chairs on their side, papers all over the floor, and one of the two file cabinets lying facedown. She entered the office, gingerly stepping around fallen items. The desk was a mess, too, and she carefully stepped through the clutter to the space behind it. The bookshelf back there was half dumped, many of the books thrown off, a black hairbrush with a mottled handle lying askew in front of a few leaning hardbacks.

Turning the flashlight of her phone on, she leaned down and noticed a red leather purse.

"No one took the purse?" Fenway called to Dez.

"CSI cataloged everything."

She looked under the desk and got a crick in her neck. *Ugh. Must have slept wrong.* The hazards of having a man in your bed. She twisted her neck farther and heard a satisfying crack as her bones realigned and her muscles stretched. She turned her head the other way.

And that's when she saw the piece of folded white paper, stuck behind one of the hardbacks on the bottom shelf, with the letters OCT handwritten on it.

She reached out and pulled the paper from the behind the books.

It said, in half printed, half connected handwriting with large loops and open letterforms:

OCT 6
Rep $27,846,577.48
Act $27,346,577.48

Fenway clicked off the phone's flashlight and took a picture of the paper.

"Hey, Dez?" She looked up.

Dez appeared in the doorway. "Did you find something we missed?"

"I don't know. CSI might have cataloged it. I pulled it out from behind these books."

"What is it?"

"Handwritten note. Two numbers, both over twenty-seven million dollars." Fenway stood up and walked to the doorway, showing the paper to Dez.

"What do you think 'rep' and 'act' stand for?"

"I don't know. This is a theater company, right? Maybe 'repertory' and 'actors'? Maybe what the company had in its account before and after the London actors did their last visit here?"

"Big difference between the two numbers. Half a million dollars." Dez scratched her nose. "Nice round number."

Fenway nodded. Something else didn't feel right. This time, she knew just what it was. "Twenty-seven million is too much for a university theater company to have, isn't it? I mean, even if they make ten grand off every person who goes on that *Guild at the Globe* thing, and even with all the ticket sales, that's maybe at the most—what, five or six million over the last ten years?"

"Maybe they get grants."

"You think they get grants for fifteen million dollars? And that their expenses don't eat up a big chunk of their revenue?"

Dez shrugged. "More forensic accounting for Piper. We should see if this matches with any of Jessica's bank statements."

Fenway nodded. "Or maybe this refers to Cygnus's personal accounts."

"You think a university Shakespeare professor has twenty-seven million in his personal account?"

"I don't know. Maybe his parents left him a lot of money. Maybe he invested it in Apple in the nineties. Maybe his wife is rich. There are a few scenarios."

"They're unlikely."

"Still, we have to consider them."

In the outer office, some postcards from Professor Cygnus to "Jessica and the NASG team," postmarked from London and Stratford-upon-Avon, lay on the floor. The sun had faded some of the postcards more than others. That handwriting didn't match the note.

Fenway went into Jessica's office and stepped to the file cabinet lying on its face.

"Help me push this upright," said Fenway.

"Think there's something in there?"

"Maybe this is where the bank statements are. Everything else seems to be in paper—checks, schedules—I bet Cygnus wants paper copies of all the financial records, including the bank statements."

They struggled for a moment but got the cabinet upright.

The second file drawer from the bottom had five years' worth of The Guild's bank statements. The bank was a small local firm, and there was a business checking account as well as a high-interest business savings account. Neither account had more than two hundred thousand dollars. Fenway suspected the checking account was used for payroll. On the savings account statement, the transaction detail showed deposits in multiples of $12,000, probably full-price payments for *The Guild at the Globe,* the summer excursion, and quite a few expenses for airline tickets, hotels, and names of people she assumed were actors paid to come speak to the classes.

In one folder, Fenway found an envelope with a sticky note on it. "Amanda, deposit this before 5 —J." Fenway pulled the envelope out and compared the writing to the note with the dollar amounts. Fenway looked at the loops on the letters, the shape of the two letter *n*s, and the way the 5s were written.

They matched.

"I think Jessica wrote both of these notes," Fenway said.

Dez came over and looked at the two notes, and then she nodded, pressing her lips together. "Those abbreviations don't refer to theater accounts. I think they stand for *reported* and *actual.* Maybe Jessica discovered that five hundred thousand dollars was missing."

Fenway went quiet for a moment. "Dez, there's something weird, and I can't put my finger on it."

"About what?"

She looked around. "For one thing, this office doesn't feel lived-in."

"Lived-in? How can you tell with all this shit all over the floor?"

"I mean there are no personal effects. No photos of parents or dogs or anything. No wall art from Jessica's hometown. This might as well be a conference room."

"Some people aren't like that." Dez looked around Jessica's ransacked office. "What is that supposed to mean, anyway?"

"You'll laugh, but I was watching this cop show once, and the murder victim didn't have anything in her house that was over three years old. The detectives thought that was odd, and she turned out to be in the witness protection program."

"You think Jessica Marquez was in witness protection?"

"Probably not, but I still think it's weird."

Dez tapped her foot. "I'll put a call in to the organized crime unit down in L.A. If one of their informants was murdered, it puts a new spin on the case."

Fenway bobbed her head from side to side. "No one's been in here yet to tell us what was here and what's missing?"

"I would ask Amanda to come over and do it, but she's too upset."

"I guess in retrospect we should have had her go through the office first."

"I don't know. With Xavier and Amanda coming over to the president's office, I don't think we could have done that without the secretary having us wait for Dr. Pruitt to come back. Yes, that would have been the right procedure, but we always have to balance it by how much resistance we'll encounter."

"Maybe *this* is how we get Professor Cygnus to come over here?" Fenway suggested. "Tell him that some award he won—or some checks that they have for the summer trip to London—are in disarray, or that we think something got stolen."

Dez shook her head. "We tried that. He said he wasn't familiar enough with the contents of the office to help us out."

"It looks like a lot of this stuff is his, though. Posters from his plays, stuff like that."

"I suppose," Dez said.

"You think maybe he's lying? That he said he *didn't* know what was in here, but he's the one who ransacked the office?"

Dez paused. "You do know you're accusing the most powerful man at this university of murder."

"I'm not accusing him of anything. I'm merely suggesting a theory of the crime." Fenway paused. "Another theory would be that Cygnus *himself* stole the half a million."

"Another theory is that there were a bunch of deposits they had on hand that didn't go through, so it was just noting that the numbers didn't match. Jessica did the books, after all."

"That theory isn't nearly as fun."

"Listen, rookie, you're not here to have fun, you're—"

"Oh, for crying out loud, Dez, I'm kidding. I *know* we need more evidence before we can come up with a reasonable scenario." Fenway put the note in an evidence bag from her purse.

"All right—well, find the murder weapon, or Jessica's laptop in the professor's possession, and then talk to me."

Fenway nodded.

Watching their feet, Fenway and Dez took a few steps into the main office, and they peered under one of the fallen desk chairs. A tower-style PC, in a matte-silver plastic case, poked up between a couple of sheaves of strewn paper.

"That's a PC right there," Fenway murmured.

"Only one in the front office," Dez said.

Fenway knelt down but it didn't provide a better view, and then she turned to Dez. "CSI didn't take that computer?"

Dez shook her head. "They didn't take anything. Wanted the inventory of what might be missing first." She looked around the office. "So, yeah. It's a real mess."

Fenway nodded. "If the laptop's missing, it makes me think there was something on it that the killer wanted, and if we can find out what this mystery twenty-seven-million-dollar account is, we might be able to get to—"

Wait a second. Only *one* PC? Fenway tried to remember what Amanda had said.

Dez folded her arms. "Might be able to get to what?"

"Hold on, hold on, hold on," Fenway said, closing her eyes.

I kind of feel bad for working so many hours when there's not that much work to do. There aren't enough computers for all of the student workers, so I usually do my homework.

Fenway opened her eyes again. "Amanda said there weren't enough computers for all the student workers."

Dez nodded.

"Isn't that a strange thing to say if there's only *one* computer for everyone? Why not say 'There's only one computer for all of us to share'?"

"Maybe they're on cheap Chromebooks that they take home."

"No, I don't think so. I think one of the computers is missing." She cautiously stepped around the room and went to the first empty desk. She shined her phone's flashlight behind it. "There's a power strip here. I think there was a PC on this desk."

"All right, so what do you want to do?"

"I think we should take the other PC in. See if there's any indication if there are files on the hard drives that someone might want to take."

"The file in question might just have been on that other machine."

Fenway nodded. "Probably."

"But yeah, we'll take it in anyway. Maybe Piper can find some user data that will help us."

"Yeah, that's a possibility, too, and I didn't see the other award."

"What other award?" Dez asked.

"The one that The Guild won for *The Merchant of Venice* last year. The crystal award that might be the murder weapon."

They carefully wound their way through the maze of papers and furniture and books. They left the main office, went down the hall and then down the stairs.

Fenway clicked her tongue. "What now?"

Dez thought for a moment. "That note—with the twenty-seven million dollars. I can't think of why in the world Jessica would write that note. What in the hell could it refer to?"

"I don't know. Maybe it has something to do with the university and not with The Guild."

"But," Dez mused, opening the door of the stairwell to the outside, "if it was an account with the university, Jessica wouldn't have access to it. That would be the university accountants, not this independent organization on campus."

They walked across the quad. "Are we going to the station?" asked Fenway.

"I don't think there's anything else for us to do here until we can wrangle the professor and the other students after rehearsal. I can get moving on Jessica's phone records."

Fenway's phone rang and she dug it out of her purse.

"Oh, no." Fenway closed her eyes. "I forgot I was supposed to meet Charlotte at noon."

"What's with you forgetting everything all of a sudden?" Dez flashed a grin at Fenway. "I'm twice your age and I've got a better memory than you do lately.

Fenway answered the phone. "Hi, Charlotte, did you—"

"Fenway, where the hell are you? I've been waiting in your office for fifteen minutes, and no one seems to know when you'll be back."

"I'm sorry. I went to interview a couple of suspects and I'm running behind."

"So, you don't know?"

"Don't know what?"

"Your dad's being released this evening. They told us it would be around six o'clock."

"They arraigned him?"

"No. They said Tuesday."

"At least he'll be home for the weekend. Oh, good. I'm happy for you."

"Did you have anything to do with getting him freed?"

Fenway paused. "Well, I did talk to the lead detective from Washington state, but I don't think he had anything to do with the release."

"Did your father tell you what he wanted you to look into?"

"He asked me to do some research. Nothing specific."

"I suppose we can wait to talk about it until this weekend."

"Wait, wait, Charlotte, I'm trying to chase down a couple of murder suspects. I can't make plans for the weekend."

There was silence on the other end. Finally, Charlotte cleared her throat, and then she spoke softly but firmly. "I can't say I'm surprised that you're acting like this."

"Acting like what?"

"Please, Fenway, let me finish. Your dad is reaching out to you right now. No, he's not a perfect man, but you have to understand what his words and actions mean, what he's trying to show you. He's always done things his way, but if you could just see past your own anger, you'd know that the things he does show his love for you. I don't think you even want to meet him halfway. You're making excuses instead of helping him. I know you're angry, but you're not prioritizing him, and he's the only father you have. You'll look back on the way you're acting right now, and you'll regret it."

Stunned, Fenway didn't know how to respond.

"Fenway, are you still there?"

"You're breaking up, Charlotte," Fenway said. "We're driving into a canyon right now—can you repeat—" and then she clicked End.

Dez looked over at her. "Everything okay?"

Fenway nodded. "Of course, Dez. I should have known my father would pick the judgmental type."

They arrived at Dez's Impala and she drove them out of the lot. As they turned onto Nidever Expressway, Fenway's phone rang again and she sent it straight to voicemail.

Fenway looked out the window and ground her teeth. Her father wanted her to be his own personal private investigator. Even if she wasn't angry at him, she was drowning in open murder cases of her own without worrying about her father being accused. She felt the sting of Charlotte's words anyway. Fenway *wasn't* prioritizing helping her father, but exactly what could she do?

"Dez," she said tentatively, "*is* there anything I can do for my father? I mean, other than visit him when I can, and that kind of thing. Should I be trying to figure anything out for myself?"

Dez shook her head. "You need to stay away from that, rookie. Unless you want everyone in the county thinking you're a hypocrite. If *you* want to recommend a private investigator for him, or if you want to be a character witness for him, then absolutely, do everything you can. But if you're looking to investigate him on your own? Hell, I've got a reputation as a maverick, but even *I* think that's crossing a line." Dez looked over her shoulder and moved into the left lane, passing a box truck. "And besides, if you find any evidence, everyone will think it's tainted because it was found by his daughter, not by an unbiased detective."

Fenway looked out the window, only half paying attention. She still had Detective Deshawn Ridley's contact information, and besides, he was probably still at the Phillips-Holsen Grand Hotel until the arraignment. Maybe she could call him up and sweet-talk him into giving her more information.

CHAPTER THIRTEEN

Dez and Fenway grabbed lunch at Dos Milagros and took it to the office.

They walked in, and Sergeant Mark Trevino looked up from his phone. "You just missed your stepmother."

Nope, I didn't miss her at all. Fenway bit her tongue to stop from saying it.

Migs wasn't in the office, but it was just past twelve thirty, so was probably at lunch.

Dez sat at her desk, pulled the tacos out of the paper bag, and started to go through phone records for both The Guild office and for Jessica Marquez's cell phone.

Fenway went into her office, and Mark followed her. He briefed her on where he was with the Tassajera case. Besides the payments for Global Advantage Executive Consulting, and several falsified customer records—all of which documented large cash payments to Tassajera, multiple times a week—no information looked out of place. A search of Tassajera's home—he was divorced and lived alone, and his ex-wife lived in San Miguelito—turned up little. The one interesting item was a cheap cell phone in the drawer of Tassajera's bedside table. Mark strongly suspected it was a burner phone and was in the middle of researching it.

Fenway spent the next few hours typing up her notes, downloading the pictures from her phone, and researching the social media profiles of the student actors in the play. She thought for sure there would be something connecting one of the student profiles to Jessica, but she had no luck.

It was almost four o'clock and Migs hadn't returned to the office. That wasn't like him.

Oh.

Perhaps Migs was with Piper.

She was sure that Piper Patten was still working, and she hoped that Piper wouldn't do anything stupid like admit to trespassing at Central Auto Body. Migs, who was taking law classes at night, would be concerned as well.

She walked down the hall and opened the door into the IT office.

Migs stood at Piper's workstation, and Piper leaned on him, head bowed and shoulders shaking.

"What is it, Piper?" Fenway asked. "Are you all right?"

"No, she's not all right," Migs said softly, an edge of anger to his voice. "Piper showed up for work this morning, and an officer took her over to the courthouse where they interrogated her for three hours."

"What?" Fenway said. "Three hours?"

Migs nodded. "They asked her what she stole—"

"Please, Migs," Piper interrupted, sniffling, "I can tell Fenway what happened myself."

"I just wish you had let me go over with you," Migs said through gritted teeth.

"You're not my lawyer."

"But I know the law a lot better than most people. I would have been able to get you out of there."

"Neither the sheriff nor I got a call about this," Fenway said. "You would think they'd want some sort of police corroboration before they hold you for three hours."

Piper waved her hand in dismissal. "Please. I brought this on myself. I shouldn't have been there."

Migs scoffed. "You are a representative of the sheriff's department, and you knew that a crime was likely to be committed. You were attempting to prevent the destruction of evidence."

"But I broke in."

"Exigent circumstance. That's an exception to the warrant rule."

Piper shook her head. "I don't even think that applies to me. I'm not a police officer."

"You're still a representative of law enforcement."

"Well, Migs," Piper said, "when you pass the bar, you can represent me."

"What do they want from you?" Fenway asked.

Migs and Piper looked at Fenway. "What do they want from her?" Migs repeated.

"Yes. I mean, based on all the evidence here, I'm shocked that the D.A. is even *considering* charges."

"Well, she's not."

"Oh—you got ADA Kim?"

"I bet she has something to prove," Migs said.

"So will you when you first get onto the scene, Migs, so don't throw stones." Fenway folded her arms. "Does she think you know something you're not telling her? Maybe that you've got the ledger and you're hiding it?"

Piper's eyes went wide. "I don't have any ledger!"

"I know you don't," Fenway said. "The room was locked, a pile of boxes was over the crawlspace where the ledger should have been, and there's no way you could have moved it off and back by yourself." She paused. "Maybe *I* should call ADA Kim."

"Maybe they're trying to make an example out of Piper," Migs muttered.

Piper blanched.

Fenway pinched the bridge of her nose. "If they wanted to set an example, it should be someone with more visibility in the department

—and for something a lot worse than trespassing." *Barry Klein would be a good choice.* She looked at Piper. "Did they tell you anything?"

"They said my career with the sheriff's department was over," Piper said miserably.

"What?"

"Yeah. I could either resign, or get arrested for felony burglary."

"*Felony?*" Fenway said, aghast. "That's ridiculous. *Maybe* a misdemeanor."

Migs shook his head. "No—we just had a session on this in class. That's intended for shoplifting, when the place of business is open."

"Well, yeah, that's what McVie said, too, but intent *has* to figure into this," Fenway said. "Intent is why they made the exception for shoplifting in the first place." She turned to walk into her office. "I'm calling ADA Kim about this right now."

"I don't know if that's a good idea," said Piper. "She was so angry when she talked with me. She was treating me like a serial killer. She barely let me get a word in edgewise."

"But this is ridiculous. She didn't even call me to corroborate what happened!"

"Maybe she figured that you and the sheriff would be on my side," Piper said softly.

"We're on truth's side," Fenway said.

"I don't know." Piper hesitated. "You seem to think that we should sweep this under the rug."

"I do. I know there's the letter of the law and all that, but you did the right thing. You were at least *trying* to do the right thing, and you're catching hell for it."

"I should have let the real police handle it." Piper's tone went flat.

"We'll fight this, *cariña*," Migs said.

"I don't know," Piper said.

"I'll go call the ADA right now." Fenway patted Piper on the shoulder and then turned and walked to the coroner's suite. She went into her office and shut the door behind her.

Fenway dropped her purse on one of the guest chairs in front of her desk and then sat heavily in her chair. None of this would have happened if she had just kept her word and met Piper like she promised. She felt sick.

She had met ADA Jennifer Kim a handful of times over the last six months, and it was always for misdemeanors, or nonviolent felonies, based on ancillary information she found in the course of her investigations: a couple who was squatting in an abandoned house where a young man had overdosed on heroin; a DUI on a man who'd called in a motorcycle accident that he had passed on the way home from a bar. While Kim was hard-edged, Fenway assumed she had to be in order to survive, especially when she had to deal with abrasive men like Barry Klein on the county board of supervisors—and now in the mayor's office.

Fenway glanced at the clock. It was a quarter after five, but she was sure Kim would still be in her office. Sure enough, the phone was picked up on the first ring.

"ADA Kim."

"Jennifer, hi. It's Coroner Stevenson."

"Oh, hi, Fenway. Sorry to hear about your dad."

She had practically forgotten, and the reminder sent a bolt of electricity up Fenway's spine. "Oh—right. Thanks. Yeah, it's tough on everyone."

"I hope you know I don't have any information on his case. The Bellingham police are being tight-lipped about it. Of course, I couldn't tell you even if I knew, but I don't know anything."

"That's not why I'm calling." Fenway leaned forward on her desk and closed her eyes. She'd have to be mindful of her tactics. "You had a conversation this afternoon with our forensic technologist."

"Your what?"

"Piper Patten. I don't know what her real title is, but that's what she does for us—figure out who's accessed what, figure out where the hackers have been, figure out where people have tried to hide money."

"Oh, yes, Miss Patten." Kim's voice lost all friendliness in its tone. "She's in trouble."

"I don't see why. You haven't even taken my statement. The business owner hasn't even pressed charges—she was grateful that Piper was trying to preserve evidence." Fenway might have been stretching the truth, but Marisol Velásquez would back her up. Probably. Mrs. Velásquez *would* be grateful that Piper had tried to prevent the ledger from being stolen.

"I haven't been able to confirm any of that," ADA Kim said. "And I can't ignore a civilian employee breaking and entering a private business, especially when one of the two primary owners of the business is missing. It looks like we're trying to cover something up."

"Cover something up? She was trying to save the case!"

"Maybe she told you that's what she was trying to do—"

"That *is* what she was trying to do! I was there!"

Kim scoffed. "You weren't there the whole time. You came after Peter Grayheath had already found out that someone had broken in."

"Grayheath? You took his word about what happened? He wasn't even supposed to be there!"

"I'm not sure who's in the right about this, Fenway, but I do know that Miss Patten shouldn't have been in the building."

Fenway drummed her fingers on her desk. "Okay, listen, what if I talk to the building owner and she tells you that Piper had permission to be there?"

"I'd say I don't believe you. You can't give retroactive permission to a trespasser."

"I think you can," Fenway said. "And besides, you wouldn't have any way to counter the owner's statement."

"Why are you trying to make my life hard? Look, I gave Miss Patten a choice. Either she resigns, or we charge her with burglary."

"Come on, Jennifer. You know intent plays into this. What kind of message will we send if you prosecute this?"

"That civilians shouldn't take the law into their own hands, even if they work for the cops."

Fenway pressed her lips together. "It's almost like you want her to resign."

"Given what she did, she's lucky we gave her the choice. Look, *you're* the one who pushed out Miss Patten's colleague six months ago."

"You can't be serious. He was taking bribes from a *murderer* to install remote access software on our PCs!"

"Yes, and Miss Patten was caught breaking and entering." She coughed. "Look, it's out of my hands."

"It's out of your hands? You mean this decision comes from higher up?"

"I didn't say that. In fact, I shouldn't be talking about this anymore. You tell Miss Patten that I either have her resignation on my desk by the end of the day tomorrow, or I'll draw up a warrant for her arrest. Either way, her career in the sheriff's office is over."

Kim hung up.

Fenway stared at the receiver for a moment before setting it on its cradle. She stood up and the weight of the situation hit her full force. She'd have to go in and tell Piper that she failed. That she couldn't do anything. Piper would have to resign.

Her heart felt heavy as she walked to the IT department. Migs and Piper were sitting in two office chairs, facing each other, Migs holding Piper's hand.

"I don't know what's going on," Fenway said, "but ADA Kim isn't budging. Either you resign by end of day Friday, or she's issuing a warrant for your arrest."

Migs set his jaw. "Something else occurred to me."

"Occurred to *you*?" Piper said.

Migs smiled sheepishly. "Occurred to Piper, and I think it's possible. Scary, but possible."

"What is it?" Fenway asked.

"Well," Piper said, "I've connected the dots so far between these murders and Global Advantage Consulting."

"Right."

"In fact, the payments list for Global Advantage is the only thing tying these deaths together." Piper straightened up and let go of Migs's hand. "If I hadn't found them, it would look like three unconnected murders."

"Four," Fenway said.

"Right, Jessica Marquez makes four." Piper scrunched up her face. "So, I don't know, this might sound crazy, but do you think the money launderer thinks that if they get me out of the way, they'll be able to— I don't know, get away with it?"

"You think they have some big last score they have to do, and then they're out? This isn't a heist movie."

"Well, no—"

"The sale of the embargoed oil is netting them *literally* billions of dollars a year."

Piper nodded. "Maybe that's why they want to quit. It's starting to get visibility. You can't spend all that money if you're in jail."

"Or dead," Migs said.

Fenway thought for a moment. "Okay, let's say you're right and they want you out of the way. I've tried talking to ADA Kim. I can maybe get McVie to talk to her, but he hardly has leverage now that he lost the election and his term is up in eight weeks. How do we keep you employed here?"

Piper and Migs looked at each other.

"I don't think you can," said Piper.

"But you're phenomenal," Fenway said. "We couldn't have solved the mayor's murder a few months ago without you. We couldn't have come as far as we did on *this* case without you."

"There are other smart, computer-literate people out there," Piper said.

"Not that we can hire two weeks before Thanksgiving," Fenway said.

"Good luck trying to find a job this time of year," Migs said. "Not only are they unfairly trying to force you out, but it's right before the holidays. They're evil."

"Don't worry about me," Piper said. "I've got some savings. Plus,

California is a vacation-accrual state, and I hardly ever took time off. I have six weeks of vacation to get paid out."

"That makes me feel better about you," Fenway said, "but I'm worried about the investigation also. We don't have anyone else who can do this work."

"Which is the point," Migs said under his breath.

"You can get a contractor," Piper suggested.

"Not someone who has access to things like arrest records and DMV data."

"There are a lot of freelancers who wouldn't need official access to stuff like that."

Fenway shook her head. "If they don't want someone with your computer skills and ability to piece together information," she said, "they won't replace you with someone competent. They'll get someone who can fix Callahan's blue screens of death and that will pretty much be it."

"Remember," Piper said thoughtfully, "I said this went pretty high up."

"You did," said Fenway, "and now I think you were right."

"But high up might only go to ADA Kim. Or her boss. It doesn't mean HR. It doesn't mean the head of IT. You should talk to Jordan. He'll want to replace me with someone competent. He knows how important that is."

Fenway nodded. "Okay. Jordan is a good guy."

"Best manager I've had, and I'll see him right now," Piper said, a determined look on her face. "See if he'll authorize a ton of overtime for tonight. I may have to resign by the end of the day tomorrow, but I can get a lot of research done between now and then. That's if I don't have to go home."

CHAPTER FOURTEEN

Piper said she would text Fenway as soon as she finished with Jordan, so Fenway bit the bullet and went to the jail to see her father. As she left her office building, she noticed the streetlights coming on, casting shadows that shrank and lengthened as she walked through them. The shadows stretched and shortened, elongated then snapped back, with the painfully blue LEDs that illuminated the plaza.

Fenway had a lot on her mind, turning over how she'd find a replacement for Piper—or how in the world she'd close the case without her.

Quincy greeted her as she walked into the foyer of the jail building, in front of the metal detectors. Fenway was lost in thought and missed the jokes about Aunt Dez; she didn't even give Quincy an empty promise of coming over for Sunday dinner one of these weeks.

"You okay, Fenway?" Quincy said, snapping her out of her reverie.

Fenway blinked and looked at Quincy. "No, not really. The murders are piling up, one of the best people I've been able to count on is getting forced out of her job, and my father was arrested for murder."

Quincy winced. "You're here to see him, I take it."

"Yeah."

"Official capacity?"

"Sure."

Quincy looked at the logbook, flipped around a little, and then looked up. "Room one. I'll have him in there in a few minutes."

"Thanks, Quincy. Sorry. I'm not myself today."

"You've had a rough week."

Fenway shrugged. She had at least won her election.

In the jailhouse interview room, Fenway felt claustrophobic. Room one was the smallest of the four rooms available, with one of the walls at a forty-five degree angle, cutting off a good chunk of space.

The man who came in wearing the orange jumpsuit was much more like the rich, confident, arrogant businessman she knew from the outside than the meek, depressed man she had seen on the inside the day before. Nathaniel Ferris nodded at Fenway and quickly sat down, his back straight, his knees bent, leaning forward slightly. Fenway studied his face. His eyes had lost every trace of the haunted look that had worried her the last time she had seen him.

"You seem like you're ready for a fight, Dad," Fenway said.

"I'm ready to stop feeling sorry for myself," Ferris said. "Do you know the name Imani Ingram?"

"I don't think so. New witness?"

"My new criminal lawyer. She loves the law, she doesn't trust the system, and she believes I'm innocent."

"That's refreshing. Usually defense attorneys don't want to know."

Ferris grinned, one of his million-watt disarming smiles. "Okay then, she believes she can get an acquittal. Same thing."

Fenway paused. "Are you drunk?"

Ferris guffawed. "Where in the world would I get a drink?"

"From bribing a guard. Or maybe Charlotte slipped you something. Or you're making jailhouse gin. I don't know."

Ferris stood up and rocked back on his heels. "None of the above. Just excited because I see a few ways out of this, and they all go through Imani Ingram."

"Well, you'll get out of here in just about an hour." Fenway scrutinized Ferris's face, but found little to go on. "Why do you think you'll be acquitted?"

"Because they have nothing," he said. "No evidence on the body of the professor. No photos, no receipts, no money trail. It's a circus. Everyone knows that the D.A. is in need of a big win."

"The D.A. just got reelected in a landslide," said Fenway. "There's no need for a big win."

Ferris waved his hand dismissively. "It's a 'what have you done for me lately' constituency. It's ridiculous and combative, and I'm caught in the middle."

Fenway's phone buzzed, and she pulled it out of her purse. It was a text from Piper.

Jordan signed off on overtime but I have some bad news for you

"Hang on, Dad, I need to deal with this."

"Take your time. I'm not going anywhere until the paperwork is done."

She texted:

What's the bad news?

Three dots appeared, meaning Piper was typing, then they disappeared—had Piper deleted everything? Then:

I found a payment going from one of your father's accounts to Peter Grayheath

Fenway thought for a moment.

How much?

She wasn't sure she wanted to know, but Piper replied almost immediately.

$50,000

Fenway's eyes went wide. Her father noticed.

"Fenway? What is it?"

She turned and looked at him. "You paid Peter Grayheath fifty thousand dollars."

"What?"

"Peter Grayheath. Does that name ring a bell?"

"Sure it does. He works for me. Or he used to. He was on the security team at Ferris Energy. Got a better offer somewhere else."

"Why did you pay him fifty thousand dollars from your personal account?"

"What? I never paid him a cent beyond his salary." Ferris crossed his arms.

"Did he go to Bellingham on the company dime around the time Professor Delacroix was murdered?"

Ferris grimaced. "He was the one who drove your car from Sea-Tac."

Fenway stiffened. "*Grayheath* drove my car to Estancia?"

"Yes. As part of the job. Ferris Energy reimbursed his expenses for the trip—meals, hotels, gas—but I didn't pay him anything that he didn't get through salary or bonuses. If someone says I paid him fifty grand, they're lying."

"No payments from your personal accounts?"

"No."

"Not murder for hire?"

"Is this what they're using as evidence? A payment to Grayheath when he was in Seattle? And they're saying I hired him to kill your professor?"

"I don't know what they have on you, Dad. I'm saying there's a money trail to a man who was in Seattle the same day Solomon Delacroix was murdered. I don't know how the police are connecting the dots."

Ferris sneered and shook his head. "I never hired Peter Grayheath to kill anyone."

"But you sent him to Sea-Tac to pick up my car."

"Yes."

"Is he another one of your super-secret executive vice-presidents in charge of security? Maybe another one who takes special measures into their own hands?"

"Come on, Fenway. That's not fair."

"Well, is he? You sent him there in your private jet."

Ferris ran his hands through his hair and stared at the table. "Holy shit," he said under his breath, lifting his head. "I'm being framed."

Fenway looked into her father's face. He didn't seem like he was lying, but the facts weren't in dispute. Grayheath went to Seattle. The next morning, Professor Delacroix was murdered. The next day, fifty thousand dollars transferred from an account in her father's name to Grayheath.

Yes, it was circumstantial, and yes, Grayheath would need to testify to convict her father of murder for hire, but Fenway couldn't think of another scenario that fit all the facts.

"Did anyone else stay with Grayheath in Seattle?" Fenway asked.

"No. The pilot and the staff of the plane were with him only until he disembarked."

Fenway shook her head. She knew it cost him over twenty-five thousand dollars for the plane to take off and land, and she couldn't believe he just snapped his fingers and sent a lackey there.

Ferris kept talking. "He was supposed to go right to Sea-Tac to get the car, get dinner, get to the hotel, and start driving down the next morning."

"Why did you pick him?"

"I thought I could trust him. I was—look, the whole thing was kind of spur-of-the-moment."

"Did the guy have a particularly good interview with you?"

"I don't remember. You'd have to talk to HR, I guess."

"I thought you were hands-on with your security staff. Picked people you trusted."

Ferris narrowed his eyes. "Some people wanted to have a little more oversight into my hiring practices."

"Are you talking about the board of directors?"

"Yes."

"Cynthia Schimmelhorn, or someone else?"

"I don't know who started the idea. I got a memo from the board that all security personnel would be vetted by HR before hiring."

"But you still interviewed them, right?"

"The high-up people, yes, of course, but not someone like Peter Grayheath."

"You had a complete stranger drive my Accord two thousand miles from Seattle." Fenway paused. As unlikely as a frame-up was, she couldn't contain her curiosity. "Could he have gone up to Bellingham to kill Professor Delacroix without you knowing about it?"

"If you mean whether he had time to do it—I guess he could have. I wasn't tracking him. I figured he'd stop for a good meal and dawdle a while, stretch his legs every couple of hours. Upgrade his hotel room on the company dime, maybe." Ferris shook his head. "But I don't think he'd drive to Bellingham and murder someone."

"It's almost two hours from Sea-Tac to Bellingham," Fenway said. "Plus he had to find the professor, kill him, take his body to the Squalicum Waterway, dump it, and make it look like an accident. That would take an extra five hours. You didn't notice?"

"He didn't arrive late." Ferris scratched his head. "Listen, I told him I wanted him on the road by nine or nine thirty. I figured I didn't want him fighting through rush-hour traffic. I suppose he could have gotten up early."

Fenway nodded. "Yeah. He could have gotten up at four or four thirty, been to Western Washington in time for the Professor's swim."

"And there wouldn't be much traffic that early."

"On the way back, there would be, though. Even if the body was in the waterway at seven thirty or eight—which is pretty fast, if you ask me—that puts him in that shitty Seattle traffic."

Ferris shrugged. "Maybe it puts him two hours off schedule. So he grabs fast food instead of a sit-down place for lunch and dinner and makes it to the hotel in Ashland in plenty of time."

Fenway nodded, though the timeline did nothing to prove her father's innocence. "Yeah, that works."

Ferris looked down at the table. "Did he provide any details? Did he confess to what he did?"

"I don't know. I wasn't there. I think the Bellingham police are the ones who followed the evidence on this one."

"Didn't that black detective question you?"

"*Black* detective, Dad?"

Ferris coughed. "You know what I mean. That detective down from Washington. He had the deep voice, kind of like Barry White."

Fenway closed her eyes and took a deep breath. "Yes, Dad, I know who you're talking about. Detective Ridley."

"Right. Ridley. That was his name. You talked to him a few times. Maybe you built a rapport with him."

"A *rapport*, Dad? You think since we're both black we built up some kind of *rapport* with each other? Maybe we have some secret *jive* hand-shake? Or bust into an improvised rap contest?"

"Dammit, Fenway!" Ferris stood up and shouted. "You *know* I didn't mean it like that, and you know I don't *think* like that. I'm not perfect, I know that, but give me the benefit of the doubt!"

Fenway looked away from him. The guard on the other side of the window had cocked his head slightly at the yelling but hadn't other-wise moved. "No, you're right, Dad. You don't think we have a black handshake. You think because I'm a pretty girl and big bad Detective Ridley is a mouth-breathing Neanderthal who thinks with his dick, I can get him to give me information he wouldn't ordinarily give out."

Ferris shifted uncomfortably. "I *definitely* didn't say that."

"No," Fenway said, "you didn't say that. Because that would be uncomfortably close to pimping your daughter out."

"NO!" her father roared. "You're reading things into—"

"I shouldn't have come," Fenway snapped. "I'm still pissed off at you, and this conversation hasn't helped." She walked toward the window and knocked.

"I implied no such thing, Fenway."

The guard turned around, and Fenway motioned for him to come in. "Last time I left," she said, "I didn't leave on a good note. So I'll say this: I love you, and I'll do what I can to make sure justice is done. If that means I get you out of this mess, then that's what I'll do."

"I promise you, Fenway, I didn't mean it like you took it. I'm sorry."

"Don't be sorry, Dad. You're always sorry for everything. You always want to throw money at every problem that comes up." Fenway gritted her teeth as the guard came in. "I just wanted you to be *there* for me. You know how much it bothers me that you missed pretty much every milestone in my life, and now that we live ten miles away from each other, you're still missing out." She folded her arms. "And if you get put away for this, we won't have any time together at all."

"Fenway, I didn't do—"

She held up her hand. "I really don't want to hear it, Dad." Clearing her throat, she looked in his eyes. "I don't want to say anything I'll regret. So."

Ferris looked bewildered. "Oh—okay. I love you, too."

Fenway nodded and left the room.

Fenway found herself breathing heavily as she walked out of the jail into the dark and misty November evening. She hated what he implied she could do with Detective Ridley to help him out. Sure, she wanted to know the details of the case, but there wasn't any way she'd flirt with Ridley to get it.

She turned everything over in her mind as she walked to her building. She wanted to see what Piper had uncovered about her father's finances before she made her next move.

Her stomach rumbled. She had just had tacos from Dos Milagros a few hours before, but the thought of the slight char on the *lengua*, the tang of the cilantro, the sting of the onions—it started to make her salivate, even as she had a bad taste in her mouth from visiting her father.

What the hell did he expect from her, anyway? To invite Detective Ridley to dinner? She pursed her lips. There's no way he'd give her the information, if she kept it professional. The interaction played out in her mind, but the skeptical look never vanished from Ridley's face.

Of *course* her father would think she should seduce him to get him to talk—it was so typical of his mindset. Despite her hunger, Fenway felt nauseated. Maybe Ridley *would* talk if he were seduced, but Fenway couldn't—wouldn't—do it. The very thought of seducing the investigator of her rapist's murder repulsed her. It was a bad strategy, not just because of her knee-jerk reaction, either, but because Ridley would see through it right away.

She'd have to think of something else.

She pulled out her phone and called Dez, who answered on the first ring.

"Hey, rookie. You went home?"

"No, I'm coming back to the office. I just went to visit my father in jail."

"Oh." Dez paused. "I'm glad you're taking care of personal stuff. You okay?"

Fenway gritted her teeth. "Not really. My father had the nerve to suggest that I should *seduce* that detective from Bellingham MCU to see what evidence they have against him."

"He did *what?*"

"Yeah. He wants information before his lawyers go through discovery, I guess, and he's not afraid to make his only daughter do his dirty work."

"He didn't actually say you should seduce him, did he?"

"Well, no." Fenway scoffed. "Strongly implied, maybe."

"What *exactly* did your daddy say, Fenway?"

"He said—" Fenway stopped and thought. What had her father said? He talked about some sort of magic communication system with Ridley. And...

She realized that he hadn't said she should seduce Ridley. He had said he thought that Fenway and Ridley had a *rapport*.

A rapport.

Holy shit. Had she—had she made all of that up in her head?

"You still there, Fenway?"

"Uh," Fenway said. "Uh, yeah. I'm still here."

"What did your daddy say?"

"He—I guess he said I had a rapport with Detective Ridley. That maybe I could use that rapport to talk to him."

Dez didn't say anything.

"Dammit, Dez. He didn't say what I thought he said, did he?"

"Well, now, it doesn't sound like it, but I wasn't there. Sometimes a person's tone of voice can mean more than their words."

Fenway squeezed her eyes shut. "I have to go apologize to him."

Dez took a quick breath, and her tone was gentle when she spoke again. "Why did you think your daddy was suggesting you seduce Detective Ridley?"

"Because—" Fenway stopped. She knew she was angry. She knew her father had *never* been there for her. She also knew everyone said she had to support him in his hour of need. Well, what about *her* hour of need? What about when she and her mother were on food stamps in Seattle? What about when the free lunch she got at school was the only thing she had to eat for a couple of weeks when her mother was between jobs? What about when her mother's car died on the side of the road in Tacoma and it took them four hours to get home?

And now she was supposed to drop everything—drop her *murder* investigations—just because her father wanted to play hero, kill her rapist, and get off scot-free? No. She wouldn't stop feeling angry about that.

"Because of everything, Dez," Fenway said. "Because I'm supposed to be the dutiful daughter now, and all he thinks about is himself."

The silence on the other end of the phone was long and heavy. Finally Dez spoke. "I think you might have some things to work through with your dad."

"Yeah, well, my shrink got himself murdered, so that's not really an option."

"Don't you snap at me, Fenway. I get that you're upset, but you are *not* giving me attitude just because I'm on the other end of the phone."

Fenway could feel hot tears just behind her eyelids and she blinked them back. "Sorry, sorry."

"It happens to the best of us, rookie, just don't do it to me."

"Sorry."

"It's okay, Fenway," Dez said. Fenway heard a beep in the background. "Oh—that's the M.E.'s office in San Miguelito. I've got to take this."

"All right. See you soon."

Fenway ended the call and took a few deep breaths. The entrance to her building was right in front of her, but she had to calm down first.

She stopped and looked around. Walking downtown didn't have the idyllic peacefulness of the path through the butterfly grove to the ocean at the end of her street, but it was better than going inside for the moment. Fenway looked up at the dark, cloudy sky, and she wasn't sure she'd beat the rain before she returned, but she decided to risk it anyway.

She walked down the street, past Java Jim's, then turned away from the parking garage. How had she jumped to such a wrong conclusion with her father, and so quickly?

Was he guilty? The payment to Peter Grayheath had definitely been made, but her father insisted that he hadn't made it.

Something else didn't seem right to Fenway, either.

Grayheath was walking around Estancia a free man.

If the police had built their case on the payment of a murder for hire and arrested her father, wouldn't Grayheath be behind bars, too? But putting Nathaniel Ferris behind bars while the supposed hit man went free didn't make sense. Even a lenient plea bargain would have resulted in *some* jail time.

The other explanation was that someone was framing her father for the murder of Fenway's former professor. In that scenario, someone would have opened an account in Nathaniel Ferris's name and sent Grayheath the money. But that didn't make sense either—what was the money for, if not for a hit? What possible reason would Grayheath have for killing Professor Delacroix if her father hadn't hired him? And who had fifty grand to throw around like that?

Of course, maybe someone else paid Grayheath to kill Fenway's former professor, but that seemed unlikely, given the connection to her father. Fenway briefly toyed with the idea that Professor Delacroix was in on the money laundering scheme, but Piper would have found a connection by now.

And if her father was being framed for hiring Grayheath to kill Professor Delacroix, the same question bothered her: why was Grayheath not in prison?

Fenway looked up. She had walked in a circle and found herself back in front of her office building. She straightened up and went through the entrance.

She walked past the coroner's suite and down the hallway to the IT area, where Piper had commandeered two other monitors and stared at several spreadsheets on the screen.

"You look like you're hard at work," Fenway said.

"My last twenty-four hours at a job I love," Piper said, a rough edge to her voice. "I'll miss being here."

"Not as much as I'll miss you, Piper. This sucks."

Piper nodded, and they were silent for a moment. Fenway looked at two stacks of papers on the desk. She picked up the top sheet from the short stack.

"You found the payments from my father to Peter Grayheath."

Piper nodded. "I did."

"Not random payments from some weird account in the Caymans?"

"No. Which is kind of strange, isn't it?"

"I don't know. Sometimes I think my father is arrogant enough to pay a hit man with a personal check and think he can get away with it."

"Yeah, but that's because you don't like him very much."

Fenway grimaced. "I guess."

"He's way too savvy for that. We're talking about a man who performs multimillion-dollar transactions on a regular basis and does it so that his tax liability in minimized."

"You mean hidden."

"I do. Which is why he'd never pay a hit man from a U.S.-based bank with a transaction record that's so out in the open."

"He thinks someone is framing him. What do *you* think?"

Piper was quiet.

"You don't have any proof," Fenway said, "do you?"

"Not yet," Piper admitted. "But I'm still working on it."

CHAPTER FIFTEEN

W HEN F ENWAY GOT BACK TO HER OFFICE, D EZ AND M ARK WERE both heading out the door.

"What'd I miss?" Fenway said.

"We're headed to San Miguelito," Dez said. "They're doing the autopsy on Jessica in about an hour, and Mark's taking the phone over to the lab."

"Six o'clock? That's pretty late for an autopsy."

Dez tilted her head. "Yeah, I thought so, too, but Michi said it needs to be done."

Mark raised his eyebrows. "I told you it was weird."

"You sure you don't want me to go instead?" Fenway asked.

"Well—" Dez started.

Mark interrupted. "Dr. Yasuda said that since Dez was the one to collect most of the evidence from the body, she should be at the autopsy to answer questions, and she's staying *late*. Combining the personal and professional, if you ask me."

Fenway shot Dez a look—Dez had been avoiding Dr. Yasuda for months. "I can go instead," Fenway said in a low voice.

"Stop whispering," Dez said. "Both of you know Michi is my ex, so stop walking on eggshells. Yes, I've been avoiding her, but damn, it's time for me to put on my big girl panties and talk to her like an adult. So that's what I'll do."

"Call me if you need to talk later," Fenway said.

"Thanks, rook—boss," Dez said quietly. "I'll be fine, but if I'm not, I might take you up on that offer."

"Heard anything from Pruitt yet? Am I still interviewing the students and the professor after dress rehearsal tonight?"

"No news is good news, but that place is like talking to a brick wall. Good luck trying to pin down the professor."

"I'll need it."

Dez and Mark left, and Fenway walked into her office, sitting heavily in the chair behind the desk. She checked her email, scanning her inbox for lab results or perhaps an update on her car. No luck.

She pulled out her phone and texted McVie.

Rehearsal ends in 2 hours if you want to head to Nidever with me

Three little dots appeared—and then vanished. She bit her lip and sent another text.

I have some ideas on how we can kill 2 hours if you're up for it

She sent the text, and the three dots started up again and disappeared once more. Finally, a quick series of three responses arrived.

Megan's got a volleyball game at 7
Sorry I can't come with you to Nidever tonight
Or kill 2 hours with you

Fenway bristled, and immediately she hated herself for it. McVie had chosen to spend the evening with his daughter over Fenway, but that was the right decision. She was angry with her own father because he always chose Charlotte and his business and his fun over spending time with his own daughter.

So why did this feel like such a personal affront?

Disgusted with herself, Fenway wondered if Amy McVie would be there too. Her heart started beating faster. No, Craig didn't want to be with Amy. He tried to make it work and couldn't. He'd moved on.

Oh, but that nagging voice in the back of her head wouldn't stop. Maybe Craig hadn't moved on. Maybe Amy realized her mistake and would try to get McVie back with the promise of her lithe, lean body, and her perfect blue-eyed blondness, and the structure of the nuclear family that Fenway couldn't give him.

She told her brain to shut up.

Folding her arms, Fenway leaned back and forced her thoughts onto the case. If she could talk to Professor Cygnus, she'd love to have Piper there to grill him on financials, although she didn't know exactly what to dig for. But with Dez and Mark gone, and Piper forced to resign—and apparently working around the clock until she had to leave—Fenway would just have to go by herself.

Her phone dinged again. This time it was a text from Charlotte. She was coming to pick Ferris up from the jail; his release was imminent, and Charlotte insisted on Fenway joining them for a family dinner at the mansion.

Fenway read the texts through half-lidded eyes. She didn't want to go, but with two hours before she could try to interview someone —*anyone*—at Nidever, she had no reason to say no.

And this might finally get Charlotte off her back.

Sure I'll be there in 30 min

Her phone dinged in her hand as she was putting it back in her purse, and she looked at the screen, expecting a response from Charlotte, but it was Rachel.

Hey I'm off at a decent time tonight

Margaritas? Happy hour?

Fenway sighed. Of all the nights Rachel would be free, it had to be the one night her father was coming home.

Sorry Dinner with my father

Fenway shut her laptop down, turned the lights off, and locked up the office, walking across the street to the jail where she'd see Nathaniel Ferris and the love of his life reunite after a harrowing week.

———

Even through Ferris grilled Fenway about standing up for herself and getting her car back, she accepted the ride to the mansion, trying to ignore all of her father's admonishments. She couldn't tell if her growing nausea was the result of the twists and turns in Las Manzanitas Drive, or from the display of affection Charlotte and her father were giving each other in the back seat of the Mercedes while Fenway rode shotgun next to Roderick, who was especially stoic in his driving duties.

The scent of spices and cooking fruit hit Fenway's nose as soon as they walked into the house. Ferris barked out a laugh. "Oh, Charlotte, that's too much! I'm not even out of the clink for an hour and you've already got pheasant roasting in the oven."

"Well, it *is* your favorite," Charlotte said, tracing her hand from Ferris's collar all the way down his chest to his stomach. Fenway averted her eyes.

Ferris was his old self again, regaling Fenway with stories of the days before the election. He offered Fenway wine three times, and Fenway refused as she wanted to be on her toes for any interview she might wrangle.

Sandrita dished out the family dinner that Charlotte had insisted on, but the meal quickly devolved into Fenway eating her apple-and-fig-stuffed pheasant with, Fenway grudgingly admitted, a delicious bordelaise, while Charlotte and Ferris looked deeply into each other's eyes, held each other's hands, and acted as if Fenway weren't there.

She finished her last bite and then clapped her hands, startling Charlotte. "All right," she said with finality. "I've got to get an Uber to take me to Nidever." She called into the kitchen. "Thanks for dinner, Sandrita. Wonderful as always." And then to Charlotte and her father, she said, "I appreciate the invitation, Charlotte. Good to have you home, Dad."

"Wait, wait, wait," Nathaniel Ferris said. "You still don't have your car back from evidence. I can't have you taking an Uber in the middle of the night."

"It's barely nine o'clock, Dad."

Charlotte turned to face Fenway. "Don't be stubborn about this. Your dad and I have seven cars for the two of us. Borrow one of them."

"I don't think—"

"Oh, please. It will make your life easier, and your dad and I will nag you less."

Fenway paused for a moment. "Okay, fine. But I don't feel right borrowing the Mercedes. You love that car, Dad."

Charlotte nodded. "Then take the Porsche." She said it properly, with two syllables.

"I can't take the Porsche—that's too much."

"What do you mean, too much? It's the cheapest car we own."

Ugh. Fenway had a habit of calculating just how much her father's toys cost. She knew the Porsche 911 in the garage, hardly ever driven, cost over a hundred thousand dollars new. *Maybe my father will let me keep it and I can trade it in for my college loans.*

"Fine," Fenway said, and she heard the ungrateful tone in her voice. "I mean—I appreciate it. I'm just not used to the fancy cars."

"Good. I'm—I'm glad we could help," Charlotte said, and smiled at her husband.

He looked at Fenway. "I know you and I don't always get along, Fenway, but you're my daughter and you mean the world to me."

A lump started to rise in her throat and Fenway forced it back down. "Yeah, thanks for the offer, Dad. It will—uh, it'll make my life easier."

Ferris nodded. "Remember—premium fuel only."

———

Fenway was used to driving her Accord, with the smooth, if soulless, continuous variable transmission. So when she turned on the engine of the Porsche 911 Carrera s and put the seven-speed manual transmission into gear, she was unprepared for the pure adrenaline rush from the raw power and control that coursed from the gearshift through her fingers. Sure, she had a manual transmission in the decade-old Nissan Sentra she had driven when she lived in Seattle, but the Porsche's gearshift was buttery-smooth, visceral, sexy—a little dollop of magic between the front seats.

After leaving her father's driveway and slaloming down the twisty road toward the freeway, Fenway's heart pounded with excitement. "I guess I know why my father likes his expensive cars," she muttered, although part of her wanted to scold herself for enjoying it so much.

She slowed down when Las Manzanitas Drive straightened out in its approach to the freeway. She passed a Volkswagen GTI, and the driver eyed the Porsche enviously.

She shot around a box truck as she took the exit onto Nidever Expressway and quickly arrived at the DiFazio Theater. She looked at the clock on the dashboard. Rehearsal should be over, and sure enough, several of the student actors were leaving the theater. She got out, locked the car, and rushed over to the lobby, avoiding the students until she could get in.

There, at the back of the large room, with notes scattered everywhere, was Professor Virgil Cygnus, no students around him. She walked up to the desk and smiled. He looked up at her, and his gaze hardened.

"Listen," he started, "I already told you—no questions about Jessica until after the play is over."

If the direct approach hadn't worked with him before, maybe a little sweetness would work. "I understand, Professor," Fenway said, widening her eyes and nodding. "I had my share of Shakespeare classes in college, too. I'm a former lit major."

"Interesting," Cygnus murmured, picking up his notes.

"I never had the chance to do anything like this when I was in school. Making these plays work for a modern audience is tough."

"Hah. You don't know the half of it."

"But you show everyone—every year—that you can still attract an audience with Shakespeare. I heard you even got a live monkey for last year's performance."

"I paid a hefty political price for that one," he said.

"Was it worth it?"

"Oh yes," Cygnus said, a little more softly, and Fenway had him.

"I bet it was," she purred. "When you're in the middle of a project like this, it's the most important thing in the world."

"That's absolutely correct."

"But, Professor, I don't think you're seeing what a help this could be to you."

"Help? You intend to distract me from my life's work, and you have the nerve to call it help?"

"Oh, Professor," Fenway said, leaning forward on the desk, "at this very minute, Nidever parents are wondering why you haven't made a statement yet. The Guild office remains closed. You *must* keep parents on your side. After all, before you were here, this was just a stupid little liberal arts campus. You *must* have enough actors to continue your life's work. People should flock to your London trips, not wonder why you won't talk to the police, no?"

"Well, I—"

"It's a great tragedy, Professor. One of your employees was found murdered, and we can't clear your name yet. Listen, Professor, you're done for the evening, right?"

"I need to sleep. Opening night is tomorrow, and I have to—"

"We can spend another twenty minutes arguing, or we can take ten minutes and be done with it."

Cygnus ran his palm from his forehead over his face to his chin. "Let it never be said that you're not tenacious."

"*Perseverance, my dear Lord, keeps honour bright.*"

"Oh, *Troilus and Cressida.*" Cygnus laughed. "You're both tenacious *and* charming."

"That's nice of you to say, Professor."

"I just call them like I see them. You have your ten minutes."

Fenway smiled. "I'll make this quick. I just need to know your whereabouts between eleven o'clock and two o'clock on Tuesday night, or Wednesday early morning, if you prefer."

Professor Cygnus nodded and rubbed his chin. "Eleven o'clock?"

"Yes."

"On Tuesday night, you say."

"That's correct."

Cygnus acted like he was stalling for time, but then he dropped his hands to his side and spoke confidently. "I daresay that was just about an hour after rehearsal ended. I believe I had my things packed up by about ten thirty and I was on my way."

"Did anyone see you leave?"

The professor shrugged. "I turned the lights off and locked the doors," he said. "I walked to my car and drove home. Then I got ready for bed, quietly, so I wouldn't wake my wife, and then I was in bed until morning."

"Did you stop anywhere?"

"Stop anywhere? At ten thirty at night?"

"Fast-food places are open. Maybe you were hungry. Long rehearsal and all."

He chuckled. "I intend to be studying the Bard on my hundredth birthday, and I won't do that by eating burgers and fries."

Fenway smiled back. "No," she said, "I'm sure you won't. You didn't stop for gas, either?"

The professor laughed. "Had I known I'd need an alibi, I wouldn't have been so careful to be quiet around Judith, would I?"

"No," Fenway said, "I suppose not. I wonder—would you be able to tell if anything is missing from The Guild's office?"

"On the second floor?" Professor Virgil Cygnus shrugged. "I'm not sure. To be honest, I don't go there too often."

"But you're the executive director."

"I'm also a full professor here," he said, "but I only teach this single class in the fall, yet I get paid a full salary. Sometimes titles can be deceiving."

Fenway nodded. "By my watch, we have seven minutes left of the ten you've agreed to give me. Let's go up and see. It'll be good for us to see it through your eyes. I mean, you've been doing this so long, you must have those offices memorized like the back of your hand."

"I doubt that," the professor said. "When you only see the office a couple of times a month, it's quite unfamiliar." He coughed. "And, as you can see, it's late, and I don't want to be tiptoeing around my bedroom again, stubbing my toe on the nightstand."

"I believe you agreed to ten minutes, Professor," Fenway said.

Professor Cygnus looked at Fenway, then heaved a sigh. "Very well," he said. "Let's take a trip up to the second floor and see what we can see."

The two of them turned and walked to the side of the lobby to the entry of the stairwell where Jessica Marquez's body had been found. Fenway pushed the door open, and the professor went through.

Fenway noticed that for a sexagenarian, Professor Cygnus was in excellent shape—and it wasn't just the muscles in his arms. The professor raced up the stairs like a man half his age; Fenway took the stairs a little slower. Cygnus took the last three steps to the second-floor landing all at once and opened the door for Fenway. She tried to keep up.

Fenway reached for the light switch on the hallway wall but had trouble finding it. The professor reached out with a practiced hand and turned the light switch on with ease. The second-floor hallway lit up, and they walked down the corridor until they came to the office of the North American Shakespeare Guild.

"Professor?" Fenway asked. "Do you have a key?"

Cygnus pulled a key chain out of his pocket and quickly unlocked the door. It swung open, revealing the mess inside.

Fenway watched the professor's face closely, looking for any telltale signs of surprise, of remorse, or of playacting.

But she didn't see any clues that the professor had seen the room in such a state of disrepair. Professor Cygnus's eyes narrowed into two slits behind his glasses, and he took a deep breath and released it in a loud exhalation.

"I can't imagine who would have done this," the professor murmured. "I don't know this office as well as I should, but these files hold letters from Shakespearian actors, directors, stage managers. Others hold interview transcripts. The Guild's most prized possessions. Is anything specific missing?"

"We don't have an inventory of what's supposed to be in here," said Fenway. "We didn't come across any letters, but we did, for example, discover one of your awards from the West Coast Theater Professors."

"Educators," the professor said automatically.

"Right, Educators. It was for *Macbeth*. Was that the only award of theirs you won?" She wondered if the professor had *The Merchant of Venice* award somewhere else.

The professor shook his head. "Those awards are all window dressing. Trying to get us to join their sham of an association. They don't care about Shakespeare; they just want me to pay my thousand dollars in dues every year."

"Did you have any awards displayed that you *did* appreciate?" asked Fenway.

"Sone are in my study at my home," said the professor. "I'm sure there must have been something worthwhile here, besides the letters, I mean." He scrunched up his face in thought. "I know we applied for a grant with a national Shakespeare theater association, but I'm not sure what happened to the application. Surely I would have been told if we had won, but I don't think we ever received a trophy or a plaque."

"Professor," asked Fenway, "would you take a look through the office—and Jessica's as well—and see if anything is missing?"

"Oh, I don't know if that will help. As I've said, I don't come into the office often, and when I do, I don't stay long."

"Even if you took five minutes, it would help."

The professor shook his head vigorously. "I know I promised you a full ten minutes, but once I get started, I'll most assuredly get wrapped up in some piece of memorabilia, or I'll come across an old photo, or I will think about poor Jessica, and I'll get sidetracked, and my concentration for opening night will wane." He pressed his hands together as if he were onstage thanking the audience. "Now, if you'll be kind enough to excuse me, I must collect my things and head out. I'm well on my way to being a grumpy old man, and if I don't get my beauty sleep, I'm afraid I'll turn from lovingly irascible to a plain old pain in the ass."

III
———————
FRIDAY

CHAPTER SIXTEEN

As odd as it felt to have McVie wake up in her bed on Thursday morning, Fenway was equally out of sorts when he didn't spend the night.

She was up early and went for a run, but her knee twinged in pain after a mile. She hadn't even made it to the butterfly waystation. She walked home, took her time getting ready, and while brushing her teeth, typed out a text to McVie.

How was Megan's volleyball game?

Was that too needy? If she didn't send it, would it seem shallow, or that she didn't care about his daughter?

Exasperated, she tossed her phone on the bed without sending the message and decided it was the day for one of her favorite dresses, one that she had been waiting for the weather to get cold enough to wear: a purple knee-length long-sleeved knit sweater dress with a generous cowl neck. She finished getting ready and walked out to the parking lot, startled by the Porsche 911 parked in her space.

Fenway forgot how difficult sports cars were to get into wearing a dress, but she managed. She got to the office in record time, a few minutes before seven, and walked straight to IT.

Piper, wearing the same clothes as the day before, had three large paper coffee cups in front of her keyboard, next to a stack of printouts three inches high.

"Oh, you have *got* to be kidding me," Fenway said. "You worked all night?"

Piper nodded. "Jordan signed off on the overtime yesterday, and I'm taking full advantage of my access while I have it." She looked at Fenway and grinned. "In fact, I've been getting double-time since two this morning."

"What a way to spend your last day," Fenway said.

"You can take me to lunch next week," Piper said. "I've got a ton of research to finish and only nine hours left."

"You packing your personal effects?" Fenway asked.

"I've got some photos and some knickknacky-type stuff. Less than a box. It'll take me ten minutes."

"When are they making you leave?"

"Five o'clock, although I'm sure they'll start breathing down my neck after lunch."

"That's a big pile of research," Fenway said, eyeing the stack on Piper's desk.

"I'll need to go over it with you," Piper said. "Explain what some of it means."

"You'll have time this afternoon?"

"No. I'll talk you through it over the weekend. Or next week."

"But you won't be working for us."

"I'll explain it to you for free. Maybe you can buy me lunch *and* dinner on Saturday."

"You can't go over it with me this afternoon?"

Piper clicked her tongue. "I won't have access to this computer system after five P.M. I *will* have access to my brain after that. I can explain this stuff to you *after* I lose computer access." She looked at

Fenway. "Don't take this the wrong way, but I've got a ton of shit to do and you're distracting me."

Fenway was a little taken aback. "Oh, sorry."

"No problem. Hey, can you go to Java Jim's and get me an extra-large drip?"

"Uh—sure." Fenway leaned forward and squinted at the screen. "Is that a list of the automated payments that went into Grayheath's account?"

"Uh—yeah." Piper looked up at Fenway. "So, that coffee?"

"Sure."

Piper stared at Fenway's face.

"Oh, now?"

"I've been up all night, Fenway. Working on *your* investigation."

"Yeah, yeah, of course. Large drip coffee."

"*Extra*-large."

————

When Fenway delivered the coffee, Piper grunted thanks but didn't invite her to stick around. As Fenway was leaving the IT office, her phone dinged: it was McVie, asking her to meet at Jack and Jill's. The promise of a decent breakfast—and, to be honest, seeing McVie again—put a smile on Fenway's face. She sent an affirmative reply and sped over to the diner. She parked the Porsche on the other side of the lot, far away from the other cars, and walked in with her laptop bag over one shoulder. McVie was already there, a steaming mug of coffee in front of him, looking at papers spread on the table.

The server gave her a knowing smile and mouthed "Coffee?" to her as she sat down.

Fenway nodded and turned to McVie. He had three file folders on his right, next to the salt and pepper shakers, and he looked up.

"Wow," he said, his eyes widening slightly. "You look fantastic in that dress."

"Thanks," Fenway said. "Thirty bucks."

"So look at this," McVie said, tearing his eyes away from Fenway and sliding the folder over to her. She opened the file and the photo of Rose Morgan stared back. "Look at her college records and work experience."

Fenway looked at the papers inside. Before she worked as the accountant for Central Auto Body, Rose had grown up in San Luis, New Mexico, and had attended the University of Texas El Paso as an accounting major.

"Right, accounting," Fenway said. "That all tracks with her HR file."

"No," said McVie. "It didn't say UTEP in the HR file. That file said she got an associate's degree at PQ Community."

Fenway furrowed her brow. "Why would you say you have a lower degree than the one you actually have?"

"I don't know, but it's suspicious, isn't it?"

"Okay, yes, that's suspicious." Fenway scanned down the page at Rose's work history.

"Petrogrande. They're—what, Venezuelan?"

McVie shook his head. "Colombian."

"But she worked out of Houston."

"Right. About twenty years ago they were bought by Van der Meer Energie, and they've got their American operations in Houston now."

"Van der Meer—they're Dutch, right?"

"Yep." McVie set his jaw. "Before I came to breakfast, I stopped into the IT department and Piper filled me in on the rest of the oil tanker story."

"Oh, right. I was going to tell you, I swear."

"Well, we got—" McVie looked at Fenway and smirked "—distracted with other things." He cleared his throat. "That Dutch company—do you remember when Homeland Security threatened them with sanctions a few years ago?"

Fenway thought about it but shook her head. "That might have overlapped with the winter I pulled graveyard shift in the ER. I don't remember much from those months. I saw so little sun, people started thinking I was white. Banks started sending me loan applications."

McVie rolled his eyes. "*Anyway,* Homeland Security threatened Petrogrande because they kept doing business with oil fields in La Mitad that were owned by the government."

Fenway nodded. "Right, that kind of rings a bell. Human rights abuses. I knew La Mitad was on the sanctioned countries list."

"This happened right after La Mitad was sanctioned. Petrogrande made excuses that they signed a contract before the sanctions, and Van der Meer kept saying that they weren't responsible for what an independently operating subsidiary did."

"They're not even an American company, so how can Homeland Security threaten that?"

"They can shut down their U.S. operations, and that's just what they said they'd do. Van der Meer called their bluff—but they weren't bluffing. They rolled out the National Guard. VDM Fuel stations stayed closed all over the Northeast before Van der Meer caved."

"Oh, right, I remember that. I didn't realize that was about Petrogrande. Rose used to work for them."

"Yes. In something called 'midstream accounting' for two years, and then got promoted to—uh, what does that say?"

"'Asset and fund accounting project manager.'"

"You ever heard of a job title like that?"

Fenway shrugged. "I bet I haven't heard of fifty percent of the job titles in the oil industry."

"Well, *I've* never heard of that."

"I don't suppose the consulting company is in here," Fenway said, turning the page.

"No," McVie said, "we're not that lucky."

The server came by, setting a full mug of coffee in front of Fenway. "Morning, Sheriff. Morning, Coroner. Refill, Sheriff?"

"Please," McVie said, pushing his nearly empty cup over.

"You ready to order?"

"The Jill's Favorite, no sour cream, English muffin," Fenway said, eyes still on the page.

The server nodded at McVie. "Anything for you this morning?"

"Just the coffee, thanks."

She turned and walked away.

Fenway frowned. "There's a gap of six months between when Rose left Petrogrande and when she started at Central Auto Body."

"She rented her house about two weeks before she got that job, too."

Fenway looked back at the cover page. "On Sunrise Terrace, no less. That's a nice neighborhood. Overpriced. I'm surprised she can afford it on an accountant's salary at an auto body shop."

"Maybe she has roommates."

"Maybe."

"Or maybe Domingo Velásquez pays Big Four rates. If he's involved in the whole money laundering thing, he can probably afford to."

"Maybe." Fenway turned to the middle of the report. "When did she move?"

"It's kind of fuzzy. She left her job at Petrogrande in March and then came on with the auto shop in October. Between those two dates, she obviously left Houston and came to California, but the report isn't complete."

Fenway pulled her phone out and put her finger under the Petrogrande section. "Maybe her last supervisor can tell us what happened." She started to tap the numbers into her phone. "Dor Trejo. Been with Petrogrande for—oh wow, it was twenty years last week."

"I don't know, Fenway. A lot of these big companies get their HR departments involved and they can only confirm when people have started and departed. Especially if the employee left on bad terms."

"I'm sure I'll get his voice mail."

The phone rang and a voice immediately answered. "Bobby! Don't tell me the shipment was delayed. You told me there'd be no more—"

"Mr. Trejo?" Fenway interrupted.

There was a pause. "Yes?"

"I'm sorry, sir. I'm not Bobby. I just have a quick question for you."

There was a sigh on the other end of the line; Fenway was sure Dor Trejo thought she was a salesperson. "Sorry, I saw the Seattle area code and thought you were one of my suppliers."

"No sir, but I promise I won't take up much of your time. My name's Joanne Stevens, from the accounting department here at Northwest Gas and Electric, and we've been impressed with a woman named Rose Morgan, who's applied for an accounting position. I understand she reported to you at Petrogrande?"

Another pause. "She did. I can direct you to our human resources department where they can confirm her start and end dates."

"Oh, I see." Fenway clicked her tongue, her mind working fast. "She said you'd probably have some sort of policy like that where you wouldn't be able to recommend her. I understand that—my last company was all about the rules, too. You couldn't even leave work to go to a dentist appointment without getting a note from the doctor. It's too bad that good, responsible employees like Rose Morgan can't even get something as simple as a recommendation from their former supervisors. Well, I won't take up any more of your time—"

"Wait," Trejo cut in, "she told you that I would *recommend* her?"

Fenway felt the tug on her fishing lure and tried to let the line out just a bit more. "It's not a problem if you're not allowed to recommend her, sir. She told us this would happen. I'll just assume—"

"I wouldn't assume *anything* if I were you," Trejo snapped. "If that little *bitch* thinks she can get away with—" And then, he stopped. Fenway heard a large exhale of breath on the other end—but she knew he was hooked.

"Mr. Trejo? Are you still there?"

"I'm here," he said, then paused for a beat. "I'm not able to tell you anything about her conduct or the type of employee she was, unfortunately. That's against not only our policy but an agreement we hammered out with Miss Morgan when she left."

"I don't understand," Fenway said. "You hammer out these agreements with all employees who leave?"

"Not all employees, no," he said. "Northwest Gas and Electricity—you're a utility, right?"

"That's correct."

"You don't do anything with oil drilling, refining, or reselling?"

"No, we don't."

"That's good," he said. "I wouldn't want Miss Morgan to be in violation of the agreement."

"Agreement? You mean to say that if we were in oil drilling, that would be in violation of some agreement you have with her?"

"I never said that, Ms. Stevens. I just said I wouldn't *want* her to be in violation of our agreement. Whatever it might say."

Fenway paused for what she hoped was an acceptable amount of time. "Is there anything else you hope that Rose Morgan *doesn't* do while in the employ of Northwest Gas and Electric?"

He laughed. "You're a monopoly in Seattle, right?"

"We're a tightly regulated utility," Fenway said, trying to sound annoyed. "Almost a million households in western Washington."

"I just meant that you don't have a lot of competition."

"Not as many competitors as other industries."

"All right, just—uh—just be sure that Miss Morgan isn't on anyone else's payroll when she works for you, and you'll be fine."

"What does that mean?" Although Fenway thought she knew what he was implying.

"Think about it for a minute," Trejo said. "Consider how important trust is to the accounting department there."

"I see," said Fenway. "Well, Mr. Trejo, I won't keep you any longer. I appreciate your time."

"Nice talking to you," he said, and hung up.

Fenway dropped her phone in her purse as the server put the omelet in front of her. She looked at the plate. The Jill's Special was fantastic; she could see the zucchini and chopped tomatoes bursting out of the sides of the omelet, where the pepper jack cheese was still melting. The avocados were out of season, and ever since Fenway's birthday, they started putting in only half the amount they had over the summer months. Fenway frowned—there was a dollop of sour cream in the center of the omelet right on top, with pico de gallo slathered underneath it. She was sure she'd ordered it without sour cream.

"What's wrong? Something the matter with your food?"

Fenway smiled at McVie. "Just thinking about the case. Everything's fine."

She grabbed her knife and scraped off the sour cream, although most of the pico de gallo went with it.

"Don't start eating without telling me what that conversation was about," said McVie.

"Corporate espionage," Fenway said, and she put a forkful into her mouth.

CHAPTER SEVENTEEN

McVie drove. Fenway sat in the passenger seat, thinking about what might have happened two years before.

"So you're thinking that your father convinced Rose to turn on her company."

"I don't know," Fenway mused.

"Tell me again what you think the situation is."

Fenway took a deep breath. "Someone—let's call them *Person x*—convinced Rose to steal information from Petrogrande."

"Okay. But you don't have any idea who Person x is, or how they got in contact with Rose."

"I think Person x is here in Dominguez County, or close to Ferris Energy, anyway."

"And why do you think that?"

"I think the connection is La Mitad. Petrogrande had the business relationships there, they knew the logistics, but they had to stop importing oil from La Mitad because of the sanctions." Fenway paused. "And I assume Piper showed you the photo of the tanker in La Mitad that she thinks is the same tanker as the phantom one at Ferris Energy."

McVie nodded. "That makes a certain kind of sense, I suppose."

"Only because Domingo Velásquez was one of the people who was laundering the money," Fenway said. "So far we know—well, we highly suspect—at least three companies of laundering the oil money: Kapp Landscaping, Dr. Tassajera, and Central Auto Body."

"And you said there were more."

"If Piper can get us the financials today, we'll be able to tell better."

McVie turned off the freeway toward the hills, where Rose's rented house was. "I'm not sure this is the best time to tell you this, Fenway, but I think I'll need to suspend Piper for a week without pay."

Fenway looked at McVie. "You can't be serious, Craig."

McVie looked over at Fenway. "She broke into a place of business, Fenway. If this investigation isn't aboveboard, it could come back to bite us."

Fenway shook her head. "That's not what I meant. I meant that ADA Kim forced Piper to resign."

McVie's mouth fell open. "What? But—they haven't even interviewed me! I don't—I mean, I know she broke the *letter* of the law, but with intent and with Mrs. Velásquez—"

"You're preaching to the choir, Craig. It's completely unfair."

McVie set his jaw. "You and I should go talk to ADA Kim."

"You can try. I already went down that path with her. She said it's above her head."

"Above her head? What does that mean?"

"I don't know. She wouldn't say any more."

McVie was quiet as they turned onto Sunrise Terrace, and a moment later, the Highlander pulled up next to the curb in front of a small but elegant Spanish-style house, in a sand color with brown trim.

"I'll figure out what's going on." McVie looked at Fenway. "You ready?"

"No," Fenway said. "That worked me up. Hang on." She took a few deep breaths, still annoyed, and still feeling her pulse race a little, but after about thirty seconds, she nodded. "Now I'm okay. Let's go see if we can find those ledgers."

"And maybe find Domingo Velásquez, too."

"Right, of course." She opened her door and got out. The sun came out for a moment and reflected off the front windows. One of the sheer curtains moved.

"Someone's home," she said.

"A Mazda 6 in the driveway," McVie said. "That's Rose's car."

"How do you want to play this, Craig?" *That would have been a better question to ask on the way.*

"It'll just depend on how she responds to my questions. Hang back, Fenway."

"Hang back?"

"Just for a minute. If Domingo Velásquez is here and doesn't want to be found, I don't want to put you in danger."

"But you're okay going up there?"

"I've got a badge and a gun," McVie said, "and I know how to shoot."

Fenway stepped to the side to let McVie pass.

"Around the front pillar," McVie said.

"I know," Fenway said. "On my way." She stepped to the side of the porch, putting a stuccoed pillar between herself and McVie. She couldn't see him, but she heard his footfalls as he stepped up to the front door.

Fenway faintly heard the doorbell ring. She listened intently, and then heard the door open, and a woman's voice say, "Yes?"

Craning her neck around the pillar, Fenway watched McVie nod to the woman in the doorway. She was the same woman from the pictures on the desk at Central Auto Body.

"Rose Morgan?" McVie asked.

"Uh, yes, that's me." She glanced over at Fenway.

McVie looked over at the pillar that Fenway stood behind, then briefly closed his eyes. "As you can see, Miss Morgan, I'm here with the county coroner."

"Fenway Stevenson," Fenway said, walking forward and holding out her hand. Rose took it, suspicion in her eyes.

"You work for Central Auto Body?" McVie asked.

"That's right," Rose replied.

"We've gotten word that your PC is missing from the office."

Rose didn't react.

McVie frowned. "You're not surprised to hear it?"

"Not really," Rose said. "Did it get repossessed?"

"No," McVie said. "You didn't take it home with you?"

Rose laughed. "Take it home with me? It's not a laptop."

"The reason we're concerned, Miss Morgan, is that we believe there's financial information on it that might put the user of the PC in danger."

"In danger? Are you for real? I'm an accountant for a mechanic. Why would I be in danger?"

McVie glanced around behind him. "Listen, I would rather talk about it inside. I don't want to worry the neighbors. Especially in this neighborhood."

"Worry the—what?"

"Why don't we talk about it inside, Miss Morgan—"

She put her body in front of the sheriff. "Nuh uh," she said sharply. "I didn't invite you in. You got a warrant?"

"No," he said, "but I'd rather not discuss the danger you're in where all your neighbors can—"

"Unless you want *me* to start talking about my fourth amendment rights in my outside voice, you'll stay on the porch, officer."

"Sheriff."

Rose cocked an eyebrow. "Not for much longer."

McVie flinched and then visibly relaxed again. "You're right. I shouldn't have assumed you'd be okay with discussing this inside."

Rose's eyes narrowed. She looked at Fenway. "Are you okay with what he just did?"

"No," Fenway said, stepping forward, "but it's kind of my fault."

"Your fault?" Rose said.

"Sure. I found evidence that you and Domingo Velásquez are having an affair."

"A *what?*"

"His wife filed a missing persons report yesterday," Fenway lied. "We also found a pile of evidence that he's booking business that he's not performing. After his car blew up, killing his son, we found evidence of criminal activity in his business files." Fenway stepped up onto the porch. "You control the money in that organization." She looked at McVie. "Now, the sheriff here, he wanted to wait until he got a warrant, he wanted to have you dead to rights before he even showed up." She tapped her temple. "But I thought you might want to tell your side of the story."

"*My* side?" Rose asked.

"You know—an older man, a younger woman, you fall in love, he tells you he'll leave his wife, but he never does. That kind of thing. He asks you if he can have access to the financial files, and since he owns the company, you say sure. He changes a cell in a spreadsheet here, books a couple of questionable accounts there. But he sweet-talks you and says it's nothing, and suddenly you realize that it looks like he's doing something illegal, and if the hammer comes down, it'll come down on *you*. Then you realize: he'll *never* leave his wife. Then his car blows up with his kid inside, and *he's* the one who's been skimming money. So you get your ducks in a row before the cops find the spread-sheets that don't match and send you to prison for a crime you didn't commit."

Rose pressed her lips together in concentration; Fenway could see the gears spinning inside her head. She had just given Rose a way out. Now Fenway just hoped that she would take it.

"How am I doing so far?" Fenway asked.

Rose hesitated. Fenway saw the calculation in her eyes, like a master chess player thinking twenty moves ahead.

"You know," Rose said, "you tell a good story. You might even be able to convince yourself it's true." She drummed her fingers on the edge of the door as she slid her hands down. "But you have no proof. Because *none* of that is true. None of that happened. And speaking of not wanting to go to prison for a crime I didn't commit—I'm definitely not giving up my fourth amendment rights. You're still not getting in the door." She set her mouth in a hard line. "So don't come back here without a warrant."

She slammed the door shut.

Fenway exhaled. "Sorry, Craig. I thought that would work."

McVie turned around and started down the driveway, with Fenway following behind. "It might have worked if I hadn't screwed up in the first place," he said bitterly. "I can't believe I read her wrong. I know better than that."

Fenway was silent and waited at the passenger door for McVie to unlock it. But McVie passed the Highlander and walked across Sunrise Terrace, stepping onto the sidewalk and looking at the large yellow house opposite Rose's, in the same Spanish style but much more opulent.

"Craig?"

He stood staring at the front of the house, looking from one corner of the house to the other.

Fenway looked both ways and walked across the street too. "What are you doing?"

"Would you look at that," McVie muttered under his breath.

Fenway followed his gaze to two security cameras, one at each corner of the house, aimed at the street.

"We might catch a break after all."

He strode up to the front door and rang the bell. Fenway followed him.

The door creaked open and an elderly Asian man peered out. "Hello, Officer. What can I do for you?"

"I'm sorry to bother you, sir," McVie said, "but I noticed that you've got security cameras out here."

"Oh, yes," the man said, nodding vigorously. "About a year ago, my car got broken into there on the street. Some other cars did, too, down the block. I put in the camera system then. We caught one of them.

The other one, you never saw his face." He clicked his tongue. "Turns out it was a boy from the neighborhood. His parents are rich—he drives a BMW. Just wanted the thrill of taking things that weren't his."

"I remember being young and stupid," McVie said.

"I do too," said the man, "but never *that* stupid."

McVie laughed, although the man didn't.

"Well, sir," McVie continued, "I believe there may have been a crime committed. Much like the problem you had—stolen property."

"And you think my cameras might have caught it?"

"Perhaps," he said. "How much of the street do those cameras cover?"

"All the way across—even part of the house over there," replied the man. "I want to make sure I get as much of the street as I can."

"Do you record it?"

"I do."

"And do you keep the recordings?"

"For about two weeks," he said.

"I don't suppose I could review the footage?" McVie said.

The man opened the door wide, and McVie and Fenway walked into the house.

———

The hallway was dark, and Fenway's eyes slowly adjusted to the light. A low table on her left featured three framed photos, all of the same young man at various ages. The first was of a high school graduation, at what looked like the field at Estancia High, with the man who had let them in standing on one side of the boy and a woman on the other, all grinning. In the second photo, the young man wore a suit a little too large for him and stood next to a large trophy, shaking hands with an older white woman in a prim turquoise dress. Finally, he appeared in dress blues, a serious look on his face.

"Is your son a police officer?" she asked.

"Yes, he is." The man beamed. "Been with Long Beach P.D. five years. He's taking the detective exam next month." He coughed. "You know, I didn't like telling the sheriff's office who I was before my complaint was taken seriously. I appreciate that you caught the kid who broke into the cars, but I didn't like the police treating me like I didn't know what I was talking about. If I hadn't reminded them that my son was a police officer and that I've supported several police fundraisers, I don't think they'd have followed up."

McVie nodded as the man led them through the living room and down another hallway. "I remember that. It was embarrassing. The officer who took your complaint was written up. He's moved on from the sheriff's department; I don't think the work was a good fit for him." McVie rubbed his chin thoughtfully. "And I remember the incident, too. You had a Lexus SUV, right? But forgive me—I can't remember your name."

"Raymond Le," the man said, holding out his hand. "I voted for you for mayor. My wife liked you, too. I'm sure she would have voted for you."

"I appreciate that, Mr. Le," McVie said. "I'm so sorry about your wife."

"Yes," he said, blinking. "Liver cancer. She didn't suffer too long, fortunately. She liked you, though. Voted for you for sheriff every time you ran." He crossed his arms. "Will Barry Klein be as bad for the city as I think?"

"Worse," Fenway said under her breath.

"I don't know." McVie crossed his arms. "I hope to do everything I can to make sure the city stays on track, though."

"Okay," Mr. Le said, turning into a side room used as both a shrine to the Los Angeles Dodgers and an office. A PC sat on a large desk, amidst at least forty bobbleheads of different Dodgers players. A stack of hard drives hummed quietly beside the large monitor. Los Angeles Dodgers pennants and banners covered the walls, and a display case held at least a dozen baseballs, bats, and gloves, all covered in signatures.

"This is quite a collection," Fenway said.

"I voted for you in spite of your first name, Miss Stevenson." Mr. Le smiled.

"It was my father's idea."

"I wanted to name our son Hershiser. My wife fortunately talked me out of it." He went to the cabinet and pulled out a wooden bat. "My pride and joy. Signed by every member of the 1988 World Series team."

"That was the series where Kirk Gibson homered off Eckersley, right?" Fenway said.

Mr. Le chortled. "Oh yes. Barely made it around the bases." He walked over to the PC. "All right, don't get me started on the Dodgers. You didn't come to hear my stories. All the footage is on this machine. You can view it here." Mr. Le clicked the mouse and the system woke up. "I only keep two weeks' worth of video on the hard drives." He set his mouth in a line. "I don't have enough storage to save much more than that at high resolution. I don't want to set the resolution lower— you can't make out the license plate numbers across the street unless it's at high res." He typed in his password and double-clicked an icon. "Okay—this is the PixelImage Security Platform—are you familiar with it?" He leaned the bat against the desk.

Fenway nodded. "I am. Maybe a slightly older version, but I'm sure I can figure it out."

McVie looked at Fenway.

"We used this at the clinic up in Seattle," Fenway said. "People kept breaking in to steal the painkillers. I had to review footage a few times, and I learned how to reset the system when it hung up."

"The latest release is much more stable," Mr. Le said, a little defensively.

Fenway smiled. "We didn't have the greatest hardware at the clinic," she said. "It was probably more us than the program."

Mr. Le grunted noncommittally and pulled up a window with bins of footage. "Okay, starting from two weeks ago Friday. I have it set to delete files for any day older than two weeks. So that previous Thursday was deleted this morning." He chuckled. "I was interested in what would happen at Halloween—someone in the neighborhood usually gets their house egged or with all the toilet paper all over it. But everyone behaved themselves." He said the last sentence with disappointment in his voice.

This guy must be a lot of fun at parties. "How about showing me this previous Friday?" Fenway asked, and Mr. Le scrolled down and then opened a folder. "Do you want to start at midnight?"

"No," Fenway said, "let's see this at—uh—six A.M. That should do it."

Mr. Le stood up. Fenway nodded, slipping into the chair in front of the keyboard. "I was about to make a pot of coffee," Mr. Le said. "Would you like some?"

"I would *love* some coffee," Fenway said, a little too enthusiastically.

Mr. Le nodded and left the room.

"Okay," McVie said, "You meant six *P.M.*, right? That's when Domingo Velásquez disappeared. If he went anywhere, it was Rose's house, right?"

Fenway shook her head. "I want to see that, too, but remember, we were called out to Jeremy Kapp's body at about five-thirty A.M. I want to see if anything happened once word got out about his death."

"We didn't release Kapp's name until that afternoon. After the family had been notified."

"Right."

"So why do you think someone heard about it earlier?"

Fenway looked at McVie. "Because there's a mole in the department."

McVie looked uncomfortable. "I don't know that for sure. I *think* there's a mole in the department."

Fenway nodded. "Right. Look—if nothing shows up on this video, then we still won't know for sure if there's a mole. But if something *does*, it supports the theory that someone's leaking confidential police information to at least one person involved in the money laundering."

McVie cocked his head. "Yes. That makes sense. I can't believe I didn't think of it." He grabbed a straight-backed chair and pulled it over in front of the desk, sitting down next to Fenway. They both turned to the screen.

The street was still dark at six in the morning, and the streetlights shone off puddles on the road and the sidewalk. No cars were in Rose's driveway.

"Is she even home?" Fenway said. "Her car isn't there."

There was no movement for several minutes, except for a single SUV driving from the left side of the screen to the right, out of the development; someone beginning a morning commute. Fenway scrubbed the video forward bit by bit. The sky lightened; a few more cars went past, also driving toward civilization and the promise of a paycheck.

At 6:23 A.M., a blue Acura ILX came from the right of the screen *into* the development, pulled into the driveway, and parked in front of Rose's garage. Fenway stopped fast-forwarding and backed up to where the ILX entered the picture. "I've seen that car before," muttered Fenway.

A woman with long, wavy hair, dressed in a gray hoodie and black jeans, got out of the Acura with a large gray duffel bag. From the way she carried the bag, it seemed heavy. Fenway couldn't see her face, as she had her back to the camera almost the whole time. She hurried to Rose's front door and knocked. The door opened and Fenway could barely make out a figure in the doorway; the figure was Rose's height, with long hair. Fenway paused and zoomed in, and sure enough, it was Rose.

"Who's the *other* woman?" McVie's eyes were transfixed on the screen.

Fenway shook her head. "I didn't get a good look at her. But when she leaves, she'll have to show her face."

They didn't have to wait long. Ten minutes later, the sky even lighter now, the front door opened once more and the Acura driver stepped out onto the porch, no longer holding the duffel bag. The woman lifted her chin and Fenway hit pause and zoomed in again.

"Holy shit," McVie mumbled.

Jessica Marquez.

CHAPTER EIGHTEEN

McVie flinched. "Isn't that—"

"Yes," Fenway nodded. "That's our murder victim."

"What's the general manager of a university Shakespeare group doing with an auto-body shop accountant?"

"Maybe they're friends."

"Jessica is at least a decade older than Rose."

"I've seen romantic relationships that have a more pronounced age difference," Fenway said. She shot a look at McVie, but he seemed oblivious to the jibe.

"Sure," McVie said, "but this doesn't look like they're lovers. This looks like a business transaction. What business would they have together? Even if Rose is spying on her employer, how would Jessica be involved?"

Fenway shrugged. "We know Central Auto Body was involved in the money laundering. The only theory that occurs to me is that somehow The Guild was also involved in it. Rose managed the books at the auto shop, and Jessica managed the books at The Guild."

McVie nodded. "But we haven't gone over their books yet. Nidever is fighting the warrant."

"Why? Isn't the warrant narrow in scope?"

"I thought it was clear to Dr. Pruitt that we only wanted to look at the North American Shakespeare Guild, but apparently there's a scholarship fund with donors who want to keep their gifts private."

Fenway chuckled.

"I know," McVie said. "The scholarship fund is the perfect place to launder money without drawing suspicion. That fund could have anonymous donations of millions of dollars and then have The Guild hire that Global Advantage consulting firm for—jeez, anything. Script consulting, set design, talent booking, travel scheduling—I bet *millions* of dollars are being laundered through this fund, and it all looks aboveboard."

"And since it's a private organization that runs separately from the university, there may not be any oversight. If there is—maybe it's only oversight from Dr. Pruitt." Fenway looked at McVie. "Have we determined where Dr. Pruitt was the night of the murder?"

"He says he was at home asleep."

"So no." Fenway hit Play again, and the ILX backed out of the driveway and drove out of the development the same way it had come in. "I wonder if we can get the names of any of the scholarship fund students?"

"We'd have to get the name of the fund first," McVie said. "I got the feeling when I spoke to Dr. Pruitt about it yesterday, he thought he'd given up too much information even saying that."

"Okay," Fenway said, "I'm sure there's a way we can find out what that scholarship fund is. For now, let's go through the rest of this footage and see if there's anything else happening with our friend Rose." She paused for a moment. "Hey—this scholarship fund—I wonder if it has anything to do with the note I found in Jessica Marquez's office."

"Why do you say that?"

"Because the note referred to something that was over twenty-seven million dollars. Maybe it was referring to the balance in the scholarship account."

"I don't know. We'd have to get a lot more information to see if we can get some confirmation on the account."

"If you knew the actual amount in the account on a particular date, would that help?"

"Most definitely."

McVie turned and looked at Fenway, a glint in his eye. "You know, you've got—"

Fenway's head whipped back to the screen. "What? Something I missed?"

"No, no." McVie looked down at his hands. "Ah, forget it."

"What?"

"You didn't miss anything." He stopped, hesitated, and began again. "I started to say that you've got a fire lit under you on this case. You're intent on figuring this out."

"That's me, Little Miss Nose-to-the-Grindstone." She looked in his eyes. "What's bothering you?"

He grimaced and shook his head. "Don't worry about it. It's stupid."

"If it's bothering you, it's not stupid."

He looked out the window and squinted. "You've got a passion for the work that I haven't had in a while. I have no idea what I'll do after January first. I've been a police officer all of my adult life."

Fenway reached out and took his hand in hers. "A lot of people in this town love working with you, Craig. You'll figure something out. You'll be drowning in opportunities before you know it."

"I guess." He rubbed his hands together. "Anyway, let's see if that duffel bag makes an appearance when Rose leaves."

They both watched in silence, fast-forwarding through the next two hours, watching dozens of cars leave the development until a black Lincoln entered from the right and pulled up next to Rose's house.

"Curiouser and curiouser," Fenway said, pausing the video, backing it up to the Lincoln coming into the frame.

"You're enjoying this."

"This case is a big deal, Craig. I'm taking this seriously." Fenway hit the space bar.

"I didn't say you weren't. I'm just saying that you're enjoying it. Your eyes lit up just now."

"Well, sure. That's Peter Grayheath's car. He's visiting Rose, too." McVie nodded.

Grayheath walked up to the door, which opened for him. Less than five minutes later, he walked out with the duffel bag, popped his trunk, put it inside, then got in the car and drove off.

"Did Peter Grayheath just accept payment for a hit?" Fenway asked.

"That's a stretch."

"It's impossible to prove from the video, for sure." Fenway fast-forwarded more.

Twenty minutes after that, the garage door opened slowly, and Rose's Mazda 6 backed out, onto the street. She drove away as the garage door closed.

McVie nodded. "So Rose car parked in the garage Friday morning. Why do you think she left her car in the driveway today?"

"Could be for any number of reasons."

"Like there's something else in the garage."

"You're thinking Domingo's car?"

"Right."

Fenway fast-forwarded more, and started to go faster. She watched the time code as the hours went by. "Okay—this is lunch time... no one came home. Now it's two o'clock, three o'clock...."

The Mazda 6 came back into the frame and pulled into the garage.

"She came home early," McVie said.

"Right," Fenway said. "I wonder if she went into work or if she went somewhere else."

Fenway fast-forwarded past four o'clock. The sky started to darken, then it was five o'clock and the streetlights came on. It was completely dark by six o'clock when an older Chrysler 300 with its headlights on parked in front of Rose's house. Domingo Velásquez got out.

"So he came to see his accountant after he heard about his son's death," McVie muttered.

Fenway heard Mr. Le clearing his throat behind them and hit pause. They turned around; Mr. Le held two steaming mugs, one in each hand.

"Sorry, I didn't want to interrupt," he said, "but I have your coffee."

Fenway stood. "Thanks so much," she said, smiling. She took the two mugs and gave one of them to McVie.

"Let me know if you need anything else," he said.

"We may need some of these videos for evidence," McVie said.

"I'd be happy to make copies for you," he said.

"Thanks," McVie said. Mr. Le turned and left the room.

"I guess we should get our own hard drive and copy the files over instead of confiscating all this equipment," Fenway said.

"We'll do the least intrusive thing that still meets chain-of-custody requirements."

Fenway nodded and turned to the screen.

They watched as Rose opened the door and met Domingo Velasquez in the driveway. They couldn't hear, but the man collapsed into Rose's arms. He looked like he was sobbing.

"He just found out about Rory," Fenway said, her throat tightening.

"They look like more than coworkers to you?" McVie took a sip of his coffee.

"I don't know what they look like," Fenway said. "The two of them are close, for sure."

"Why not go home to your wife? Why go to Rose?"

"I don't know."

"I'll tell you. It's because they're sleeping together. He might even think he's in love with her."

"Maybe it's because he thinks someone's after him, and he can't go home."

McVie shook his head. "He might think someone's after him, but that's not why he's at Rose's house. He's there because he needs emotional support and he wants to see her, not his wife."

Fenway set her jaw and kept watching the screen.

After a few minutes, Domingo Velásquez stopped crying. Rose Morgan started kissing the side of his face, then on the lips, briefly, and then she said something to him and they went inside the house.

A few minutes later, the garage door opened. Rose backed out of the garage, parked the Mazda on the street, then went over to the Chrysler, opened it, started it up, and pulled the car into her garage. The garage door closed a few moments later.

"Think it's still there?" Fenway asked.

"I think we've got another six days of footage that can tell us that," McVie said.

"This is enough for a warrant?"

"So far, all this proves is that Rose comforts her boss and hides his car. Looks like they're having an affair, which isn't illegal. That wouldn't even get us a warrant to look at her financials."

"But it does tell us where Domingo Velásquez went."

"Yes."

"We should take this as evidence," Fenway said.

The doorbell rang.

McVie stiffened. "I hope that's not Rose."

"How would she know we're over here?"

"We left my car parked in front of her house. Plus, she might have seen us out her front window."

They heard the door open, then a man's voice spoke. Fenway thought it sounded familiar.

"Everything okay?" McVie called.

There was silence for a moment.

"Mr. Le?"

"Just a package," Mr. Le called, haltingly. "Something my wife ordered."

Liver cancer. She voted for you every time you ran, though.

"Shit," Fenway said. She clicked off the old footage and brought up the current camera view. Parked behind McVie's Highlander was a black Lincoln.

Fenway heard a thump from the living room.

McVie rose up and unholstered his gun, shifting around to the entry of the office. He raised his Sig Sauer with both hands.

"I see you, McVie!" The voice of Peter Grayheath clearly rang down the hallway. "Put the gun down!"

"Drop your weapon!" McVie said sharply.

"You know I'll kill the old man, McVie. You know I'll do it."

Fenway grabbed the bat and shifted to the other side of the room, her back flat against the wall, next to the door frame, across from McVie. She looked at him, trying to get on the same page.

"You'll give me all the camera footage, McVie, or the old man's brains are going all over the hallway." Grayheath's voice was closer now.

McVie hesitated and then put his arms up.

"Slide the gun over to me."

McVie had the gun in his right hand, and he clicked something with his thumb. The magazine of bullets fell to the floor. Then he threw his gun into the hallway. Fenway hoped it was out of Grayheath's reach.

"Now back up," Grayheath said, and Fenway heard his voice right on the other side of the wall that she had her back against.

McVie took two steps back.

"Farther into the room," Grayheath said. He started through the doorway, his right elbow appearing first. "Don't be a hero, Sheriff."

Fenway held her breath. The Louisville Slugger, covered in signatures, was heavy in her hand. She looked at the names; most of them were scrawls that she couldn't make out, although she did see Kirk Gibson's autograph. She wanted to smash Gibson's name through Grayheath's elbow, but didn't know if he had the gun against Mr. Le's temple, and didn't want to risk the gun discharging.

McVie took another step back.

"Three more steps," Grayheath said, and he raised his right hand, the one holding the gun, to motion McVie into the room.

Fenway swung hard, pulling with her left arm, bringing the bat over her right shoulder, and putting her body weight behind the blow.

The bat connected with the cap of Grayheath's right shoulder, and Fenway heard a sickening pop and a crunch.

Grayheath screamed and dropped the gun. McVie leapt in front of Grayheath and grabbed the gun off the floor.

Fenway stepped forward; Mr. Le had scrambled away from the scrum and sat on the hallway carpet, a few feet away. He looked up.

"You hit him with my World Series bat," he said.

"I hope I didn't damage it," Fenway said, her left shoulder starting to throb. "It was the only thing—"

"Bless you, Tommy Lasorda," Mr. Le said, casting his eyes skyward. "You just saved my life."

———

McVie called for an ambulance, and Fenway examined the damage to Grayheath's shoulder. She found at least three bone fractures, including the clavicle. He also had a dislocated shoulder and couldn't feel the tips of his fingers. Mr. Le was effusive in his praise for the sheriff and Fenway—and he enthusiastically recreated the scene for the deputy who came to take his statement. He expressed dismay that the bat would be taken into evidence.

"They've got to make sure that the story happened like we said it did," Fenway said, soothing him. "You'll have the bat back in no time. A day or two, tops." Although she remembered her Accord, still gathering dust in evidence.

They also had to take the hard drives in, which left Mr. Le worried about the ability of his system to record the area in front of his street. McVie talked him down from that.

"So," Fenway said, "what should we do about Rose?"

"We'll take her in for questioning," McVie replied. "After the police action here at this house—I'm betting she saw Peter Grayheath come over—she's definitely a flight risk."

"Didn't she *send* Grayheath over? Can we arrest her for, uh, I don't know, conspiracy to commit burglary?"

McVie rubbed his chin. "We'll see what ADA Kim says. If Miss Morgan doesn't come with us, we'll regroup. Let's see what she has to say for herself."

McVie and Fenway walked up to the door and rang the bell.

After a moment, the door opened. It was Rose.

"I've got nothing to say to you without a lawyer," she said.

"You can do it down at the station," McVie said. "Officer Callahan can give you a ride."

"I respectfully decline," Rose said.

"I would encourage you to help us out on this," McVie said.

"Am I under arrest?"

"I'd rather not put you under arrest," said McVie. "I've got two weeks of video footage, however, that makes it pretty clear you participated in a conspiracy to commit murder."

"What video footage?"

"Please, Miss Morgan. I'd rather not arrest you. I'm interested in what you know and what information you can provide."

"You're interested in putting a target on my back, is what you're interested in," spat Rose.

"We need information," McVie said. "That's all."

Rose considered for a moment. "Maybe we can work something out."

"Excellent, I'm glad to hear that. Why don't you come with us? We'll give you a ride to the station."

Fenway stepped up and said softly in McVie's ear, "Can I talk to you for a second?"

McVie nodded and took a few steps away from the door.

"Are you going to take a look in the garage?"

He shook his head. "I don't have a warrant."

"Not the house. The garage. We have probable cause that the Chrysler 300 belonging to Domingo Velásquez is in there."

"Of course we do, but we'd need his wife to file the missing persons report first."

"He's a person of interest in an ongoing investigation," Fenway said.

"I think as peace officers we have a right to figure out where he's gone. I don't think any judge would believe we'd need a warrant to look in the garage after the video footage we saw."

McVie nodded. "Yeah. A little creative for my tastes, but okay."

He radioed for Callahan, who crossed the street.

"Miss Morgan," McVie said, stepping onto her front porch, "we have reason to believe that Domingo Velásquez's missing car is in your garage."

Tight-lipped, Rose didn't say anything.

"After viewing video footage of the street from last Friday, we know his Chrysler is in there." He tapped his foot. "So, will you open the garage, or will we have to break the door down?"

"You need a warrant."

"We have probable cause, Miss Morgan, but if you insist on a warrant, I don't have any problem sticking around here for a couple of hours. I know a judge who'd love to sign off on this."

Rose shook her head. "Cops are all the same." She scoffed. "Fine. If you'll go in there anyway, Dom's car *is* parked in there."

"We'd like to see it for ourselves."

Rose looked at the ground, tapping her foot. Then she looked up. "Fine. Open my car, push the first button on the left on the ceiling right next to the rearview mirror."

"Where are your keys?"

Rose opened her purse, pulled her keychain out, and pushed a button on the car remote. The Mazda emitted a quiet clicking noise.

"Thank you. Fenway, do you want to do the honors?"

Fenway walked around to the driver's door, opened it, and pushed the button. The garage door grunted and squeaked as it rose.

The Chrysler 300.

"Pop the trunk," McVie called to Fenway.

"What?"

"Pop the trunk. Let's make sure that Miss Morgan isn't hiding both Velasquez's car *and* his body."

Fenway looked inside the Chrysler for a moment and found the trunk release. She walked around, a bit gingerly, to the back, and held her breath as she peered inside.

A Samsonite weekender and nothing else. Fenway exhaled with relief.

"No body," she called. "A small suitcase, though. It might belong to Velásquez."

"Enter it into evidence at the station," McVie said. "Maybe we'll get lucky with a fingerprint."

"So," McVie said, turning to Rose Morgan, "we know where his car is. Now we need to know where *he* is, and, for that matter, where the missing ledgers are."

"Not to mention your work PC," said Fenway.

Rose's eyes went from the Chrysler to McVie's face. She pursed her lips and folded her arms. "I'm exercising my right to remain silent. You can talk to my lawyer."

CHAPTER NINETEEN

AFTER A DEPUTY DROVE OFF WITH ROSE IN THE BACK SEAT, MCVIE and Fenway got into the Highlander.

"And here I thought you said this would be a slow morning," Fenway said.

"Yeah, I lied." McVie looked at Fenway. "Thanks for what you did back there with Mr. Le and the baseball bat. That was quick thinking."

Fenway shrugged. "Oh, please. I had to be a quick thinker after a few years in the ER. I know you're good under pressure, too."

McVie started the car. "You're good at a lot of things, Fenway, but you're shitty at taking compliments."

"It's one of the things that makes me me," Fenway said, leaning her seat back. Her left shoulder was hurting her; she had been babying her whole arm ever since she had broken her left hand three months before, and now her shoulder was complaining. "Are we going to the station to see if we can get Rose to open up? Or to the hospital to question Grayheath?"

"I don't know. I don't think he'll exactly be forthcoming with anything to either of us."

"That's right," Fenway said. "I forget how fragile male egos are when they get beat by a girl."

"In this case, literally." McVie thought for a moment. "Maybe we should check in with Dez."

Fenway nodded and pulled her phone out. "That's a good idea. She knows about the ledgers—besides Piper, she's the only one in the office who does. I'll put her on speaker."

Dez answered on the first ring. "Fenway Stevenson, as I live and breathe. Finally living up to your name and doing some good with a baseball bat."

McVie chuckled. "Hey Dez. I swear, you gossip worse than Megan's friends."

"Good day, Sheriff. You better make sure Fenway doesn't leave the county to sign a major league contract. Heard she can hit some real nasty stuff."

"You got that right." McVie paused for a moment. "Listen, Dez, we need a favor."

"A favor?"

"Well, a professional favor. You're working the Jessica Marquez murder, we were looking into the Central Auto Body stuff. But we need to get a statement from Peter Grayheath before the medical staff puts him under."

"And you're thinking he won't talk to the woman who played whack-a-mole with his head?"

"It was his shoulder," Fenway cut in.

"Whatever," Dez said. "Sure, Sheriff, I'd be glad to. You know how charming I can be."

"I do," McVie replied, "so I must be pretty desperate."

Dez hooted. "That was weak, Sheriff. I threw a nice, easy fastball right over the plate, and you just fouled it off. Have Fenway give you some pointers."

Fenway smiled. "You heard from Mark?"

"Interviewing the property owner at Tassajera's office, and then heading to San Miguelito to interview the ex. He should be back in a couple of hours."

McVie nodded. "He can try interviewing Rose when he gets back. It won't hurt to have her sit and stew for two hours. We've got to wait for her lawyer anyway."

"How about you and Fenway?"

"I thought we might head to Nidever. We didn't talk to the students Wednesday night after rehearsal."

Fenway nodded. "I got the professor to say he went home at ten thirty and was in bed by eleven thirty, but he wouldn't look at the office. I'd like another crack at him."

"That's okay with me," Dez said. "Fenway's better interviewing the students than I am, anyway." She exhaled loudly. "Okay—I better get over to the hospital before they dope Grayheath up with the good stuff."

"Thanks, Dez," Fenway said.

"See ya, boss." Dez clicked off.

Wow. *Boss.* Not *rookie.*

"It's eleven thirty now," McVie said. "I could use lunch, and then we can go find the students before they have to show up to prep for opening night. Someone there must have known Jessica Marquez well enough to hear her secrets. Also, we need to see if any of the students —or the staff, for that matter—has seen Rose Morgan around."

"Amanda said there was a younger woman hanging around Jessica Marquez. We can ask her if that was Rose."

McVie ran one hand through his hair. "If Morgan and Marquez were working together on something with Central Auto Body, maybe they've been doing something with The Guild, too." McVie sighed. "Plus, that'll give us some time to try to get the warrant for Rose's house and financial records. It'd be nice if we found something else besides the Chrysler."

Fenway nodded. "Don't you think we need to find out what was in that duffel bag?"

"Yep. I asked for warrants to be drawn up for Peter Grayheath's home and car."

Fenway straightened up as McVie took the George Nidever Expressway exit. "I thought we were stopping for lunch."

"We'll stop for lunch."

"Before we go to the university."

"The university has some great places in the student center."

"I thought we were getting *real* lunch."

"There are places to eat other than Dos Milagros, you know."

"I know. Like the Argentine steak house."

"I liked Ernesto's. Let's go there again."

Fenway rolled her eyes. "I assume you want to eat lunch at Ernesto's as an excuse to talk to Xavier Go."

"Sometimes people can be a lot more forthcoming if you catch them away from their comfort zones," McVie said. "I've also found that when people just want you to leave so they can do their jobs—like, perhaps, keep their head above water during a lunch rush—it's amazing how they can forget to lie."

"Remind me not to get on your bad side."

McVie smiled.

They parked in a visitor space in the student center parking lot and went inside. A wall of noise washed over them. A few minutes before noon, crowds of amped-up students flooded the center. Fenway looked at the line in front of Ernesto's; it was already ten people long, and she could see the cashier behind the counter, taking orders as quickly as he could—but it wasn't Xavier.

"We got here too late," McVie said. "It's way too crowded now. I thought we'd hit right before the rush."

Three young men, two in jeans and hoodies and one in a tight muscle shirt and shorts, ran from their table toward Micah's Deli. Laughing, they almost knocked the lunch tray out of the hands of a young, curly-haired woman in a gray NIDEVER FOREVER sweatshirt.

"That's Emilia," Fenway said, motioning to the woman who melodramatically sighed, looking after the three men, while pointedly ogling the one in the muscle shirt.

"Who?"

"The woman who plays Emilia in *Othello*," Fenway said. "You've seen her, right? She's good, although Professor Cygnus sure tore into her yesterday."

"Oh, right." McVie squeezed his eyes shut, thinking, then opened them again. "Denise, right? Denise—uh, Delatasso."

"Impressive, Craig. You know the names of all the girls in the play, or just the pretty, talented ones?" Fenway's tone was teasing, but she couldn't keep a faint brushstroke of jealousy out of her voice.

McVie looked at Fenway out of the corner of his eye.

She said, "We should go talk to her."

"Yeah," McVie said. "We can salvage something out of this trip."

Fenway nodded. She saw Denise stop and consider the large table that the three young men had just vacated—one of the few empty tables in the student center—but the tabletop had cups, trays, napkins, and dirty plates all over the top.

McVie swooped behind her. "Hi, again," he said. "Here, let me clear that for you." He scooped a couple of plates onto a tray and lifted it off the table.

"Oh!" Denise said. "Sheriff! I didn't see you there."

Fenway went around the other end of the table. "Hi," she said. "I don't think we met. I'm Fenway Stevenson."

"The pleasure is mine," Denise said. "Are you an officer, too?"

"The county coroner." Fenway picked up the other two trays.

"Oh, of course!" Denise said. "The recent election. How perfectly silly of me."

Fenway fought the desire to roll her eyes at Denise because it was almost like she was faking a British accent through her grandiose word choice. She steeled herself for the conversation. "Don't apologize for not following politics," Fenway said, stepping over to the trash and dumping the contents of the trays. "If I weren't running, I'm not sure I'd have followed it myself."

When Fenway turned back to the table, McVie was sitting across from an uncomfortable-looking Denise, a steaming rice bowl sitting between them.

"I guess this is about Jessica," Denise said as Fenway slid into the seat next to the sheriff. "It's tragic what happened to her."

"Did you know her well?" McVie asked.

"Not as well as I might have liked," Denise said, tearing the paper off her chopsticks. "Certainly some of the other students knew her better than I did."

"Like who?" Fenway asked.

"Amanda, for one, obviously." She took a bite from her rice bowl.

"Obviously?"

"Of course. She worked in The Guild office. She put in far more hours than any other student. A regular Girl Friday."

McVie smiled. "How many hours did Amanda put in?"

"At least twenty or twenty-five every week. She wanted to go on the London theater trip, and working for The Guild not only gave her enough money to go, but also cut her ticket price in half."

"In half?" Fenway said.

"The lodging and the activities in the U.K. Not airfare. Still—hotels, theater tickets, classroom events—it's all quite expensive."

McVie nodded. "Six thousand dollars, right?"

"Assuming you aren't one of The Guild's lucky employees, yes."

"So for Amanda it was what? About three grand?"

"Given what I know of the program, that sounds about right."

"Did *you* want to go?" Fenway asked.

Denise crinkled up her nose. "I enjoy performing in the Bard's great plays, but attending eighteen theater productions in a little more than a fortnight? That's not exactly my idea of a pleasant summer vacation." She sniffed. "Especially not with the great Professor Cygnus ejaculating his self-righteous Shakespeare interpretation all over his fellow travelers."

Fenway almost laughed out loud but suppressed it. "So it's like one of Professor Cygnus's Shakespeare classes, but compressed into three weeks?"

"That's correct." Denise ate another bite and swallowed thoughtfully. "I must admit that I'm surprised that Professor Cygnus is leading it this year."

"Really?" McVie said. "He seems like this Shakespeare stuff is the only reason he gets up in the morning."

Denise smiled. "It certainly is. I just didn't realize that it was more important to him than spending time with his wife."

"His wife?"

"Surely you've discovered by now that the professor's better half was diagnosed with leukemia a few months ago." Denise looked from McVie's face to Fenway's. "No? My understanding is that she has about a year to live, perhaps less. If it were me, I'd rather spend those three weeks in the summer with my dying wife instead of a busful of entitled, rich theater snobs and nineteen-year-old students. Students who'd rather drink cellar-temperature ale at a pub than sit through a lecture with some of the greatest Shakespearean actors of our time."

McVie leaned back. "He didn't have a backup? He didn't want Jessica to go in his place?"

"To lead the theater tour? Good heavens, no. I've always had the impression that enduring a Shakespeare play would have been Jessica's embodiment of hell." Denise laughed. "Jessica made the excuse that a responsible adult had to stay to attend to The Guild's day-to-day functions."

Fenway put her elbows on the table. "Xavier isn't traveling to London, either, is he?"

"No," Denise said. "There are six students going, and they seem to be Cygnus's pets."

"Xavier's not one of his pet students?" asked McVie.

"Just because he was cast as the lead? No. He's the best actor—*male* actor—in the play, but you can certainly tell that he doesn't subscribe to Cygnus's more, shall we say, creative interpretations of the text."

McVie leaned forward. "Creative interpretations?"

"Surely you're familiar with the more controversial elements Professor Cygnus puts in his Shakespeare plays? I thought that's how Nidever found its place on the literary map."

McVie grinned. "Do I look like I'm familiar with the literary map?"

Denise's eyes raked McVie's torso and arms. "I'm sure I don't know, Sheriff. Don't judge a book, and all that."

"So," Fenway said, trying to mask her annoyance, "tell me about these innovative interpretations that Professor Cygnus does."

"Certainly," Denise said. "Perhaps his most famous—or should I say *infamous*—interpretation came last year with *The Merchant of Venice* production."

"He won a West Coast Theater Educators' award for that, right?"

Denise nodded. "I was a sophomore when I went to see that, and I couldn't *wait* to be in his play this year." She looked at McVie. "Do you know the play?"

"Uh—no, I don't think I do."

"That's the one with Shylock and the pound of flesh," Fenway said to McVie.

"And *The Quality of Mercy*," Denise said, a little too dreamily for Fenway's taste. "I must say that even though I'm not too keen on some of the things he does, Cygnus possesses an unequaled ability to pull beautiful emotional performances from students with absolutely no acting experience. The woman who played Portia—she and I have shared several literature classes—folds in on herself, she's so introverted. When she speaks in class, it's only at the behest of the instructor, and even then a more mousy, whispery voice you'd be hard-pressed to hear again. And yet, the way that woman commanded the stage—unbelievable."

"So," Fenway said, trying to keep her on track, "what made the production of *The Merchant of Venice* so infamous?"

"Of course. I apologize; I get carried away every now and then," Denise said, putting her hand on Fenway's elbow. "It was the monkey."

"Oh," Fenway said, "I think I heard someone mention that."

Denise nodded emphatically. "There's a scene where Shylock's daughter—oh, her name is Jessica too, just like Jessica Marquez!"

"What about the scene?"

"Shylock bemoans the fact that Jessica has left him. He feels completely betrayed. He goes on and on and on about how she's rejected him, her own flesh and blood, her own father, and she's gotten a pet monkey." Denise cleared her throat. "It's where Tubal says to Shylock, *'One of them showed me a ring that he had of your daughter for a monkey.'* And Shylock responds, *'Out upon her! Thou torturest me, Tubal. It was my turquoise. I had it of Leah when I was a bachelor. I would not have given it for a wilderness of monkeys.'*" She stopped, looking pleased with herself. "Now—most interpretations just have Shylock performing the speech. It may be metaphorical—Jessica's new husband could be a monkey in Shylock's eyes, I suppose. Most directors assume that Jessica is simply frivolous, and gets a pet monkey because it's something her father never let her have—or perhaps she just *told* him she got a monkey to spite him. He's not the greatest father in the world, and maybe Jessica knew that it would hurt him more that she traded her mother's ring for a monkey than that she married a gentile."

"So how did Cygnus interpret it?"

Denise guffawed. "Our dear professor *procured* a live monkey. He contacted a local wildlife rescue organization and eventually persuaded them to lend The Guild one of their capuchin monkeys. He insisted that Sarah have that infernal monkey on her shoulder the very next scene she was in."

"Sarah?"

"Oh—Sarah Harding."

McVie's brow furrowed. "Sarah Harding. That name sounds familiar."

"She was a senior last year—she played Shylock's daughter." She shook her head, perhaps in disbelief, or maybe in shock. "She's simply a wisp of a girl, ninety pounds soaking wet."

"Was there an issue with the monkey?" Fenway asked, hoping the exasperation didn't creep into her voice.

"Only that Professor Cygnus made her *bond* with the monkey," Denise said. "And by bond, I mean he insisted she take it home. When the wildlife organization objected, he refused to give the monkey back. But the truly nefarious part is that he didn't tell Sarah that they objected. Of course, she got into a huge fight with the professor—her apartment didn't allow pets—never mind a capuchin monkey. If she had known the wildlife organization objected, she would have given it back gladly. Instead, the very first night she took the monkey home, she got *arrested*."

A look of dawning comprehension came into McVie's eyes. "Of course. *That* Sarah Harding."

Fenway felt the shock on her face. "*You* didn't arrest her, did you?"

"I didn't, but I had to run some interference between that wildlife preserve and the university."

Denise frowned.

McVie folded his arms. "Listen, it's not like I could do anything about it. Morris was their property—"

"Morris?" Fenway said. "Morris the monkey?"

"—and the wildlife organization insisted on pressing charges."

"For taking home a monkey?"

"For stealing an animal worth fifteen thousand dollars," McVie said.

"What?" Fenway said. "Why in the world would they agree to let a fifteen-thousand-dollar monkey perform in a Shakespeare play?"

"Professor Cygnus can be charming," said Denise. "Besides, the monkey seemed to enjoy performing."

"You mean to tell me," said Fenway, "that even after all that, they *still* let him use the monkey?"

"The university provided a large donation to the wildlife organization," said McVie.

Fenway shook her head.

"And the monkey performed wonderfully," Denise said. "Well-trained. They had a little speech at the end about endangered wildlife and they had donation boxes in the lobby."

Fenway looked at McVie, who shrugged.

"At any rate," Denise said, "apparently it was the first *Merchant of Venice* production in over two hundred years that had used a live monkey, and it even got a write-up in the L.A. *Times*. It was a big deal. People were writing in to tell The Guild how much they loved or hated the monkey, Sarah even had her picture in *Theater Now*. She got that role on *Until Proven Guilty* because of that exposure."

"Wait—Sarah *Marie* Harding?" Fenway cocked her head at McVie. "You arrested a famous actress?"

"Correction," McVie muttered. "I worked out a politically charged situation to *free* a famous actress. Who wasn't famous at the time, I might add."

"How well does Cygnus know Jessica Marquez?" Fenway said, a note of double entendre in her voice.

Denise's laugh turned into a giggle. "The great Virgil Cygnus and Jessica Marquez?"

"It's not such a strange concept. Older men go for younger women all the time."

"A tiresome trope, indeed," Denise said, "but, alas, it's an open secret that Cygnus is having an affair with Leda Nedermeyer."

"Leda Nedermeyer?"

"She's nothing less than the head of the Nidever English department," Denise said. "'If the stacks are a-rockin', don't come a-knockin',' as the literature majors say. It's true that Professor Nedermeyer is a younger woman, of course, but Cygnus is sixty. She's in her late forties."

"So basically robbing the cradle."

McVie, tight-lipped, said nothing.

Fenway tapped the table. "He started the affair even though his wife was diagnosed with cancer?"

"No, no," Denise said. "This is not a recent development. In fact, to hear Jessica tell it, Professor Cygnus and Professor Nedermeyer have been having an affair for more than a decade."

Fenway's eyes widened.

"So," McVie said, "you think there was absolutely nothing happening between Jessica Marquez and Virgil Cygnus."

"Nothing," Denise said. "She's quite the gossipmonger about him, as well, and in my experience, the other woman does not gossip about her beau."

"Fair enough," said McVie. "So was Jessica Marquez seeing anyone?"

Denise squinted. Fenway saw it in her eyes—she knew about Jessica's affair with Xavier.

"What is it?"

"I don't think anyone's privy to this knowledge, but I entered in The Guild office one day and Jessica and Xavier were engaged in, uh, sexual congress."

"It's always a shitshow when Congress gets involved," Fenway deadpanned.

"No, I meant—"

"I know," Fenway said. "I was making a bad joke. Had you heard that Xavier and *Amanda* are dating?"

"It *is* true that I have seen the two of them together, and it doesn't surprise me that they've been intimate. Let's put it this way: Amanda gets assigned a lot of hours when Xavier is free." Denise rested her chin in her hand. "And Xavier is never there observing when Desdemona and Emilia rehearse their dedicated scenes."

"So how did you walk in on them?" McVie asked.

"It was during rehearsal for a scene between Desdemona and Brabantio."

McVie leaned forward. "Who?"

"Sorry. Amanda's character—Desdemona—and the young man playing Desdemona's father. So I wasn't in the scene. I went to retrieve some flyers from the office—I planned to put them up in the Java Jim's over off University Avenue—and when I opened the door, the two of them were positioned *in flagrante delicto,* on top of the desks, 'making the beast with two backs,' as Iago would say."

"I see." McVie looked over at Fenway. "Are you aware of any others?"

"Any other paramours, you mean?" Denise took another bite.

"Friends, lovers, enemies, whatever."

Denise chewed for a moment, a thoughtful look on her face.

"What about this woman?" McVie said, taking his phone out and showing Denise the picture of Rose Morgan.

Denise swallowed and looked at the picture. "Well, I don't think Jessica was bisexual, if that's what you mean."

"We were told they were friends," McVie said. "In fact, if you've just seen this woman around, that would be great for us to know."

"I can't be absolutely certain," Denise said. "I've been by the office a couple of times when visitors have been in whom I failed to recognize. She looks like a woman who was in there."

"When was this?"

Denise shrugged. "I don't recall. Perhaps two weeks ago. Perhaps a month."

"But you're not sure."

"It's a big campus, and I'm sorry to say I don't always pay attention to everything. It's one of my flaws. Apparently I've been in three different classes with the woman who plays Bianca, and I didn't recognize her."

"Okay," McVie said. "Fenway, you have anything else for Miss Delatasso?"

Fenway shook her head and had a thought.

"Oh—sorry. Just one more thing. Do you own a Kendra Quinlan top?"

Denise laughed. "One of those famous two-thousand-dollar blouses with that gaudy logo on all the buttons? Heavens, no. I'm afraid you've identified the wrong student actor."

Fenway cocked her head.

"By that I mean it isn't me who has the expensive clothing." Denise lowered her voice. "I know that Amanda has been pinching pennies to go to the theater tour in London, so I'm not sure what *she's* doing with such an expensive blouse. I assumed she purchased it at Goodwill, or perhaps she has a rich uncle who prefers buying her expensive clothes for her birthday rather than a theater trip. Who knows? If you want my opinion, she looks hideous in it—as if she's about to purchase a minivan and join the Junior League. I'm sure she only wears it because she wants people to think she has more money than she does."

"Have you seen her wear it lately?"

Denise expertly swept up the last few grains of rice on her chopsticks. "Perhaps earlier this week. Monday or Tuesday. She doesn't wear it often."

Fenway nodded. "Great, Denise. Thanks. Oh—it's opening night tonight, isn't it?"

"It certainly is."

"Well, break a leg."

Denise smiled, wiping her hands on her napkin. "I appreciate the sentiment, though I can't say I hold much stock in superstition. But thank you." As Denise gathered her books and walked off with her tray, McVie looked at the line at Ernesto's, which had shortened considerably. "What do you think?"

"I think it's time for us to find out where Xavier is." Fenway's stomach growled. "And to order a super burrito."

CHAPTER TWENTY

McVie and Fenway stood in line at Ernesto's, but didn't see Xavier. The student center started to empty, and no one stood behind them. They patiently waited while the young man in front of them— dressed in board shorts and flip-flops even on this chilly November day —dithered between *bistec* and *pollo asado* for far too long, and then asked for an exhaustive list of ingredients inside the burrito before finally finishing his order and stepping to the side.

The two of them ordered super burritos with *horchata* to drink.

"I don't see Xavier," Fenway whispered to McVie as they stood off to the side, waiting for their food.

"I don't, either. I thought maybe he'd be in the kitchen."

After a few minutes, the chef placed two super burritos, wrapped in foil, onto a tray and dinged a bell. The cashier grabbed it and placed it on the counter, then ladled out *horchata* into two paper cups. He looked up at McVie. "It's ready, sir."

"Thanks," McVie said. "Say, is Xavier around?"

The cashier shook his head. "He's not scheduled today. He'll be in on Saturday. The morning shift."

McVie nodded, picked up the tray, and walked over to the nearest open table, about thirty feet from the front counter. Fenway followed close behind.

Fenway spoke to McVie in a low voice. "Makes sense. He's the lead in the play—probably want to focus on his performance. So now what?"

"Now we eat our burritos," McVie whispered. "We've got some time before Cygnus's office hours start."

Fenway sighed, a long, slow exhale.

"Oh, please," McVie said. "I know you've been wanting a burrito for hours. Be happy and take it."

"I need some salsa." Fenway scooted to the side and started to get up.

"Get me some too."

She looked at McVie out of the corner of her eye.

"Please."

Fenway nodded and walked up to the salsa bar, spooning two scoops of habañero and a single scoop of mild verde salsa into squat clear plastic containers, snapped the tops on, turned around—and almost smacked into Dr. Pruitt.

"Miss Stevenson!" he said, taking a step back and putting a hand up to his chest, probably to check for any spilled salsa on his suit or dress shirt.

"Sorry!" Fenway said. "I was just grabbing some lunch before we, uh, follow up on some leads."

"Leads?" Dr. Pruitt said. "Getting closer to finding out what happened to poor Jessica?"

The wheels spun in Fenway's head. "Dr. Pruitt, maybe you can help us."

"Oh, of course." But his face betrayed his lack of enthusiasm.

Fenway went over to the table, putting the salsa down, and pulled her phone out of her purse.

McVie looked up, chewing a big bite of burrito, but didn't say anything.

"We met a person of interest," she said to Dr. Pruitt, tapping the photo app on her phone, "and we've got witnesses who put her with Jessica Marquez last week." She double-tapped on the photo of Rose Morgan and her picture filled the screen. "Here you go," she said, holding the phone up so he could see the picture. She stared at his face while he saw the picture.

"Oh," Dr. Pruitt said, his eyes flitting across the phone screen. He hesitated and then finally spoke. "No," he said, sounding puzzled. "I, uh, wanted to say that she looked familiar, but I don't know, a lot of the students here look so alike."

Fenway almost said something. She noticed—and Xavier had pointed out—how the Nidever students lacked diversity. She looked around the student union. Had Xavier been working, he would have been one of maybe four or five black students in the whole building, and just like Xavier, Rose Morgan would have stood out like a sore thumb. "Take a closer look, Dr. Pruitt. She looks young, but she's actually not a student."

"Oh, that's surprising. She looks like a senior, or maybe a grad student."

"Nope, she's twenty-eight. She's got several years of experience as an accountant. Maybe you know her in a professional capacity? Maybe she interviewed for a position in the finance department?"

Dr. Pruitt laughed. "You know, that must be it. I must have seen her in the building when she was interviewing."

"That's great," McVie said, standing up, his burrito half finished in the foil. "I appreciate the HR department being so forthcoming with Ms. Marquez's records, although the records were sadly incomplete—we didn't even find a résumé or a filled-out job application. Do you think we can stop by and see if there are any records of this woman?"

Dr. Pruitt blanched. "I honestly don't even know if we'd keep records of anything like that."

"That's okay," McVie said. "I can ask your HR director."

"Um... sure," Dr. Pruitt said. "I'll make sure that the director knows to make any files available to you. Can't make any promises, though."

He coughed. "I don't think we keep records on people who just interview if they don't get the job."

"Yes, you said that," Fenway replied, nodding.

"Oh—did I? Well, it's true. We may have had some trouble in the past of records getting into the wrong hands—"

"The wrong hands? You mean someone stole the records?"

"Uh—no, not that," Dr. Pruitt stammered. "I mean, we suspected —that is, it turned out—oh, it doesn't matter."

"What did you suspect?"

"No, no, forget it." A trickle of sweat ran down Dr. Pruitt's forehead. "I'm just thinking out loud. Of course, I'd be happy to get you whatever we have on Miss Morgan."

"We'd appreciate it," McVie said.

"Hang on," Fenway said.

Both Dr. Pruitt and the sheriff looked at her.

"We didn't mention her name." Fenway looked in Dr. Pruitt's eyes. "We just said she talked with Jessica Marquez last week."

All the color drained out of Pruitt's face. "No, no," he said, "I'm sure you mentioned it."

"She didn't," McVie said.

"So, Dr. Pruitt," Fenway continued, "you *do* know who she is. You just don't want *us* to know that you are familiar with the accountant for Central Auto Body." She set her jaw. "And that makes me think you have something to hide."

"Now, just wait." Dr. Pruitt held up his hands in front of him. "I don't want to give you the wrong idea."

McVie's jaw clenched. "You've already given us the wrong idea by lying to us, Dr. Pruitt." He took a step forward. "We've been nothing but accommodating. You didn't want classes on the second floor interrupted the day before yesterday, so I brought an extra crime scene tech on the scene so we could finish faster. You didn't want us to disrupt the rehearsal schedule that Professor Cygnus put in place, so we've worked around it—which, if I can be frank, might have jeopardized the investigation."

"I appreciate it," Dr. Pruitt mumbled.

"I don't think you do," McVie said. "I think you've taken advantage of your political clout to get yourself some distance from whatever it is you're trying to hide."

"Maybe he's trying to get rid of evidence, Sheriff," Fenway suggested. "I wonder if a judge will think there's enough here to approve a forensic accountant going through Nidever's—"

"Now, there's no need for that!" Dr. Pruitt drew himself up to his full height, although his eyes still looked up at Fenway. "If you want to get attorneys involved, sure, keep talking about forensic accountants."

McVie took another step forward. "Forensic accountants? Do you think that's all we'll do? You're already in danger of an obstruction charge, and now we've got a person of interest who might connect Jessica Marquez's death to some other recent murders in this town. This would be a good time to start talking."

Dr. Pruitt's mouth opened and closed several times. Finally, he leaned forward and lowered his voice. "Let me take care of a couple of things, and then we can speak in my office. Meet me there in forty-five minutes."

He spun on his heel and left Fenway and McVie standing there in disbelief.

"What do you think?" Fenway asked McVie.

"I think Dr. Pruitt's got a lot of explaining to do."

"Do you think he killed Jessica and he's trying to escape?"

McVie shook his head. "No. I don't think he killed Jessica, but I think he knows more than he's letting on about the money laundering."

"Do you think he went back to his office to get rid of some evidence?"

McVie thought for a moment. "I think what he has to say to us is more valuable than whatever evidence he thinks he can get rid of. If he *does* get rid of evidence—especially if it's on his computer—we can find it in no time. If we follow him over there, he'll definitely clam up."

"Are you sure we shouldn't follow him to his office?"

"No—especially since I've already made some bad judgment calls in the last couple of days. But it's my best guess."

Fenway nodded. "Then before we go over there, I think we should talk to the students—and to Professor Cygnus—again."

McVie looked at his watch. "Forty-five minutes. That'll be two o'clock. We've got enough time to follow up with Amanda Kohl."

"Isn't she working in The Guild office today?"

McVie shook his head. "The office is officially closed until further notice. Still a crime scene."

"Shall we go to her dorm?"

"Yep. Plus we can look for that Kendra Quinlan blouse. Even if it's not missing a button, maybe I can see where she bought it. You never know—perhaps I can save myself some money on Megan's Christmas gift."

"This is turning into quite the adventure."

McVie elbowed Fenway and grinned. "And you thought having lunch in the student center would be a waste of time."

CHAPTER TWENTY-ONE

THE TWO OF THEM TREKKED ACROSS CAMPUS WITH MCVIE consulting the map on his phone, until they arrived at the San Sebastian Residence Hall. Just as they came upon the walkway, Fenway's phone dinged. It was a message from Dez.

"Shit," Fenway said.

"What?"

"Rose Morgan. Her lawyer got there and insisted they leave. No information, no discussion."

McVie's phone dinged next. He glanced at it and grimaced. "At least Dez keeps us both in the know."

They walked into the residence hall, and a rosy-cheeked young blond woman at the front desk greeted them brightly.

"Hi, officer! Welcome to San Sebastian Hall. Can I help you with something?"

"Good afternoon," McVie said. "I'm Sheriff Craig McVie and this is Coroner Stevenson."

"Coroner?" the woman said, her smile faltering.

"We're here to talk with Amanda Kohl. I understand her room is in this residence hall."

"It sure is," she said. "I can call up and have her come down."

"No need." McVie held his hands up. "We'd prefer to go up ourselves."

"Um, hang on." The woman picked up the phone and turned halfway in her chair, lowering her voice. Fenway couldn't make out more than a word or two—*sheriff, privacy, student,* and *rights.* After a couple of minutes, she hung up and turned to them, her smile back on her face.

"Someone will be right with you to take you up."

"We can find it ourselves," McVie said.

"Our elevators need card keys to work," the woman said. "I'm sure you understand."

McVie smiled.

A minute later, an equally rosy-cheeked young man appeared. His face bore the remnants of acne on his pallid skin, but he radiated enthusiasm. He strode toward them with his hand out. "I'm Toby, one of the resident advisors here at San Seb. I hear you'd like me to take you to a resident's room?"

"Amanda Kohl," McVie said, his voice pleasant enough, although Fenway detected frustration a layer underneath. In most people the equivalent would have been gritted teeth.

After an elevator ride to the sixth floor, they stood in front of a door. *618* was prominently affixed about five feet up, and the sign on the wall, next to the door at doorknob-height, said KOHL / JENSEN.

"Well, Sheriff, here it is," Toby said. "Shall I leave you to it?"

"Thanks, Toby," McVie said, taking a step forward and knocking loudly on the door.

Toby hustled down the hall and went around the corner before the door opened.

Amanda Kohl's face appeared in the opening between the door and the jamb. "Oh—hello." She was mostly in shadow, but she had on a crisp white-collared oxford shirt over black leggings. Her feet were bare.

"Hi, Amanda," Fenway said, smiling as genuinely as she could. "I hate to bother you, but we have to get this investigation moving, and those students who were closest to Jessica Marquez are next. I was hoping we could continue our conversation from yesterday morning."

"Uh... sure, I guess."

"Mind if we come in?"

Amanda took a step back and looked around the small dorm room. "I don't know—this is my roommate's stuff too...."

"We just want to have a private conversation," Fenway said, taking a step forward.

Amanda let go of the door and took a backward step into the dorm room. "It's kind of a mess. With opening night and all."

Fenway pushed the door open. A few clothes lay on the floor, and one of the beds wasn't made, but the room was otherwise tidy and clean. Even the nightstand was organized, with a vintage-style alarm clock, a small art deco lamp, and a Magic 8 Ball artfully arranged on it. Fenway looked at the closet at the foot of the unmade bed; its door was pulled shut.

"We figured you'd be available since you were scheduled to work," McVie said, following Fenway inside.

Amanda laughed nervously. "I suppose that makes sense."

Fenway nodded. "I wondered how you got along with Jessica."

"What do you mean?"

"Well, you worked for her, didn't you? What kind of boss was she?"

"Fine, I guess. She gave me hours, which was great, since I was saving up to go on that theater trip. Of course, she slept with my boyfriend, too, which wasn't great."

"But you didn't know until yesterday?"

"No." Amanda's shoulders slumped. "I get it. He and I weren't exclusive. I just—I guess I thought we were heading that way."

Fenway nodded sympathetically. "I still have to ask about what kind of boss she was, though. Was she demanding? Was she friendly?"

Amanda shrugged. "She wasn't that demanding. It's not like we were working on world hunger or anything. I'd open the mail, I'd update the website, I'd keep track of who signed up for the trips and whether they'd paid or not."

"That pretty much sounds like accounting work."

"I guess some of it was. Jessica oversaw the books, too, I think."

"You think? What did she do for The Guild?"

Amanda looked confused. "What do you mean?"

"Well, if she had the students do the majority of the work for her, what did she do all day?"

Amanda sat on the unmade bed and grabbed the Magic 8 Ball off the nightstand. "I don't know. I assume she had to do some fundraising, or maybe coordinate the actors visiting the groups in London. We had Carter Henson do a version of *Christmas in St. Louis* last year; I know she did a lot to coordinate the venue, the flights to get Mr. Henson here from New York, stuff like that." Amanda thought for a moment, turning the Magic 8 Ball over in her hands. "Although I think a student picked him up from the airport."

Fenway nodded and took a breath. "Are you sure you didn't know about Jessica and Xavier? Other students knew."

Amanda took a sharp breath. "I didn't know for sure. I didn't—I didn't want to believe it."

"Did you ever talk to Jessica about her sleeping with Xavier?"

Amanda bowed her head again.

"If I open that closet door, Amanda, will I find a Kendra Quinlan blouse with a button missing?"

Amanda looked up, surprised. "I, uh…"

McVie stood up and pulled the closet open.

"Hey!" Amanda shouted. "You need a warrant to do that!"

McVie shook his head. "Not in a university-owned dormitory. You signed a bunch of paperwork when you agreed to live here."

Amanda's eyes turned dark, but she said nothing more.

"Oh," McVie said, turning to the closet, "my daughter wanted this exact blouse." He pulled out a black-and-white tulip-sleeved blouse with a large collar and four large buttons with the KQ logo down the front. "But I seem to remember there were *five* buttons on it."

Fenway piped up. "That fifth button ended up in the second-floor hallway, outside of the stairwell where Jessica's body was found, Amanda."

"I didn't kill her."

Fenway saw something black and rectangular on the top shelf of the closet, above the hanging rod, and walked over to the open closet. She looked more closely; it seemed to be the same type of crystal award that had been on display in The Guild's office.

"How did you lose the button?" Fenway said, turning around and looking directly in Amanda's eyes.

Amanda opened her mouth and closed it again.

"Do we need to take you down to the station?"

"No," Amanda said. "It was Tuesday night. I found a text on Xavier's phone from Jessica the night before. I worked that day, and right when I left, I told Jessica to stop seeing him."

"And what did she say?"

"She—uh—she laughed at me. She said I was just a little girl and Xavier wanted to be with a real woman." Amanda's voice became small. "She said she was teaching him lots of adult things, and I should —uh—just enjoy the things he was learning."

"What did you do?"

"I threatened to tell the administration, and then I stormed out."

"And you lost the button in the office?"

"I don't know, but it was probably in the hall. Jessica ran after me and grabbed me—hard. She told me to think about what I was doing, and think about what I wanted. I thought she was threatening my trip to England!"

"Well," Fenway said, "it sounds like you could have lost the button then. How hard did she grab you?"

"So hard she left bruises on my arm."

"Let me see."

Amanda unbuttoned two buttons on the oxford shirt—she had a tank top underneath—and slid the shoulder of the shirt down to her elbow. Fenway took a step closer and saw two finger-shaped bruises on the front of her bicep.

"That's from Jessica?"

"Yes."

"Did you fight back?"

"No."

Fenway paused. "Are you sure?"

Amanda raised her chin and stared at Fenway. "Sure I'm sure. I got the hell out of there. I didn't even know if I still had a job."

Fenway stepped in front of the closet and looked up. "Amanda, what's that on your top shelf?"

"The top shelf?" Amanda looked at the open closet and her eyes widened. "Oh, I don't—"

"You don't what?"

Amanda bit her lip. "It's an acting award I won in high school. I thought I had put it somewhere else, that's all."

"Is that from the Western States Theater Association?"

"You mean the West Coast Theater Educators?"

"Yeah, sorry," said Fenway.

"Yes. I won it last year. Professor Cygnus won best director for *Merchant* at the same ceremony. That's how I decided on Nidever. He called me a couple of days after I won and told me I'd be perfect for The Guild, and he was willing to make an exception for me."

"An exception?"

"I don't know if you noticed, but I'm a freshman. Everyone else is an upperclassman. He never let underclassmen be in his plays. He got me a special waiver for this—it's a design-your-own-major."

"They let you design your own major at Nidever?"

"They do."

"What's your major called?"

"Shakespeare Performance."

"What'll you do with a major like that?"

Amanda set her jaw. "Hopefully become artistic director of the RSC."

"By RSC, you mean *the* Royal Shakespeare Company? The one in London?"

"Um, the one in Stratford-upon-Avon, you mean. Yes."

Fenway turned around to face Amanda. "They've never had an American artistic director, have they?"

"They haven't had a *female* artistic director, either, but that's what I want to do."

"And you won this West Coast award last year."

"Right."

Fenway looked around the room. "Why don't you have it displayed somewhere? On your shelf over there? Maybe even in The Guild office?"

"I. uh...."

"Well?"

"I don't have an answer for that. To be honest, I could have sworn I brought it to work to put in The Guild office next to the other Bardies."

Fenway searched Amanda's face for signs of dishonesty, but found nothing. "Is it all in one piece?"

"Is what all in one piece?" Amanda asked.

"The award."

"What do you mean? Like, is it broken?"

"Yes."

Amanda motioned to the top shelf. "Take a look if you want." She sighed. "I was probably stupid to bring it to school, but I'm proud of it."

Fenway snapped on a glove and took two large evidence bags from her purse.

"What are you doing?"

"I'll bag the award and the blouse and take them in as evidence."

Amanda's jaw dropped open. "Evidence? Evidence for what?"

Fenway reached up and pulled the award off the top shelf. "For our investigation."

"You can't just take that award. It's mine!" She set her jaw.

"The dorm room isn't your property," McVie said, "it's the university's. We can search your room and take anything as evidence."

Fenway turned the award over in her hands. It was clean. The top edge of the award had some minor zigs and zags, but she couldn't tell if there was a sliver of crystal missing or not. She suspected that this wasn't the murder weapon, but if there were any microscopic traces of Jessica's blood on the award, the lab would find it.

"I'll get a lawyer," Amanda seethed, as Fenway placed the award in the bag then pulled the hanger with the Kendra Quinlan blouse off the rod and put it in the other bag.

"Be my guest," McVie said. "I'll provide him the chain of custody records."

"Her," Amanda said.

"Her," McVie said. "Whoever. This is by the book."

"We'll see," Amanda said.

"We'll run some tests," Fenway said, "and if we don't find evidence of a crime on the award or the blouse, we'll get them back to you as soon as we can."

"I can't believe this," Amanda said.

"Use it for method acting," McVie said. "When you have to get angry on stage, just think of Coroner Stevenson pulling your award down from the shelf."

Fenway winced. Amanda's mouth tightened as she narrowed her eyes at McVie. "I have an alibi."

"Xavier is your alibi," McVie said, "and he has a reason to lie for you. He's already lied to us."

"Why me and not him?"

"Does he have a Kendra Quinlan blouse?" said McVie. "And a heavy hunk of crystal?" he added, taking the bagged award from Fenway and holding it up.

Amanda was silent, staring right into McVie's eyes. She broke from the stare and looked out the window.

"Sorry to inconvenience you," Fenway said. "Break a leg tonight." She shut the closet door. "And, you know, don't leave the area."

McVie secured the evidence in a lockbox in the back of his SUV, and they walked to the administration building. Fenway saw McVie's shoulders tighten and his jaw clench as they got closer to the building.

"Everything okay?" Fenway asked.

"I shouldn't have let him have that forty-five minutes," McVie said. "He's probably shredding documents as we speak."

"We'll see. Nothing we can do about it now."

They arrived in front of Dr. Pruitt's office five minutes after two o'clock.

"Hi, Belinda," Fenway said to the secretary. "Is he ready for us?"

Belinda gestured to a set of resin-and-steel chairs by the door.

"Dr. Pruitt is finishing up a call," she said, glancing up from her typing. "He'll be with the two of you in a moment."

McVie folded his arms and stared at Pruitt's closed office door. "He's the one who asked us to meet him."

Fenway looked at McVie; it was uncharacteristic for him to lose his cool, especially before an interview. "Maybe we should do this another time," Fenway said, putting her hand on McVie's arm.

"I'm sick of being jerked around by these entitled pricks," McVie replied. "They think their money and the word *president* or *chief* on their business card makes it okay to get around the rules."

"Keep your voice down."

McVie ignored her. "They think they don't have to tell the police the truth. They think they can bend the rules and we'll look the other way. And then when we *do* go the extra mile to gain some goodwill, they screw us over."

Fenway looked at Craig, appalled. "Wow—I didn't expect that coming from you."

"What are they going to do, fire me?" McVie spat. "This Boy Scout is sick of it, Fenway. Dr. Pruitt better start giving us some damn answers, or I'll drag him out of here in cuffs." The lines of his brow were creased; his mouth was turned down at the corners; his jaw was clenched. Fenway's gaze dropped to his hands; he made a fist, released it, made a fist again.

"Listen," she said, a steely tone in her voice, "you need to calm down, Craig. I don't know if you're second-guessing yourself, agreeing to meet here instead of walking back with him, but it won't help if you go in there guns blazing. You won't get Dr. Pruitt to answer you if—"

McVie's head snapped around to look at Fenway. "He doesn't respond to us being nice, Fenway. We need to go in there mad as hell and put the hammer to him."

Fenway took a step back. "Okay, Craig. You've been doing this a lot longer than I have."

"Damn right," McVie said under his breath.

Fenway walked over to a table spread with magazines and looked through them. They were all print issues of *The Blue Dolphin*, the Nidever alumni magazine. Fenway spied a familiar face on the cover of one.

"Cynthia Schimmelhorn," she mumbled to herself, taking a seat. The statuesque woman she had met at the Nidever-hosted political dinner a few days before. In a cashmere sweater against a backdrop of trees, with the new Nidever engineering building slightly out of focus in the background, Schimmelhorn looked as elegant as she had in an evening gown. Fenway leafed through the magazine until she found the article on page 26. "Titan of Oil," read the title.

The article was little more than a puff piece, but Fenway read it with interest. It talked about her roots growing up with four brothers in a rich suburb of Los Angeles, being the only female student in the petroleum engineering major at Nidever University, but graduating at the top of her class in three years, then getting her MBA from Stanford when she was barely old enough to drink.

The article touched on her personal life, discussing her brief marriage to an oil executive, the birth of her daughter, Nerissa, the tough balance of 'having it all'—raising her child while shuttling back and forth to South America, having to prove herself as a new Petrogrande executive, and then a single line of text referencing Nerissa's suicide. Fenway heard a gasp and realized it was hers.

"What?" McVie said.

"I'm reading this bio on Cynthia Schimmelhorn. I didn't know her daughter committed suicide."

McVie's eyes widened a bit. "Oh. I didn't know that either."

"That would explain her walking away when we brought up her daughter at the candidates' dinner. Ugh." Fenway shook her head. "Open mouth, insert foot."

Belinda cleared her throat. "Sheriff? Dr. Pruitt is ready to see you now." She stood and opened the door behind her.

Fenway followed the sheriff into Dr. Pruitt's office. The university president sat behind the large mahogany desk, thoughtfully resting his chin in his hand, his two large bookcases towering imposingly behind him.

Fenway looked at the bookcase on the left, noticing the knick-knacks scattered among the leather-bound tomes: a crystal jaguar, about eight inches tall, next to *Gulliver's Travels* and *The Wealth of Nations*. On a lower shelf, a signed baseball on a black granite stand stood beside several business hardbacks whose covers looked more worn and used, including *Blue Ocean Strategy* and *Order Without Design*.

"I don't make this decision lightly," Dr. Pruitt began, indicating the two straight-backed chairs in front of his desk. As McVie took the chair on the left and Fenway settled into the one on the right, she could sense a speech about to rev up in Dr. Pruitt's voice and immediately detached. Her eyes lost focus for a moment, and then she locked in on the other bookshelf behind Dr. Pruitt. She remembered the intriguing wire sculpture of the 1890s-style man-on-a-bicycle, as well as the photo of Dr. Pruitt with his wife. Next to it, a tiny beige-and-orange ceramic pot with a succulent—

Oh no.

It hadn't been there two days before. And Fenway would have recognized that succulent right away. She sat up perfectly straight, her mind racing.

"...and I know you think I haven't been completely forthcoming," Dr. Pruitt was saying. "So I've decided to—"

Fenway stood up.

"Drop your act, Pruitt," she shouted. "Stop stalling. You'll give us access to Cygnus now, or we'll get a subpoena."

"Fenway—" McVie started.

Fenway's head snapped around to look at McVie as her finger flew in front of her mouth to shush him. Fenway looked at Dr. Pruitt, too, tapping her vertical finger against her lips a few times. He looked thoroughly confused.

"You've given us one too many excuses on how *important* the great professor is, to your program, to your school. I'll tell you something, Pruitt, your diploma isn't worth shit when you're in jail fighting an obstruction charge."

"I don't know what you—"

"Save it for the judge," Fenway said. "Take us to Cygnus right now."

Fenway walked around the rear of the desk.

"Hey," Dr. Pruitt said, "what do you think you're doing?"

"I'd like to know that myself," said McVie.

She stopped at the bookshelf and pointed at the succulent in the small ceramic pot. McVie's eyes grew wide, then he too stood up and nodded.

"Yep," he said. "You're right. Time to go, Dr. Pruitt. It's an interview with Professor Cygnus, or else."

"I don't have to go—"

Fenway grabbed Dr. Pruitt's elbow. His head spun to look at Fenway as she put her finger to her lips again.

"Trust us," Fenway whispered.

McVie stepped to the office door and opened it.

Dr. Pruitt, still with a skeptical look in his eyes, stood uncertainly, but walked out the door, followed closely by Fenway. The three of them stood in the foyer.

"Dr. Pruitt?" Belinda asked. "Is everything all right?"

"Certainly, certainly," Dr. Pruitt said. "I'm taking our guests over to the DiFazio Theater."

"You have your three o'clock."

"I'll be back in plenty of time," Dr. Pruitt replied. To Fenway, he said under his breath, "You better have a good explanation for this."

They walked out of the main door into the chilly afternoon. The sun had given up shining through the clouds and the air was heavy and wet. Fenway pulled out her phone, opened a web browser, and went to the Desert Sands Spy Gear web site. They walked about fifty feet away from the building, through a grassy area, finally stopping next to a brick planter box.

"Okay," Dr. Pruitt said. "Do you want to tell me what this is about?"

"Someone bugged your office," Fenway said. She held up her phone and scrolled past an ad for night vision goggles—now with improved body heat sensors—and a pop-up for diversion safes, with a book, a hairbrush, and a soda can. The ceramic pot was the third listing on the page. She turned the screen to Dr. Pruitt. "This is the same beige-and-orange ceramic pot that's in your office. You see how it's really a hidden microphone and a transmitter?"

Dr. Pruitt swallowed hard.

"We found one just like it in the office of the psychologist who was murdered a few days ago."

Dr. Pruitt's face went ashen.

"After Dr. Tassajera was murdered—beaten to death with a golf club, if you must know—we took a look at his financial records," Fenway continued. "You'll never guess what we found."

Dr. Pruitt was quiet.

"We found he was billing clients who didn't exist, and we also found he was making suspicious payments to an organization based in the Cayman Islands."

Dr. Pruitt opened his mouth but no words came out.

"I wonder what we'd find in your bank accounts," Fenway mused.

"Probably not his *personal* accounts," McVie put in. "Dr. Tassajera—

in fact, everyone who we've found murdered so far—has had those strange payments from their *business* accounts."

"That's right," Fenway said, nodding. "I wonder if you've used the university's accounts for that activity. Maybe you've been charging tuition for students who don't exist."

"No," Dr. Pruitt said, "you won't find any anomalies in the university's finances."

Fenway looked closely at Dr. Pruitt's face. "It's not the university's finances, then." She peered into his eyes and noticed a bead of sweat run from his temple. "But it's *something* related to the university. What would that be?"

"Maybe a scholarship fund," McVie suggested.

"Right." Fenway nodded. "Maybe there are payments made to a bogus scholarship fund. Maybe with a balance of around twenty-seven million dollars."

Dr. Pruitt gasped.

So it *was* the scholarship fund.

"You know what would be perfect for this type of money laundering?" said McVie.

"I'm racking my brain," Fenway said, still looking in Dr. Pruitt's face.

"An organization based on campus that functions largely without oversight. That takes in large sums of money in donations, and has to pay large sums of money for travel expenses, lectures, or perhaps to consulting companies for script consulting, or business advice."

"I like the way you think," said Fenway, a smile spreading across her face as she looked in Dr. Pruitt's eyes.

"You don't have any proof," said Dr. Pruitt. "You certainly don't have the right to look in Nidever's books. My lawyers are confident about that."

"We wouldn't be looking in the right place anyway, would we?" said Fenway. "Fighting that subpoena is just a ruse to make us think you have something to hide in there, but that's not where the financial anomalies are at all, are they?"

Dr. Pruitt swallowed.

"But what I don't get is why they're bugging *your* office," said Fenway. "You're not in charge of those payments. Those payments are for The Guild."

"Unless there *is* a line of oversight," said McVie.

Fenway nodded. "Maybe the university has put you in charge of making sure everything with The Guild's financials is on the up-and-up." She crossed her arms. "But that didn't sit well with whoever's in charge, did it? You must have gotten a communication. A phone call. A letter. Something."

"You know, Dr. Pruitt," McVie said, "if you've said anything in your office in the last couple of days that you wouldn't want certain people to hear, we might be the only people who can protect you."

Dr. Pruitt was quiet.

McVie, standing next to him, stroked his chin absently. "Am I getting warm? Did they bribe you? Did you think it was something you could get out of after a month or two?" He looked into Pruitt's face. "Or maybe you're embezzling from the scholarship fund." McVie said, his voice so soft next to Dr. Pruitt that Fenway could barely hear him. "They'd be angry with you if you did that, wouldn't they?"

Dr. Pruitt looked down.

"Ah. Maybe that's it. What happened, Dr. Pruitt? Credit card debt? Gambling problem?"

Dr. Pruitt shook his head quickly from side to side, as if readying himself before a race.

"And Jessica Marquez found out about it, didn't she?"

Pruitt looked up defiantly at McVie.

"I refuse to answer on the grounds that I may incriminate myself," he said.

CHAPTER TWENTY-TWO

McVie and Fenway prodded Dr. Pruitt for answers for over fifteen minutes, but by three o'clock, they knew they weren't getting anywhere. They also had nothing to arrest Dr. Pruitt for—as much as they thought he had embezzled the scholarship funds, they had innuendo, but no proof. Fenway and McVie continued to throw out hypotheticals, but each theory seemed to be further away from the truth, and Dr. Pruitt was becoming less and less responsive. Finally, they let him return to his office, a few minutes late for his appointment.

"Well, that was frustrating," Fenway said.

"I can feel them circling the wagons," McVie said. "There's nothing we can do with Dr. Pruitt right now, though, and he'll make our lives more difficult until we figure out why he won't answer our questions."

"I think you were spot on with your embezzlement theory," Fenway said. "His body language, just about everything—he physically reacted when you said *embezzlement*." She thought for a moment. "Where do you think the money could have gone?"

"I don't know, but we'll have to look at The Guild's financial records, especially if there's a scholarship fund. I'll get a warrant written up just for that—keeping the Nidever's main records out of it."

"With Jessica Marquez and Rose Morgan sniffing around both Central Auto Body and The Guild, it certainly would seem like that's the right thing to do."

"Let's talk to Professor Cygnus before they start getting ready for opening night," he said. "Maybe he can tell us if there's a scholarship fund. If not, maybe we can talk to other students who worked in the office."

"After the third degree we gave Amanda and Xavier, I'm not sure how helpful the other students will be."

"There's only one way to find out," said McVie.

They rushed over to the DiFazio Theater. Fenway sensed the frenetic energy of opening night, even in front of the building. The box office windows were lit and two student-age young women in black milled around behind the glass.

"What time do the students start prep for the play?" asked McVie.

"No idea," said Fenway. "You're the one with the schedule."

"I think it's four thirty," McVie said. "We've got plenty of time."

Fenway pulled on the theater door.

"Locked," she said.

"Let's see if we can go in the back way."

The side door that led into the stairwell also led to the side lobby of the theater. McVie went in first, and he turned left down the hallway into the greenroom. Students walked quickly through, some in a period shirt or blouse but still in athletic shoes, some in T-shirts.

"I didn't think students would already be here," Fenway muttered.

"Anyone seen Professor Cygnus?" McVie's voice carried down the hallway.

One of the students pointed, and Fenway and McVie found themselves in another hallway, where they passed the prop table and a rack full of costumes.

Fenway passed McVie in the hall and turned right toward the stage —and ran right into Virgil Cygnus. She heard herself squeak.

"Sorry," she said. "But we wanted—"

"You can't be in here." Cygnus's voice boomed down the hallway.

"We're preparing for opening night." Cygnus, clearly irritated, straightened up as McVie came around the corner. "Ah, Sheriff. Listen, as I've told both you and your officer here—"

"Coroner," McVie corrected.

Cygnus smiled, a tired, patronizing smile. "She got her ten minutes with me. And now we're done." He folded his arms. "Let me be clear. I don't want you making excuses to talk to me. I don't want you bringing up my parking tickets from twenty years ago, or my daughter stealing office supplies from her job, or poor Jessica's senior prom escapades because you're trying to cover all the bases."

Fenway looked at McVie, whose gaze was hardening.

"I don't share your priorities, Professor," McVie said. "If the people of this county allowed me to place your precious play above solving a murder, I'd be hearing about it for *months*."

"Listen, you *fool*, I see right through your little gambit. You mean to catch me off-guard, to have me so worried about getting back to my play that I'll say I've done something I haven't, or that I know something I don't. I've told you I wasn't around that evening. I told you I know nothing of The Guild's finances. And I've told you, now, in so many words, to get out of my sight."

"I can get a material witness warrant and bring you in," McVie said, "and it might even be in the middle of tonight's play."

"The hell you will," Cygnus said. "My lawyer will be so far up your ass he'll serve a cease-and-desist to your esophagus."

"I thought Shakespeare wanted to kill all the lawyers," Fenway said.

Cygnus turned and bore his gaze into her. His jaw opened and closed, as though he knew he shouldn't respond but desperately wanted to. Finally he raised his voice. "Had you done any *serious* studying of the master, you'd know that he gave that line to a tyrant. Lawyers protect people like me *from* tyrants. Tyrants, I might add, are those in positions of power who threaten to disrupt people's livelihoods when they don't like the way things are going." He glared at McVie.

McVie exhaled. "Listen, professor, we got off on the wrong foot.

Now that we know where you were on Tuesday night, we have four, maybe five follow-up questions for you at most. It will take all of fifteen minutes. Surely you can spare—"

"Nothing but *Othello* for the next two weeks," Cygnus said, pushing past Fenway and McVie and rushing down the hall among the half-costumed students. "Talk to me after our closing show."

Fenway watched him disappear down the hallway. "The professor is hiding something. I bet he has information about that scholarship fund. We asked him about the *murder* and he said he didn't know anything about The Guild's *finances*. I never asked him about their finances. Did you?"

McVie nodded. "No. Good catch."

"Maybe he even knows why Pruitt isn't answering our questions."

McVie looked thoughtful. "But you think he knows a lot more than he's letting on? What's that saying? *Methinks he doth protest too much?* That's Shakespeare too, right?"

"Yep. The Scottish Play."

"The what?"

"The Scottish Play. We're inside a theater. We're not supposed to say the actual name of that play inside a theater. Old superstition. You call it 'The Scottish Play.'"

McVie rolled his eyes and grinned. "Your knowledge of Shakespeare is dangerously close to nerd territory, Stevenson."

"Yeah, well, when we started college, some of us didn't know what we wanted to be when we grew up." Fenway thought for a moment. "Didn't Professor Cygnus say his wife was his alibi?"

"Uh... you know, I don't think he did," McVie said. "If I remember right, he said he went home and tried not to wake his wife up."

Fenway paused. "But his wife has cancer, right?"

"Yeah, leukemia—at least, that's what Denise told us."

"Right, and a lot of times, cancer patients have messed-up sleep patterns."

"I've heard that."

I've lived it, Fenway thought. "So—if what Cygnus says is true, that he was home by eleven, and if he truly doesn't do anything but eat, sleep, and breathe *Othello* right now, maybe his wife woke up when he came home but she didn't say anything."

"Oh—yes, I see. Well, let's go confirm it."

"You're suggesting that we go talk to her?"

"I am."

"I don't know, Craig."

"What don't you know? A potential suspect gave us a statement. We're trying to confirm the timeline."

"But with his wife so sick? It feels a little like we're crossing a line, invading privacy."

"No way," McVie said. "This is a murder investigation."

Fenway nodded. She'd had little time with her mother between diagnosis and death. Professor Cygnus had been given a year—maybe even longer—yet was wrapped up in his work, not in spending time with his wife. "We won't compromise the investigation, will we? Cygnus already doesn't want to talk with us. You think he'll be any better if we interview his dying wife before contacting him?"

"Hey," McVie said, "we gave him a chance to talk without bothering her. As far as I'm concerned, this is his own fault." He clapped his hands together. "All right, let's get his address and get over there. Maybe his wife can shed some light on this case."

————

On the way to the car, McVie called the station to get the warrant application started for The Guild's finances, and then asked for the Cygnuses' home address from the professor's DMV records.

"That's crazy," McVie said after ending the call. "They live in your neighborhood. Just up Chumash Falls Way." His phone dinged. "That's the address—let's go." McVie started the engine and backed out of the parking space.

It didn't take long for them to get off the freeway onto Broadway, McVie's phone announcing the upcoming turns. In the gray light of the late afternoon, they passed the turn for Fenway's apartment and The Coffee Bean, and turned right two streets later, into a cozy neighborhood of single-family homes with two-car garages jutting at the front of the houses. McVie made two more turns and the phone dinged as its disembodied robot voice said, "You have arrived."

McVie parked on the street, and they walked up to the door. The porch light was on although the sun hadn't quite set.

Fenway reached out and rang the bell.

The door opened slowly to reveal a short white woman, a kerchief of lime green, aquamarine, and cerulean blue paisley wrapped around her head, her thin body swimming in a blue linen blouse and navy blue athletic pants.

"Can I help you, officer?" she said, looking at McVie in his uniform. Her cheeks were sallow, but her eyes were bright.

"Yes, ma'am," McVie said. "You're Judith Cygnus, Professor Virgil Cygnus's wife, correct?"

"Guilty as charged," said Judith.

"I'm Sheriff Craig McVie, and this is the county coroner, Fenway Stevenson."

"Fenway? Like the ballpark?"

"Yes, ma'am," Fenway said.

"We're just trying to piece together a timeline for Tuesday night," McVie continued. "Were you home then?"

"Is this about the woman who works with Virg? That's the night she was killed, wasn't it?"

McVie shifted his weight from foot to foot. "Yes, it is, ma'am."

"Virg isn't giving *me* as his alibi, is he?"

"We'd just like to know what your recollection of that night is."

"All right." She shivered. "Goodness, it's getting cold. It wasn't too bad today, especially when the sun was out for a bit. Oh, well. You might as well come in." She held the door wide.

"I don't want to disturb your dinner or anything, ma'am. I don't think this will take more than a couple of minutes."

Fenway suspected the woman might be starved for company, especially at this time of the year, with her moderately famous husband all but living at the theater.

"I'm not standing out here a minute longer than I have to," Judith said. "This rag on my head looks like a chimpanzee threw paint at a canvas, I know, I know. But it's warm, and I'm a lot more sensitive to the cold than I used to be."

McVie motioned for Fenway to enter first, and she was hit by a blast of hot air as soon as she stepped into the small entryway.

"Can I get you anything? Our daughter gave me one of those single-cup coffee pod dispensers for my birthday. I can get both of you a cup of coffee, if you like."

"No, thanks," Fenway said, "I'm fine."

"Good. It tastes like shit anyway." She sighed and walked into the living room, with a beige sofa and a royal blue recliner facing a small flat-screen television. She eased herself down on the recliner, then motioned them over to the sofa. Fenway sat on the sofa and immediately sank distressingly deep into the soft cushion.

"So," she said, as Fenway leaned back, trying in vain to get comfortable, "what is it you want to know? Where I was that night?"

Fenway glanced at McVie, perched on the edge of the sofa. He shrugged slightly.

"That's a good place to start," Fenway said.

Judith struggled a bit with the chair, but on the third try, she managed to push hard enough to get the back to recline and the footrest to spring forward. She took a long breath and exhaled loudly. "Don't ever get cancer," she said. "The bullshit you have to go through is obnoxious."

"I'll keep that in mind." Fenway leaned forward and gave Judith a weak smile.

"Okay," Judith said. "Tuesday night. I came home from the treatment center at about five-thirty."

"Did you drive yourself?"

"Oh no, after the treatments, I'm too tired to drive. Sadie drove me."

"Sadie?"

"My daughter. She lives over in San Miguelito, but she drives me to my appointments."

"Professor Cygnus doesn't?"

Judith smiled, though her eyes were sad. "I knew when I married Virg that he was in a tangled mess of a relationship with Billy the Bard. It's like being married to a superfan of a sports team." She raised her eyebrows at Fenway. "I suspect much like being married to your father. At least Virg didn't insist on naming our daughter *Hermia,* or *Lady Macbeth,* or something ridiculous."

Judith was ridiculing her, but Fenway laughed—a big, hearty laugh, which Fenway saw earned her a disbelieving stare from the older woman. "I like you," Fenway said. "You cut right through all the bullshit, don't you?"

Judith sniffed, a twinkle in her eye. "I suppose I do."

"I bet that is both incredibly infuriating and incredibly attractive to your husband."

Judith barked a laugh and then coughed. "It sounds like you do your fair share of cutting through the bullshit, too, Coroner."

"Anyway." Fenway smiled and tilted her head. "What time did Sadie leave?"

"She left right away. She wanted to get home to her kids."

Fenway nodded. "And what did you do?"

"Me? I made myself some vegetable soup for dinner. Wait... *made,* who am I kidding. I opened a can. If I'm eating by myself, I can't be bothered to expend effort on anything decent." She coughed lightly, but something caught and she gave several long, loud hacks before she stopped. "Sorry about that," she rasped. "Anyway, I put on the television when I was eating. I'm binge-watching one of those hospital dramas where everyone is sleeping with everyone else."

"And then what happened?"

"I went to bed. I think I dozed off in my chair, here, about when the head of surgery was being wooed by the hotshot med student." A mischievous smile flitted across her face. "That actor who plays the med student is sure easy on the eyes. If only I were four decades younger. And didn't have cancer."

"What time did you go to bed?"

"I know I put the hospital show on about six fifteen, maybe six thirty, and I got through about an episode and a half before I fell asleep. So that's what? Seven thirty, eight?"

Fenway nodded, although she was calculating a little earlier.

"But I don't know what time I woke up. The TV had a little marker that said, 'Are you still watching?' My first thought was, 'Screw you, Netflix,' but then, of course, I was happy it hadn't gone through the entire second season."

"Then you went to bed?"

"Yes."

"You weren't curious what time it was?"

"Honestly, I didn't think about it."

"You didn't think it was strange that Professor Cygnus wasn't home yet?"

Judith cocked her head. "What do you mean?"

"I mean, if it had been midnight and he hadn't come home, wouldn't that worry you?"

Judith scoffed. "You haven't been around the professor long, have you?"

Fenway tilted her head. "What do you mean?"

"I mean when that man is in the middle of directing one of his precious plays, nothing gets in the way of his 'singular vision,' as he calls it. Why, last year he was able to convince a wildlife refuge to lend him a live rhesus monkey."

Capuchin monkey, Fenway silently corrected.

"He eats, sleeps, lives, and breathes the play," Judith said. "He sleeps in his office during the play. He showers in the Nidever locker rooms. He can't be bothered coming home." She grimaced. "Truth is, it's like a six-week vacation for me. You can imagine the—let's see, how can I put this?—*intensity* he has sometimes. Not that it's always a bad thing, but sometimes I need a break, and when he's in the final month before the play opens, it's just the break I need."

"Even now?" The words were out of Fenway's mouth before she could stop them.

"You mean, because of the cancer treatments?" Judith crossed her arms. "Truth be told, he's the only one who treats me like I'm normal. Sure, for the first few weeks he was railing about how unfair it all was, but he got it out of his system. He doesn't keep harping on the cancer. He doesn't tiptoe around me like I'm fragile. Sometimes I hate him for not dropping everything and taking care of me, and sometimes I'm grateful."

"But as things progress—"

"Well, they haven't progressed enough for me to ask him to sacrifice his life's passion," Judith said. She stared hard at Fenway, daring her to judge the choices a devoted wife had made. Fenway looked down at the carpet.

"So," Fenway said, "you didn't expect him home. Not Tuesday night, and not for another two or three weeks."

"That's correct."

McVie said, "But he *did* come home Tuesday night?"

Judith turned to look at McVie and shook her head. "No, of course he didn't. He had rehearsal late, and he always wants to make some tweaks and changes, right up until the very last show on the very last day."

Fenway frowned. She thought she had remembered Cygnus saying he had gone home. She closed her eyes and tried to recall the conversation.

But she knew she wasn't remembering it correctly; she had thought Cygnus used his wife as an alibi, and McVie had been clear that he hadn't. "Maybe you were asleep when he came in, and maybe he left before you woke up."

Judith adamantly shook her head. "No. That night, as soon as I went to bed, I had a lot of trouble staying asleep. I dozed again, and when I woke up it was one in the morning. I was alone in bed. I got up to go to the bathroom—I thought I might have to vomit, but I didn't —and then I came back to bed and lay awake until about two thirty. I finally got up and went out to the living room here to keep watching that hospital show. And, of course, I had to find the place in the show where I'd fallen asleep, and then, after watching another, I don't know, ten or fifteen minutes, I fell asleep in the recliner again. When I woke up this time, it was four in the morning, and I went to the bathroom again before I went to bed. No sign of Virg." She took a breath with effort. "And yes, I suppose it's technically possible that he could have come in and gone out again, but that man is like a hurricane. He has no concept of picking up after himself. If he'd been here, I'd be able to trace his steps by the piles of crap all over the house."

Fenway smiled. "Okay. So he might not have come home."

"No," Judith said, "he most definitely did *not* come home that night."

Fenway glanced at McVie. He started to speak, then hesitated.

"What is it?" Judith said.

McVie leaned forward. "Do you have any idea why the professor would tell us that he went home that night?"

Judith's brow furrowed. "He said that?"

"He said he got home quietly and that you didn't wake up."

A look of confusion came over Judith's face. "I can't—no, I have no idea why he'd say that." She shook her head. "Listen, I know the medication, the chemo, all that messes with me. My attention span, my sleep cycles. I'm not always all there. But Tuesday night, I know Virg didn't come home."

"Okay," McVie said.

Fenway thought for a minute. Why would Professor Cygnus lie about such an easily disproved story, especially one that didn't help him out? "Do you know if there's a university rule against sleeping on campus?"

"If there is, I'm sure they've made an exception for Virg," Judith said. "Virg put Nidever on the map, in the eighties when they were a piddly little school known for not giving real grades and being too expensive." She sniffed. "It used to be a college where rich parents sent their underachieving children when they couldn't bribe their way into an Ivy."

"There are quite a few famous, successful people who are Nidever alumni," McVie said.

"Just because they didn't get into Yale doesn't mean their parents weren't still well-connected," Judith said. "I remember one little obnoxious student of Virg's. This would have been in the early eighties, just when he was getting started with The Guild."

"The Guild goes back that far?" asked Fenway.

"It does. Anyway, this cute blond girl with Farrah Fawcett hair and perfect skin does her whole thing, batting her eyes, wearing low-cut tops, looking like a model in a music video. Virg was sure that it was just her *modus operandi*. Don't do any work in class, flirt with the teacher, skate by with a C. Maybe higher, depending on how far she was willing to go." She coughed, once, then twice, then a rolling series of coughs that petered out after ten seconds or so. "Anyway, Virg saw something in her. He broke that girl down. She thought she'd get to play a beautiful lady-in-waiting, recite a few lines, look glamorous onstage, and get eight easy units."

"I take it your husband didn't make it so easy on her."

"No, he didn't. And that girl fought him tooth and nail."

"What happened?"

Judith cackled. "You've met my husband. What do you *think* happened?"

I think he might have slept with the student. Fenway bit her tongue.

"He tamed her," Judith said.

"Sorry?

"Oh, come on." Judith rolled her eyes. "Tamed her like the shrew. He showed her the ridiculousness of her behavior. Showed her, ultimately, that she was better than what she was showing the world of herself. Taught her that she could get what she wanted without hurting others, or hurting herself."

"So she... changed her ways?" Fenway hated using the cliché, but it seemed exactly where this story was going.

"She did. She got her master's degree from Stanford, I believe it was, and she started working at oil companies. She rose up in the ranks, and now she's one of the most respected people in the industry."

"Wait—are we talking about Cynthia Schimmelhorn?" Fenway said.

"Well, back then, she was Cynthia DiFazio," Judith said. "But yes. The ironic thing is that she didn't even major in performance or English. After taking Virg's class, she switched to something like biomedical engineering."

"Petroleum engineering," Fenway said automatically.

"That's right. She's a big oil executive. That makes sense. But I have no doubt that Virg's class changed her whole life—her outlook on everything. She went from an entitled little rich girl whoring herself out on her looks to one of the most powerful businesswomen in the nation."

"Do they still keep in touch?" Fenway asked.

"They did for a little while. When Cynthia moved back after the South American job she had, they met once or twice for dinner or coffee. But I don't think they've seen each other much lately."

"Did you know Cynthia's daughter?"

Judith rolled her eyes. "How do you think I know what a big influence Virg was on her? You know what her daughter's name is, don't you?"

"Nerissa."

"That's right. Almost as weird as *Fenway.*" Judith chuckled. "Do you know who Nerissa is?"

"Sure. Portia's lady-in-waiting in *The Merchant of Venice.*"

"That's the part Cynthia played."

Fenway tried not to let the surprise show on her face. "I thought he did *Merchant of Venice* last year."

"He's done *Merchant* five times now. At least Cynthia didn't have to perform it with a monkey."

"I thought it would have been a big, juicy part like Gertrude, or

Ophelia in *Hamlet*, or Cordelia in *King Lear*. Not a bit part with twenty lines."

Judith shrugged. "That's Virg. That's why he was so brilliant. That's how he transformed students."

Fenway thought of Denise and of the professor pitching a fit during dress rehearsal. *Didn't seem that transformative to me.*

Fenway's phone rang in her purse. She cursed under her breath for not putting it on silent. She fumbled with it as she pulled it out. It was Charlotte.

"I'm sorry," she said. "I have to take this."

She heaved herself out of the sofa's quicksand and went into the entryway, where she clicked ANSWER and began to pace back and forth along the tile floor.

"Hi, Charlotte," she said. "Listen, I'm with—"

"I don't care who you're with," Charlotte snapped. "Your dad got out of jail yesterday, and when he gets arraigned on Tuesday, I don't know if he'll be coming home. So while dinner last night was fine, I think you'd better plan to spend time with us this weekend."

"I'm right in the middle of a—"

"Did you know that apparently someone is willing to say that your dad hired him to kill that professor? *That's* why he might not be coming home Tuesday."

"Someone actually confessed to the murder and said my father hired him?" Fenway's eyes went wide—and her mind immediately went to Peter Grayheath. But maybe it was someone else. Surely Grayheath couldn't be free if he confessed to the murder of Professor Delacroix. "Who said that?" Fenway took a step back and bumped a table in the entryway, knocking a stack of opened mail onto the floor. She knelt down to pick up all the papers.

"No one is telling me anything," Charlotte said, and her voice wavered. "If I don't get answers by tomorrow, I'll get one of your dad's private investigators."

"To be clear, Charlotte, is my father repeating what I told him in jail, or did someone actually come forward?" Fenway remembered how angry her father had been two days before, ranting about wanting to kill Delacroix himself, how he would never leave it up to someone else. Fenway hadn't believed him at the time, but now she wasn't so sure.

"He said someone confessed. He took a call earlier today from his lawyers." Charlotte's voice was noncommittal, but Fenway nonetheless heard the echoes of disappointment and judgment. "Fortunately, Imani Ingram thinks it's just a bump in the road."

"Do you like the lawyer?"

"I don't know. What do I know about what makes a good lawyer? Your dad likes her."

Fenway put all the papers in a single stack. "Does he seem okay?"

"Your dad?"

"Yes. Did the news get him down at all?"

"A little agitated, maybe, but okay."

"Good."

Charlotte clicked her tongue. "So are you coming for dinner tonight?"

Fenway, papers in hand, stood up as she tried not to let her annoyance show in her voice. "I can't. I'm in the middle of a murder investigation."

"You're *always* in the middle of a murder investigation, Fenway."

"I'll do what I can, Charlotte. I can't promise anything."

Charlotte sniffed. "I suppose that's better than nothing."

Fenway hung up and immediately called Dez.

Dez picked up. "Hey, Fenway. I don't have an update yet. They won't let me in to see Peter Grayheath."

"I just heard from Charlotte that someone accused my father of hiring him to kill my professor at Western Washington. It wasn't Grayheath? It wasn't from your interview?"

"It wasn't me."

"Okay. Let me know if you can get in to see him. Don't wait around all day, though—if he's going into surgery, it'll be hours before he's ready to make a statement."

"You got it, boss. I'm about to ask the staff again. Hey, here's the doctor now. Talk to you later."

Dez clicked off, and Fenway looked at the table next to her and the stack of mail and papers she'd put back. The top paper caught her eye.

THANK YOU FOR YOUR PAYMENT in blue printing, from the oncology center at Querido Canyon Medical Center, and a payment in full of the former outstanding balance of $473,256.00.

That's some expensive cancer treatment. Fenway's mother had gone so fast, she hadn't even been able to take advantage of a ridiculously expensive treatment program.

But still—how did Professor Cygnus pay for this?

The total was awfully close to the difference on Jessica's note. It couldn't be a coincidence.

Fenway stopped and thought. Of all the people who had access to that scholarship fund—maybe it was Cygnus, not Dr. Pruitt, who had embezzled the funds—and now, neither man had an alibi.

She needed to find who had transferred half a million dollars out of the account.

Piper still had another hour before she had to clear out her desk. Maybe she could pull out a miracle.

CHAPTER TWENTY-THREE

IN THE OFFICE A FEW MINUTES LATER, FENWAY STARED OVER PIPER'S shoulder at the computer screen. "Okay," Fenway said. "What else have you come up with?"

Piper, looking wired, but with deep black circles under her eyes, smirked. "How much do you want to know?"

Fenway looked at Piper's face. "Everything that won't land you in jail."

Piper smiled. "No worries. The warrant came through."

"I thought Dr. Pruitt was fighting it."

"Not that one—the new one McVie called in on The Guild's finances."

"Wow, that was quick."

Piper nodded. "And a good thing, too. I've been digging through these files for half an hour."

"What did you find?"

"I found out The Guild doesn't tell the public exactly accurate information."

"What does that mean, 'exactly accurate'?"

"It means," Piper said, "that The Guild has a public scholarship fund that supposedly provides money to about ten students a year. Full cost of tuition, room and board, and job placement as well."

"That's a *public* fund?"

"Yes. And for those ten students, everything seems pretty legitimate. Xavier Gonsalves and Amanda Kohl are recipients, for example. That's the guy who was sleeping with the victim and his girlfriend, right?"

"Right, but you said it's all legitimate?"

"I said *some* of it was legit. I dug into the bank server's files and records for the scholarship fund—and tens of millions of dollars are going in and out of that fund every *week*. Payouts to dozens of students who don't exist, but who have bank accounts in the Cayman Islands. Millions of dollars paid to consultants, actor groups, theater companies—they're all just fronts with offshore accounts. The public reports only report the legitimate transactions—they leave out everything else."

Fenway paused for a moment. "So where does the money go?" she asked. "It doesn't surprise me if Dr. Pruitt's been cooking the books. We think he's embezzling money from the scholarship fund. Are Amanda and Xavier involved?"

"It's complicated. Let me show you what I'm looking at." Piper pointed to several lines on the screen. "Okay. This screen shows the financial statements from the scholarship fund."

"All right."

"And this window"—Piper clicked and a different set of numbers appeared—"shows the spreadsheet data that gets fed into the public reports. The ones that Nidever gets to brag about during university tours."

"So that's the spreadsheet that Pruitt might have altered?"

Piper shook her head. "I don't think so. The spreadsheets got uploaded—I can see the original files—and I can see the revision history. About four hundred changes, entered by students, Jessica Marquez, and a couple of the finance admins at Nidever. The spreadsheets have had errors in them, but mostly for transposed numbers on checks or a missing number here or there."

"So you don't have anything."

"Seriously, Fenway, are you always this impatient?"

"Impatient? You have less than an hour left here."

"Thanks for reminding me, sunshine," Piper said. "Now, different spreadsheet files are associated with the master scholarship fund statement—the *real* one, with the millions going in and out all the time." She clicked on a column header and a row of numbers appeared, all in the millions. "You can see a bunch of large cash deposits are *entered* as anonymous donations to the scholarship fund." She clicked again and the rows and numbers changed. "These are the payments going to student accounts in the Cayman Islands."

"What about accounts owned by Global Advantage?" Fenway asked.

"I've got to cross-reference some things, but yes, I think money is going there, too."

"Okay, so this is all interesting. The scholarship fund looks like a major cog in the money laundering scheme."

"Yes. If my calculations are correct, it's how they're laundering more than half their money."

"And it ties into Jessica's murder?"

Piper nodded. "I think so. Every month, The Guild receives a statement about this." Piper pointed to the screen. "These codes mean that a statement was mailed."

Fenway squinted. "I'll take your word for it."

"And look—here, on October sixth, at the close of business, there's an anonymous donation of over two million dollars."

"Right. Two million, seven hundred and seventy-seven thousand."

"Okay. Now—and this is where the magic happens—I query the database for the snapshot taken at noon." She clicked and typed in a command, and another window popped up.

"Same number," Fenway said. "Two million, two hundred and seventy-seven thousand. What does that prove?"

"*Is* it the same number?"

"Yes, Piper, it's—" Fenway broke off and stared at the screen. "Hold on, no. It's five hundred thousand less."

"Bingo," Piper said. "Someone got the bank to deposit part of that payment into a separate account, but with the same transaction number, and kept the full amount in the information window. Tricked the bank into thinking it received the full amount."

"Holy shit," Fenway said.

"I know."

"Why didn't Jessica see this before?"

"She probably trusted the bank statement."

"How did she find out the money was missing?"

"The bank issued a correction on Monday."

"A correction?"

"Right. As in, the balance previously reported was wrong. The bank posted a correction of exactly half a million dollars. After the bank issued the correction, someone logged in with Jessica's credentials and checked the balance on October sixth."

"Which was?"

"Before the correction?" Piper typed and clicked. A new window popped up. "Close of business on October sixth: $27,846,577.48."

Fenway pulled up the photo on her phone of Jessica's note. "But after—half a million less. And that matches these two numbers." She thought for a moment. "Do you think she figured out who it was?"

Piper bought up the student spreadsheet and tapped the screen. "I think the answer lies in Jessica's spreadsheets. The ones we can't find. She might be getting statements directly from those Cayman Island accounts. Or she might have seen the correction from the bank and made the same mistake you made, assuming two long numbers were the same. She might have recognized the account number."

"Who's authorized to deposit funds to different accounts?"

"As far as I can tell, it's just Jessica Marquez and Dr. Pruitt."

"So—you're saying that this important spreadsheet, with payment information, addresses, phone numbers, all of which could destroy the money laundering scheme if it gets out—all of these were just kept on one machine's *hard drive?*"

"That's what it looks like."

"Do you think it's possible that *Jessica* stole the money?"

"It's possible. I don't have a line on that other account yet. Dr. Pruitt is possible, too. Or—someone could have broken through the security here, just like they exploited a back door on the bank's firewall."

"You know how it was done?"

Piper shrugged. "I know how *I* would have done it, but anyone could have gotten in there. The hack is on YouTube—step by step instructions. It's a script you can copy and paste. Anyone could have done it."

"Someone without hacking skills?"

"I saw the video. My two-year-old nephew could do it, if he could sit still long enough to follow instructions."

"Something like this doesn't get patched?"

"Well—a patch for the firewall came out months ago. It obviously didn't get applied."

"This is brilliant, Piper." Fenway said, and it suddenly hit her that Piper wouldn't be around to connect all these dots anymore, and she felt punched in the stomach. "I just wish we could find Jessica's spreadsheet. But if the only copy was on her laptop hard drive, it might be lost forever."

Piper screwed up her face.

"What?"

"I just—well, look, I work all day with computers, so maybe I'm biased, but for a file that important, Jessica must have a backup file *somewhere.*"

"Would she?" asked Fenway. "It *is* a file tracking something illegal. She wouldn't want anyone to be able to find it. If she backed it up, that increases the chances of someone finding it."

Piper shook her head firmly. "Too much can happen to a file like that. Spreadsheets get corrupted. Laptops get stolen. Jessica wouldn't just access and make changes to the main file that kept track of the illicit payments without backing it up."

Fenway sucked in a breath through her teeth. "Okay, let's say you're right. Where would the backup file be? We haven't found it anywhere."

"There are a bunch of options—none that *I* would use if I were doing something illegal, but I guess I'm not most people." Piper rested her chin on her fist. "The university supplies a shared directory—that's where all the employees are supposed to back up their files." She grimaced. "You wouldn't believe some of the stuff we find on our shared file servers here."

"Try me. I used to be an ER nurse." Fenway sat down on an extra chair. "But that's too public. Jessica would think there are too many unknowns. What about a USB stick?"

"We haven't found anything yet."

"Maybe she hid it somewhere we haven't looked."

Piper nodded. "Just like the ledgers at Central Auto Body were under the floorboard."

"Right." Fenway rested her chin in her hands. "If she had a physical backup, where would it be? In a fire safe? Maybe on her person—somewhere that only she could find or get to."

"What about a safe deposit box?" Piper suggested.

"At a bank? I don't think so. She'd need it somewhere she could access quickly. She can't go into the bank every time she needs to add a fake scholarship payment, or record a false donation."

Piper paused. "You think they were looking for the backup file when they tossed the place?"

Fenway thought a moment. "It makes sense. Do you have the crime scene photos of the office?"

Piper nodded. "Yes. The initial ones from Dez, and then the rest we got from CSI. Let me pull them up."

A moment later, Piper had a set of twenty-four photos stretching across her two screens.

"Are there more?"

Piper snickered. "Only about two hundred. These are the ones that give you the best overview of most of the stuff in the room."

Fenway looked at the photos, seeing the whole room in context. Her face moved between the screens, and then she pointed. "They tossed the whole room. Both of the rooms."

"Right."

"Once you've found what you're searching for, don't you stop looking?"

Piper shrugged. "Maybe they wanted to throw people off the trail, or maybe they just wanted to mess up the office. It could have been personal against Jessica, right? Didn't I hear that she was sleeping with the lead actor in the play?"

"You heard that?"

"I did." Piper smiled. "Come on, Fenway, you know I look at the sheriff's notes as soon as he comes in."

"Right."

"So you're looking at the guy's girlfriend, right?" Piper tilted her head. "The blonde?"

"Amanda." Fenway sat back in the chair. "You know, maybe we should see if anyone else was romantically involved with Jessica?"

"Jessica was single."

"Are you sure? Have you looked? Social media accounts, dating apps, anything like that?"

Piper smiled. "Yes, I have, Miss Smartypants, and no, I didn't find anything. Jessica doesn't seem to have been involved with anyone since she's been here."

"Except Xavier."

"Right, but no one publicly. No official boyfriend."

Fenway turned to the screen and something caught her eye. "Hold on."

"What?"

"All right." Fenway looked again and squinted, deciding if what she was about to say made sense. "Can you kill all the photos from the outer room and bring up a few more from Jessica's office?"

"Sure." Piper clicked on a few items and brought up another six pictures from Jessica's office.

Fenway stared again, looking at one of the pictures of the bookshelf directly behind Jessica's desk.

"What is it, Fenway? Come on, spit it out."

"Fine." Fenway took a deep breath. "Jessica was *professional*, right?"

"You call banging a student actor professional?"

"No—that's not what I mean. I mean her appearance. Her office. All work and no play."

"I never met her."

"No, but look at the stuff in her office. She's got the plant in the corner, she has her desk arranged to maximize efficiency, she's got corporate art on the wall. Her books are all on strategy, economics, theater management—not a novel in sight. This is a woman who means business. There isn't a single personal effect in her office. No photos of her family, no tchotchkes she picked up at conferences, nothing. She works for a theater company, yet there's nothing that so much as hints at a personal life."

"Yeah, that's weird, but you guys had a theory about that, right?"

"We did. We realized that Jessica worked for the money launderers you found. That means she was involved with the oil shipping from La Mitad, the refined fuels going to East Timor, and with the money coming back into the country. She made sure that The Guild was an effective front for the money laundering."

"A hypothesis without proof."

"True," Fenway said. "Which is another reason we need to find that backup file." Fenway pointed to the picture, her finger landing on the bookshelf behind the desk, second shelf from the bottom. "Can you zoom in on that?"

"Sure." A couple of clicks later, the screen was filled with nothing but the second shelf.

"That's a hairbrush," Fenway said.

Piper squinted. "Yes, that's sure what it looks like. But so what? She needs to brush her hair for visitors."

"Would she have it out in the open like that?"

Piper looked at Fenway out of the corner of her eye. "Are you forgetting the room was tossed? It could have been in a drawer."

"True enough. Maybe it was in a drawer." She squinted and looked closer at the photograph. "Even so, I don't think that's *just* a hairbrush."

"Not—what?"

"It's—well, hang on. You've got a regular ol' browser on this warp drive-powered monster PC, don't you?"

Piper clicked. Fenway typed *Desert Sands Spy Gear* into the search window, then clicked on the first website. The page came up and she scrolled around the menu until she found *Diversion Safes*.

"Isn't this the place that makes those beige-and-orange planters that hid those microphones?"

Fenway nodded, scrolling through the product list. "I checked out their website earlier, and I think I remember something. Maybe it was an ad, I don't know."

"What was it?"

"It was a hairbrush," Fenway said. "And it looked just like—"

And there it was. A black hairbrush with a silver band and a mottled handle.

"Thirty-nine dollars with free overnight shipping," said Fenway.

Piper stared over Fenway's shoulder. The top of the hairbrush screwed off, leaving a cylindrical hole. Piper scrolled to the specifications. "Listen to this. 'Perfect for cash, rings, jewelry, USB drives, and more.' It comes in an array of fashion colors, too. Oh, look, it even includes a 'smell-proof' bag."

"Can't have the K9 units stealing your hairbrush," Fenway said. "I bet there's a USB stick in the one in Jessica's office. *And* I bet the stick contains the spreadsheets that track the cash deposits and payments that Marquez was using to launder the money."

Piper sat back. "That's a lot of conjecture."

"Still, it's worth checking out."

Piper hid the browser and brought up the financial reports. "Let's see if I can track any orders from Jessica's bank accounts."

"Before you do that," Fenway said, "I wondered if you'd had a chance to look at the PC that Dez brought from The Guild's office."

Piper shook her head and motioned to a lonely-looking PC tower connected to a small monitor. "They just logged it into evidence and brought it over here—I don't know, maybe five minutes before you got here. I have it connected, and I ran a preliminary scan, but I haven't looked at anything yet. It's up and running, though, if you want to take a look."

"Sure." Fenway walked over to The Guild's PC and woke it up. "No password?"

"I'm in admin mode. I bypassed it."

"So you didn't break Jessica's password."

"No. I don't have time." Piper clicked around again. "Okay, here's who had access to the bank account for the scholarship fund. Jessica, no surprise there—oh. And Dr. Alfred Pruitt."

"Who else?"

"That's it. No one else."

"Not Professor Cygnus?"

"Nope."

"Wow—I really thought Cygnus would be on there." Fenway folded her arms. "So either Dr. Pruitt embezzled the money, or Jessica did."

"Unless someone stole their credentials."

"Great—can you send me everything you've got? And copy McVie on it, too." Fenway clicked around through the applications.

"Hey," Fenway said, "did you know they've got the Windows Device Tracker running on this machine?"

"A nearly useless piece of software to run on a desktop machine."

"No, Piper—I mean, if they standardized on Windows Device Tracker at The Guild office, then it's on Jessica's laptop, too. Maybe we can log into Jessica's account and see where it is."

"Oh—yeah, that makes sense. I kind of assumed they weren't savvy enough to turn it on."

"Well, it can't hurt to try."

Fenway launched the tracker—and a login prompt popped up.

"Oh, crap. I can't go any further without Jessica's username and password."

"Her username is just her email address." Piper walked over and typed it in. "All the naming conventions are the same for staff."

"Now we just need her password."

Piper nodded. "Right. Well, I've got a password cracker but that will take a while."

"A while?"

"Two or three days, maybe. You can get started on that if you want, but I'll focus on tracking as much financial information as I can before they drag me out of here."

"Maybe I can figure out Jessica's password."

Piper scoffed. "Good luck."

Fenway thought, but she had no idea what Jessica would choose. People often choose personal things—and, of course....

She typed in *password* and hit Enter. No luck.

Fenway stood up. "I'm going to my office, Piper. Let me know if you find anything—and I'm for sure coming to say goodbye."

CHAPTER TWENTY-FOUR

FENWAY LEFT PIPER IN THE IT ROOM AND WALKED INTO THE coroner's suite, thinking about what Jessica might use as a password. People tended to use personal information, even if most of them knew better than to use a birth date, or the name of their father.

Ugh. Now she was thinking about *her* father, and how to get the information he wanted her to get out of Detective Ridley.

She pulled her laptop out of its bag and plugged it in. The old Acer slowly woke up, and after launching a browser and logging into the police information system, Fenway researched the life and habits of Detective Deshawn Ridley, writing certain facts on a small yellow notepad. She found him on Facebook and searched a few of his work records, but after about fifteen minutes, she had no new ideas about how to weasel the information out of the detective from Bellingham.

She didn't have the element of surprise; Ridley would recognize her and what she was up to right away. She couldn't get the information herself.

Oh—but maybe there was someone who could.

She closed her eyes, picked up the phone and then exhaled slowly as she opened her eyes and dialed.

Rachel picked up on the first ring. "Wow, they haven't let you go home yet?"

"Hey, Rachel. Looks like they haven't let *you* go home either."

"It's been a big week. Elections, Barry Klein getting installed, the whole deal. And you know how Klein loves his press releases. He'll keep me busy for the rest of his term." Rachel sighed. "What I can I do for you?"

Fenway was silent. She thought the way to broach the topic would magically come to her as soon as she heard Rachel's voice, but no such luck.

"Fenway? You still there?"

"Yeah," Fenway croaked. "There's no easy way to tell you about the favor I need from you, Rachel."

"You need a favor from me?"

"Yes."

"It's totally fine. Name it."

"No, you haven't heard it yet. I need you to, uh, see if you can get some information from a visiting police detective."

"That guy from the Bellingham MCU?"

"Right."

"He's still in town?"

"I'm not a hundred percent sure, but I think so. His department wants my father extradited to Washington state, and—if I can read him as well as I think I can—he'll bring him in himself."

"And you can't ask him?"

"No. He already deflected when I tried to ask him about it yester-day. He'll see right through me."

Rachel clicked her tongue. "What's the information you need?"

"Details about the evidence they have against my father. Right now, he thinks it's just a bank transfer to the supposed hit man. My father heard rumors that someone confessed to the killing and said my father hired him. But that makes no sense, because the hit man was walking free when my father was in jail."

"You don't think the hit man got immunity, do you?"

"For murder? I can't imagine how that would go down. ADA Kim would fire whoever was responsible for that."

Through the phone Fenway could hear the suspicion in Rachel's voice. "Why do you think this detective will talk to me if he won't talk to you?"

"Well—uh—he doesn't know who you are."

"But as soon as I tell him I'm the public information officer—" Rachel paused and then laughed. "Oh, you want me to be a *spy*."

"Uh—yeah, kind of."

"And you want me to—what?"

"I don't know. I was kind of hoping you could help me brainstorm something."

"Like what? Pretend to be an FBI agent and insist that he tell me all about the evidence?"

"Uh—no, I don't think so."

"Why? Don't you think I can pull it off?"

"No, because impersonating a federal agent is a felony."

Rachel laughed. "As cool as that would be, I guess I don't want to go to jail." She paused for a moment. "Maybe I could come up to him in a bar in a slinky black dress? Fawn all over him? Slip him a mickey?" Rachel giggled and affected a breathy voice in a higher register. "Oh, Mister Big Strong Detective Man, I just need to know one *eensy weensy* bit of evidence you have."

"Ugh," Fenway said, disgusted with herself. "Sorry, Rachel. This is a bad idea. I shouldn't have asked. It's ridiculous. Not to mention more than a little skeevy."

"Hang on, hang on. I mean, yes, it is a little skeevy, but—uh, it kind of sounds fun."

"No, Rachel. I feel like I'd be pimping you out." She remembered using the same word in the conversation with her father in jail, and she felt a little ill.

Rachel laughed. "I haven't had the chance to use my feminine wiles for evil in a long time."

Fenway paused. "You're telling me you're seriously considering this?"

"Um, I guess I am. I mean, I fooled everyone with the whole ATF thing a few months ago. Even though it was serious, that was a lot of fun."

"I know what you mean," Fenway admitted.

"Exhilarating, right?"

"Well, yeah."

They were both silent for a minute.

"So," Rachel said, "where do you need me to be?"

Fenway hesitated. The sick feeling in her stomach abated slightly. "His name is Deshawn Ridley, and he's staying in the Phillips-Holsen Grand Hotel downtown."

"Wow, nice hotel for a public servant."

"I know. It's off season, I guess. Anyway, I think you should go down to the hotel bar tonight, probably around seven thirty, or eight. My guess is that he'll be hanging out there—he said it was a 'nice bar,' and I get the impression he's lonely."

"Lonely? Why? Is he single?"

"Divorced."

"Ah. So how do you want me to play it? That's a nice hotel, so I could get dressed up. How about that red dress I wore when we went dancing last month? I look good in that."

"No, that's overdoing it. Something first date-worthy. Not a slinky red dress."

Rachel laughed. "Okay, fine. I'll wear something tasteful. You have a picture of Detective Ridley?"

"I found one on his Facebook profile. I'll text it to you."

"How old is he?"

"If I had to guess, maybe thirty-five."

"Yeesh. That's, like, ten years older than I am."

"I know." Fenway paused, the creepy feeling sliding over her again. "You know what? This is a bad idea. I feel gross just talking about—"

Rachel scoffed. "I can do this, Fenway."

Fenway's stomach turned over, and she tasted bile in her mouth. "No. Ick. Forget it. I'll think of something else."

Rachel laughed. "Fine. No impersonating an FBI agent, no flirting. Spoil my fun." Rachel paused for a moment. "Is there a specific type of evidence you think Detective Ridley has?"

"I think they've probably found a payment from my father to the guy who said he was the hit man, but the guy worked security for my father, and then he quit. I can't imagine that any D.A. worth his salt would go to trial with just the word of a former employee who supposedly kills people for a living. They *must* have something else, right?"

"I guess so."

"I mean, my father told me that he sent the guy up to Seattle to drive my car home. My father just has the ridiculous kind of money to pay him more than the Accord is worth to do that."

Rachel paused. "But... even if it's not strong enough to stand up in court, why else would your dad pay the guy—what, thirty thousand dollars or something?"

"Fifty k."

"Yeah—so if not for a hit, then what?"

And then it came to Fenway. The notation in the ledger: "Grayheath—SEA." *Sea* didn't refer to the ocean, or a body of water. SEA was the airport code for Seattle-Tacoma International Airport. The ledger kept track of Grayheath's movements in Seattle. She shook her head and snapped to the present. "I'm sorry, Rachel, what did you say?"

"I said that if the fifty thousand isn't for a hit, then what did your dad pay him for?"

"That's just it. I don't think it's his bank account."

"You don't think it's—what?"

"I don't think the payment came from his real account. I think someone opened a bank account in his name and paid Peter Grayheath fifty thousand dollars."

"Really?" Rachel paused. "Who would do that?"

Fenway hesitated. Another challenge with the idea that Ferris got framed was that very few people had fifty thousand dollars lying around. "There are a lot of people in this town who want my father gone." A name finally came to her. "Barry Klein, for one."

Rachel's tone was skeptical. "I don't know about that—he just won the mayorship. He should be happy—and he was so consumed with the election, he wouldn't have had time to frame your dad for a murder for hire. Besides, he doesn't have fifty thousand dollars for something like this."

"Don't be so sure." Fenway bit her lip and thought. "Klein's been obsessed with my father ever since I got here. He thought I was working to collude with my father for—I don't know, something. And he's got a campaign war chest, right?"

"I mean, I know Klein is an arrogant ass—"

"You don't know the half of it."

"But," Rachel continued, "the timing isn't right. It just doesn't make sense why he'd do it now—or during the election—and not after."

"Professor Delacroix was killed in late July," Fenway pointed out. "That was right *before* Klein announced that he was running for mayor."

"Uh... Fenway, wasn't Klein in jail the night before he announced? Didn't you *put* him there?"

Fenway smiled wryly. "Yeah, we tried to keep that under wraps, but I guess word got out."

"Not only did word get out, but I'm the public information officer, Fenway. After Klein announced he was running, I had to field about twenty calls about Klein spending the night in jail." She grunted. "And it's not like *you* were any help."

"You remember I was in the middle of a murder *and* a kidnapping investigation," Fenway said. "It's not like I was well-equipped to deal with a PR nightmare of Klein's own making."

"Okay," Rachel said. "Well, I can't think of another way to wheedle that information out of him, but call if you think of anything. I've got to finish some work."

"Thanks, Rachel."

Rachel hung up, and Fenway sat at her desk, thinking.

If she was right, and if Nathaniel Ferris hadn't opened that bank account, that meant someone was trying to frame him. Why would anyone do that?

Barry Klein? He certainly hated her father, but Rachel was right: Klein was getting everything he wanted, without having to get Ferris out of the way.

What about his wife, Catherine Klein? *She* wasn't in jail the night before Delacroix was killed, but she didn't have a motive.

It was also possible—unlikely, but possible—that Nathaniel Ferris didn't know of the illicit oil going through the Ferris Energy port. He was the most powerful man in the county, but for how much longer? Every month Fenway had been coroner, Ferris's power ebbed a little.

Perhaps, Fenway thought, someone at Ferris Energy thought they'd make a better CEO than Ferris. Someone who needed him out of the way.

Perhaps it was someone who had the ear of the board of directors. Ferris had been complaining the board had it in for him, and perhaps someone had the board in their corner. Fenway went to the Ferris Energy website and looked at their Board of Directors.

Yes, Ferris was still the chairman, but Cynthia Schimmelhorn was obviously an aggressive second. She clicked on LEADERSHIP TEAM and saw Bryce R. Heissner as the chief operating officer. He was likely the next CEO-in-waiting. She wondered if Heissner had Schimmelhorn in his corner, or if it was one of the other C-level employees or vice presidents.

Another thought flitted across Fenway's mind: it might have been a competitor.

She went to the Petrogrande website, and sure enough, Dor Trejo—Rose Morgan's former boss at Petrogrande—was now the chief financial officer. He would know whether Petrogrande was in financial shape to buy a weakened Ferris Energy. Maybe the story about Rose Morgan being a corporate spy was all subterfuge. Maybe instead of Morgan stealing Petrogrande intellectual property, as Trejo had strongly implied, she was inflicting damage on Ferris Energy's reputation to leave them wide open for a buyout.

She called McVie. He picked up on the second ring.

"Fenway, hey. Just about ready to call it a night?"

"Not quite, Craig. I found out that only two people had access to that scholarship fund—Jessica Marquez and Dr. Pruitt."

McVie let out a low whistle. "Someone just shot to the top of our suspect list. Didn't he tell us that he didn't have access?"

"I've got one more thing to do over at Nidever, too."

"What is it?"

"I think I know where The Guild's secret payment ledger is."

"You think the ledger is somewhere besides on the stolen laptop?"

"I do."

"Where is it?"

"On a USB drive, hidden in plain sight. I think it's in a hairbrush."

"Did you say it was in a *hairbrush*?"

"Yes, it's one of those secret 'distraction safes.' That place that sold the potted plant microphones has them in stock."

"A hairbrush safe?"

"I saw it in a photo from the crime scene. It looks just like the one on the website. At least from the angles we can see."

"I don't think I've seen a hairbrush safe before. You need a ride?"

"I, uh, borrowed one of my father's cars."

"Oh—nice. The Mercedes?"

"No, the Porsche. The 911 Carrera s."

"That's an expensive car." He paused for a moment. "Would you like some company? Maybe we can head to dinner after you find that hairbrush—and after we search Dr. Pruitt's office."

"You're not just using me to ride in an expensive Porsche, are you?"

"No. I'm using you for other things." His voice lowered a couple of registers.

Fenway rolled her eyes. "Oh, gee, you sure know how to make a girl feel special, Craig."

"Glad to be of service."

"Great." Fenway paused. "I'm in the parking lot over on Fifth."

"Way over there?"

"Yes, way over there. I'm not leaving my father's hundred-thou-sand-dollar car on the street."

"Okay. What do you think—ten minutes?"

"Make it fifteen. Judge Baker is still here, and I bet I can get him to sign a search warrant for Pruitt's office with what we have."

They hung up, and Fenway looked one final time at the photo of Detective Deshawn Ridley, and thought about his divorce, and then she had a flash of inspiration.

CHAPTER TWENTY-FIVE

"Piper—" Fenway said, bursting into the office.

A sheriff's deputy Fenway didn't recognize was standing guard over Piper's computer as she forlornly put her personal items into a bankers' box.

"Oh no," Fenway said.

Piper raised her head. "Yeah. It's time. I copied everything I researched onto the file server."

Fenway walked over to Piper's desk and hugged her. Piper awkwardly hugged her back, a GIRLS WHO CODE mug in one hand and a stuffed Kirby in the other.

"It's not goodbye," Piper said. "You're taking me to lunch tomorrow, remember?"

"Yeah. I'm so sorry, Piper."

"It's my own damn fault. Mostly."

"Can I help you pack?"

"No. This is all of it. What did you need?"

"Oh—I've got a couple of passwords to try."

"It's past five, Miss Patten," the deputy said.

Piper picked up her box. "Let me know how it goes." She turned and walked out of the office, the deputy following behind her.

The tears welled up in Fenway's eyes and she fought them back. She wouldn't cry. She wouldn't let anyone see this get to her.

She turned on her heel and walked to the PC.

Everyone uses personal information for passwords, except for the nerdiest of the cybersecurity geeks. Even hard-to-break passwords usually have personal elements to them.

But Jessica had no personal life to speak of.

Almost.

At the login prompt, Fenway typed:

XavierGo

Her finger hovered over the Enter key. When she left her office, she'd thought for sure that was it, but as she typed it, doubt crept in. It was close—but it wasn't right. Not personal enough. She deleted what she had typed and stared at the screen.

Oh, yes. That was better. That had to be it.

ItsGoTime

And Fenway was in.

———

McVie had never been in Fenway's passenger seat when she had so much vehicular power under her command. She downshifted and shot past a minivan as they took the George Nidever Expressway toward the university.

"You okay?" Fenway looked over at McVie from the corner of her eye. He had his right arm braced against the door.

"Fine," McVie said.

"Performs a little better than your Highlander, right?"

"Yeah, just a little," McVie said. "You've got—"

"I see it," Fenway said, slaloming around a chair lying on its side on the road, half in the fast lane and half on the shoulder. "Probably some student that didn't tie the chair down in the back of their pickup."

"Right."

Fenway could feel the road beneath her hands, through the steering wheel. The engine alternated between purring and roaring, like a beautiful Bengal tiger at a zoo who wanted you to scratch its ears one minute, and claw your heart out the next. It was delightful.

"Okay—so tell me why you don't think it's Dr. Pruitt," McVie said.

"Because he doesn't have her laptop."

"How do you know?"

"Because Jessica had installed the Windows Device Tracker." She grinned. " I got in."

"And you know where the laptop is?"

"It was last used on Wednesday morning at an address on Chumash Falls Way."

"Chumash Falls—that sounds familiar."

"It should. We were there just a few hours ago."

"Professor Cygnus?"

"Yep." Fenway turned off Nidever Expressway onto the campus.

"So," he said, "to be clear—"

"To pay for his wife's cancer treatment, I think Cygnus stole half a million dollars from the scholarship fund—the same fund that Jessica was hired to oversee the money laundering for."

"And Jessica found out Cygnus stole it."

"Yes." Fenway began to list points on her fingers. "She confronted him, and he killed her and stole her laptop to destroy the files."

"But his wife says he wasn't home!"

"I have a theory about that, too. I think he went home—but never went into his house. I think he used his workshop or the garage, opened up the laptop, and trashed the file. Then he either hid it, or destroyed it. But when he opened it—"

"The device tracker gave him away." McVie paused. "So, you think it was Cygnus and not Pruitt who embezzled the money?"

Fenway nodded. "I think the professor figured out Jessica's password the same way I did. Cygnus taking the money makes more sense. It explains the medical bill being paid off, for one thing. Piper never found anything in Pruitt's accounts to suggest a big windfall."

There were no parking spaces next to the theater. "Oh, that's right, it's opening night," Fenway said. "It'll be a madhouse in there." She reversed out of the lot and continued down the university lane.

"So why do we need the hairbrush?"

"If I'm right and it has Jessica's ledgers in there, we should be able to track a lot more than just the deposits and withdrawals from the scholarship fund. We'll be able to get full account numbers, names and businesses associated with the money laundering—hopefully everything we need to take down the whole operation." The Porsche came to a stop sign but she wasn't sure which way to go. "Okay, Craig, you've come here a lot the last couple days. Where should I park?"

"Park in the open visitor spots by the administration building."

Fenway saw the left arrow labeled ADMINISTRATION and turned. "What did you have Pruitt do with the microphone?"

"Nothing," McVie said. "I thought we might use it to our advantage. Maybe throw whoever's listening off the scent."

"Feed them false information, you mean, and then try to catch them in the act."

McVie grinned. "Because I'm sneaky like that."

"What sort of false information do you plan to give them?"

McVie shook his head. "First, we'll serve this search warrant on his office, even though you think Cygnus is the killer."

"What do you think that will do?"

"It might convince Pruitt to talk if he thinks he's compromised," McVie said.

Fenway pulled into a visitor space and killed the engine. "Okay. You think Pruitt's still here?"

"Maybe not in his office." McVie looked at his watch. "It's past five now. The admin offices are probably all closed."

The two of them walked to the double doors in front, and sure enough, they were locked.

"Dez is getting here with the search warrant soon," McVie said.

"You know where I bet Pruitt is?" Fenway said. "He and Cygnus are so tight, he's probably got a front row ticket to *Othello*. I bet that's where he'll be."

"And even if he's not," McVie said, "that's near where The Guild's office is, so that's where we need to go."

"You think we can get the key from someone? Maybe Amanda Kohl?"

McVie put a hand in his pocket and his keys jingled. "I might have neglected to return the key after we fingerprinted it. Besides, it's still officially a crime scene. The office won't open again till Tuesday."

They walked toward DiFazio Theater but took a left before the entrance and went into the stairwell.

"The scene of the crime," McVie muttered under his breath.

Fenway looked around as they ascended the staircase to the second floor.

"What are you looking for?" McVie asked.

"I don't know. I feel like I missed something."

"This staircase was open all day today and most of the day yesterday. Even if there *is* something to find here, it'll be tough to use at a trial."

"Still."

McVie reached the second-floor landing and held the door open for Fenway. The corridor stretched out before them. "You know, Fenway, there's one thing that bothers me. Professor Cygnus said he didn't have an alibi because he didn't wake his wife up when he got home."

"Yeah—that bugs me too. Because his wife was awake, and she just told us he never came home."

"So what's that about?"

Fenway thought. "You know, it's pretty common knowledge that he's had a mistress for a decade. Leda Nedermeyer—the head of the English department."

"Hmm," McVie said. "Maybe he thought we'd uncover his affair, and so that would explain his lie—that he lied to cover up his affair, not that he lied to cover up the murder he committed."

"You think he coached his mistress to say he was with her all night?"

"Maybe, or maybe he *was* with her all night."

"Fine," Fenway said. "Let's go find out what she has to say. I bet she's still here. She's probably coming to the preview tonight, too."

"Okay," McVie said, "I'll go see if Professor Nedermeyer gives Cygnus an alibi. In the meantime, you go get that super-secret spy hairbrush and see if it's got something in it."

"I'll take pictures and bag it up," Fenway said.

McVie fished the key out of his pocket and handed it to Fenway, then opened the stairwell door and left.

Fenway turned everything over in her mind as she continued down the hall. She came to the door of the North American Shakespeare Guild's office and put the key in the lock. She didn't even have to turn the key before the knob turned all the way.

Fenway paused. Was it really unlocked? Had McVie forgotten to lock it when he left last time? Maybe Dr. Pruitt or a student had gone into the office. After all, it *was* opening night; perhaps some props or costumes the student actors had stashed in the office were still here.

But Professor Cygnus ran a tight ship. Would he tolerate his students leaving necessary equipment in the office? At a crime scene? Especially after the tantrum he had thrown at dress rehearsal?

Fenway texted McVie:

Did you leave the door unlocked?

She listened carefully at the threshold. There were a million explanations for the door not being locked; she was just being paranoid. Her phone dinged and she cringed—if anyone was inside the office, they might have heard it. She looked at the screen, expecting a return text from McVie.

! Not delivered

Fenway exhaled. It was probably for the best; she didn't want McVie to think she was spooked—or that she hadn't thought about the student actors going through the office. She pushed the door open and peered inside. The lights were off, and only the streetlights from outside gave any light to the room.

She flipped on the lights, then stepped over the fallen books and papers and shelves, and over to the closed door of Jessica's office. Teetering awkwardly, she looked at the ground next to the door, where a stack of binders had fallen, for a place to put her foot.

Wait.

The students wouldn't access the office in this state. It was far too messy; it would have been impossible to find anything in here, especially in the few minutes before the show. They wouldn't have unlocked the door.

And secondly, she was *positive* that she and Dez had left the door to Jessica Marquez's office open when they had left yesterday.

The door swung open and a book—a big, heavy hardback book—came hurtling at her head.

Fenway tried to duck, but not in time, and the book hit her in the jaw, knocking her off-balance onto her rear, flattening a file box.

A figure, cloaked in black, leaped out of the office, bounding over the papers and books and holding a black cylindrical object in its right hand like a relay baton.

The hairbrush.

And that wasn't Professor Cygnus. The figure was too short, too agile, too *feminine* to be Virgil Cygnus.

Fenway tried to pull herself up, but the thief was already out the door, and she could hear the footsteps racing away. She swore at herself and got unsteadily to her feet, tripping over another box, pain shooting through her knee again. She reached the door and broke into a run down the hall, just as the door to the stairwell was closing.

How had she been so wrong about the professor?

She reached the stairwell and slid down the first rail, almost falling on the dismount, and heard the sound of an opening door below. She couldn't see who it was—and then, the sound of a different door opening. She ran down the last flight of stairs and reached for her phone.

It wasn't there.

She must have dropped it when the book hit her—in fact, she was sure of it. She'd had it in her hand when she saw the book come at her, and her hands had been empty when she got up.

She got to the ground floor and looked at the two doors: one going out to the portico in front of the DiFazio Theater, and one leading inside to the hallway with the dressing rooms on one side and the theater lobby on the other.

Fenway opened the door to the portico. The night was dark, with excited opening night patrons milling around in front. No one was looking shocked, as if a black-clad woman had just sprinted by.

She slowly opened the door from the stairway into the hallway next to the theater lobby. Fenway looked through the glass doors on the right; two of the student actors were warming up, running lines from the looks of it, but neither of them was behaving as if a strange figure had just run through.

The door in front of Fenway, leading to the greenroom and the dressing rooms, and ultimately the stage, was closed. Fenway had a hunch the thief had gone through the door.

The mystery figure could be armed. Fenway had no way to contact McVie, but also knew that there were perhaps fifteen or twenty students behind that door who might be in danger.

Taking a deep breath, she strode toward the door, and yanked it open.

An empty hallway.

She could hear students' voices in the dressing rooms, and the doors were all open. She walked down the corridor and stuck her head in the first one. Denise Delatasso looked up from hand-sewing a section of a cream-colored fabric.

"Miss Stevenson?"

"Hi, Denise. Did you happen to see someone come by here, dressed all in black, maybe twenty seconds ago?"

"Uh—I can't be sure. I was sewing up a rip I found in Iago's tunic."

"You can't be sure?"

"I think I heard footsteps and saw a shadow, but I have no idea who it was."

Fenway cocked her head. "You've been here for a few minutes?"

Denise chuckled. "For three hours. Apparently, I'm the only one who can sew."

"Okay. Break a—I mean, best of luck tonight."

"Thanks."

Fenway walked on; in the next room, Xavier was rehearsing an early scene with another actor. The next room was empty. Amanda was in the final room, doing vocal exercises. She glared at Fenway.

"What do you want now?"

"Did you see somebody dressed in black run by here?"

Amanda nodded. "Yeah, about thirty seconds ago."

"Did you recognize who it was?"

"I've seen her around, yeah. But I don't know who she is."

"It was a woman? You've seen her around?"

"With Jessica. She's come into the office a couple of times, and I think they go to lunch together."

"You know her name?"

Amanda scrunched up her face, thinking.

"Is it Rose Morgan?"

Amanda's face sparked with recognition. "Maybe. Rose sounds right. I don't think I ever heard her last name."

"Thanks, Amanda."

"When am I getting my award back?"

Fenway didn't answer, but ran.

She came to the end of the hallway and there was nowhere to go except up the three steps that flanked stage right. The front curtain was closed to the audience. She took the stairs cautiously and pulled back the dark side curtain.

There, in the middle of the stage, stood Rose Morgan, dressed all in black, facing the front of the stage, arms stretched out to her sides, the hairbrush in her right hand.

Fenway took four steps out onto the stage and stopped.

Professor Virgil Cygnus was pointing a gun at Rose.

CHAPTER TWENTY-SIX

"THAT'S FAR ENOUGH, CORONER," PROFESSOR VIRGIL CYGNUS SAID.

"What the hell is this?" Fenway looked at Rose.

"This is where I take what I deserve," Cygnus said. "Hand me that brush, dear," he said to Rose.

"No," Rose said. "You're not getting the files, and you're not getting away with robbing us."

"You're using the scholarship fund to launder money," said Fenway.

"No," said Rose.

"Yes," said Cygnus.

Fenway nodded. "And you've taken more than your agreed-upon share, Professor."

"Yes," said Cygnus.

Rose's eyes narrowed at the professor.

He laughed. "You think a dirty look will stop me? You think that will *hurt* me? Don't be ridiculous."

"We were paying you well," Rose said.

"It doesn't matter," the professor said.

"No one gets a raise," Rose sneered. "You agreed to the terms. No surprises."

"Yes, yes," he said, waving the statement away with his left hand as his right hand held the gun steady. "Too bad my financial circumstances changed."

A questioning look appeared on Rose's face before she replaced it with a stoic countenance.

"An experimental treatment for Judith," Fenway said. "Insurance wouldn't cover it."

"Very good, Coroner," Cygnus said. "I obviously hadn't hidden that secret well enough."

"The health care records are sealed, of course, but the billing records go to your house." She pointed at Rose. "And she's got the last backup of the files that show how you embezzled from the money launderers."

"What good is it to give my wife another six months if I can't spend it with her?"

"That's kind of selfish, Professor."

Cygnus chuckled. "*I am not bound to please thee with my answers*," he quoted.

Fenway's mind raced. Surely McVie would be back soon, see The Guild office, and come looking for her. Maybe he'd even call her and find her phone on the floor and know something was wrong. She wanted to keep Cygnus talking.

"How do you plan to get out of here, then?" Fenway asked. "Rose knows you've taken the money. *I* know you've taken the money. Are you going to kill us the same way you killed Jessica?"

A grin spread over Cygnus's face. "I have a more effective weapon this time. I find a gun isn't quite so messy as a blunt object."

"So you won't brain us with the award you got for *The Merchant of Venice*," Fenway said.

Cygnus chuckled. "Your reputation as an excellent detective is well-earned, Miss Stevenson."

"You said you went home that night, but you didn't. You didn't even tell your wife to lie for you. Jessica found out about the money and confronted you that night, didn't she? She waited until after rehearsal, and then she threatened to destroy you."

"I built the North American Shakespeare Guild from the ground up," Cygnus said. "If I hadn't come along, this university would be a podunk bottom-rung college famous for intramural dodgeball."

"So ask Pruitt for a raise. Or an advance. Or better health insurance."

"He's just waiting for me to retire," Cygnus said. "When Global Advantage came to me—"

"Don't say anything else, Virgil," Rose warned.

"I agreed to their terms, but I fear I was tricked. I didn't agree to have a babysitter for the transactions, and certainly not one I had to pay like a staff member. It cut my profits down considerably." He shook his head. "In a way, it was self-defense. Jessica told me how those others ended up dead last week. The boy who was killed in the car bomb. The doctor bludgeoned to death in his office. I won't end up like that. *My wife* won't end up like that."

"Okay," Rose said, jerking her hands up. "You win. I'll give you the hairbrush. But you have to let us go."

Cygnus considered it for a moment. "Promise to call off your dogs."

"I promise," said Rose.

"And you," he said to Fenway, "shall arrange for my wife and me to go to Mexico without pursuit. There's a clinic there. Then I promise to come back after she's gone."

"Okay, it's a deal." Fenway's eyes darted back and forth between the professor and Rose.

"Superb," Cygnus said. "Give me the hairbrush, and we'll initiate the first stage in this agreement."

Rose, her arms above her head, took several small, deliberate steps toward Cygnus. She was now within arm's reach.

"That's good," Cygnus said. "Now slowly, slowly, open up the top of the hairbrush."

Rose lowered her arms carefully and twisted off the cap of the brush. She turned it upside down, and a USB drive fell out into her hand.

"Now hand me that USB stick," Cygnus said.

Rose reached out toward the professor.

And Cygnus grabbed her wrist and forced her down to the floor. Fenway could see the muscles in his arms flex.

"Hey, hey, hey!" Rose yelled, dropping the USB drive. "That's not—"

"Shut up," Cygnus growled. "Now get up. Slowly. Leave the USB stick where it is."

Rose stood, and Cygnus, still gripping her wrist, held the gun to her head. "No sudden movements. I'm old. I wouldn't trust my reflexes, if I were you."

"You said you'd let us go," said Fenway.

"But I need to make sure the agency won't come after me for the money," Cygnus said. "Right now, she's the only one at the agency who knows that the money is even missing."

"Is this what your wife would want?" Fenway said. "Do you think she'd want to spend the last six months of her life with a thief and a murderer?"

Cygnus smiled. "My dear," he said, "I am assured of it."

He stepped forward, hard, and the USB drive made a nauseating crunch underneath his shoe.

Rose's face was livid. Fenway saw the barrel of the gun against her temple, the young woman straining against Cygnus's hold.

Even in his sixties, the Shakespeare professor was strong; Fenway could see his sinewy biceps bulge large and taut under the short sleeves of his red-and-black plaid shirt, easily holding Rose.

"Professor," Fenway said, straining to keep her voice even, "this isn't what you want. You're better than this. You think there are exigent circumstances? That's fine. But don't force our hand. We can show you mercy, but you have to meet us halfway."

There was a whispering sound from the roof. It had started to rain, gentle and soft.

"They wouldn't give me what I needed," the professor said. "My wife is dying, but Jessica didn't care. None of them did."

"This isn't the way to do it," Fenway said, taking a step closer to the professor. "You let Rose go, and the sheriff and I will make sure the D.A. understands the circumstances."

"You might *understand* the circumstances," Cygnus spat, "but unless I have a hostage, no one will *care*. No one will let me extend Judith's life." He tightened his grip around the handle of the gun. Fenway saw it digging into the flesh at Rose's temple.

"Oh, but we do care," Fenway said. "My mother died from cancer earlier this year. I was lucky to be able to spend her last days with her, even though I didn't know what my future held for me." She took another step toward Cygnus. "I was angry at the world, I was angry at God, I was angry at my father, I was angry at everyone. Just like you must be angry. Just like you must be pissed off at every Jessica, at every Rose, at every Fenway who gets between you and your loved ones." Fenway held her hands at her sides. "But letting go of that is the only way you get better, Professor. Healing yourself is a decision *you* have to make."

"I was ruler of this kingdom," whispered Cygnus. "The director chair my throne, the cap on my head the crown, the pencil in my hand the scepter. I had power. My students were in awe of me. The actors in London respected me. The rich bastards on those Stratford trips sat in dread and fear of me."

"And now you have to look in your heart for mercy for others," Fenway said. "Look above all of what you have. Look at everything you've learned about human nature through the plays you've taught. The plays you've devoted your life to understanding. You know that rising above those feelings of revenge and pettiness is something that's bigger than you. It's bigger than your enemies. It's even bigger than your wife's cancer."

At that, the professor blinked hard; a tear threatened to run down his face.

"You want fairness, you want justice—I know. I've been there, too," Fenway said, "but I've never heard of anyone who wanted justice to find peace through *revenge*. They don't become better people; they don't sleep better at night. It's letting go that brings that peace. It's forgiveness that brings you the calm and the quiet you've been desperately wanting."

Rose's breathing, too, had slowed. She seemed to understand that Fenway was talking Cygnus down.

"You won't feel better if you pull that trigger," Fenway said. "You might think you're getting justice, but you won't feel it."

Fenway saw the doubt in Cygnus's body language, saw his hand loosen its grip on the handle slightly—and she saw the determination return to Rose's eyes.

Rose snapped her head back, hard, and caught Cygnus in the chin. He dropped the gun in surprise and took a shocked step backward as Fenway dove for the gun.

Fenway expected a scramble for it, but she grabbed it before either of them could react. She rolled on her back, gun pointing into the air, more or less in the direction of Professor Virgil Cygnus.

"Back away!" Fenway yelled, but he was already five steps back, holding his mouth and partially doubled over. He didn't even look at her as he pulled his hand away, blood on his upper lip.

Rose scooped up the broken pieces of the USB drive and started running across the stage.

"Hey!" Fenway yelled, but it was too late; Rose ran down the stage-left stairs and Fenway heard a door open, then footsteps running away, and then the door slam. Rose was getting away, and Fenway couldn't do anything about it.

"I guess it's just you and me, Professor," she said.

"I need another six months with Judith," he whispered. "Another six months. Is that so bad? Jessica would have given me up." He used the back of his other hand to wipe his bleeding lip, and Fenway, gun still trained on Cygnus, pulled herself into a sitting position. "I thought

I understood Jessica. I thought I meant something to her. But, no, I didn't mean nearly as much to her as the promise of a bigger payday."

"Virgil Cygnus." Fenway got to her feet and gritted her teeth. "You are under arrest for the murder of Jessica Marquez."

IV

SATURDAY

CHAPTER TWENTY-SEVEN

THERE WAS NOTHING BUT DARKNESS AND HEAT AND THE GENTLE sound of rain against the bedroom window. Then a dull ringing sound. Then an elbow in her back.

"Your phone," McVie said.

"Ugh," Fenway mumbled, rolling over and reaching blindly in the direction of the ringtone. "Sorry." Her fingertips caught the edge of the phone, and she pulled it toward her an inch or two before getting her hand around it. She lifted her head, the pillow on top of it, and saw the screen.

"Charlotte."

"You better get it. She'll call again until you do."

"I know." She hit Answer. "Hi, Charlotte."

"Fenway—are you planning to come to your father's arraignment on Tuesday?"

"What?"

"I didn't wake you, did I?"

"Yes, as a matter of fact."

"Are you planning to sleep all day?"

"It's Saturday, Charlotte."

There was silence on the other end of the line.

"Look," Fenway said, "I know you're worried, but you've got a great criminal lawyer now. When my father shows up for the arraignment, they'll set reasonable bail and then you can work on the defense."

"Of course you're right," Charlotte said. "Sorry to wake you."

"Anyway," Fenway continued, "if I get any more information on the case, you'll have it as soon as I do."

"All right," Charlotte said.

"Anything else?"

"Are you enjoying the Porsche?"

"Yes, Charlotte. Thank you for letting me borrow it. They're returning my Accord to me any day now." She elbowed McVie in the ribs, and he grunted.

They said their goodbyes and Fenway rolled onto her stomach. "What time is it?"

"Almost eight," McVie said, turning onto his side to face Fenway.

"Charlotte's up early." She yawned. "I guess we should get moving too. I need to finish the paperwork from last night. And we've still got open cases to solve."

Something was different. Fenway didn't feel anxious with McVie in her bed. Was it really just another two days of working the case with McVie that had loosened the knot in her chest and made her human again?

"We've had few late nights in a row," McVie said. "We can sleep in." He traced his hand lazily up the side of her calf to her knee, and then her thigh.

Fenway smiled. "I get the feeling you don't intend for us to sleep."

McVie shifted his weight and planted a kiss on Fenway's shoulder, and then another closer to her neck.

His phone dinged.

"You don't have to get that," Fenway said, her breathing coming heavier.

"Let me just make sure it's not an emergency," he said, picking up the phone off his nightstand. "Ah."

"What is it?"

"Cygnus's arraignment has been set for Tuesday."

"Hmm. Maybe he'll get arraigned with my father. It'll be like a parade of celebrity murderers."

McVie looked at Fenway. "You want to be there?"

"I kind of do, yeah."

McVie leaned in and kissed her neck, one hand on her shoulder, the other on her hip, and Fenway shuddered with anticipation.

————

After Cygnus's arrest, Fenway didn't want to work on Saturday, but she hadn't submitted the paperwork on the arrest Friday night, and thought she could finish it with an hour in an empty office. Fenway took the Porsche, arrived a few minutes past ten, and found Rachel waiting in her office, two large cups from Java Jim's on her desk.

"Been here long?"

Rachel shook her head. "Only a few minutes. I knew you'd be cleaning up the paperwork on your arrest last night. I thought I'd catch you in time for your midmorning latte." She slyly smiled. "But I didn't think it would be your first of the day."

Fenway blushed.

"Solving the murder in the first forty-eight hours. Very nice."

"Not quite. First seventy-two, maybe, but thanks." Fenway sat down at her desk and gratefully reached for the latte. "I wish Cygnus would give us information on who's paying him and who's behind the accounts. I wish we had caught Rose Morgan, too. It would have been nice to play the two of them off each other. See which one would crack first."

"It'll be good for Cygnus to spend the weekend in jail," Rachel said. "Make him realize how serious the crime is, see if he'll name names."

Fenway shook her head. "If he doesn't get to spend the next few months with his dying wife, I don't think he cares about anything else."

Rachel was quiet for a moment, a morose look on her face.

"What is it?"

"Well—look, Virgil Cygnus was a dog, wasn't he? I mean, he was sleeping with Leda Nedermeyer for over a decade. He's been cheating on his wife for ten years—and yet, he wants to risk going to prison for the rest of his life just to be with her at the end of hers?"

"I know," Fenway said, "and he wouldn't even stop directing the play. People are funny."

"Do you think Cygnus truly loves his wife?"

Fenway looked into Rachel's eyes, saw the searching and desperation there, and knew Rachel wasn't just asking about the Shakespeare professor. Fenway took a breath. "I think it's possible for a person to truly love someone else and still cheat. It's horrible for the person who's being cheated on, of course, and it signifies something kind of screwed up about the cheater, but just because"—she paused and lowered her voice—"just because Dylan cheated on you doesn't mean he didn't love you."

"I can't believe I didn't know," Rachel said miserably.

Fenway nodded. Dylan hadn't been dead quite six months, so Rachel's wounds were still open—not as fresh as they once were, but still raw. "Yeah," Fenway said. "I'm sorry."

"Anyway," Rachel said, straightening up, shaking her hair out, and lifting her arms. "I didn't come over here to have a pity party for myself. I came here to tell you what I learned from Deshawn."

"What you learned—what? Tell me you didn't—"

"Yeah. I took matters into my own hands."

"Rachel—no! I didn't want you to—"

Rachel waved her hand as if shooing a fly. "I'm a big girl. I make my own decisions."

Fenway paused, gaping at her friend, and then sat back in her chair. "And you're calling him *Deshawn?*"

Rachel shrugged. "He's a nice guy, Fenway. He was in the bar when I walked in, and he couldn't take his eyes off me. *He* was the one to approach *me.*"

"Tell me you weren't wearing that red dress."

Rachel laughed. "I *did* try it on before I left, but you were right—it was too much. Like the girlfriend in a bad gangster movie."

"I can't believe you, Rachel! I told you I'd think of something else."

"You needed the information, and I thought it would be fun."

Fenway covered her eyes with her hands.

"I pretended I had been stood up on a blind date. I looked sad. He sent over a drink to my table, and then we started talking."

"What the hell, Rachel?"

"He's lonely. His wife left him a couple of years ago and he hasn't even dated. We talked about how much it sucks to start dating again."

"Rachel, I didn't want you to—"

"Relax, Fenway. It's fine. He was on his third bourbon before I even asked him what he did for a living."

Fenway paused. "And did he tell you anything?"

"He said he was a homicide detective, and that he was trying to get the guy who'd hired a hit man."

"What did you say then?"

"I told him I saw an episode of a cop show where they had to let the bad guy go because the hit man wouldn't talk."

"Holy crap, Rachel, that's brilliant. And he bit?"

"Hook, line, and sinker. He said the hit man *did* talk—and gave up the guy who hired him."

Fenway's jaw dropped open. "Well, then, what the hell was he doing out of jail?"

"I'm not done with my story yet, Fenway. I said, 'Oh, Detective, that's wonderful—getting two killers off the street!'"

Fenway shook her head and laughed.

"And he said that the ADA was so intent on getting the rich guy who hired him that she offered the guy *immunity* before she realized he'd confess to murder."

Fenway sat back. "You've got to be kidding."

Rachel shook her head.

"ADA Kim offered Grayheath immunity just to get something on my father?"

"That's sure what it sounded like. Deshawn was mad about it, too. He said they had a ton of evidence tying the hit man to the murder, and he was *pissed* that the ADA threw it out the window."

"Evidence?"

Rachel nodded. "They've got video."

"Video? Of what?"

"He searched video feeds of ATM cameras in Bellingham, then he found what he called a 'secret account' that proved the guy in the video was hired to kill the target."

"Did he say how he found it?"

"He went on about it for a while. How hard he worked, elbow-grease, ear-to-the-ground detective work. Then he said that none of it mattered, and it was an anonymous tip a couple of weeks ago. A copy of a bank statement he found under his office door one day."

Fenway nodded. "He didn't think that was fishy?"

Rachel shrugged. "I don't think that even crossed his mind. He thought he had finally caught a break on the case." She tapped her foot. "He didn't have nice things to say about the victim. At one point in his investigation, he thought you were behind it."

"Me?"

"Well—he said the murder victim had sexually assaulted several young women at the university during his time there, and that he had a bead on a couple of the women who had ties to Estancia. One who parked long-term at the airport."

"I guess that would be me." Fenway paused. "Wait—a *couple* of them? Professor Delacroix assaulted *another* woman who lives in Estancia besides me?"

"He'd had another bourbon by then and he was pretty happy. Maybe he was embellishing."

"Maybe."

"If I'd been in his shoes, I would have looked at myself as the main suspect, too," Fenway said. "That makes me think my father *didn't* do it. Because of how likely it would be for the hammer to come down on me." She paused. "You know, my father can be a real ass, and he missed my graduation and everything, but he'd never hang me out to dry."

"No, he wouldn't," Rachel said.

"What else do they have? Tapped phone conversations? Video of my father meeting Peter Grayheath in a park?"

Rachel shook her head and then paused. "They've got the confession from Grayheath and the payment from your dad's account—but now that I think about it, he said there were payments. Multiple payments."

"To Grayheath?"

"I—I'm not sure. Like I said, he was pretty drunk by then. He was slurring his words."

Fenway looked sideways at Rachel. "It makes a lot more sense if there's more to their paper trail than a single payment. My father's lawyers would tear that apart."

Rachel nodded. "Yeah, they must have something else. Maybe they wanted to get your father in custody while they built the case against him."

"Think the D.A. will ask for remand?"

"It's what I'd do," Rachel said. "Your dad's an obvious flight risk—more money than the Queen of England, and access to airplanes that could have him sipping margaritas on the beach in the Caymans before the weekend is over."

They sat in silence for a moment.

"Did you get anything else from Ridley?" Fenway finally asked.

Rachel blushed.

"No," Fenway said. "You didn't. You kissed him?"

"Well, *he* kissed me, but I didn't say no."

"You didn't, huh?"

She smiled. "He's a pretty good kisser. Even after all those bourbons."

"Did you do anything else?"

Rachel rolled her eyes. "You know I'm not that kind of girl."

"Oh, come on, Rachel, for the right guy, we're *all* that kind of girl."

Rachel's eyes grew wide.

"Well," Fenway said, "maybe I'm just speaking for myself." She tapped her fingers on the desk. "Will you see him again?"

"No. I don't know. He said he'd leave in the next few days."

"After the arraignment, probably," Fenway mused.

"Probably."

"And if you're not that kind of girl in the next couple of days—well, Bellingham's an awfully long way away."

"Hah. True enough, I guess."

Fenway thought of Officer Brian Callahan, mooning over Rachel a few days before. "Besides, there are other options."

"Other options?"

"Locally, I mean."

"Really?"

"Really."

"Well." Rachel stood up. "I think I'll head over to the bar at Phillips-Holsen again tonight. Just to see what happens. But I might be asking you more details about these options I have." She smiled and walked out of Fenway's office.

———

Fenway typed up the last paragraph of her report, leaned back in her chair, and shook her latte cup. There was one last sip in it.

The phone on her desk rang. She looked at the number; it was from the San Miguelito county offices.

"Fenway Stevenson."

"Hey, Fenway. It's Melissa from the lab. It's about that award you sent us."

"You're working on Saturday, too, huh?"

"The lab's backed up. I'm sure you're not surprised."

"Right." Fenway bit her tongue to stop herself from asking about her car. "So, the award. This is the *Macbeth* award? Or is it the acting award from Amanda Kohl's dorm room closet?"

"The acting award you sent us yesterday."

"You got the results already? Wow, that was fast."

"It's only fast because there weren't any prints on it."

"Wait—what?"

Melissa laughed. "Just what I said. No fingerprints on it, at all."

"That can't be right. Amanda loved that award. She put it on the top shelf and everything." Fenway paused. "Why would someone wipe the fingerprints off it?"

"I don't know. That's why *you* get the big bucks."

"Wow. Okay, thanks."

"You still don't have a murder weapon, do you?"

"I know what it is—I'm almost positive it's the missing award. The one from last year for *The Merchant of Venice*."

"Oh—one other thing. The base had a big scratch in it."

"Is that significant?"

"It is when there's paint transfer in it. It's a dark gray paint with a metallic finish. Don't quote me on this since we haven't done the official analysis yet, but I've only seen this kind of paint come from machine sprayers, like in factories. Cars, appliances, that kind of thing."

Fenway emptied the last of her latte in her mouth, thinking.

"Fenway? You still there?"

"What? Oh, yeah, Melissa, sorry. Thanks for the information."

"Any time."

Fenway couldn't help herself. "Hey—if you hear anything about when I'll be able to pick up my car..."

"You'll be the first to know."

"Thanks."

Fenway hung up, glanced through the completed form on her screen, and hit the SUBMIT button. She got up and stretched, then walked over to IT to tell Piper everything Rachel had said.

Halfway there, she realized there'd be no Piper. When Fenway had told her goodbye the night before, she wasn't coming back.

Fenway returned to her desk, a wave of nausea coming over her, and sat down. She stared at her computer screen for a moment, then brought up her email.

Dozens and dozens of messages from Piper. Scans of documents, photographs, financial records. Detailed analyses of what everything meant—not formatted well, and with a bunch of typos, but apparently thorough and certainly voluminous.

The emails were on many different subjects—Dr. Jacob Tassajera, the financial records of the North American Shakespeare Guild, a file on each of the students. Piper had found the work history and education of Jessica Marquez, too—not an empty folder like Nidever's HR department had.

But nothing on Nathaniel Ferris, and Fenway knew that Piper had done some digging. Maybe she had taken that work home with her.

Her phone buzzed. It was a text from Rachel.

Forgot to tell you, your gray hairbrush was on top of your desk when I walked in
I didn't want anyone to take it so I put it in the top left drawer

Gray hairbrush? Fenway didn't own a gray hairbrush.

Fenway opened the drawer, and sure enough, a gray hairbrush with a silver band and a mottled handle sat on top of the cables and cords. She took it out. Except for the color, it looked exactly like the hairbrush safe she had seen in The Guild office. She twisted the top, and it came off.

A USB drive skittered out onto the desk.

She put it in the computer and gasped. Dozens of financial records from Peter Grayheath were listed, and several banking records from her father as well—banking records she suspected were faked. But the trail of her father's wrongdoing was impressive.

Fenway paused. It had to be from Piper. She didn't know how Piper got the hairbrush there so fast, but it had to be her.

Fenway pulled her phone out of her purse. She dialed her father's cell phone, but after several rings it went to voicemail.

She debated with herself for a moment, then dialed Charlotte's cell phone.

After three rings, Charlotte answered. She sounded out of breath. "Hi, Fenway. I didn't expect to hear from you."

"I'm in the office, so I can't talk long," Fenway said in a low voice, "but you need to hire someone to do research for my father's case."

She heard Charlotte breathe out, then a man's voice, mumbling and low—sounding an awful lot like her father—and then it occurred to her exactly why her father hadn't picked up. She closed her eyes and felt a little nauseated.

"Sorry, sorry, Fenway. Can you say that again?"

Fenway swallowed hard, the bad taste in her mouth abating. "You need to hire a researcher for my father's case."

"I'm sure that Imani—"

"No," Fenway said, "a researcher who knows financial systems well. Someone who can trace those transactions that the prosecution is saying my father made."

"Oh—I take it you have someone in mind."

"That's right. She just got fired by the county."

"She—she what? That's not exactly a ringing endorsement of—"

"It's because she was getting too close to the people who are trying to take my father down." Fenway didn't mention the trespassing incident—let Charlotte figure that out for herself.

Charlotte was silent for a moment.

"Well?" Fenway asked. "Do you want to know who it is?"

"You think this person could help prove your dad is innocent?"

"I do."

Charlotte let out a long exhale. "I—I guess I'd better do it."

"You'll need to buy equipment. A top-of-the-line laptop. Access to some international financial databases. It won't be cheap."

"But you're saying it's necessary."

"I am."

"And she's good?"

"The best."

"Then I'll do it."

Fenway paused, thinking about Piper's savings account going up in smoke while she searched for a job during the holidays. "And *she's* not cheap, either."

"If she's the best, I assume it'll cost us."

Fenway closed her eyes. It wasn't the most aboveboard thing to do —she knew there was a gray area here, and Piper would need to walk a fine line.

But this was her father's best chance.

ACKNOWLEDGMENTS

Many thanks to Max Christian Hansen and Ki Brosius, who edited the living daylights out of this book. Thank you to all the other early readers who spent their valuable time catching errors and getting my book to be the best it could be. I'd also like to thank Cheryl Shoults and A.L. Book Promotions for helping this book (and others I've written) rise as high on the booksellers' charts as they have.

To all my former compatriots from the 1993 American Shakespeare Company production of *A Midsummer Night's Dream*: I hope you enjoyed this, and I hope you agree that Professor Homer Swander would be delighted and (mostly) flattered by his doppelgänger. And no, none of you are in this book, despite your names showing up as characters and places.

Finally, to my wife, my kids, and my mom: I'm deeply grateful. I couldn't have written these books without your encouragement and support.

WANT MORE FENWAY?

The Fenway Stevenson Mysteries

Book One: The Reluctant Coroner

Book Two: The Incumbent Coroner

Book Three: The Candidate Coroner

Book Four: The Upstaged Coroner

Book Five: The Courtroom Coroner (coming soon)

Collection

Books 1–3 of The Fenway Stevenson Mysteries

Dez Roubideaux

Bad Weather

To order more books in the Fenway Stevenson series, go to

www.books2read.com/rl/fenway

Sign up for *The Coroner's Report,*

Paul Austin Ardoin's biweekly newsletter:

www.paulaustinardoin.com

I hope you enjoyed reading this book as much as I enjoyed writing it. If you did, I'd sincerely appreciate a review on your favorite book retailer's website, Goodreads, and BookBub. Reviews are crucial for any author, and even just a line or two can make a huge difference.

CPSIA information can be obtained
at www.ICGtesting.com
Printed in the USA
LVHW041158141019
634125LV00006B/2636/P